Fatal Knowledge

A Collegiate Murder Mystery

Daniel P. Hennelly

iUniverse, Inc.
Bloomington

Fatal Knowledge
A Collegiate Murder Mystery

iUniverse books may be ordered through booksellers or by contacting:

iUniverse
1663 Liberty Drive
Bloomington, IN 47403
www.iuniverse.com
1-800-Authors (1-800-288-4677)

ISBN: 978-1-4759-6052-5 (sc)
ISBN: 978-1-4759-6054-9 (hc)
ISBN: 978-1-4759-6053-2 (e)

Library of Congress Control Number: 2012922729

Printed in the United States of America

iUniverse rev. date: 12/17/2012

Author's Note

This book is a work of fiction. All characters are fictitious; any resemblance to real individuals, living or dead is a coincidence. Although set in a real locale, with the exceptions of well known national chains, all other businesses and places are a creation of my imagination. My portrayal of the investigative and legal process is intended to move the story along and is not a real representation of how the process works.

Dedication

This novel is dedicated to my wife, Mary Bride, who provided much love, inspiration and support during the writing of this novel.

Acknowledgements

I'd like to acknowledge John A. Parker, Jr., the Emeritus Head of the Reference Department at the now demolished Kirn Memorial Library in Norfolk, Virginia, who read my manuscript and made many comments and suggestions on how to improve it. His editorial comments vastly improved the final manuscript.

I'd also like to thank my neighbor, Dr. William S. Rodner, Chancellor's Professor of History at Tidewater Community College, Virginia Beach, Virginia, who read my manuscript from start to finish and frequently cautioned me, "Dano, you're out of control again."

My parents, Patrick J. and Ann L. Hennelly, also read my manuscript. My mother, an avid reader of mysteries, cautioned me that I may've have tipped off readers too early to the identity of the murder so I revised the manuscript to bury the clues deeper. I wish to thank them for their support and love over the years. Who knew when they bought all those Hardy Boys books years ago where it would lead.

I would also like to acknowledge my cousin, Sister Mary Anne Foster, SC, who read a draft of my novel and caught a number of spelling and grammatical errors with her red pen.

My employer of over twenty-eight years, Old Dominion University, using funds from a generous benefactor, annually sponsors an Employee

Dream Fund contest to help employees achieve their dreams. A generous award from the Dream Fund helped make publishing my novel a reality.

Finally I would like to thank the members of my Writer's Group that meets at the Barnes and Noble Store in the Virginia Beach Town Center. They have listened to my three novels over the last ten years and have provided criticism that has helped me hone my skills as a writer.

Two Matters of Pronunciation

In the New Jersey dialect of the English language, Kearny, New Jersey is pronounced Carney.

Taliaferro is pronounced Tolliver south of the Mason-Dixon Line.

CHAPTER I

I NEVER ASPIRED TO BE Chair of the History Department. Academics only become administrators if they have no other choice; we earned our Ph.D.s to spend our lives pursuing esoteric scholarship not pushing papers. Rick Hanson, my predecessor, enjoyed being department chair and probably would've served indefinitely. His love of bacon cheeseburgers and French fries altered my career path. If Rick hadn't dropped dead during a pickup basketball game at the campus rec center, I would've happily continued as a tenured professor in the department till retirement.

Those outside academia believe being department chair is the pinnacle of a professor's career. They envision a chair mentoring junior colleagues, nurturing students and moderating scholarly discussions. Instead, a chair referees petty squabbles between faculty in the department, resolves problems for clueless students who've never bothered to read the university catalog and allocates scarce resources to no one's satisfaction.

Emily Worthington, the only other full professor in the department, had already served a stint as chair. During her tenure, she clashed constantly with Tollie Monroe, the Dean of the College of Arts, Social Sciences and Humanities (abbreviated as CASSH in the university's lexicon). Tollie unceremoniously sacked her like Harry Truman firing Douglas MacArthur, complete with Emily's farewell address at her last department meeting as chair. As a tenured professor, Emily returned to her former office and conducted guerilla warfare against the university's administration. Rick's untimely death coupled with Tollie's visceral hatred of Emily meant I was the logical; make it only, choice to assume the burden of leadership.

I'd spent Monday at the National Archives in Washington researching my new book on slavery in Southern industry. It had been a productive day; I'd found documents relating to the Tannehill Ironworks in Alabama. A workforce of almost 600 slaves labored in hellish conditions in the iron works at the height of production during the Civil War.

Arriving home late in the evening, I found an e-mail from the department secretary Janet Hodges, indicating her daughter had gone into labor on Sunday evening and she was in North Carolina awaiting the birth of her first grandchild. She'd not been in the office on Monday to photocopy the mid-term exams I'd left her on Friday afternoon.

I went in early on Tuesday morning to get the exams photocopied before my section of American History met at 8:00 AM. Counting the cars in the faculty parking lot, I was the third faculty member to arrive. A trash truck emptying the dumpster blocked my reserved parking space behind Russell B. Jordan Hall and I had to wait until it was finished. Dr. Jordan was the first president of Chesapeake Bay College and at the end of his twenty-five year tenure, the board of trustees named the Stalinist style edifice in his honor. Undoubtedly one of the ugliest buildings in Virginia and a testament to the doctrine of the lowest bid, Jordan Hall was a ten story office tower flanked by classroom wings of three stories. After starting the college in a shuttered boys' orphanage at the end of World War II, Dr. Jordan perceived the building to be the crowning achievement of his presidential career. During most of the 1950's the college had functioned in the aging buildings of the orphanage with surplus military barracks added to handle surging enrollments. The completion of Russell B. Jordan Hall marked the metamorphosis of Chesapeake Bay College into Chesapeake Bay University.

"You're in early Dr. Stanard," greeted Vivian Underwood, one of the housekeeping workers as I exited the elevator on to the 6th floor. Pine cleaner fumes lingered in the corridor from the recent mopping of the floor.

"Good morning Vivian. How are you doing?"

"I don't know how they expect me to get everything cleaned by 8:00 AM. Some people take their sweet time doing their business," muttered Vivian as she emptied the trash can next to the copier.

"What's wrong?" I asked thinking I'd offended her.

"Someone is in the women's restroom; I can't clean until she finishes."

I wondered who else had come in early; Janet was usually the only one on the floor this early. Of the female faculty in the department, only Emily Worthington had an 8 o'clock class on Tuesday. The last thing I wanted was a run in with Emily before I'd digested my breakfast.

Vivian moved her cart to the men's restroom and began cleaning it instead. Unlocking the department office, I found the envelope containing the exam still sitting on Janet's desk where I'd left it on Friday. I unlocked my office and put my brief case down on the floor next to my desk. Sitting on the corner of my desk were the blue books from the midterm exam for my American history survey class taken on Monday. Leafing through a few of the exams, I cringed at the answers from the class composed mostly of freshman. Hopefully today's exam would go better; usually only history majors signed up for America from 1880 to 1919. I searched my desk drawer and found my copy card. After putting on a pot of coffee in the file room, I went across the hall and turned on the copier to warm it up.

The copier came to life and drowned out Vivian cleaning until the paper jammed. I spent several frustrating minutes trying to clear the jam in the aging machine, a problem encountered daily by everyone in the department. Much of the last department meeting involved Emily hectoring me about when the department would be getting a new machine, especially since the English Department received a top of the line model the month before. Emily believed Tollie favored the English Department when allocating resources because he'd been an English professor before becoming a dean.

"She's still in there," complained Vivian as she waited impatiently outside the women's restroom. "She doesn't care that someone has to clean."

I found the scrap of paper jamming the machine and removed it; the machine gave me the green light to resume copying. As I shuffled the papers to resume copying, the silence of the deserted floor was pierced by Vivian's scream from the women's restroom. Rushing down the hall, I pushed open the door to the women's restroom to find Vivian frozen in the center of the room.

"What happened?"

"She's dead!" Vivian panted as if trying to scream again.

"Who's dead?"

"She's on the toilet, in the third stall against the wall."

I looked at the stalls and saw a pair of legs behind the third door; the odor of stale urine hung heavily over the room. Slowly I pushed in the door to the stall with my elbow and found a young woman, fully clothed, propped up on the toilet. Her bruised neck, bulging eyes and contorted face indicated she'd died violently. Suppressing the urge to vomit, I helped Vivian, still in shock, out of the restroom. Once in my office, I seated her in my chair and dialed campus police. "This is Professor Stanard of the History Department. Send a police unit to the sixth floor of Russell Jordan Hall. One of the housekeeping workers found a dead woman in the restroom. I think she was strangled. She needs an ambulance."

"If she's dead, why would she need an ambulance?" asked the dispatcher.

"Vivian needs the ambulance."

"Is Vivian the victim?"

"No, she's the housekeeping worker who found the body. She's in shock."

"I've dispatched a unit; they'll be there in a minute. I'll call for an ambulance too."

I went over to the coffee maker and poured a cup for Vivian. She probably needed a shot of bourbon but coffee was all I had to offer. "Here drink this."

In between sips of her coffee, Vivian kept muttering, "I can't believe she's dead."

A few minutes later, the elevator doors opened and I went down the hall to meet the police. Harley Simpson, the Chief of the Campus Police Department stepped off the elevator with two of his officers. I knew Harley from the campus recreation center; like me, he usually worked out at noon. A retired Army officer, he came to CBU after a career in the military police. "What are you doing here?"

"I was down the street when the call went out."

"The body is in the women's restroom."

"Did you find the body?" asked Harley.

"No, Vivian did."

"Where is she?"

"I took her to my office. She's badly shaken up."

"Stay with her till the ambulance arrives," Harley directed the female officer.

"Do you want me to question her?" asked the officer.

"She's probably too traumatized; give her a few minutes."

"Where's the body?"

I pointed to the women's restroom. Harley went down the hall and came out a few minutes later. "Secure the building; don't let anyone in or out. It's only 7:30; there shouldn't be too many people in the building. Get every officer over here and call the nightshift back in. Call the city police; we need a crime scene team to survey the bathroom."

"Most departments have scheduled mid-terms today," I interrupted.

"We have a murder to investigate; the building is locked down till further notice!"

"Can I call my faculty and let them know classes are cancelled?"

"No. We're keeping the lid on until we know what happened. Don't talk to anyone about what you saw."

At the next department meeting, I imagined being raked over the coals by my colleagues for not notifying them the building was shut down and they drove to campus for nothing.

"Do you want a cup of coffee?" I asked.

"It's going to be a long day, might as well."

We went into my office and I poured two Styrofoam cups. "Do you have any creamer?" asked Harley.

"I thought police drank it black."

Harley gave me an irritated look. "Do you feel up to talking?" he asked Vivian.

She nodded reluctantly.

"What happened?"

"God it was horrible!" Vivian started sobbing and the police woman put her arm around her.

Harley waited for her to regain her composure. "What time did you arrive this morning?"

"Our shift starts at 5:00 AM; we clean the classroom wings first since we have to get them finished before classes start. It's impossible to keep this building clean with classes going till ten at night. After we finished the classrooms, we started on the office floors. Since most of the professors don't get in till eleven or so, we have more time."

"Many professors have night classes," I interrupted.

"I started on the fifth floor; Stella took ten through eight. When I got here, I saw the ladies room was occupied. So I swept and mopped the hallways first. When I got back, she was still in there."

"That didn't seem unusual?"

"Dean Monroe takes his sweet time in the bathroom reading his damn books. I thought she may have been reading poetry too."

Harley looked over at me, and I confirmed Vivian's statement by nodding in agreement. An unrepentant English professor, Tollie found his morning stint on the toilet an ideal time to read poetry.

"I waited almost fifteen minutes for her to finish her business. When I called in to her and got no answer, I thought she might be sick."

"Was it unusual that someone was in the building that early?"

"Some professors come in at seven; they have keys to the building," replied Vivian.

Harley turned to me, "Was anyone else on the floor?"

"I didn't see anyone," I replied.

"Do either of you recognize the victim?"

"I've seen her around the building but I don't know her name," replied Vivian.

"She's a doctoral student in Economics; she's dating Brendan, one of my students. Her first name is Jenny; she has an Italian last name. Badoglio? No, he was the Italian general who took over after Mussolini was deposed. I'm too rattled to remember her last name."

"You've met her before?"

"The first week of school, we held a tailgate party at our house on Friday afternoon for the department."

"The football game wasn't until Saturday."

"That was the theme my wife chose for the party." CBU was one of the largest universities in the South without a football team until the alumni pushed the President and the trustees to get one off the ground this year. "Brendan brought Jenny; as I recall she talked with Laura. After that, I've seen her around Jordan Hall with Brendan."

Despite being only five foot six inches tall, it was hard not to spot Jenny around the building; her long blond hair and blue eyes stood out in the sea of female students. I assumed her family's roots were in Northern Italy rather than Sicily.

As part of her unassigned duties as department secretary, Janet enjoyed keeping track of the romances of our graduate students sometimes to the detriment of her assigned duties. When I was looking for Brendan one day last spring, she directed me to the 9th floor since he'd become involved with Jenny. I saw no need to share with Harley Janet's wealth of information on Brendan's activities under the sheets.

The elevator opened in the hall and two paramedics arrived with a stretcher. The female officer directed them to Vivian and they began checking her blood pressure.

"Is there someplace else we can talk?" asked Harley.

I directed him down the hall to the conference room. "What's your graduate student's name?"

"Brendan Healy."

"Do you know his complete name?"

"His middle name is Ryan."

"His date of birth of birth and social security number would be helpful too."

"It's in the student information system."

"Do you have an address for him?"

"He shares a house with two or three other graduate students over on 80th Street in Jefferson Terrace."

"Get his address and date of birth for me."

"Do you have a picture of him?"

"There's one on the bulletin board in the hallway; my secretary put up photos of all the teaching assistants."

"Grab it!" Harley ordered one of his officers.

Janet wouldn't be happy that her bulletin board had been tampered with.

"Who would know more about Jenny?"

"Dr. Ruiz is the department chair in Economics."

"Did either of you see a purse or wallet? She has no identification on her."

"I don't recall seeing it in the restroom," I replied.

"I didn't find anything while I was cleaning," answered Vivian.

"Do you think it's a robbery? Remember the student mugged in the stairwell last week; the mugger took her purse. It wasn't the first mugging we've had on campus this year."

"Crack addicts don't murder someone to steal a purse nor do they go to the trouble to dump the body in the restroom."

"Maybe he mugged her in there."

"You saw the body Andy; it doesn't look like a mugging."

One of the officers came in the room, "Chief, Channel 8 has their satellite truck out in front of the building. They want to know why we've shut down the building."

"Damn it! How did they find out so quickly?"

I kept my mouth shut; Harley had obviously missed the article in the campus newspaper about the Communication Department students working as interns at Channel 8. One of their duties was to monitor the police bands for potential news stories.

Deciding it best to leave, I went back to my office to find the paramedics finishing with Vivian. Although her blood pressure was slightly elevated, she was doing better. The officer called the housekeeping supervisor to take her home. The crime scene technicians were surveying the bathroom. Turning on my computer, I opened the student information system to find Brendan's address and printed it off for Chief Simpson; I also wrote down his date of birth and social security number.

Back in the conference room, I found Harley huddled with Dick Torelli, the university's balding director of media relations. "I have to tell the reporters waiting outside something; Channel 8 wants to break into their morning talk show with a news bulletin."

Torelli was a former local television anchor until his acrimonious divorce from his longtime co-anchor forced him out of the anchor chair. His comeback as a reporter with a rival station ended when a vicious wind gust blew off his toupee while covering a hurricane that struck Norfolk one August. His career in shambles, he managed to land on his feet and found his true calling on the other side of the camera as CBU's spin doctor.

"I'll give you a statement when we're ready. We only found the body a half hour ago."

"You still haven't arrested the crack addict who mugged that girl last month. The Admissions Office is having an open house on Friday. How do think the parents of prospective students are going to react when they hear about this murder? You'd better stop this crime wave fast; I need your cooperation not more yellow tape!"

Torelli pushed me aside as he left the room. Looking out the window, I saw knots of students and faculty in the parking lot talking. Spread by iPads and text messages, all sorts of rumors would be soon moving along the campus grapevine.

"Asshole," muttered Harley under his breath.

"Here's Brendan's address," I said as I handed Harley the paper.

"Tell me about him."

"He finished his masters' degree three years ago; he's working on his doctorate. Before getting his undergraduate degree, he did a stint in the Marine Corps. He's originally from New Jersey."

"Not too many academics enlist in the Marine Corps."

"He dropped out of high school when he was seventeen; he earned his GED after boot camp. Then he started taking college courses on the base and finished his degree after his enlistment ended. You've probably seen him at the rec center; he lifts weights."

Harley arched his eyebrows as if lifting weights and serving in the Marines gave him further justification for making Brendan the chief suspect. "Describe him."

"Brendan is in his late twenties, six feet tall, sandy blond hair and blue eyes."

"Most jarheads have tattoos; does he have any?"

"He has two Chinese characters tattooed on his upper right arm." Harley's questions pointed in one direction. "Are you putting out an all points bulletin for him?"

"For now he's a person of interest; I'm sending someone over to his house to bring him in for questioning. Usually the victim knows their killer. Caesar knew his killers; Brutus may even have been his son."

"Doubtful, Brutus was around ten years old when Caesar began his affair with his mother. Don't believe everything you see on the History Channel."

One of the policemen entered the room. "Dr. Ruiz is on his way up."

"Have the men found her purse?"

"No sir. They fanned out through the building but nothing yet."

Dr. Ruiz was escorted into the conference room.

"I have some bad news for you; one of your graduate students is dead. We need you to identify the body."

Jake's face turned ashen. "One of my students; are you sure?"

"Dr. Stanard thinks her name is Jenny."

"Dios mio!" The shock caused Jake to lapse into the language of his native south Texas. "Jenny Biggio is one of my graduate students. What happened to her?"

Harley took a deep breath, "She was murdered. Dr. Stanard and one of the housekeeping workers found her body early this morning."

"Murdered!"

Once Jake regained his composure, Harley escorted us to the restroom to view the body. The crime scene technicians had already covered Jenny's hands with plastic bags. Harley noticed my curiosity.

"It's in case the killer left any skin under her fingernails; we'll do DNA tests."

Jake confirmed Jenny's identity; he looked sick to his stomach and I took him back to my office. "Fortunately the police will notify her family; there's no way I could handle telling someone their only child is dead. I'll call her parents later; our department will hold a memorial service."

I noticed Jake was tearing up. "Where was Jenny from?"

"Cleveland, her dad worked in the Ford plant there. Jenny's dissertation is incredible; the economic models she created are cutting edge. She is scheduled to defend it next month; she already has three interviews scheduled for tenure track positions at top tier schools."

I noticed that Jake still talked about Jenny in the present tense; I didn't have the heart to correct him.

"I've offered her a visiting appointment to replace Cynthia Wallach while she's on sabbatical during spring semester."

"It's a tragic loss all the way around." CBU had difficulties attracting top students; more prestigious schools offered higher graduate assistant stipends. If Jenny had landed a position at top research university, it would've enhanced the reputation of Jake's department.

"I took charge of her dissertation from Art Campbell. That fool failed to see her potential."

Art Campbell marched to his own drummer. The only Marxist in the Economics Department, the collapse of the Soviet Union in the late 1980's left him high and dry intellectually. At any college meeting, Art could be counted on to spout off about capitalist abuse of workers or a rote denunciation of Wal-Mart. His prize possession was a poster of Fidel Castro tacked to his office wall; he considered framing it too bourgeois. Unfortunately Art had tenure and would remain a thorn in everyone's side until he retired.

Chief Simpson entered the conference room. "Thank you for your assistance Dr. Ruiz. Please don't talk to the media; we'll issue a statement shortly. I don't want to release any more details than necessary; details often help us trip up the killer."

"I understand. May I inform my colleagues of her death?"

"We're attempting to contact her family in Ohio; I'll have one of my staff notify you when we reach them."

"You have my cell phone number." Jake looked as if he'd aged ten years since being summoned. I could only imagine how hard it would be to talk with her parents.

"Am I free to go?"

"I have some more questions for you. It looks like your student has flown the coop; my officer went to his house and found no one there."

"He's the teaching assistant for Dr. Worthington's 8:00 AM section of European History; he's probably out in the parking lot." I pointed out the window to the throng of students and faculty milling around the parking lot behind the building. The smart ones had gone to the Student Union and picked up a cup of coffee. Satellite trucks from Channel 4 and Channel 12 had joined the truck from Channel 8 to complete the circus like atmosphere.

"Why are you so quick to defend him?"

"He's not the type to viciously strangle someone."

"The neighbors of Son of Sam said he was a nice Jewish boy, not the type to go around shooting people."

"Brendan has come a long way; he grew up in a working class neighborhood. No one ever encouraged him intellectually in high school. His dad abandoned the family leaving his mother to raise three kids on her own. He quit school and joined the Marine Corps to help out his family."

"How noble," Harley replied.

He looked out the window at the satellite trucks; Dick Torelli was already putting a full court press on him to wrap it up quickly and prevent a public relations disaster. "You play hunches in police work. I hope to God Healy isn't the killer but in my career I've seen too many women killed by their boyfriend or husbands. One of my first assignments as an investigator, I went to base housing and found a young wife beaten to death with a baseball bat by her drunken husband. He was a year out of boot camp; his life story sounded a lot like your student. At his court martial, they sentenced him to forty years at Leavenworth."

"Let me look around campus and see if I can find Brendan."

"I'll send one of my investigators out with you. Does Healy have an office on this floor?"

"Six of the teaching assistants share an office across the hall from the bathrooms. Each one has a small cubicle."

Harley face lit up as if I just given him the winning numbers for the lottery. "I need to look it over."

"Don't you need a search warrant?"

"His cubicle isn't his residence; employees have no expectation of privacy on their employer's premises."

We walked around the corridor to the office. I unlocked the door with my master key and turned on the light. With the desk chairs in the aisle, there was barely room for the two of us. "Brendan's cubicle is the middle one on the left."

Harley seemed disappointed that the cramped room was in general order and nothing seemed amiss. He went over to Brendan's cubicle and rummaged through all the drawers. "I'll need the technicians to go over this room."

"Chief," interrupted the female officer who'd helped Vivian.

"What is it?" replied Harley wearily.

"A student just found the victim's purse in the bushes on the east side of the library; the wallet is missing. That's where he dumped the purse he stole on Thursday."

Jordan Hall had been plagued all semester by a rash of purse snatchings attributed to a crack addict stealing to feed his habit.

Harley pointed his index finger at the officer. "Don't assume the same perpetrator committed both crimes."

My hopes were dashed that the news just delivered by the officer cleared Brendan from the list of suspects. It was easier to pin the murder on the victim's boyfriend than finding an elusive crack head in a city flooded with more than its fair share of addicts.

CHAPTER II

"OFFICER BENTON WILL GO WITH you; just point Healy out to her."

Intellectually I understood Harley's mind-set that made Brendan the prime suspect; it disturbed me that he did it within minutes of arriving at the crime scene without any physical evidence linking him to the crime. It seemed like the rush to justice that ensnared the Duke University lacrosse players. "Will Brendan be arrested?"

"At this point we just want to question him," Harley replied.

"How much longer will the building be closed?"

"It will be secured the rest of the day."

"By the way, how many women work on this floor?"

"I did some rough math in my head. "Eight of our seventeen professors are women. Our secretary Janet, the two student workers, four doctoral students and most of my adjunct faculty are women. Also on Monday nights, the Women's Studies department uses our conference room for its graduate seminar."

"I guess all the students in the seminar are women."

"All eleven plus the professor, not many men earn a graduate degree in Women's Studies."

Jordan Hall had more traffic than any other building on campus. With classes held from 8:00 AM to 10:00 PM, thousands of students daily tramped through the building. The housekeeping crew's early morning efforts probably obliterated much of the evidence.

Officer Benton and I took the elevator down to the lobby. Outside we were besieged by the television reporters; they knew a body had been found but little else. I looked up and saw the helicopter from Channel 12 circling the campus; it must be a slow news day. Hopefully the helicopter would leave once the morning news was over.

"Where are we heading?" asked Officer Benton.

"Over to the bike racks; Brendan doesn't own car. He gets around town on his bike."

"Is he some kind of eco-nut?" Officer Benton took advantage of being outside and lit a cigarette. I decided not to tell her he was a vegetarian.

Scanning the bike rack, I failed to spot Brendan's battered mountain bike. A red and yellow Marine Corps bumper sticker on the frame proclaiming Semper Fi usually made it instantly recognizable among the other bikes. "I don't see it."

"He may already be a fugitive and hit the road."

"I doubt he'd get very far on a bike."

It was a chilly morning for mid-October; a shift in the wind direction over night had brought in a cold front from Canada. Students still dressed for Indian summer, milled around the parking lot trying to keep warm and waiting for word about when the building would reopen. About half of CBU's undergraduate students were commuters and the lot was already full. Some students took advantage of their class being cancelled by sacking out in their cars; others listened to their I-Pods or chatted on their cell phones. Despite the chill, a group of male students had doffed their shirts and played Frisbee on the lawn in front of the library. Life went on for everyone but Jenny Biggio.

"Dr. Stanard! Are we going to have our midterm today?" asked Alan, a student in my 11 o'clock class.

"It's cancelled; the building is going to be closed the rest of the day. Tell anyone you see the mid-term is rescheduled for Thursday. I'll post it on my web site."

"Is it true they found a body in one of the classrooms?"

"Head home if you have classes in Jordan Hall," ordered Officer Benton.

Alan looked at Officer Benton and took her advice to move on.

"Shall we look over in the Student Union for Brendan? He may've headed there for a cup of coffee."

"I could use a cup too," replied Officer Benton who had several drags left on her cigarette.

As we passed through the parking lot I scanned it for any sign of Brendan but only spotted Art Campbell sitting on the hood of his red Volvo drinking a vente coffee from Starbucks and munching on a cranberry scone. Bumper stickers enumerated the various left wing causes he supported. Art drove a Volvo because the former Soviet Union never exported its poor quality autos to the United States. He justified his purchase by noting his car was manufactured by the good socialists in Sweden. I couldn't resist taking a jab at Comrade Art.

"Good morning Art! Are you showing your solidarity with the proletariat by joining them for a latte at Starbucks?"

"Cute," he replied. He seemed embarrassed that I'd noticed he'd joined the haute bourgeois at Starbucks for his morning fix of caffeine instead of uniting with the proletariat at 7-Eleven.

"Didn't Marx warn that lattes were the opiate of the masses?"

"Religion is still the opiate of the masses. If you'd ever bothered to read Marx you wouldn't be making your sophomoric jokes. For your edification, I've been going to Starbucks to research my book on the exploitation of workers by large multi-national corporations."

I never particularly thought Starbucks exploited it workers. Most baristas sported several visible tattoos and body piercings that limited their employment options; if it wasn't for Starbucks they'd likely be unemployed.

"What the hell is going on?" I noticed Emily Worthington coming down the row of cars toward me out of the corner of my eye.

"We've closed the building due to an ongoing investigation," replied Officer Benton saving me the trouble of responding to Emily. It didn't surprise me that Officer Benton knew Emily; her frequent complaints to campus authorities over the past twenty years gave her a high profile among the 750 members of the faculty.

"Have you seen Brendan around?" I asked.

"No doubt he's off with that girlfriend of his." She tossed her Gauloise on the ground and ground it out with her stylish maroon pumps. As the department's resident French historian, Emily was a dedicated Francophile down to her cigarettes. When the local tobacconist who carried them went out of business, she made frequent trips to Washington D. C. to stoke her addiction. Emily was forced to buy an Acura when her beloved Peugeot was totaled in a rear end collision since Peugeot had ceased exporting cars to the United States in the early 1990's.

Emily failed to make the connection between Office Benton and my questions about Brendan's whereabouts. After Officer Benton and I reached the Student Union, we fruitlessly searched the building for ten minutes without finding him. Officer Benton seemed anxious for another smoke and I decided to press the case for Brendan's innocence. "I think your chief is wrong to make Brendan a suspect; he's a former Marine."

"My first husband was a Marine; that scumbag cheated on me with a bargirl at one of the taverns outside the main gate at Camp Lejeune. Smartest thing I ever did was kick his ass out of the house."

Obviously Semper Fi was the wrong card to play with Officer Benton; her beefy physique suggested she didn't use the phrase "kick his ass" figuratively. She left to make her report to Harley and I headed upstairs to grab a cup of coffee in the faculty dining room. As I filled my mug I noticed Dean Monroe motioning for me to join him at his table.

"Good morning Tollie."

Taliaferro Monroe had been Dean of the College of Arts, Social Sciences and Humanities for ten years, a long tenure for a dean. Born and bred in Richmond, the holy city of the Confederacy, his first name was pronounced Tolliver in the old English fashion. (Those born above the Mason-Dixon Line incorrectly pronounced it Tal-i-a-ferro.) A true southerner, Tollie held a bachelors degree from the University of Virginia and like me, his masters degree and doctorate from the University of North Carolina at Chapel Hill. He'd been chair of the English Department at the University of South Carolina before coming home to Virginia to assume the deanship.

"What the hell is going on in the History Department?"

I motioned for Tollie to move to a table in the corner of the room away from everyone. "Chief Simpson told me not to speak to anyone until they contact the victim's next of kin but you need to know what's going on. It's pretty bad. A housekeeping worker found a graduate student dead this morning."

"One of your students?"

"No, she's one of Jake's students."

"Did that crack addict kill her?"

"The police are still investigating; one of my graduate students, Brendan Healy, is at the top of their suspect list."

"Why?"

"He's been dating her for the last five or six months."

Tollie stroked his white beard. "Is that all they have?"

"Do they need any more?"

"This is all the college needs after the art show fiasco last year."

A professor in the Art Department displayed her latest paintings at the university's gallery and a member of the Board of Trustees attended the opening. She saw tableaus of tits and asses in the abstract shapes on the canvas and complained to the university's president. Tollie was caught between defending artistic freedom and placating a large contributor to the university. He ordered the offensive paintings removed; the faculty was dismayed by his craven caving in to President Clayton. Tollie's ulcer put the two events in the same league although I failed to see any connection.

"I came in here to hide out; Emily Worthington almost caught up with me in the parking lot by. Usually Tammie handles her complaints and I don't have to speak with her. If the campus police are looking for a suspect, they ought to put that psychotic bitch on the top of the list!"

"We need to support Brendan."

"I must consider the college's reputation; we don't need a scandal at this time."

"What if he's innocent?"

"Don't get the college involved. I have to fight for every dollar the college gets in the budget. Doug Clayton is always touting the other five colleges and treats us like a bastard child."

Seeing I was getting nowhere with Tollie, I finished my coffee and decided to head to the library to see my wife, Laura, the Head of the Reference Department. In front of the library, I spied Brendan's mountain bike in the bike rack. I shook my head; I should've figured

Brendan had headed to the library. The library was more crowded than usual with Jordan Hall closed. I made my way to the reference desk and asked the librarian on duty, "Where's Laura?"

"She's up in her office, Dr. Stanard."

I took the stairs to the mezzanine and knocked on Laura's office door.

"Come in."

Laura seemed relieved to see me. "I've called your office and got no answer, what is going on? All the university's web site says is that Jordan Hall is closed until further notice. Channel 12's web site says a body was found in the building."

I closed the door behind me. "One of the housekeeping workers found the body of an econ graduate student in the women's restroom on our floor. She'd been strangled."

"That's horrible! Who?"

Even though I'd been told by the police not to say anything; I trusted Laura to keep it under wraps. "Jenny Biggio, she came to the house for the cookout for the graduate students over Labor Day."

"I saw her just yesterday in the library."

"The campus police have settled on Brendan as the prime suspect."

"She clung to him at the cookout. Brendan has cut a wide swath across the female students on campus. Last spring he dated one of the graduate students from the library school who worked in cataloging. I heard he unceremoniously dumped her."

Anyone who wronged a fellow librarian, even one in training, had to answer to Laura and her colleagues. A primarily female profession, librarians were notoriously protective of their sisters in distress. One professor who cheated on his wife, a librarian at the university, found he was persona non grata in libraries across the state. If he ever had an overdue book, her colleagues would've found a way to put him in front of a firing squad.

"Can you help me find Brendan? The police want to question him and they've jumped to the wrong conclusion when he wasn't at his apartment. I don't have time to search all five floors by myself."

"What makes you think he's here?"

"His bike is out front."

"I'll take the fifth and third floors, you take the second and fourth. We'll meet on the first floor. What do you want me to do?"

"Call me on my cell phone if you find him. Tell him nothing other than I'm looking for him; I'll take him to Chief Simpson."

The fourth floor was familiar territory; the history section was located on it. It was empty, except for two students making out on a couch in a remote corner, due to a carpet replacement project. I took the elevator down to the second floor where the journals and periodicals were situated and found Brendan going through a volume of *Harper's Weekly* in the microfilm room. He appeared not to have a care in the world; he didn't realize his world was about to come crashing down around him.

"Good morning Dr. Stanard?" he greeted me. Ten years away from northern New Jersey had failed to polish the rough edges off his accent. I looked him in the eyes; no doubt Harley Simpson saw on the History Channel that Hitler had piercing blue eyes like Brendan.

"I need to talk with you."

"Is Dr. Worthington pissed at me again?"

"No, there's been some trouble over in Jordan Hall and the campus police need to ask you some questions."

Brendan stiffened. "What's going on? There are all sorts of rumors about a body being found."

"It's best you talk directly with Chief Simpson."

"Why do they want to talk with me?"

Brendan's demeanor struck me as strange; he seemed rattled after I mentioned that the campus police wanted to speak with him. It was as if he had something to hide.

"They're questioning everyone on our floor," I said trying to put him at ease.

"All right, let's get this over with sir."

CHAPTER III

BRENDAN AND I WALKED OVER to Jordan Hall and found a police officer barring the entrance.

"No one is allowed inside."

"I'm Professor Stanard; I'm Chair of the History Department. This is Brendan Healy; Chief Simpson wanted to have a word with him." From the dubious look on the officer's face, my position as Chair of the History Department failed to impress him.

"Let me check." He pulled his radio off his belt. "Dispatch, put me through to the Chief."

Brendan looked around apprehensively; he tried to appear nonchalant but his nerves betrayed him.

"What is it?" squawked Harley's voice over the radio.

"Chief, I have Professor Stanard and Brendan Healy down at the main entrance. He says you wanted to see them."

"Send them up."

After the door to the elevator closed, Brendan asked, "What's going on? You need to level with me."

I couldn't tell him that his girlfriend was dead and he was at the top of the Chief Simpson's list of suspects. "I'm in the dark too."

Harley was waiting for us at the elevator; Brendan appeared surprised to see the floor crawling with police. "Come with me Mr. Healy."

"I'd like to know what's going on."

"It would be best if we spoke in private. We'll use the conference room."

"I'd like to have Dr. Stanard present."

"Fine," he replied.

I could tell Harley didn't want me there but he realized putting Brendan at ease would get more information out of him. Harley took a seat across the table from Brendan and me. Once of his investigators slipped into the room and closed the door. Brendan eyed them warily as if he had a reason to fear them.

"This is Sergeant Ramsey, my chief investigator."

"Good morning, sir." As he'd been trained in the Marine Corps, he always ended his responses with sir. He sat stiffly in his chair; his eyes darting around the room trying to figure out why he was there.

"There's no easy way to tell you this Mr. Healy. Your girlfriend, Jennifer Biggio, was found murdered this morning."

"No!" Brendan buried his face in his hands and started sobbing. It took two or three minutes for him to recover his composure. He was in a state of shock but embarrassed that tears were flowing from his eyes; Marines were not supposed to cry. Finally he asked, "What happened?"

Harley intently watched Brendan's facial expressions and demeanor. "Dr. Stanard and one of the housekeepers found her body in the restroom across from your office. She'd been strangled."

"My God!" Brendan's mouth hung open for several seconds as if he'd just been punched in the stomach.

"We thought you could shed some light on that. When did you last see her?"

"I stopped at her apartment before I went to work."

"When was that?"

"About two o'clock sir."

"Why?"

"Just to chill, I share a house with three other guys. It's impossible to be alone there. Her roommate doesn't get home till after five."

"So you grabbed a little afternoon delight." A big smirk filled the investigator's face.

Harley glared at the investigator to tell him his comment was inappropriate. Brendan looked down at the table with a sheepish expression on his face.

"What time did you leave her apartment?" asked Harley.

"I left a little after five, sir."

"What time did you get to work?"

"Around seven; I work as a banquet waiter at the Convention Center. They've had a nursing convention there since Saturday. It was an awards dinner; the cocktail hour was from six to seven."

"If you didn't have to be at work until seven, why'd you leave at five?"

"Jenny needed to go to the library."

"Where'd you go?"

"I went back to my apartment to change and take a shower."

"Were any of your roommates home?"

"No, they were all out."

"Who's your supervisor at the Convention Center?"

"Ken Walton is the banquet manager."

I noticed the investigator writing everything down in his notebook. Harley's questions were trying to pin down Brendan's whereabouts last night. Depending on when Jenny had been murdered, Brendan seemed to have an alibi for most of the evening.

"What time did you finish up?"

"It was after nine; we had to wait to clear the tables until after the awards were presented."

"Did you go straight home after work?"

"I stopped at the library to pick up a book from the interlibrary loan office."

"What time was that?"

"Just before they closed at ten o'clock."

"Did you see your girlfriend after work?"

"I tried to call her cell phone last night and this morning but couldn't reach her."

"You didn't think that was odd?"

"She'd been having trouble with the battery charging; I left messages on her voice mail."

"Jerry, check with the phone company to see if you can access her messages."

"Yes sir," replied Sergeant Ramsey.

"Where did you go after the library?"

"I went home."

"We find it strange that Ms. Biggio was found across the hall from your office. When were you last in your office?"

"About one o'clock yesterday."

"That seems rather early to call it a day."

"Graduate assistants are required to work 20 hours a week for their stipend," I interrupted.

"Was Ms. Biggio in your office yesterday?"

"No, I went to her office after my ten o'clock class. We chatted for a few minutes."

"Do you know why she would be on this floor last night?"

"No, Jenny knew I was working at the Convention Center."

I looked at Brendan and noticed large damp circles spreading across the armpits of his yellow cotton polo shirt. His left hand clenched the arm of his chair; his right hand held tight to the edge of the conference table.

"Did you call her and tell her to meet you here after you finished work?"

"No."

"Would she have met anyone else in Jordan Hall last night?"

"Not that I know of; maybe she went up to her office in the econ department."

"That seems more logical," I interjected.

"Professor Stanard tells me you're an ex-marine."

"Yes sir, I did a four year enlistment and was discharged as a corporal."

"Were you honorably discharged?"

"Yes sir; my DD 214 is at home if you need to see it. The Veteran's Counselor in Financial Aid has a copy too."

"I'm retired from the Army," replied Harley trying to gain rapport with Brendan using the military connection as a leaver.

Harley motioned for the investigator to go out into the hall. Brendan shot me a worried look. They inadvertently left the door ajar and I could overhear parts of their conversation. After years of barking orders in the military, Harley was unable to modulate his voice to a lower decibel.

"Until the medical examiner pins down the time of death, we don't have any probable cause to hold him," said Harley.

"He seemed evasive to me at times Chief."

"His answers seemed too pat."

"What do you think about him crying when we told him?"

"Jarheads aren't the sentimental type. Those looked like crocodile tears to me."

Sergeant Ramsey snickered. "He could have left those messages on her cell phone to throw us off the trail."

"You have a point Jerry. He's a lot smarter than our usual suspects. We're not going to trip him up very easily. Start checking his alibi; I see several gaps in it."

"We also have to trace her movements; we know nothing about her whereabouts yesterday. Start over at the library; see if she ever made it there."

"He only needed a minute to strangle her."

Harley pushed against the door and returned to the conference room.

"I have one more question for you."

"Sure."

"How long had you been dating Ms. Biggio?"

"We met at the Graduate Student Association keg party at the end of April."

Before Harley could ask another question, he was interrupted by a knock on the door. Officer Ramsey opened the door and Officer Benton stepped in the conference room.

"Chief, the city police just radioed in. They picked up a woman at the Wal-Mart trying to use the victim's VISA card."

"What?" Harley seemed clearly stunned by this development.

"The security manager recognized the woman when she came in the store. She'd been in about two weeks ago and filled a shopping cart with merchandise. After the clerk rang up everything, she tried to pay for it with a Discover Card. When the transaction was rejected, she just walked out of the store and took off in a waiting car."

"The credit card had been reported stolen?"

The officer nodded affirmatively. "This morning he spotted her on the monitors as she filled the cart with DVDs and clothes. When she got to the checkout, he had the clerk ask for identification. She gave a song and dance about how she'd left her license in the car; the security manager said he'd be glad to escort her to her car. The suspect bolted but he grabbed her in the parking lot. He got the license plate number of her accomplice but he sped out of the parking lot when he saw her being chased. When the city police arrived, they recognized Ms. Biggio's name from our bulletin about her missing wallet."

"Where are they holding her?"

"They're processing her at central booking for possession of a stolen credit card."

"Jerry, go over and see what you can get out of her. See if they've traced that license plate yet."

"Mr. Healy, we're through with you for now. Give Officer Benton your contact information in case we have any more questions for you."

"Yes sir."

"We're doing everything we can to find the killer of your girlfriend."

"Thank you sir; has anyone contacted Jenny's parents in Cleveland?"

"We haven't talked with them yet. Please don't say anything to anyone including the media."

"Yes sir."

Once out in the hall, I said to Brendan, "You're still in shock over what happened. You might want to talk with one of the counselors over in the counseling center."

"Thank you for staying with me in there; they questioned me like I murdered her."

"It's probably standard procedure."

"You're right; I shouldn't take it personally."

I sensed Brendan's tough persona was beginning to crack. "Let's go get a cup of coffee over at Nick's."

"That's a good idea sir; I need to talk with someone I can trust."

CHAPTER IV

WE WALKED ACROSS THE STREET to Nick's Diner and took a booth at the back of the restaurant. Nick's, a Norfolk landmark, was open around the clock and was a favorite student hangout. It was only a little after eleven and the lunch crowd hadn't started drifting in. A few students were nursing cups of coffee as they read or listened to their I-Pads.

"Two coffees," I told the waitress.

"I can't believe she's dead," said Brendan. "We were going to be married at Christmas."

I noticed tears welling in his eyes but he managed to hold them back. Their marriage plans compounded the tragedy of her murder. Still his statement surprised me after Laura's comment earlier in the morning. Women usually kept track of these things better than men. According to Laura, Brendan had broken up with his previous girlfriend in the spring. Less than eight months after hooking up with Jenny, he would've been walking down the aisle. Brendan seemed to enjoy the freedom of the graduate student lifestyle and didn't impress me as someone itching to settle down in domestic bliss.

"I need to level with you."

His voice came close to breaking. He was sweating again just as he'd been when questioned by Harley and the investigator. Brendan looked nervously around the restaurant.

"When the police start probing into my background, they're going to find things out about me that I'm not too proud of. I wanted to tell you so that you wouldn't be caught off guard. It's probably going to kill any chances for a career in higher education; I should've been honest from the start."

"What do you mean?"

"As a historian, you would term me a revisionist. My life before the Marine Corps wasn't what I've made it out to be."

Brendan had been my student for over six years and was now admitting that he lied to me. His deceitful behavior surprised me, but it was best to hear him out. It put his demeanor while questioned by Harley Simpson in a different light.

"Here are your coffees," said the waitress as she put them down in front of us.

Brendan took a sip of his before continuing. "I told you I joined the Marine Corps because of my home situation. That was only partially true. I had no choice; the judge gave me the option of either the Marines or prison."

"I thought they only did that in the movies."

Brendan laughed. "It's more common than you imagine; I ran into a lot of guys in the Marine Corps who shared a similar conversion experience."

I wondered what Brendan had done that he faced time in prison.

"Part of what I told you about my past was true; my dad left my mom when I was thirteen. It was a real struggle for her to support my two younger sisters and I; she worked long hours as an LPN at a nursing home. She later earned her nursing degree at a community college. It was too late for me. I started hanging out with the wrong crowd, smoking weed and committing all sorts of petty crimes. When I was seventeen, I was sentenced to a year at the Mountainview Juvenile Correctional Facility. That was where I completed my GED and picked up my tattoo, not the Marines."

I could understand Brendan's predicament; the image he'd so carefully crafted to portray himself to the faculty and his peers was about to be torn apart. His juvenile misdeeds didn't make him a murderer although I could see how it could be misconstrued by the police and put him back at top of the suspect list.

"My incarceration did nothing to curb my wild behavior and within a few weeks of my release I was back to my old activities. I didn't realize it but the police were keeping tabs on me. One night to impress my girlfriend, I stole a Lexus to go joy riding and the police nailed me. They slapped me in jail and I was facing prison time. Even though I was under eighteen; they were going to try me as an adult. That's when my grandfather intervened; Judge O'Connor was an old pal from the neighborhood. My grandfather pleaded with him to take pity on an Irish boy in trouble. Judge O'Connor bought my grandfather's plan for me to enlist in the Marine Corps and reduced the charges to a misdemeanor. At the time, I figured four years in the Marines was better than two years in prison. My grandfather's plan worked and the Marine Corps turned my life around. I started taking college courses at Camp Lejeune."

It sounded like something out of a Pat O'Brien movie. The judge cut Brendan a big break; I wonder if he would have done the same for an African-American kid in trouble. "You've stayed out of trouble since then?"

"My record since I joined the Marines is spotless. If the police get hold of my rap sheet from Jersey they could jump to the wrong conclusions."

"Like what?"

Brendan paused and looked around the restaurant. "One of my buddies, Sean, was dealing drugs; we were pretty tight. A rival dealer was beaten to death with an aluminum baseball bat; the police questioned me extensively."

"Why?"

"Sean was only five foot, six; I provided the muscle to back him up when he collected his drug debts."

I couldn't believe what I was hearing; was Brendan a split personality? Did a psychopath lurk under the polished veneer of a graduate student? "You broke arms and legs for your friend?"

Brendan smiled as he rolled back the sleeve of his shirt to expose his bulging bicep. "I started lifting weights when I was fourteen. Just showing up was usually enough to get them to pay up. I used force only once; I twisted one punk's arm when he didn't respond to gentle persuasion."

He seemed almost proud of his exploits. "Why did the police think you killed Sean's competitor?"

"The police knew I was handy with a bat; I played on my high school baseball team until I was expelled."

"Did you have anything to do with the murder?"

"No, Ramon was a two bit hustler with a lot of debts. They were grasping at straws; they didn't have any evidence to tie either of us to it."

"Has anyone ever been convicted of his murder?"

"No, Sean was murdered shortly after I went to boot camp; they shot him seventeen times and stuffed his body in the trunk of his car."

"Wouldn't three or four bullets have done the job?"

Brendan laughed. "You have a lot to learn; the number of bullets sent a message to other dealers. According to the newspaper clipping my mom sent me, they used two guns on Sean. It could have been me if I hadn't smartened up and enlisted in the Marines."

"Sean's murder should've taken you off the police's suspect list; drug dealers are killed all the time in senseless turf wars."

Brendan looked around the restaurant. "You don't understand the jam I'm in. I have a two year suspended jail sentence hanging over me. The authorities in Jersey can slap me back in jail if I get into any trouble."

It explained his nervousness when questioned by Harley Simpson.

"Once the police start digging, everything will be dredged up. I won't be able to look people in the face."

I tried to reassure Brendan. "The police just wanted to question you. The fact that woman at the Wal-Mart had Jenny's credit card indicates it was a robbery. Her boyfriend is probably the one who's been doing all the muggings on campus."

"That doesn't make sense."

"What do you mean?"

"I spent seven months at Mountainview; I learned more about crime than if I'd earned a Ph.D. in criminology. Crack addicts don't strangle their victims to steal their purses; they use the element of surprise to attack their victim from behind, grab the purse and run like hell to get away."

"If an addict didn't kill Jenny, then why would someone kill her?"

"The police are going to ask the same question and point the finger in my direction. I'm Jenny's boyfriend; that automatically makes me a suspect. You saw how that female police officer looked at me; it was as if I had scumbag written across my shirt."

I thought I knew Brendan before today; now it was as if a total stranger was sitting across the table from me. Was he involved in Jenny's murder? He'd spun a clever fairy tale to cover his tracks as a juvenile delinquent. Was his protestation of innocence, just another lie?

CHAPTER V

BRENDAN'S REVELATIONS HAD KNOCKED THE wind out of me; we sat there for several minutes sipping our coffee in silence. "Do you need a lift?"

"It will help clear my head to bike home sir."

"Take a couple days off; I'll get someone to cover your classes."

"Is that a polite way of telling me I'm suspended?"

His comment surprised me; the police had questioned him since he was the victim's boyfriend. "You're still in shock over what happened. It might help you to talk to someone."

"I don't want to burden my mother; she has enough on her mind. She went through hell with me before I joined the Marines."

"Maybe you should talk to Dr. Fitzgerald in the Counseling Center."

Brendan didn't respond; he just stared at the picture of the 1976 CBU basketball team hanging on the wall next to the booth. Finally he broke the silence, "When I was locked up, the counselors at Mountainview were a bunch of head cases themselves. One of them committed suicide by closing the door to his garage and turning on his car. Go figure how he was supposed to help us when he was screwed up himself."

Clearly Brendan and the other boys weren't well served. Without therapeutic help, it explained why being incarcerated failed to curb his wild behavior. "I'm sure the salaries paid by the prison system didn't attract the best counselors. Give Dr. Fitzgerald a chance to help you."

"In the Marines we were taught to rely on ourselves."

"If you need help, give me a call. Everything you told me will be kept in confidence."

After Brendan left, I paid the bill and walked across the street to campus. With Jordan Hall still closed, I found myself at loose ends. I'd normally be finishing my 11 AM class. Since it was past noon, I walked over to the library to see if Laura had any plans for lunch. She was at the reference desk helping a clueless looking student with a skateboard tucked under his arm and a T-shirt promoting the "Boogie Till You Puke Festival".

We'd met when I was I in graduate school at Chapel Hill. Laura was working the reference desk and I needed help locating a journal article for my dissertation. Back in the Stone Age as my children called the early 1980s, there were no electronic research databases. Locating a book or an article was a time consuming task made easier by a friendly librarian. With numerous research sources accessible from a laptop today, some students manage to go through college never venturing into the library. I wonder if I'd even have the opportunity to meet Laura if I was a graduate student today.

The student had been stymied because he'd found no information on the Battle of Tannenbaum in the *Wikipedia*. I started whistling the popular Christmas carol, *O Tannenbaum*. Laura suppressed the urge to laugh and subtly signaled for me to stop my musical entertainment. I waited as she explained to the student that that his professor would prefer sources other than the *Wikipedia* for his term paper. Patiently she taught him how to search the library's catalog to locate books on the Battle of Tannenberg.

"Stick to teaching history; I don't think you have a future in the music business," said Laura after the student left.

I laughed. "Don't you want to hear my rendition of *White Christmas?*"

"I'll stick to my Bing Crosby CD. What brings you back to the library?"

"Do you have any plans for lunch?"

"I brought a can of tomato soup from home to microwave. What do you have in mind?"

"I'm in the mood for Mexican food; let's head over to Tortilla Flats." Run by a former English graduate student, the restaurant combined his love of Steinbeck and Mexican food. Down the street from Nick's, it offered plentiful servings at reasonable prices.

"Are you treating?"

"Now that I'm a department chair, I guess I can afford it." When we were dating during my graduate student days, a meal out seemed like a luxury. Although we both worked on campus, our conflicting schedules often made lunching together impossible.

We walked out of the library and headed across campus. Channel 12's satellite truck was still parked outside Jordan Hall, its reporter, Felicia Wright, waiting to broadcast on the station's midday news. Two shirtless students skate boarded with impunity behind her trying to get their 15 seconds of fame, knowing the campus police were busy inside the building. Out of the blue, Dick Torelli appeared with one of his staff and shooed them away. Laura and I paused to listen.

"Felicia has a rather huge rear," whispered Laura in her judgmental tone. I noticed a Dunkin Donuts box on the dashboard of the truck; it appeared Felicia and her cameraman had been chowing down on chocolate covered donuts.

"No wonder they only shoot her from the waist up." Felicia had been a fixture in local television for over ten years in more ways than one. She was a stolid reporter who gamely covered any assignment thrown at her; she'd hung on as flashier reporters moved on to larger media markets.

"She needs to bleach her roots; they're showing," noted Laura.

"This is Felicia Wright reporting live from the campus of Chesapeake Bay University where early this morning a cleaning lady found a young woman dead in a bathroom on the sixth floor of Russell Jordan Hall. University officials have not released the victim's name pending notification of next of kin."

"I talked with a group of students before the broadcast and they indicated that several women have been mugged this semester in the vicinity of Jordan Hall. No one has been arrested yet for those attacks. Campus police are not saying if there is a connection between the murder and the muggings."

"The southern edge of the CBU campus is adjacent to the Braxton Homes, a low income housing project troubled by gang activity and curbside drug dealing."

I looked over at Dick Torelli and noticed his blood pressure shoot up at the mention of Braxton Homes.

Felicia paused as the anchor asked her a question. We were unable to hear it since it was audible only in her ear piece.

"Campus police are not saying if the woman is a student nor have they released the cause and time of death."

The anchor asked her another question.

"Jordan Hall is home to almost 150 faculty plus 30 classrooms and an art gallery. The sixth floor of Jordan Hall is the home of the History Department according to students. Apparently all the female professors in the department have been accounted for."

She paused for another question.

"Sources close to the investigation indicate a graduate student was questioned by campus police this morning; we don't know if he's a suspect or merely a witness."

Considering their exchange this morning, I doubted Harley shared that he interviewed Brendan with Torelli. However I noticed Officer Benson guarding the entrance to the building. She may have let it slip if Felicia caught her in an unguarded moment. Brendan's fears about being dragged through the mud now seemed justified.

With Felicia's broadcast over, we walked across campus to the restaurant. "What are you going to do when the media calls?" asked Laura.

"Why would they want to talk to me?"

"They know the murder occurred in the history department; a fifth grader can look on the university's web site and find you."

"Hopefully they'll find Emily first; she can occupy them with one of her diatribes."

"You need to be careful."

"What do you mean?" I asked as we entered the restaurant. The waitress showed us to our table and handed us our menus.

"Don't go out on a limb for Brendan. You know very little about him."

I hated to admit it but Laura was right as usual. Brendan had revealed a dark side of his personality that I was unaware of.

"Are you ready to order?" interrupted the waitress as she placed a plastic basket of tortilla chips and a bowl of salsa on the table.

"I'll have the taco salad, go light on the cheese and sour cream," replied Laura.

"I'll order the tacos con chorizo."

The waitress moved on to her next table and we were free to talk. "Why do you think I'm making a mistake about Brendan?"

"After you left the library, I went over to cataloging to talk with Rita Flanagan about Brendan's relationship with her graduate student."

I scooped my chip into the salsa and managed to get it to my mouth without dripping it on the table. "What did you find out?"

"Their breakup was acrimonious to say the least."

I took another scoop of the salsa. "Which party was angry about the end of the relationship?"

"He'd been dating Kate Goodman most of spring semester; as the kids say it was a relationship with fringe benefits. We closed the library early one evening due to the air conditioning breaking down and she took advantage of it to go to his apartment. She found him in flagrante delicto with a banquet waitress from the convention center."

"If she caught them in bed, how did she know she was a waitress?"

"Her uniform was just strewn on the floor; she didn't even bother to fold it and put it over a chair."

Judging from Laura's tone, I didn't know whether her biggest offense was failing to fold her clothes or screwing Brendan. Having attended an all girls' Catholic high school and college, Laura took a dim view of others' moral failings. I took another scoop of salsa to fortify myself. "Brendan's not the first graduate student to burn his candle at both ends."

"But most have done it without police intervention," Laura replied.

"Why were the police involved?"

"Kate threw a book at them, hitting Brendan's backside; the police had to be called in to bring a peaceful resolution to the dispute."

"Isn't throwing a book against the canons of the American Library Association? Did they revoke her student membership?"

"Be serious for once. Kate was hurt badly by Brendan; he took advantage of her. The police will dig the incident report out of their files and draw their own conclusions."

The waitress delivered our order and I took a bite out of my first taco as Laura removed the excess cheese from her salad. "It doesn't make him a murderer."

"What I'm going to tell you violates all the ethics of the library profession but you need to know before the police. I checked Jenny Biggio's circulation record this morning."

"Why'd you check Jenny's record?"

"Call it women's intuition; I saw her yesterday acting furtively at the circulation desk."

"Why's that important?"

"Last week in Walgreens, I saw a teenage boy acting the same way. He kept checking the aisle near the pharmacy and waited till I picked up my prescription."

"Let me guess, he was buying condoms."

"Exactly! He was red-faced when the sales clerk left them out on the counter and didn't immediately bag them. Jenny didn't want someone she knew on the circulation desk seeing what she checked out."

In the ninth grade I went to my neighborhood library and waited for the gray haired librarian, Mrs. Summers, to go to lunch. John, the college student hired for the summer, didn't object when I checked out four James Bond novels. My curiosity piqued, I asked, "What did she check out, *Lady Chatterley's Lover* or *The Kama Sutra*?"

"No, she checked out three books on pregnancy yesterday."

"So what?"

"Women don't check out books on pregnancy for bedtime reading. Jenny was pregnant!"

Now I knew what it felt like after being run over by a Mack truck. "You think she found out recently?"

"I bet she'd just been to the student health center for a pregnancy test. Then she went to the library afterwards to check out the books."

It certainly explained Brendan's sudden rush to the altar; I never realized it was a shotgun wedding. "He told me they planned to get married over Christmas."

Laura gave me a look as if I just tried to sell her the Brooklyn Bridge. "I doubt he planned to go through with it. Marriage would've constrained him from spreading his DNA around campus."

"You're rushing to judge him."

"The police will find the books when they search her apartment and reach the same conclusion. It now gives Brendan a motive for killing Jenny."

I took a large bite out of my taco. "You're the one who's jumping to conclusions now."

"How well do you really know Brendan?"

"He's been my student for six years now." For the time being, I decided not to share with Laura what he'd divulged about his criminal record.

"Call it my women's intuition again. I've never liked Brendan; I always thought his smarmy demeanor masked something. The way he treated Kate shows he's nothing but a lying snake. His jailhouse tattoo confirms my suspicions he's a two bit thug."

I wondered how Laura knew Brendan picked up his tattoo in jail. It was doubtful she'd come into contact with anyone sporting a jailhouse tattoo at her all girls high school unless Sister Veronica conducted lessons on how to spot boys of low moral character. I decided to test Laura as I grabbed another tortilla chip. "I always thought he picked up his tattoo in the Marines."

Laura grinned triumphantly. "When we first moved here, you may recall I worked for the city library until the position at the university opened up. When the jail librarian was on maternity leave, I helped cover for her. I saw more than my fair share of jailhouse tattoos. He probably did time in the brig when he was in the Marines for all you know."

More ominously if his tattoos marked him as a two bit thug to Laura, what would the police think? "Before you send Brendan to prison, when I was with Harley Simpson this morning he was informed the city police arrested a woman at Wal-Mart trying to use Jenny's credit card."

"Are you trying to tell me she was robbed then murdered?"

"That's my guess."

"It doesn't make any sense to murder someone just to steal a credit card. Unattended purses are easy picking in the library; they're like low hanging fruit. We have two or three purses taken every month not to mention laptops."

Like Brendan, Laura discounted the robbery theory. Unless the police were totally obtuse, they'd find the pregnancy books at her apartment. The books were icing on the cake; the autopsy would confirm the pregnancy and point to Brendan as her murderer.

"I told you all this in confidence; I violated my professional ethics telling you about the books so you won't get yourself in trouble. Let the investigation run its course and stay out of it."

I sprinkled my remaining taco with habanera sauce. After lunch, I'd pay Brendan a visit. Before I helped him he needed set things straight.

CHAPTER VI

JUST AS I POLISHED OFF the last tortilla chip from the red plastic basket, I noticed Emily Worthington coming toward me. I wished I'd ordered a margarita instead of iced tea.

"Andy, I need a word with you."

"I'm surprised to see a Francophile like you in a Mexican restaurant; I thought you'd be lunching at Le Petite Jardin." One of the tonier bistros in Norfolk, its pricey menu meant Laura and I could afford to patronize it only on our anniversary. It counted the university's president as one of its best customers; he frequently wined and dined potential donors there.

Emily smiled. "I find Le Petite Jardin's boeuf bourguignonne a little too salty for my taste; no wonder President Clayton is hypertensive and forty pounds overweight."

Touché! Point to Emily; she was rarely bested in a verbal exchange.

"Please excuse us Laura."

"No problem, I was just leaving," replied Laura.

"I'll see you at the Faculty Women's Association luncheon next week."

"I'm bringing our new government documents librarian; it will be good opportunity for her to meet some of the faculty."

"We have to counter the old boy network every chance we get."

Emily was the dowager President of the Faculty Women's Association; her ardent feminism caused her to spar frequently with Tollie Monroe and led to him sacking her as department chair.

I gave Laura a good-bye peck on the cheek as Emily took the empty chairs at the table."

The waitress refilled my glass with ice tea and asked Emily, "Can I get you something?"

"A cup of coffee if you please."

Since Laura and I had already settled our bill, the waitress gritted her teeth. A hungry mob queued at the front door waiting for tables and one of her prime tables was tied up by a customer offering the prospect of a minimal tip.

"What can I do for you?"

"For starters you need to find a new teaching assistant for my lecture class."

"Why do you want to replace Brendan?" I decided to play dumb to see what Emily knew or thought she knew.

The waitress placed Emily's cup of coffee in front of her. Barely containing her surly demeanor, she asked, "Do you want cream ma'am?"

"Black is fine." Emily took a sip of coffee. "You'd think after growing it, the Mexicans would know how to brew a decent cup of coffee. Only the French know how to do it right."

No one on the restaurant's staff looked remotely Mexican; although the owner hailed from south of the border in North Carolina.

"I ran into Officer Benton taking a smoke outside Jordan Hall."

"Does she smoke Gauloises too?"

Emily gave me a withering glare. "Every year the Faculty Women's Club sponsors a self-defense seminar; Wendy volunteers her time to teach it. I asked her what was going on since the administration has suppressed all information about this tragedy."

"No one is suppressing anything Emily; let the campus police conduct their investigation." Emily confirmed my suspicion that Officer Benton leaked the details of the murder to Felicia Wright.

"The victim was Healy's girlfriend; he's the chief suspect. I'm not going to work with a strangler!"

"When I was talking with Chief Simpson, they arrested a woman in Wal-Mart trying to use one of Jenny Biggio's credit cards."

"Wendy discounted that; the girl says she found the wallet in the alley behind Tait's Market."

Located several blocks from campus, the corner in front of the grocery was a center of drug activity. Despite police attempts to shut down the open air drug bazaar, the dealers would lay low for a few days after the police sweeps before setting up shop again. "Wallets don't fall from the sky into the hands of crack addicts; she's lying to protect her boyfriend. He murdered her while stealing her purse."

"Wendy thinks Brendan planted the wallet in the alley to send the police off in the wrong direction; hundreds of women are killed every year by their husbands and boyfriends!" Emily's face reddened with rage and she pounded her fist on the table for a rhetorical flourish.

I held my tongue and fought the urge to tell Emily to cut the feminist litany. "You've convicted him without any evidence."

A look of triumph filled Emily's face. "When you get a chance to check your voice mail from Monday, you'll find a message that I wanted to meet with you about Brendan. I caught him interacting in an inappropriate manner with a freshman enrolled in my European History survey class."

"What was he doing?"

"He was kissing her in the elevator."

"You were in the elevator with them?"

"I caught them by accident; the elevator stopped on the sixth floor yesterday and when the door opened, the two of them were locked in embrace. That's a violation of the university's sexual harassment policy. It's unethical behavior to take advantage of a young impressionable student."

College coeds these days would hardly be construed as naïve waifs in the woods; they all seemed to dress in tight jeans and blouses to show off their feminine assets. Emily's charge was serious; if true, I would have to dismiss Brendan as a teaching assistant. "Did you share this with Officer Benton?"

"I wanted to discuss it with you before filing a formal complaint. Brendan should resign quietly and not cause a disruption in the department."

"Send me a memo indicating what you'd observed so I can discuss it with him and take the appropriate steps. What's the student's name?"

"Tiffany Finley; I trust you won't sweep it under the rug like Tollie."

"Let's not make any more wild speculations until we have all the facts; it doesn't justify Officer Benton's suspicion that he murdered his girlfriend."

"It doesn't? The gossip around campus indicates his saucisson has been very active since he arrived on campus."

"Saucisson?"

"I forgot you took Spanish in college," replied Emily in a condescending tone. "Saucisson is French for sausage; I was using a polite euphemism for Brendan's unrestrained male appendage."

Taken with Laura's story, Emily's assertion made it appear Brendan was thinking with the wrong part of his anatomy. Too many men in history have met their downfall when ruled by their passions instead of reason.

"Italians are very emotional people. How do think his girlfriend reacted when she found out he was two timing her?"

"You've seen too many Anna Magnani films; not all Italians posses Vesuvian tempers." If Emily knew Jenny was pregnant, she was playing her cards close to the vest. But I had to admit most pregnant women would react furiously if they found out their boyfriend or husband was cheating on them. If Emily's story were true, how did Brendan respond to his righteously angry girlfriend? Did he lose control of his temper and strangle her?

Although a sexual harassment investigation was confidential, I had no doubt the information would have to be turned over to the police if Brendan was charged with murder. Despite being sometimes clouded by her feminist perspective, Emily was usually a good judge of people. Why did I get the feeling for the second time Brendan had been less than truthful with me? Should I listen to Laura and distance myself from him?

The police had a very strong circumstantial case. Once they started digging in Brendan's past, who knew what else they'd find. The noose had already been slipped over Brendan's neck and was seconds away from being cinched tight.

I didn't have much time. I parted company with Emily and headed back to campus to retrieve my car.

CHAPTER VII

I REMEMBERED BRENDAN'S ADDRESS AFTER looking it up for Harley earlier in the day.

As I drove the mile to his house, I passed Tait's Market. A police car parked across from the store kept the drug dealers from setting up shop for the day. As Officer Benton noted, it would have been easy for Brendan to ditch the wallet in the alley behind the store as he rode past on his bike.

Brendan's house was located in Jefferson Terrace, a neighborhood that had seen better days. Originally developed in the 1920's, the neighborhood featured southern bungalows with large front porches. During Norfolk's housing shortage in World War II, a number of the houses were divided into duplexes or converted to rooming houses, beginning the neighborhood's decline. In the 1960's, houses were knocked downed and cheaply built apartment houses shoehorned onto the small lots. The mature shade trees were chopped down and the front lawn paved over for parking. Jefferson Terrace's absentee landlords violated city zoning ordinances and allowed several students or sailors to share a dwelling.

Like most houses in the neighborhood, the white paint on the once attractive bungalow where Brendan lived had turned almost gray from coal dust of the nearby coal piers. One of the front shutters was missing; its mate was rotting and close to death. Brendan's bike secured to a pillar of the front porch with a heavy chain and massive padlock confirmed that I had the right address. Instinctively I knocked on the door rather than ringing the doorbell that looked like it last worked during the Nixon administration.

Waiting for a response I looked up the street and saw an African-American man sitting in a dark blue unmarked Crown Victoria. His position in the next block gave him a clear view of the house. The police were keeping an eye on Brendan's movements. Were events moving that rapidly?

Finally the door opened; Brendan stood in front of me clad only in a pair of red sweat pants. His eyes looked red. Had he been crying?

"What are you doing here Dr. Stanard?"

"I need to talk with you."

"About what sir?"

"We may not have much time. Casually look up the street to your left; an unmarked police car is watching your house. You need to play straight with me because the police are quickly getting their ducks in row."

Brendan observed the police car and motioned for me to come in. The inside of the bungalow was in better shape than the outside. It appeared no one else was home. I took a seat in an arm chair with a frayed slip cover. Brendan sat down on the leather couch that looked rescued from the trash collectors.

"I was doing some pushups to clear my head; at Parris Island they taught us that exercise releases stress. I did forty pushups before you came; it didn't help."

Brendan's cell phone sitting on the battered coffee table went off. He picked it up. "It's one of my roommates; I'm going to take it out on the porch; the reception is better outside."

I noticed a stack of photos on the coffee table and curiously leafed through them. The date stamp on the back indicated the photos were taken in late August; Brendan and Jenny had spent the day at Virginia Beach. Jenny's blond hair and blue eyes were accentuated by the blue bikini she wore that day. Someone, a passerby perhaps, had snapped several pictures of the two of them together. They made an attractive couple; Jenny's supple curves accentuated Brendan's muscular physique in the photos. From the look in Jenny's eyes, she was clearly as smitten with Brendan as he was with her. Brendan must have taken over a dozen pictures of her alone. Nothing in their smiles and laughter that day foretold the tragedy that would unfold two months later. I put the photos down when I heard the door opening.

I got right to the point when Brendan sat down. "You didn't tell me Jenny was pregnant."

His jaw dropped. "I only found out yesterday. How did you know?"

"My wife saw Jenny checking out books on pregnancy; the police are going to find the books in her apartment and draw the same conclusion."

"Shit!"

"How do you think you could have concealed this from the police? Did Jenny go to the student health center and have a pregnancy test?"

"She had an appointment tomorrow morning; she used a home pregnancy test on Monday morning."

"That's why you were getting married at Christmas?"

"Yes sir."

"Did Jenny tell her parents?"

"Not yet; she wanted to wait until she had her appointment at the health center."

"Did she tell anyone else?"

"I doubt it."

"Do you see how this is going to look to the police?"

"What do you think I should do?"

"You need to make a clean breast of things to the police. Why weren't you honest with me?"

"I was embarrassed about getting Jenny pregnant. Everything has been such a shock; I'm not thinking straight."

"So no one knows about Jenny being pregnant or the two of you getting married?"

"Jenny and I made an appointment to meet with Father Novello on Thursday morning. Jenny wanted to get married in the Catholic Church."

"Are you a Catholic?"

"When I was at Mountainview I attended Mass; that scored points with the guards."

I thought of Henry IV of France and muttered to myself, "Paris vaut bien une messe."

"What were you doing in the elevator with the student on Monday?"

Brendan exhaled a deep breath. "I should have figured Dr. Worthington would totally misconstrue what happened. Tiffany got carried away when I told her she passed the quiz; she'd been down because she'd failed the first one."

I didn't recall any of my students hugging me when I was a teaching assistant. Standing in line in the bookstore last month, I was behind two attractive sorority girls discussing Brendan's good looks and speculating on his availability. Could one of them have been the over-enthusiastic freshman? It was not as cut and dried as Emily described it; Brendan may not have been the aggressor.

A hard rap on the door interrupted us. Brendan opened the door to find Harley Simpson with the man from the car standing on the porch. Not waiting for an invitation, they pushed past Brendan and entered the room.

"We'd like to have a word with you," announced the man from the car.

Harley spotted me. "What are you doing here Andy?"

"I'm just going over with Brendan the arrangements to cover his classes. In light of what happened, I'm giving him a few days off."

"You're a true humanitarian," replied Harley's companion. He eyed Brendan's tattoo suspiciously.

"I don't believe, I caught your name," I asked.

"Lieutenant Eddie Riddick, I'm an investigator with the campus police." He flashed his badge.

"Let me go upstairs and get a shirt on," said Brendan as he headed toward the stairs.

Lieutenant Riddick looked at Harley and seemed ready to tackle Brendan to prevent him from escaping through a second floor window. Harley stopped him with a subtle wave of his hand and Brendan darted up the stairs.

"He looked like a lawyer to me; I didn't realize he was only a college professor," whispered Lieutenant Riddick as he pointed to me.

"You made the right call; we need to question Healy before a lawyer gets him to clam up," replied Harley.

Harley and Lieutenant Riddick seated themselves on the couch; Harley opened his brief case and pulled out a small tape recorder.

Brendan returned about thirty seconds later wearing a yellow T-shirt with USMC in red letters across the chest. All he needed to do was to serve apple pie and convince the officers that Chinese characters tattooed on his arm spelled mom. He looked warily at the tape recorder as he pulled up a chair from the dining room table.

"Is it all right if Dr. Stanard stays?" asked Brendan.

Harley frowned but he knew he couldn't demand that I leave. He clicked on the tape recorder. "I want to get straight to the point. Why did you withhold from me your criminal record?"

"I never withheld any information; you never asked if I've ever been in trouble with the law. It happened when I was a teenager; my record is clean since I joined the Marines."

"Until now," muttered Lieutenant Riddick under his breath.

"You were tried as an adult for your last escapade with the law," noted Harley.

"That was over eleven years ago," replied Brendan.

"In fact you still have a two year suspended sentence waiting for you back in New Jersey," said Lieutenant Riddick.

"I'm not proud of what happened when I was a teenager. The Marine Corps offered me a chance to redeem myself."

"I talked with an old friend of yours in New Jersey, Sergeant Milkowski."

"I'm sure he had nothing good to say about me."

"It seems you're still the chief suspect in an unsolved murder in Kearny. You're quite handy with a baseball bat according to him."

Brendan surprised me by laughing. "Milkowski was as thick as a brick. A drug dealer was murdered and he thought I did it as a favor for my friend Sean. After I shipped out to Paris Island, Sean was found stuffed in the trunk of his car, pumped full of bullets. The dumb Polack failed to notice a gang of Dominicans had moved in from Newark and taken over the drug trade in Kearny right under his big nose; they put all their rivals out of business so to speak."

Brendan's use of an ethnic slur seemed out of character for him. He treated his friend's murder rather cavalierly as if his friend had merely stubbed his toe. What really lay underneath his polished veneer?

Harley jotted down something in his notebook. "Milkowski said you had a violent temper; did you lose control and strangle your girlfriend?"

"No! I loved Jenny; we were going to get married."

"No one seems to know that you were engaged," interrupted Harley. "My investigators talked with her roommate and parents; it was news to them."

"We hadn't announced it publicly; we only became engaged on Monday afternoon."

"It's customary to give your fiancée an engagement ring," chided Harley.

"I gave her my Marine Corps ring until I could afford to buy her an engagement ring."

"Check to see if she was wearing the ring, Riddick."

Lieutenant Riddick pulled his cell phone off his belt and went out on the porch. I watched him through the window. He returned with an almost triumphant smile on his face. "No ring sir, she was wearing only a watch, bracelet and pendant."

"The ring was too big for any of her fingers; she put it on a chain. It might still be at her apartment."

"Your engagement story sounds rather specious," interrupted Harley.

"We made an appointment to meet with Father Novello on Thursday."

"Get one of the investigators to call on the good padre to check it out."

"I'll get on it sir;" replied Lieutenant Riddick.

"We searched Ms. Biggio's apartment a little while ago. I'll have one of the investigators check to see if we missed the ring. By the way, do you have an explanation for this?" Harley reached into his brief case and pulled out a plastic bag containing the box for a home pregnancy test kit. "We found this in the trash can in her bedroom."

"Jenny used the test kit when she got up on Monday; she told me a couple hours later that she was two months pregnant," replied Brendan.

"It bet it pissed you off; did she forget to take her pill? Or did you forget to use a condom?" asked Lieutenant Riddick.

"That's not it at all!"

"It made you so angry, you slapped her around!"

"No!"

"Then you strangled her; a pregnant girlfriend would've tied you down. You wouldn't be able to poke your pecker in all that pussy you've been chasing all over town."

"That's crazy; you're distorting everything!"

"Is it? You seem to have a rather busy love life."

"Do you look into everyone's window to see who we're sleeping with?"

"We don't need to; the Norfolk Police indicated there was a domestic disturbance here on March 24th. It seems your girlfriend found you and another young lady in the throes of love."

"Ex-girlfriend to be correct, Kate was upset we'd broken up and was stalking me. I brought one of waitresses from the convention center here after work. Kate barged in without knocking and attacked us."

Riddick laughed. "You were lucky she was armed only with a book; I bet that left a nasty bruise on your ass."

The incident tarred Brendan as much as his former girlfriend. It also drew the unwanted attention of the police when he could least afford it.

"Kate went psycho. I didn't lay a finger on her; my roommate grabbed her and I called the police. I could've pressed charges for assault as well as my friend."

"According to the police report, your friend was Jessica Kravich of 4515 Halsey Circle, that's over in Navy Enlisted Housing. No wonder you didn't file a criminal complaint; Mrs. Kravich's husband would've come after you with more than a book if he'd found out you were screwing his wife while he's out at sea. You're a real piece of work boy!"

Brendan's face flushed with anger but he resisted Riddick's goading and held his temper. It was a clever attempt by the police to provoke Brendan and see what happened.

Harley seemed frustrated that the questioning failed to bring him any closer to solving the murder. "We have a search warrant for your room."

"Be my guest," replied Brendan. "It's at the top of the stairs."

"We also want the clothes you were wearing yesterday."

"They're in the laundry bag in my closet."

"We need to scrape under your fingernails."

"I have nothing to hide sir."

"It's time for you to leave Andy; you're starting to get in the way."

CHAPTER VIII

SINCE JORDAN HALL WAS STILL under wraps by the police, I decided to work from home. It would be quiet until my sons returned from high school. As I pulled into my driveway, I noticed my neighbor weeding her flowerbed.

"Good afternoon Julia," I called out. Dr. Julia Palmer, a retired botany professor was the first woman to be tenured in the College of Sciences at Chesapeake Bay University. Having suffered a frosty reception if not outright hostility from her male colleagues, she developed a thick skin and a sharp tongue in self defense. Until her retirement, she frequently formed a tag team with Emily Worthington to bedevil the administration during Faculty Senate meetings.

"I heard on the news there was a murder in Jordan Hall today."

"It's a real tragedy; the victim was a Ph.D. student in the econ department."

"I've already talked with Emily. She indicated your graduate student is the prime suspect."

It looked like Emily wasted no time in spreading her opinion of Brendan's guilt in Jenny's murder.

"The campus police asked me not to say anything until they've completed their investigation."

"When I arrived on campus in 1966, the campus police was headed by an ex-Navy chief who hired all his beer drinking buddies from the shore patrol. They were utterly useless. When punks from Braxton Homes started breaking into cars, Chief Parsons suggested we bring binoculars to work and periodically scan the parking lots from our office windows. He called it the Eyes in the Sky Program."

I'm sure Harley Simpson cringed every time he heard a tale from the good old days of the campus police. I feared that he would make a quick arrest to assuage the mistaken perception that his force was less than competent; Brendan would serve nicely as the sacrificial lamb.

"It doesn't look like they'll need binoculars to find the culprit this time," said Julia as we parted.

I went inside and turned on my computer to check my campus email account. Two members of the department had sent me messages asking if the rumors about Brendan being involved in the murder were true. I checked my office voice mail and found Emily's message regarding Brendan and the young lady in the elevator. Disasters usually come in threes. What was next?

To my amusement, the next phone message was from a student requesting to take the exam on Thursday because he'd been sick with food poisoning on Monday evening. Fate had intervened to grant him the reprieve that I would've denied since I didn't believe his cock and bull story. His illness was more likely caused by tequila rather than salmonella.

The rest of my emails were rather mundane; a former student needing a letter of recommendation for graduate school, an inquiry from a retired high school teacher about part-time teaching, and a student requesting a prerequisite course be waived so she could take a course in spring semester needed for graduation in May.

The mantle clock in the family room chimed two o'clock and I turned on the television; Channel 12 repeated its noon news program. We'd heard only the reporter's answers to the questions posed to her by the anchor. The anchor's questions shed no light on the day's events. Except for Officer Benton running her mouth, Harley had kept a tight lid on the investigation. Or had he authorized her to leak that a graduate student was a suspect in order to rattle Brendan's cage? It wouldn't be the first time the police played the media.

At the end of the story, the cameraman panned the crowd; as Andy Warhol predicted Laura and I achieved our fifteen minutes of fame. I chuckled when I noticed Art Campbell in the crowd sipping another latte. His Starbucks tab must cost him a small fortune every month. Over the years when television cameras showed up at the university, Art adroitly injected himself into the story and launched into a denunciation of globalization, multi-national corporations or Wal-Mart. Much to the administration's annoyance Art had become one of university's more recognizable professors. Tollie rued the day his predecessor recommended Art for tenure. Fortunately Felicia didn't seek comments from the crowd and the viewing public was spared having to listen to one of Art's harangues.

After the chilly start to the day, the sun had come out and I decided to take advantage of the Indian summer afternoon. I settled into one of the plastic Adirondack chairs on my deck and started reading the book I was reviewing for a journal. Half way into the first chapter, my cell phone rang; the three digit prefix of the phone number displayed indicated the call originated at the university but it was not a number I called regularly.

"Dr. Stanard," I answered.

"This is Natalie Wellman."

Natalie Wellman was President Clayton's secretary. Calls from the President rarely brought glad tidings. "What can I do for you?"

"I've scheduled a meeting for you and Dean Monroe with President Clayton at 8:00 AM in his conference room."

Scheduling the meeting for 8:00 AM indicated we were being shoehorned into his schedule. "May I ask what the agenda is?"

Ms. Wellman paused for a second and cleared her throat. "President Clayton wishes to discuss the investigation of Ms. Biggio's murder with you and Dean Monroe."

"I'll be there at eight sharp."

Department chairs rarely met with the President individually; my usual chain of command was through Tollie and the Vice President for Academic Affairs. If a problem reached the level of the President, it meant he was displeased with the way it was being handled or an outside constituency had put it on his radar. Tollie and I were on the chopping block.

Since I had tenure, President Clayton was limited to a terminating my appointment as department chair. I'd lose the $5,000 yearly stipend for serving as chair and a few minor perks but I would gain a more relaxed work schedule. However none of the other senior faculty in the department wanted the headaches of being chair and Tollie wouldn't permit Emily's second coming; they were stuck with me.

Still the phone call rattled me and I couldn't concentrate on the book. I kept thinking about the murder. Why was Jenny murdered? Was she the victim of a botched robbery attempt? If it wasn't a robbery, what was the motive? Did she have an ex-boyfriend who killed her in a jealous rage? Or was I overlooking the obvious? Was Harley Simpson right that the clues pointed in one direction? Was my faith in Brendan misplaced?

In the eyes of the police, Brendan would remain at the top of their suspect list. Angry at Jenny getting pregnant, he snapped and strangled her in his office across the hall from where Jenny was found. Brendan knew the workings of the criminal justice system plus his years of graduate education made him smarter than the average criminal. The Marines taught him to remain calm under fire and improvise when confronted with an obstacle. Fliers posted in the building warned about the recent muggings; Brendan decided to pin the murder on the crack addict attacking women on campus. Knowing the women's studies seminar was held in the conference room, he waited until after ten o'clock when the seminar finished before moving Jenny's body across the hall to the restroom. He went to work to build his alibi and prayed that none of the other graduate assistants came in that night. It was a neat little theory that the police developed within minutes of finding Jenny's body.

Brendan admitted he'd learned a lot about crime while incarcerated; perhaps he received a lesson from the other inmates on throwing out false leads to muddy the trail for the police. Did he drop Jenny's purse in the bushes outside Jordan Hall to mislead the police? The student found the purse shortly after Jenny's body was discovered; it was almost as if the killer wanted the purse to be found early in the morning.

Brendan passed Tait's Market when he bicycled to and from the university. The crack addicts hanging out at the corner would be unwitting accomplices in his efforts to confuse the police. To a crack addict, finding Jenny's wallet would be like manna from heaven. An addict wouldn't be able to resist the urge to use the credit cards. Did Brendan count on the addicts using Jenny's credit cards to lead the police on a wild goose chase? What he hadn't counted on was the alert security staff at Wal-Mart catching the woman using one of the credit cards? Or had he? A flesh and blood suspect was even better than a hypothetical suspect; the police had a major problem on their hand, a second suspect threw a wrench in the works.

The criminals' code of silence also worked in Brendan's favor. It seemed doubtful the girl would rat on her accomplice, in all probability her boyfriend. She would take the rap for using the stolen credit card and in today's revolving door justice system probably get probation. If Brendan ever went to trial; any attorney worth his salt would be able to use the unidentified second suspect to sow doubts into the minds of jurors.

Was Laura right that I didn't know Brendan? Did a psychopath lurk under the polished veneer? He admitted providing the muscle for his friend's drug deals; did he murder that drug dealer before joining the Marines? Did he suddenly boil over in a rage and murder Jenny when she told him she was pregnant?

Harley Simpson was no doubt having these same thoughts. In a matter of hours, he'd already uncovered Brendan's prior criminal record and wasn't buying Brendan's alibi. He believed Sergeant Milkowski's suspicions about Brendan. If Brendan had no qualms about bashing in the brains of a rival drug with a baseball bat, he'd be able to squeeze the breath out of his pregnant girlfriend without batting an eye.

Laura urged me not to get involved. Yet Brendan was my student. Who would stand up for him? I thought about the Duke lacrosse players again. If their parents hadn't stood up for their sons, they'd be behind bars now. Many professors and students at Duke automatically assumed the three young men guilty based on the statements of a woman later found to be suffering from serious mental health problems. Unlike the Duke parents, Brendan's mother would be unable to pay for a lawyer. He would likely be defended by an overworked public defender fresh out of law school.

Throughout history, from the Salem Witch trials to Alfred Dreyfuss, too many individuals have been railroaded by justice running amuck.

Someone had to stand up for Brendan; he was innocent until proven guilty. The meeting with President Clayton in the morning sounded like the lynch mob was already gathering.

***

I read the first two chapters of the book and began outlining my review. The squeal of tires in the driveway announced the return of my sons from high school. They saw me sitting on the deck and came to the backyard.

"Hey dad!" We heard about the murder at the university," said James, my oldest son, a senior in high school.

"How did you hear about it? I thought you only listened to rap stations in the car."

"I went to the library during study hall; Pete was looking at Channel 12's website."

"What do you know about it?" asked Robert, his younger brother.

"Too much, I'm afraid."

"What do you mean?" asked James.

"One of the housekeepers and I found the body this morning down the hall from my office."

"So that's why you're home early."

"Jordan Hall has been closed all day."

"Nothing like that ever happens at our school; we haven't had a snow day in four years," sighed Robert.

"Someone was killed and all you think about is a day off from school," intoned James, showing an encouraging sign of maturity.

As usual I was deluded; before I could say anything, James administered the verbal coup de grace to his younger brother. "You're such a twerp!"

Robert moved into position to take a swing at his older brother but I quickly interposed myself between them and prevented any bloodshed. I always wondered why Robert Young's children peacefully co-existed on *Father Knows Best* while my household frequently resembled an episode of *Combat*.

"James, plan to light the grill later. Since I'm home early, we'll help your mother out and grill some steaks for dinner."

I thought about inviting Brendan to have dinner with us; he needed support from his friends as he grieved Jenny's loss. Since he was a vegetarian, the gesture of a steak dinner would be wasted. Brendan was in deep trouble in more ways than one. What would a vegetarian eat before being sent to the gallows? Steamed broccoli and carrot sticks weren't my idea of a hearty repast for a condemned man.

CHAPTER IX

"YOU SHOULD WEAR YOUR BLUE pin stripe suit to your meeting with President Clayton tomorrow," said Laura after dinner.

"I have a class at 10 o'clock after the meeting; I'll look too authoritarian."

"For God's sake, don't go to the meeting wearing one of your tweed sport coats. You'll look like a history professor."

"I am a history professor."

"You want to impress Doug Clayton that you're his equal. It wasn't that long ago that he was the chair of the Accounting Department at the University of Oklahoma," pointed out Laura.

Doug Clayton had had a meteoric rise from department chair to university president in eleven years with stops in between as a business school dean at two universities.

"All right, I'll wear the pin stripe suit," I agreed after Laura's arm twisting.

"I'll press your blue striped shirt; the gold tie I gave you for your birthday will contrast nicely with it."

***

Due to my meeting with the president, I set my alarm to wake up a half hour earlier than usual. I put on the coffee maker and went out to get the newspaper. As the coffee brewed I read the article about Jenny's murder. It contained nothing that hadn't been reported on the television news except the police were questioning a person of interest in connection with the murder. Individuals were no longer suspects; for whatever reason the police preferred using the euphemism "person of interest." Although not a linguist, as a historian I noticed the distortion of the English language that began with the Nixon administration. When it was discovered that false statements had been made concerning the Watergate Affair, Nixon's press secretary instead of admitting he lied, deemed the prior statements no longer operable. Further semantic twisting continued during the Reagan and the two Bush administrations.

I arrived at the Old Main Building ten minutes before my meeting to find Channel 12's truck lowering its satellite dish; apparently they'd been interviewing bleary eyed students for its morning news program as they arrived for school. Old Main had been one of the original buildings of the orphanage; unlike the linoleum floors and cinderblock walls of the rest of campus, the building featured a marble staircase and wood paneled walls. I climbed the staircase to the second floor and found Tollie Monroe already ensconced in the reception area outside the President's office engrossed in *The Love Letters of Dylan Thomas*.

"Good morning Tollie." He briefly looked up from his book and nodded hello. His wife had not attempted to alter his appearance; Tollie wore his usual rumpled gray suit. I took a seat on the maroon leather couch across from the wing chair he occupied. I vaguely felt like the time I was summoned to the principal's office in high school. Instead of uncomfortable plastic chairs and harsh neon lights, the president's waiting area resembled a room in a private club. The leather couch was complimented by matching wing chairs, a red and black oriental rug, cherry paneling and prints of famous sailing ships. Only cigars and a decanter of brandy were missing.

I picked up yesterday's *Washington Post* off the coffee table and scanned the front page.

"Good morning," greeted the striking receptionist as she arrived for work and turned on her computer. "President Clayton has not arrived yet; he had a breakfast meeting with the mayor."

Shortly after Doug Clayton arrived on campus, the receptionist who'd served the President's Office for over thirty years retired. Her replacement's attractive figure started rumors on campus that President

Clayton had a keen eye for the opposite sex. The receptionist settled into her cherry desk polished to a high sheen. I was rather envious of it; the green metal desk in my office dated to the opening of Jordan Hall and had been designed in the 1950's to survive a nuclear missile attack rather than serving any decorative purpose.

Dick Torelli and a bleary eyed Harley Simpson entered the waiting area. Dick grabbed the seat next to me while Harley reluctantly settled on the couch next to Tollie.

"Dr. Brandt is excited you'll be teaching for her department during spring semester," said Tollie.

I wondered what course Tollie had enlisted Dick to teach for the Communication Department, Spin Doctoring 325? Would the *University Catalog* state, "It is recommended that students not take Ethics 310 prior to enrolling in this course?"

"I've blocked out my schedule; it should be fun," replied Dick.

It always irritated me when someone thought teaching a college course would be fun; it's a lot of hard work and shouldn't be done as a lark. Clearly Torelli was attempting to burnish his credentials in preparation for moving on to a well paid sinecure at another university. Higher education was a more stable gig than local television news; a rapidly receding hairline didn't negatively impact one's employment.

I put down the Washington Post. "Do you have anything new to report Harley?"

"I'd rather wait until the meeting," he replied.

Natalie Wellman stepped out of her office behind the receptionist's desk. "President Clayton is waiting for you in his conference room."

Since becoming department chair, my close encounters with the president normally occurred twice a year. Every September he held a luncheon for the department chairs where he enumerated his goals for the coming year. With thirty-five department chairs, it was relatively easy to blend in at the luncheon and avoid controversy.

Every February thanks to an endowment from a wealthy benefactor, the History Department was able to bring a noted historian to campus for a public lecture. Due to the speaker's prominence, he was invited to dinner at the President's residence before the lecture. As chair of the department, my wife and I were invited along with two or three couples identified as potential donors to the university. The two dinners I attended as chair passed without me knocking over my wine glass and I was safe till my next required appearance.

We were ushered into the small conference room; President Clayton was already settled in his red leather chair at the head of the glass topped table, a black leather portfolio open on the glass topped table. Harley took a seat in front of a lap top computer plugged into the conference room's audio visual system; he had a dog and pony show prepared for the president. Dick Torelli took a seat at the President's right elbow. Tollie and I filled the remaining chairs opposite him.

"Good morning gentlemen; we need to wrap this up quickly because I have an 11 o'clock flight to Tampa." President Clayton's drawl gave away his roots in south Texas. "Tom Terrell and I are meeting with a former resident of the orphanage; he made a fortune selling used cars down in Florida. His wife died last year and they had no children. Mr. Jennings has fond memories of his days at the orphanage and Tom is trying to persuade him to remember CBU in his will. Florida is filled with elderly widows on the prowl for a second or third husband; Tom needs to get to him first before one of them gets their hooks into him."

Having read *Oliver Twist* in junior high school, I never imagined any boy having fond memories of an orphan asylum. Tom Terrell, the Vice President for Development, was a smooth talking former lawyer. During his tenure, he'd coaxed several elderly widows to leave their estates to the CBU Foundation. With President Clayton, a former linebacker at Texas Christian University, blocking for him, no elderly widow or spinster was going to score on Mr. Jennings's bank account.

President Clayton rocked back in his chair. "Dick briefed me over the phone that you did a good job handling Felicia Wright from Channel 12 when she interviewed you this morning. It's important we keep the press at bay. Now I'd like an unvarnished update on your investigation into Miss Biggio's death."

Suppressing a yawn, Harley looked toward President Clayton's end of the table. "Although there is circumstantial evidence linking Miss Biggio's murder to the muggings that have recently plagued the campus, it is more likely she was murdered by someone she knew."

Harley didn't need to mention Brendan by name; everyone at the table knew who he was referring to.

"A woman was arrested at Wal-Mart attempting to use Miss Biggio's credit card. Her accomplice abandoned her and sped out of the parking lot after she was apprehended by the store's security manager. Her arrest ended up being a false trail instead of a lead to the killer."

Harley clicked the mouse on his lap top and a mug shot of a young African-American woman appeared on the screen.

"Lynette Tompkins has previous convictions for shoplifting and credit card fraud. After interrogation by Norfolk police and threatened with prosecution as an accessory to murder, she admitted her boyfriend bought Miss Biggio's credit card for $10 from a homeless man who frequents the area around Tait's Market."

"Why did the homeless man sell the card?" asked Tollie.

"Being in a woman's name, the credit card was worthless to him. He just wanted to score a couple bottles of Thunderbird. Individuals like Ms. Tompkins use the stolen cards to buy as much merchandise as they can before the credit card company deactivates the card; the thieves often have only a matter of hours. Before computer processing of credit card transactions; it would take weeks to take a stolen credit card out of circulation."

Ms. Thompkin's picture disappeared and a mug shot of her boyfriend appeared.

"Antonio McKinney, her boyfriend, works at the McDonald's across from campus. He has a juvenile record for possession and sale of marijuana; he has no history of violent offenses."

"Neither did Jeffrey Dahmer until they arrested him," interrupted Tollie.

Harley gave Tollie a withering glare and resumed his presentation.

"Mr. McKinney worked the day of the murder from 4 PM to almost 1 AM; due to that fact it's unlikely he had any connection to the murder. The medical examiner estimates Miss Biggio was murdered between 6 PM and 7 PM on Monday evening."

The time of the murder seemed to rule out Brendan as a suspect too; he had to be at the hotel by 7 PM. It was at least a 25 minute bike ride from campus to downtown; there was no way he had enough time to commit the murder and move the body.

"The homeless individual, who sold the credit card to Mr. McKinney, is well known on campus. We've frequently seen him scrounging half-smoked cigarette butts from the ash trays in front of campus buildings."

"It looks like my anti-smoking policy was a boon to him," laughed President Clayton.

The homeless man's mug shot appeared on the screen; I'd seen him around campus before. His long scraggily beard and battered CBU baseball cap were his trademarks along with two missing front teeth. He'd been hanging around campus for over a year; he was often confused with Whitfield Tanner, a professor in the Philosophy Department, who sported a similar beard and baseball cap. Whit also favored vintage bowling shirts that he picked up at flea markets; I never asked Whit about the connection between existentialism and his bowling shirts.

"He's bummed a few cigarettes off me when I'm smoking out in front of Jordan Hall," said Tollie.

There were more than a dozen homeless individuals who drifted around the campus. With open access to most campus buildings, they could get out of the cold in the winter or use the restrooms. If they got past the security guard at the front door of the library; they could sleep on the couches. College students were easy marks for panhandlers; with any luck they could score enough money for a pack of cigarettes or a pint of Mad Dog.

"Felton Snyder has an extensive criminal record, mostly for minor crimes like public drunkenness, trespassing, loitering and shoplifting. He did three years in the North Carolina prison system for stabbing a man in a barroom brawl in High Point in 1979. From 6 PM to 8 PM, the estimated time of the murder, Mr. Snyder was at the prayer and soup supper at The Ark Evangelical Church. After the dinner, he washed dishes and Pastor Franklin slipped him five bucks. When questioned, Snyder admitted selling the credit card to Mr. McKinney."

For a wino, Snyder was awash in cash on Monday night. He should have been able to score two or three bottles of Thunderbird. I was surprised Harley's investigators were able to get anything coherent out of him.

"Brendan Healy, a graduate student in history and Miss Biggio's purported fiancée has emerged as a person of interest in the investigation."

Harley put a mug shot of Brendan taken as a juvenile offender in New Jersey up on the screen. Back in those days he had shaggy blond hair and a surly attitude that came across in the photo.

"Mr. Healy had an extensive criminal record in New Jersey and was a person if interest in the brutal slaying of a drug dealer."

Again that damned euphemism!

President Clayton turned to me, "Andy how was someone with a criminal record like that admitted to your program?" Despite addressing me familiarly, his tone was anything but friendly.

"I don't believe the university's application for admission asks for any information about criminal offenses. His offenses occurred before his 18th birthday. He was initially admitted through the veteran's program established by your predecessor."

"He's a veteran?" President Clayton's tone indicated he didn't quite believe me.

President Clayton looked over to Harley for confirmation. "He showed us a copy of his DD 214 yesterday; he spent four years in the Marines and was discharged as a lance corporal."

"Was he honorably discharged?"

"We're checking with military authorities for confirmation."

President Clayton drummed his fingers impatiently on the table. "I want this investigation wrapped up quickly; this situation is not going to linger and fester."

"We don't want this story on the evening news every night for the next two weeks," stated Dick Torelli in unison with President Clayton. He looked across the table at Harley Simpson. "The fall ratings sweeps are coming up; the local stations are all looking for news stories to attract viewers and boost ratings. A juicy crime story is a sure bet in their eyes; remember last year when they caught Judge Tillman soliciting an undercover police woman for a blow job."

"That's why I stopped watching that drivel on the boob tube; your friends at the television stations tried to make it the second coming of Monica Lewinsky," interrupted Tollie.

Until recently Tollie Monroe was among the handful of people in America without cable television or a satellite dish; his wife finally forced him to sign up for cable due to the switch to HDTV. Tollie was right about the local television stations. In one ratings ploy, Dick Torelli's ex-wife went undercover with the police and dressed up as a street walker to trap unsuspecting johns. Norfolk's television stations employed a lot of cheap gimmicks to attract viewers.

"Not everyone spends their evenings reading *Paradise Lost*. You're out of touch with the way people get their information today. They're too busy to read newspapers; we must be concerned about the impact this story will have on the parents of prospective students. If parents perceive that CBU is unsafe, they're going to send their precious daughters elsewhere," said Torelli.

"Dick has made an excellent point; we don't want this matter spiraling out of control," stated President Clayton.

"It's important that we immediately counter the negative aspects of this unfortunate situation with positive symbolism."

It was interesting to observe a spin doctor like Torelli at work; he viewed Jenny's murder not as a tragedy but as a public relations opportunity.

"The memorial service for Miss Biggio enables us to showcase the university in a positive light and put this unfortunate episode behind us. What are the plans for the service?" asked Torelli.

"Jake Ruiz has done most of the work setting it up; the service will be held Friday at 4 PM in the Jordan Hall auditorium."

"It would be better to hold the service in the Fine Arts Building Theater; we don't want the reporters mentioning that Miss Biggio was murdered in Jordan Hall," recommended Torelli.

"The Dance Department is holding their Fall Recital on Friday evening," replied Tollie flustered by Torelli's interference.

"Move the service back an hour; that will ensure it's covered on the early afternoon news broadcasts. The Dance Department will still be able to twirl around on their toes," ordered the president.

Tollie sighed. "Very well, Dr. Crosby will direct the university Concert Choir; he's researching suitable songs for the service. Dr. Li Yang will perform a harp solo."

President Clayton nodded his head in approval. "Have you asked the Gospel Choir to perform too? It's always good to show off the multicultural aspects of CBU. "

"They have a concert scheduled in Raleigh on Friday evening and are available."

"Have you found a minister yet?"

"Miss Biggio was a Catholic; it would be appropriate to ask Father Novello, the Catholic chaplain," I interrupted.

"He's a safe choice; although he's as long winded as a country preacher. Just don't ask the Reverend Deidra Livingston-Bailey to participate; her invocation at commencement last May was an unmitigated disaster," said President Clayton.

"Deidra has been an adjunct professor in the Philosophy Department for many years," defended Tollie.

"We took a lot of flack from parents and alumni after she invoked God, our mother in heaven. That was another public relations disaster you handed us," said Dick Torelli pointing his finger at Tollie.

Deidra Livingston-Bailey was a local Unitarian minister. Her dramatic prayers reflected her former career as an actress in local dinner theaters. Being on the faculty, she was often called to pinch hit and deliver an invocation when one was needed at a campus event. In line with her feminist viewpoint, she believed that the Almighty could just as well be a woman and enjoyed provoking those who held conventional theological beliefs.

President Clayton and Dick Torelli were more concerned with containing the bad publicity from Jenny's murder; they showed little if any concern for the victim or her family.

"Will Miss Biggio's parents attend the memorial service?" I asked.

"No, the medical examiner will release Ms. Biggio's body on Thursday afternoon. Her parents plan to hold the wake on Friday evening and her funeral on Saturday in Ohio. President and Mrs. Clayton along with Dr. Ruiz will fly to Cleveland to represent the university," replied Torelli.

"It's important to make an arrest before Friday's memorial service. As Dick stated earlier, the university needs to begin the healing process. I had to call her parents yesterday and tell them their only daughter was murdered on my campus. When I meet Mr. and Mrs. Biggio on Friday night, I want to inform them that the campus police have arrested the man who murdered their daughter. How close are you to making an arrest?"

"I'd rather not say; we're still gathering evidence."

"I thought most murders were solved within the first 48 hours. Stop futzing around and get on the ball."

Harley's face flushed with anger. "You'll be the first to know when we make an arrest."

President Clayton turned to me. "If your graduate student is arrested, you need to work with Dick to minimize the fallout for the university's reputation."

"There's not going to be any bad publicity; Brendan didn't murder Jenny Biggio."

"Your loyalty to your student is admirable but didn't Chief Simpson just say that Mr. Healy is the chief suspect."

"He deemed that Brendan a person of interest." I couldn't believe I'd contradicted President Clayton.

President Clayton looked over at Harley then glared at me. "Whatever he is, why are you so sure he's innocent?"

"Brendan told me yesterday, they were planning to get married."

Harley laughed. "It's strange that no one my officers interviewed knew anything about the wedding. It was a surprise to her parents. Her roommate laughed when we asked her; she said Brendan didn't impress her as itching to get married."

"Back home in Texas, most boys are a little resentful about being marched down to see the preacher with a shotgun pressed against their back. Sounds like Mister Healy had a motive for wanting Ms. Biggio out of the way," drawled President Clayton.

Dick Torelli laughed at the president's homespun humor. "I admire your loyalty to your student but who else had a motive for killing Ms. Biggio?"

"That's what I aim to find out," I replied.

"I don't need some crusading professor interfering with my investigation in some misguided quest to clear someone who's guilty as hell," said Harley.

"I'm not interfering with your investigation!"

"Your visit to Brendan's house yesterday tipped him off that we were watching him; we were waiting for a search warrant to search his place. By the time I arrived, he'd ample time to destroy any potential evidence."

"Why'd you tip him off?" demanded President Clayton.

"I went to visit Brendan, nothing more. The investigator jumped to the wrong conclusion that I was a lawyer and moved in to stop Brendan from talking to me. Harley arrived five minutes later; Brendan had no time to destroy anything."

President Clayton's pounded his meaty fist on the table as his face turned red and the vein on his right temple pulsed. "Just stay the hell out of Harley's investigation. I'm not going to end up out of a job like the president at Eastern Michigan University because of a botched murder investigation!"

CHAPTER X

I STARTED TO WALK TO Jordan Hall after the meeting ended.

Harley Simpson hailed me from his car, "Andy, do you want a lift?"

His gesture surprised me considering what had transpired during the meeting. "Thanks."

He unlocked the door and I climbed in his unmarked patrol car. Harley expertly threaded the car through the traffic and pedestrians on the streets surrounding the campus.

"I want to apologize; I lost my temper during the meeting. Torelli has been riding me pretty hard; ever since he wormed his way into Doug Clayton's confidence, he exploits it every chance he gets."

"He views Jenny's murder merely as a public relations crisis."

"His meddling has been more than irksome; I didn't want to do the interview with Channel 12 this morning. It's best to say nothing until an arrest is made; we don't want to prejudice our case by a careless remark,"

"Are you close to making an arrest?"

Harley sighed. "Between you and me, we don't have enough evidence to charge Healy yet. We lifted over thirty sets of fingerprints from the restroom; we're still running them through the FBI. One set of prints clicked with the FBI; I thought I had our murderer until the info came back."

"Why'd you rule the person out?"

"I don't think Dr. Dalton had any motive for killing Ms. Biggio."

Linda Dalton was the head of the Women's Studies Department; I couldn't resist finding out what secret was lurking in her past. "What did she do to have her fingerprints on file with the FBI?"

"She was arrested at an anti-war rally in Washington D.C. in 1972," laughed Harley. It was the first time he'd shown any levity in the past two days.

I couldn't resist laughing too. "She was an undergraduate at the University of Maryland around that time." It was hard to imagine Linda Dalton in a tie-dyed shirt, matching head band and love beads. Every stitch on her these days came directly from Nordstrom's.

Harley pulled up in front of Jordan Hall.

"Thanks for the lift."

"Just because I don't have enough evidence to arrest Healy today doesn't make him innocent. I worked one murder where it took three months to make an arrest even though we knew the bastard did it when we arrived at the scene. A vicious killer is hiding behind the mask of a mild mannered graduate student. You don't want to be his third victim."

"I'll keep that in mind."

Harley had no evidence to make an arrest just his gut feeling that Brendan was the murderer. He was grasping at straws; otherwise he wouldn't have tried to match all the fingerprints lifted from a public restroom. Despite President Clayton pushing for a quick resolution, the investigation could drag on for weeks.

I took a seat on one of the benches in the plaza in front of Jordan Hall; I didn't feel like going upstairs to my office. Over twenty years of my life had been spent in Jordan Hall and my memories were mostly pleasant ones. After finding Jenny's body in the History Department, the 6th floor would never be the same. The nightmare of her murder clouded my perceptions; hopefully time would heal my wounds and help the others in Jordan Hall affected by Jenny's murder. The Building and Grounds Department needed to transfer Vivian to another building so she wouldn't have a flashback every time she cleaned the 6th floor restroom.

Students began pouring into the plaza as the eight o'clock classes let out and they made their way to their next classes or back to their dorm. I watched the students with bemusement. They were certainly different from students in the Dark Ages, also known as the 1970's, when I attended college.

Two skateboarders whizzed by me; I didn't recall anyone using skateboards as mode of transportation back in the 70s. Most students walked around with their ears plugged with headphones connected to their I-Pods. Messenger bags seemed to be gaining in popularity over backpacks; I surmised because many students lugged their laptops to class. When I was in college, everyone had a backpack.

Brendan's military issue backpack stood out in the sea of L. L. Bean, North Face and Quicksilver backpacks. The last time I saw Jenny with Brendan, she had a black messenger bag slung over her shoulder. I didn't recall seeing her bag when I looked around the restroom. When Harley checked the graduate students' office, it wasn't in there either. What happened to Jenny's messenger bag?

Again it seemed that robbery was a motive. A colleague's car window was smashed in the faculty parking lot when a thief thought the messenger bag on the front seat contained a laptop. Did someone try to try to steal Jenny's laptop and strangle her when she resisted?

Or did Jenny leave her bag somewhere? After leaving her apartment did she come straight to Jordan Hall or did she stop somewhere in between? If she had used her student ID card, she likely left a trail for investigators to follow. It had to be swiped to gain entrance to computer labs, the recreation center or to check books out of the library; money could be loaded on the card and used as a debit card for purchases on campus. Was Harley aware that her bag and laptop might be missing?

I took a deep breath and walked into the lobby of Jordan Hall. One of the elevators had just emptied and I rode it alone to the sixth floor. There was still yellow police tape across the door to the women's restroom. Knowing the tape wouldn't be enough to bar the curious, the police installed a padlock to seal the restroom off until their investigation was completed. The department office was locked; Janet was still in North Carolina with her daughter and new grandson. Our work study student wouldn't be in till noon to answer the phones. At one time we had two secretaries but we lost one position to budget cuts during my first year as chair, a topic Emily brought up every department meeting.

In my office, my half drunk mug of coffee from yesterday and the Styrofoam cup I'd poured for Vivian still sat on my desk. Some sort of mold or fungus had started to grow on the walls of the mug; if I was a bacteriologist, I might start researching it to see if I'd accidentally discovered the next breakthrough in biomedical science. Instead I turned on my computer and went to rinse my mug out in the sink in the workroom. I put on a pot of coffee figuring some of the faculty would be drifting in looking for a jolt to get them through the morning. My class would be starting in forty minutes and I sent my notes to the printer.

I picked up the phone and punched the numbers for campus police.

"Campus police," answered the other end of the call.

"This is Dr. Stanard, Chair of the History Department. I'd like to speak to Chief Simpson please."

"Let me see if he's available," replied his secretary.

A few seconds later Harley came on the line. "Chief Simpson."

"Sorry to bother you Harley but I just thought of something. When I found Jenny's body in the restroom, I didn't see her messenger bag."

"What about it?"

"All students carry a backpack or messenger bag; a lot of them bring their laptops to class. Her purse was found in the bushes outside Jordan Hall. Did your men find her bag on campus yesterday?"

Harley paused for several seconds. "Are you trying to throw a red herring across my trail?"

"Not at all," I replied.

"I'll check with the investigator who interviewed her roommate; she may have left her laptop at home."

"Someone could have killed Jenny trying to steal her laptop."

"We've received three reports of laptops being stolen out of offices on campus this month alone. A thief can bide his time and grab one off a desk when the owner runs to the bathroom. There's no need to strangle someone just to steal a laptop."

CHAPTER XI

"Dr. Stanard?" asked a red haired woman as she knocked on the door to my office.

"What can I do for you?" I replied trying to conceal my annoyance. With Janet still out, there was no one to screen my visitors. Around thirty years of age, her tailored pant suit was too expensive to be in a graduate student's wardrobe.

"I'm Amanda Saltzman from the *Register*; I'm covering the murder of Jennifer Biggio."

Although I'd never met her before, I recognized her byline; she normally covered the education beat for the *Register*. Did the newspaper assign her to cover the murder because CBU was her turf or did she sense a big story that she could run with? Newspapers loved sensational stories about attractive woman, preferably blond, being murdered.

"I understand you found Ms. Biggio in the restroom down the hall."

"I'm sorry; the police have asked that I not talk to the media while their investigation is ongoing."

"Rumors going around campus indicate one of your graduate students, Brendan Healy, has emerged as a suspect in the investigation of her murder."

The CBU grapevine with the assistance of email spread gossip and rumors in a matter of minutes across the campus. According to the grapevine, Amanda Saltzman was involved with Mark Sanders, a professor in the Communication Department. Brendan's relationship with Jennifer Biggio and his status in the investigation was old news by the time they bedded down last night.

After I failed to respond, Ms. Saltzman flashed me a knowing smile. "It's hard to reconcile a graduate student being a murderer. Everyone knows history students are boring and bookish, not Lotharios like Scott Peterson."

I saw the slant her story was taking. Like Scott Peterson, Brendan could have come from central casting when the call came in for a handsome, roguish murderer. Being blond and blue eyed, Brendan would stand out in the sea of African American murderers paraded daily through the media. I doubt CNN would've covered Laci Peterson's murder if she had been an African American woman living on the south side of Chicago. Brendan's good looks were the icing on the cake for a murder story.

"I'm due in class in five minutes; I need to head to the elevator if I'm going to be there in time. No doubt Mark Sanders has told you about the temperamental elevators in Jordan Hall," I replied as I grabbed my notes.

"I understand you're the chair of Brendan Healy's dissertation committee.

I headed to the door and motioned for her to leave with me. "Federal privacy laws limit what I can divulge about a student's educational record."

Ms. Saltzman followed me like a bloodhound on a scent to the elevator. "That information is on your department's web page."

Obviously Ms. Saltzman had done her homework; I wondered what else she'd dug up on Brendan on the internet. His departmental biography indicated he hailed from Kearny, New Jersey and spent four years in the Marines before enrolling at CBU. I doubted his dissertation topic interested her; if she was worth her salt as a reporter she would delve further into his background. His criminal activities in New Jersey occurred over ten years ago and his petty crimes as juvenile wouldn't have merited any newspaper coverage. She could gain access to Brendan's juvenile record with the aid of a friendly policeman. As Brendan feared, his past misdeeds were likely to be splashed across the pages of the *Register*.

"Mr. Healy was Jenny Biggio's boyfriend."

"We have 9 doctoral students, 26 masters degree students and scores of majors in the department. I don't have the time or inclination to keep track of who's dating who."

She laughed. "That I doubt Dr. Stanard; you seem to know that Mark Sanders is screwing me."

The elevator arrived and I allowed Ms Saltzman to get on first after two students exited. I pushed the button for the second floor.

"From what I've learned about Miss Biggio, she was apparently a brilliant student," resumed Ms. Saltzman after the balky doors closed.

"Dr. Ruiz spoke very highly about her," I answered.

"Even intelligent women can get trapped in an abusive relationship."

"I'm a historian not a psychologist. You might want to talk to Dr. Donaldson in the Psychology Department; I understand she recently wrote a book on that topic. But I doubt that was the case with Brendan and Ms. Biggio; they seemed very happy the times I saw them together."

The elevator door opened on the second floor.

"Will Mr. Healy be in today?"

"No, I told him to take a couple days off."

"Do you know where he lives?"

"You might be able to find his address in the city directory." I hoped to send her off on a wild goose chase; I wanted her out of the History Department. Brendan's minimalist life style kept him off the grid; I doubted she'd find him without a lot of effort. From her questions, she was clearly fishing for information. All she had was her boyfriend's tip that Brendan was the chief suspect; not enough to go public with her story.

I closed the door to the classroom and left Ms. Saltzman standing in the hall. With the door secured behind me, I was safe from her pesky inquiries. Before I could settle in behind the podium, a student still wearing his baseball cap called out from the back of the classroom, "Professor Stanard, I heard you found the victim's body upstairs."

I don't know what I find more annoying, a student who never takes off his baseball hat or a cell phone ringing during class.

"Yes, I found her body and that's all I have to say on the subject." I had no intention of letting the class deteriorate into a bull session on Jenny's murder. Immediately I segued into, "Why did the election of Andrew Jackson in 1828 signal a new era in American democracy?"

From the blank looks on their faces, I knew few had done the reading assigned in the syllabus for today. Like many freshman, they assumed they could get by as they did in high school by doing as little as possible. Most were in for a rude awakening when I graded the midterm exam they'd taken on Monday. The exams were still sitting on my desk untouched, my plan to begin grading them derailed by Harley evicting us from the building.

A couple of students had done the reading and I was able to lead the class through a discussion of the Jacksonian era. Mercifully the clock struck 10:50 and I was able to put the class out of its misery.

I took the elevator back to my office and saw my neighbor, Julia Palmer, at the end of the hall inspecting the murder scene with Emily Worthington. With their backs to the elevator, they failed to realize I was behind them.

"He probably murdered her in the graduate student's office and dragged her across the hall to the restroom to make it appear she was murdered in there," stated Julia.

"Brendan is always lifting weights at the rec center; it wouldn't have been too difficult for him to carry her; Jenny was rather petite."

"If he murdered me, he'd have his hands full."

Julia Palmer stood over six feet tall. I couldn't resist laughing at the prospect of someone trying to lug her corpse across the hall and gave away my presence.

"Good morning Andrew," said Julia.

"It was rude of you to sneak up on us," said Emily.

"I just got off the elevator and what do I find but Jessica Fletcher and Miss Marple conducting a joint investigation."

Neither Julia nor Emily chuckled at my witticism; instead they jointly glared at me.

"Julia just brought me some interesting news about Ms. Biggio's murder."

"What have you discovered?" I replied.

"It's best we go in your office, Andrew," answered Julia as a group of students came off the elevator to gawk at the university's newest tourist attraction.

With Emily and Julia addressing me as Andrew, I felt like an elementary school student again. When I was in trouble in school, my teachers always addressed me as Andrew not Andy. We went around the corner to my office; I offered them seats at my small circular conference table.

"This morning I went into the department to meet with Melinda, the doctoral student I'm helping teach Intro to Botany while Charlie Ralston is recovering from his bypass surgery. I told Charlie years ago all that beef would kill him; he should've adopted a vegetarian diet like I did. They wouldn't have had to rip his chest open."

Julia always loved to remind everyone she became a vegetarian in 1967 long before it was trendy. It was rumored that her husband tired of tofu and ran off with the hostess from a local steak house he secretly frequented.

"Melinda shares an apartment with Jenny Biggio. When the police searched Jenny's bedroom, they found a pregnancy test kit in the trash. They also found three books on pregnancy secreted under her bed."

I drummed my fingers lightly on the table. If Melinda had told Julia about Jenny's pregnancy, depending on who else she told, it was only a matter of time before the news spread over campus and reached Barry Sanders. Amanda Saltzman would be the next stop on the grapevine.

"You don't seem surprised Andy," said Emily when I failed to react in the expected manner to Julia's revelation.

"Brendan told the police yesterday Jenny was pregnant; that's why they planned to get married over Christmas."

"Hmm!" replied Julia.

"Ever since Brendan arrived here, he's acted like a stallion standing at stud. If Janet were here, she could tell us how many girlfriends he's had; I've lost count," said Emily.

Thanks to Janet, our ever efficient department secretary, we were kept informed about the bedtime activities of our graduate students.

"Melinda described Brendan as narcissistic; he was always showing off his well-muscled physique," said Julia.

I found it interesting that Melinda and Julia, both botanists, were suddenly experts on personality disorders.

"Narcissists are not the marrying kind. Jenny's pregnancy gave him a motive for her murder," added Emily, who'd also become an expert on the topic.

"Speculation like this is counterproductive. Let the police finish their investigation," I replied.

"We have another problem to deal with."

"What?"

"When are the police going to reopen the women's restroom? We have to trek to another floor with it closed. The police wouldn't have dared close the men's restroom if the body had been found there."

Although I sympathized with Emily and the other women in the department having to detour to another floor, Emily's complaint was another exasperating example of how she cast everything with a feminist slant. It seemed odd the restroom was still closed; the police had all day Tuesday to gather evidence. Did they fail to find any evidence to link their chief suspect to the crime scene? "I doubt the police had misogynist motives in closing the restroom."

"As usual you have your blinders on."

"It's time for guerilla tactics," declared Emily. "We're staging a coup d'état and seizing control of the men's bathroom. We'll paste a women only sign on the men's restroom door; now the men can take a hike!"

"A stroke of genius," seconded Julia.

I rolled my eyeballs and decided I had more important things to do than fight the takeover of the men's restroom by the feminist proletariat. "In your new role as restroom commissar, please send an email to everyone in the department announcing the temporary bathroom arrangement."

Emily and Julia left my office smug in their triumph. I needed a breather and since it was almost lunch time I decided to head over to the rec center. Walking across campus, it appeared everything had returned to normal; I didn't see any satellite trucks setting up for a noon broadcast.

"Afternoon Andy," greeted Art Campbell when I entered the faculty locker room. He was toweling off after a swim. A fitness fanatic, he swam every day and was a martial arts enthusiast. I never recalled Marx or Lenin expounding on the virtues of physical fitness although the Soviet Bloc had promoted athletic competition with the West during the Cold War.

"How's everyone holding up in the econ department?"

"It's pretty grim; everyone liked Jenny. Jake Ruiz was jealous when I recruited her to the department. Until she was seduced by the dark side of the force, I was her thesis advisor."

His comment perplexed me. "What do you mean seduced by the dark side of the force?"

"Jake converted her to capitalism and forced me out of the picture." Art faked a laugh but it was clear he perceived her change of viewpoint as a betrayal. Like many intellectuals, Art could not draw the line between a professional dispute and a personal one. Art and I joined the university the same year but over the years he'd estranged himself from most of his colleagues in the economics department with his diehard devotion to Marxism.

"I've heard your graduate student was screwing Jenny. Is he the suspect mentioned in the newspaper this morning? "

"I believe he was deemed a person of interest."

"It's another example of the debasement of the English language, it's like the Bush administration using the term 'stress positions' instead of calling it torture."

"It's like Stalin imprisoning the 'rich peasants' who opposed his collectivization efforts."

Art slammed his locker shut and stalked out of the locker room.

After changing into my gym clothes, I headed to the cardiovascular room to ride an exercise bike before doing the circuit training machines. Entering the room, I was hit by a blast of heavy metal blaring from the sound system. Since the kid checking ID cards controlled the music, we had no chance of hearing classic rock. The music seemed to alternate between rap and heavy metal depending upon who was on duty. I wrinkled my nose; as usual the room smelled of a mixture of the rubber floor mat and the antiseptic spray used to clean the machines after each use. College students these days seem to be germ phobic compared to the laissez faire attitude of my generation during the 1970's.

I was surprised to find Brendan doing pull-ups on the bar at one end of the room. Intently watching his pull-ups on the mirrored wall, Brendan failed to notice me. As usual he was dressed in one of his red Marine Corps PT shirts with the sleeves cut off. I'd always assumed he favored sleeveless shirts to show off his tattoo. Or were the sleeves cut off to display his bulging biceps? Was he in love with his muscles as Jenny's roommate claimed?

"Good afternoon Dr. Stanard," he grunted. "Twenty!" He let go of the bar and dropped to the rubber floor with a resounding thud.

I walked to the end of the room. "How are you doing Brendan?"

"All right I guess. I couldn't sleep last night; I kept thinking about Jenny." Brendan's voice cracked and he struggled to maintain his composure. "I know what you're thinking; what is he doing here the day after his girlfriend died? It was pretty grim sitting in the house alone after my roommates left for class. I had to get out of there."

"Have you called Dr. Fitzgerald in the Counseling Center?"

"I told you already I don't believe in that sort of help."

"What about your mother?"

"I talked with her last night; she's driving down this weekend from Jersey."

I hoped his mother would be able to convince him to see Dr. Fitzgerald; he needed to drop his macho façade and seek help. If I pressed him too hard, it would only stiffen his resistance.

"Do you see my shadow over there?" Brendan pointed to a dour looking man in slacks and a windbreaker sitting on the bench by the entrance leafing through a magazine. "Dave noticed him sitting in an unmarked police car across from the house this morning. When I got on my bike to come over here, he started following me. I was tempted to go the wrong way down a one way street to screw him but I decided not to piss him off. Instead I got off my bike and told him where I was heading so he wouldn't run me over by accident."

"He even followed me into the locker room to make sure I didn't make my escape through one of the other exits. I hope he doesn't follow me into the shower after I finish working out."

I laughed even though I knew it wasn't a good sign that Harley had detailed a man to keep tabs on Brendan. He wouldn't waste an officer's time unless he believed it necessary.

Harley wasn't letting go of his suspicions. Was he hoping Brendan slipped up and led them to evidence linking him to Jenny's murder? He needed time for the DNA and fingerprint evidence to be processed. Was he looking for a hole in Brendan's alibi? What was Harley missing to make an arrest? When he was ready to make an arrest, the tailing officer would ensure that Brendan hadn't flown the coop.

Or was Harley merely bowing to Doug Clayton's pressure and putting a tail on Brendan out of frustration. Would Harley make an arrest just to call off the dogs yapping at his heels? Harley impressed me as possessing integrity but when Amanda Saltzman went public with her story, the pressure might be more than he could handle.

CHAPTER XII

AFTER MY WORKOUT, I PICKED up a sandwich at the Student Union and headed back to my office. My plans to quietly eat my sandwich and grade mid-terms were derailed when I was accosted by Woody Farrell, the longest serving member of the department, as I exited the elevator.

"This is an outrage Andy!"

A native Virginian, Woodrow Wilson Farrell was the department's resident Southern historian. His father had named him for Woodrow Wilson, the last native born Virginian elected President. Woody's bright pink face indicated he'd probably enjoyed a glass of Rebel Yell or two during lunch at the Faculty Club. Southern historians had only two interests, bourbon and the Civil War.

"Good afternoon Woody."

"I'm going to Tollie; Emily cannot dictate who's going to use the men's restroom. I have arthritis and prostrate problems; I can't be running downstairs every time I need to take a piss, pardon my French!"

"It's only for a few days until the police finish their investigation and reopen the women's restroom. I thought it was a good compromise."

"Everyone thought the Compromise of 1850 would avert conflict between North and South. Ten years later, the North began its war of aggression against the South."

As usual Woody failed to remember the Confederacy fired the first shots in the Civil War at Fort Sumter. "Please be patient for a day or two."

"She can't even use the damn urinal," Woody shouted as he stomped back to his office.

I heard his office door violently slam shut as I unlocked my office. Sitting down at my desk, I took a bite out of my sandwich as I picked up the last blue book from the stack. Usually the student who finished the exam first was either a speed writer or grossly underestimated what was needed to correctly answer the questions. The latter was true and I gave the student a D.

Grading the first dozen exams, I found only one A in the group and two dismal Fs that indicated neither student had bothered to open the book. It was likely both students would be home permanently in January.

My phone rang and Caller ID indicated Laura was on the line. "Hello dear."

"Have you read the *Register* this afternoon?" Laura replied.

"You know I only read the *Washington Post* and *New York Times*; the only thing the *Register* is good for is lining the bottom of a bird cage."

"Brendan Healy hasn't made the web page of either the *Times* or *Post* yet; he's featured prominently on the *Register's* web page."

I wished I'd bookmarked the *Register's* web page as I fumbled typing the address. The page opened with the headline, "Ex-Con's Background Probed in CBU Student's Murder" splashed across the top. Underneath was Amanda Saltzman's byline. Staring out from the page was a head shot of Jenny Biggio, probably copied from the Economics Department homepage. To her right was a different mug shot of Brendan from the one Harley showed at the meeting this morning. Brendan was holding a placard marked Kearny Police Department. He sneered defiantly at the camera; looking every inch a cheap thug with his torn tank top and unkempt blond hair. The story had been posted about ten minutes earlier.

"What do you think?"

"It doesn't look good for Brendan."

"Isn't Amanda Saltzman the reporter who's screwing Barry Sanders?"

"She was snooping around the department this morning after I met with Doug Clayton; no doubt Barry clued her in on the gossip swirling around campus."

"As usual you never tell me anything."

"I'm sorry; I'd meant to call you."

"Brendan looks really creepy in that mug shot; if he'd come into the library looking like that, I'd direct the staff to keep an eye on him."

As Laura frequently pointed out, libraries in addition to serving as a center of intellectual exploration were also magnets for all orders of perverts. Years of working in libraries taught her to keep a wary eye for those with interests other than books.

I quickly scanned the story. It related Brendan's sentencing to a juvenile correctional facility and his later conviction for stealing the car. Ms. Saltzman conducted a phone interview with Sergeant Vincent Milkowski of the Kearny Police Department, "Mr. Healy had an extensive record with our department as a juvenile; he ran with a gang called the West Side Boys that was involved in every criminal activity imaginable. He's still a person of interest in the unsolved murder of a rival drug dealer who was beaten to a pulp with a baseball bat. In retaliation, the leader of the West Side Boys was pumped full of bullets; Healy saw the handwriting on the wall and enlisted in the Marines to get out of town."

Amanda Saltzman struck gold interviewing Jenny's roommate Melinda. "Jenny and I were very close; we shared an apartment for three years. She wouldn't have knowingly dated a criminal."

"It surprised me when Jenny started dating Brendan. He had a bad reputation on campus for carving notches on his bedpost. Jenny was finishing her Ph.D. this semester; she was excited about starting her career."

"When the police searched our apartment, they found a pregnancy test kit in the trash and three pregnancy books. She was murdered before she could share with me that she was pregnant."

"The story is nothing but a hatchet job," I said when finished.

"Any woman reading the story will come away with a negative impression. Brendan took advantage of Jenny; he concealed his criminal record and used her like all the other women he bedded. He murdered her when he found out she was pregnant."

Laura had raised an interesting point. Due to the vagaries of our jury system, many juries have a female majority. Before any testimony was heard, Brendan had six to nine votes against him. The pool of potential jurors was poisoned before Harley Simpson even made an arrest.

Someone close to the campus police had tipped Amanda Saltzman off to some of the details of the investigation. Was one of Harley's investigators trying to ratchet up the pressure on Brendan?

Or was Dick Torelli behind the story? He wanted a quick arrest to end the negative publicity for the university. Dick already had a connection to the Communication Department due to his planned teaching assignment. Knowing Barry Sanders's link to Amanda Saltzman, it would only take one phone call to pass the information he wanted disclosed.

Sergeant Milkowski couldn't resist taking a shot at his old nemesis. Other than his suspicions, Milkowski had no evidence linking Brendan to the drug dealer's murder or he would've arrested him years ago. If Brendan was arrested for Jenny's murder, Milkowski's might revive his long dormant case.

"I know you think Brendan is innocent. You're getting involved in something you know nothing about. Please be careful, the police may be right about him being a murderer."

"He wasn't much older than our boys when he got in trouble in New Jersey."

"Our boys don't go around beating people to death with a baseball bat. I'll see you at home; I have a department heads meeting in ten minutes."

I reread the article to see if I missed anything during my hurried first reading. Brendan's reputation as a rake was well known on campus according to Melinda. Opposites attract; was Jenny the classic good girl attracted to the bad boy? As a graduate student, Jenny had seen the difficulties female faculty members had in finding suitable mates. Most tended to marry other academics. Did Jenny mistakenly see Brendan as suitable marriage material while Brendan saw her as only another in his long string of conquests? Had Jenny been blind to the Brendan's faults?

My phone rang again; Caller ID indicated Tollie Monroe was on the line. I took a deep breath and put the speaker phone on. "Good afternoon Tollie."

"Woody Farrell was just in my office complaining about the bathroom situation on the 6th floor."

"We have more important things to deal with; Amanda Saltzman went public in the *Register* with Brendan Healy being a suspect in the murder of Jenny Biggio. It's already posted on their web site."

"Judas betrayed Christ for thirty pieces of silver; Barry Sanders sold us out for a romp in the hay with a reporter who cannot string two grammatically correct sentences together."

Tollie judged a person's worth by their grammatical abilities. One administrator's memo to Tollie was sent back with all the mistakes marked in red pencil like a paper for a freshmen composition class.

"Give me a minute to take a look at it."

I could hear Tollie breathing heavily as he perused the article; every so often he muttered under his breath at something he read. "I don't know if Barry served as a conduit to Saltzman; with all the information out on the web, even a second rate reporter like Saltzman would be able to dig up Healy's criminal record in a matter of hours."

"I'm afraid there's a rush to judgment before there's any evidence linking Brendan to the murder."

"You need to step away from this Andy. Healy has a history of violent behavior. From what the police sergeant in New Jersey said, it's not a stretch to see him killing Ms. Biggio when he found out she was pregnant."

"So you've joined the lynch mob too?"

"Take a step back and look at things clearly. Healy's background says a lot about him. He had a great role model for a father. His old man skipped out on his mother; I bet he probably beat her too. Healy is even suspected of murdering a rival drug dealer. God knows what else he did!"

I couldn't believe Tollie's reaction; he'd been a member of the ACLU for years. Instead he was acting like an arch-conservative who wanted to lock up all criminals and throw away the key. "The police in New Jersey are just blowing smoke about a ten year old murder they failed to solve."

"Have you ever considered Healy might be conning you?"

"Brendan is no longer the person he was before he joined the Marines; he's almost finished his Ph.D. If he wanted to pursue a life of petty thuggery, he would've returned to New Jersey after his enlistment ended."

"I can't run interference for you on this one; you're on your own."

Clearly Doug Clayton's meeting with us this morning was influencing Tollie's decision to back away from supporting Brendan.

"Amanda Saltzman's story is conjecture, nothing more."

"Harley Simpson hasn't made public any of the evidence he's gathered. I'm warning you; don't do anything that's going to embarrass the university."

"I've always been a loyal soldier." I would have to be more discreet in aiding Brendan and work under the radar to avoid Doug Clayton's ire.

"I might as well tell you now; I'm waiting for the Dean of Students to send over a letter indefinitely suspending Mr. Healy from the university under Policy 157. The University Attorney is reviewing the final draft."

Policy Number 157 was implemented by the university in response to the mass shootings at Virginia Tech and Northern Illinois University. It gave the university wide latitude to remove students from campus when they might pose a danger. A review panel would determine when and if he might be reinstated; a process that could take up to ten days. It was clear that Brendan's suspension was at Doug Clayton's instigation. Dick Torelli had anticipated the press would quickly learn of Brendan being the focus of Harley Simpson's investigation and would be able to show that the president had taken decisive action and removed the menace from campus.

"Brendan is not a psychotic murderer; he stole a car when he was a teenager."

"Or so he claims; the university needs to review his prior criminal record to see if he poses a danger."

"Who's being appointed to the review panel?"

"I've asked Anita Dickerson to represent the college."

Anita Dickerson was the Associate Dean of the College of Arts, Social Sciences and Humanities; by reputation, she was fair minded and thorough. She'd add a voice of reason to the panel.

"Who else will be sitting in judgment?"

As you know, the Dean of Students chairs the panel. Dr. Fitzgerald from the Counseling Center has been appointed as well as Bonita Sutton-Fontaine.

"Who is Bonita Sutton-Fontaine?"

"She was recently hired as Associate University Attorney; I understand she formerly worked for the Commonwealth's attorney's office."

With a former prosecutor on the panel it looked like there was already one vote for hanging him.

"The Dean of Graduate Studies will be a member too."

"I'd appreciate it if you delivered the letter to Mr. Healy; Tammie will bring it down to you when it arrives. By the way, what in God's name is Emily going to use the urinals for?"

"It was easier to give in to Emily and save my energy for other battles."

Tollie laughed. "You can't forestall Armageddon forever. I'll back you this time. Woody Farrell's brains settled in his ass years ago; it would do him some good to get off it once and a while."

***

I went back to grading midterms periodically checking the Register's web site for any updates to the article on the murder. Brittany, the department's student worker knocked on my door. "Come in."

"Dean Monroe's secretary is here to see you."

"Send her in."

Tammie McMillan entered my office carrying two large envelopes and handed them to me. "One is your copy; the original needs to be delivered to Mr. Healy as soon as possible. His address is on the envelope. Please have Mr. Healy sign the memo acknowledging receipt of the letter."

"Will do," I replied.

I'd lost interest in grading the midterms anyway; leaving now would enable me to get home and see the evening newscasts. Delivering the letter personally would hopefully allow me to soften the blow and gauge Brendan's reaction to the *Register* article.

I opened the envelope addressed to me and began reading the letter to Brendan.

Mr. Brendan R. Healy
5412 80th Street
Norfolk, VA 23528

Dear Mr. Healy:

Pursuant to University Policy Number 157 you are suspended indefinitely pending a review of your prior criminal convictions and whether you pose a danger to the university community. During your suspension you are banned from the university grounds and all university buildings. You are also suspended without pay from your employment as a Graduate Teaching Assistant.

A panel consisting of Dr. Peter Fitzgerald, Director of the Counseling Center, Dr. Anita Dickerson, Associate Dean of the College or Arts, Social Sciences and Humanities, Ms. Bonita Sutton-Fontaine, Esquire, Associate University Counsel, Dr. Elias Yang, Dean of Graduate Studies and myself will conduct a review of your fitness to continue as a student at Chesapeake Bay University.

Under Policy Number 157, the review must be completed within ten days of your receipt of this letter. You must provide all requested information and documents to the panel in a timely manner. In addition you are required to undergo a psychological assessment with a psychologist in the Counseling Center within five days of the receipt of this letter. A hearing before the panel will be scheduled before the eighth day of the ten day period. Failure to comply with any request from the panel or missing any scheduled meeting will result in your immediate expulsion from Chesapeake Bay University. If you are found on university grounds or inside any university facility you will be immediately arrested for trespassing. If you are required to appear on campus, you will be escorted by a member of the campus police department.

If cleared by the panel, you will be reinstated as a student. However your reinstatement may be conditional. Failure to comply with any conditions imposed upon you may result in your expulsion.

I have appointed, Serena Alston, Student Ombudsman, to advise you during this process. All requests for information and documents must be submitted through her. If you desire, you may retain an attorney to represent you during the hearing.

The university must take these steps to ensure a safe and secure learning environment. I hope you understand the necessity for this action. Attached is a copy of Policy 157 for you to review.

Sincerely,

Harold J. Noble, Ph.D.
Dean of Students

cc: Dr. Anita Dickerson
Dr. Elias Yang
Dr. Peter Fitzgerald
Ms. Bonita Sutton-Fontaine, Esquire
Ms. Serena Alston
Mr. Harley Simpson, University Police
Dr. Taliaferro Monroe
Dr. Andrew Stanard

The administration delegated me to deliver the bad news to Brendan. It was absurd to invoke Policy 157; his petty crimes as a teenager paled in comparison with the acts of a psychotic mass murderer. Brendan had no recourse; he was left twisting in the wind while the review was conducted. Although President Clayton's name was not on the document, I had no doubt he was slated to receive a blind carbon copy of the letter as well as Dick Torelli.

***

I told Brittany I was leaving early; she smiled since she'd be able to chat on her cell phone without interruption from me. I headed to the elevators and pushed the button; the elevator door opened and Cynthia Wallach, a professor in the Economics Department was inside. We'd both been hired the same year and over the years we served together on several university committees. When we first moved to Norfolk, Cynthia and her husband Stan, a finance professor, lived in the same apartment building near campus. Our sons had played same soccer together and she and Laura had been active in PTA. Later Cynthia and I collaborated on a book on the Roman slave economy.

"How are you doing?" I asked as I got on the elevator.

"It's so sad; I can't stop thinking about Jenny." Cynthia stopped to dab her eyes with a tissue. "Jenny was so brilliant; brilliant people have a tendency to be arrogant but Jenny was just the opposite. She was always very kind and helpful to everyone."

"I never realized the cause of Art's arrogance before."

Cynthia laughed, breaking the gloom in the elevator. "No, it's genetic in Art's case. Do you remember when we were all down on the third floor?"

The third floor of Jordan Hall served as an overflow floor and housed first year and visiting faculty who lacked accommodations within their departments. Cynthia, Art and I all had offices on the third floor during our first year at the university. We moved upstairs to our respective departments when offices opened up during our second year.

"You remember that awful shag rug Art has had in his office ever since he arrived?" asked Cynthia.

"It was a swirl of maroon, orange, red and gold; he was so proud he found it at Goodwill for $2.00."

"Housekeeping had to fumigate the third floor for fleas after he put it in his office."

The elevator door opened and we stepped out into the lobby.

"He finally got rid of it over the weekend."

"Did it die of mange?"

Cynthia laughed. "He replaced it with a faux oriental rug he bought at Wal-Mart."

Art's new Oriental rug and Starbucks' lattes showed his tastes were more petty bourgeois than proletarian. "Comrade Art is always ranting against Wal-Mart."

"Stan saw him at Wal-Mart buying it. I couldn't believe it but Stan showed me the rug in Wal-Mart's Sunday sales circular; the rug was on sale for $15.99."

Art, a dedicated Marxist, didn't attend church on Sunday and was able to beat the churchgoers to the bargains at Wal-Mart.

Cynthia and I left the lobby and headed to our cars in the parking lot. Channel 12's satellite truck was already in the parking lot raising its dish for its first evening newscast at 5 o'clock. With Amanda Saltzman's article already on the internet, the other stations would be dispatching their trucks as well.

I'd have to make a trip up to the eighth floor and check out Art's new rug as well as chide him on his shopping habits.

CHAPTER XIII

I turned into Brendan's street around 4:30 and saw an SUV with the markings of Channel 5 parked across from his house; his police shadow sat in an unmarked car sipping a coffee as he kept watch. Two African-American boys on bicycles stopped to check out the intruders in the neighborhood.

Channel 5 Action News according to its commercials had a young dynamic news team that got to the bottom of the story. With the lowest ratings among the local stations, Channel 5 couldn't afford experienced reporters. It hired recent journalism school graduates on the basis of their good looks and willingness to work for a low salary; the eager young reporters took the job to gain exposure and hopefully be noticed by a major market station. Shane Alvarez, Channel 5's young Hispanic reporter leaned against an SUV with the station's logo and smoked a cigarette while he chatted with his cameraman. His fitted Armani suits, coal black hair and dark brown eyes made him a favorite of female viewers according to a recent feature story in the television section of the *Register*.

I walked over to Shane. "What's going on?"

"We're staking out that house across the street; the suspect in the murder of that CBU coed lives there," said Shane in his slow Texas drawl. "I tried a Mike Wallace style ambush but he wouldn't open the door. See that police car over there; he's dogging him too. If we can't get some footage of him in five minutes, we'll have to use an old mug shot my editor dug up in New Jersey."

The *Register's* story indicated Shane grew up in the exclusive River Oaks neighborhood of Houston. Coupled with his degree from Rice University, his pedigree indicated his ancestors crossed the Rio Grande long before the Alamo. He was obviously itching to pack his bags and leave Norfolk for greener pastures.

"We have to get back to the station. Are you ready to film?" asked the cameraman.

"Let me finish my cigarette; try one more time to get him to come to the door."

The cameraman strolled lackadaisically across the street. Shane looked at my pinstripe suit suspiciously; I was definitely overdressed by the standards of Jefferson Terrace. "You look like a lawyer; are you here to see your client?"

Although I hated to lie, I needed to conceal my identity to avoid being questioned about Brendan and the murder. "I own several rental properties in the neighborhood; I thought you might be doing a story on the city's redevelopment plan for Jefferson Terrace."

"You're a slumlord? That's a cut above a lawyer."

I laughed. "Someone has to provide low cost housing; I think of it as a public service."

Shane laughed too and threw his cigarette on the pavement; he crushed it with the heel of his polished cowboy boot.

"This story is going to go national and I'm stuck on a stakeout with little chance of getting more than 30 seconds of airtime on the 6 o'clock news. Amanda Saltzman with the *Register* broke the story. I heard she's banging a professor over at CBU; he tipped her off about the suspect's identity. She's doing a guest appearance on Channel 12 at six o'clock. Media National owns both the *Register* and Channel 12; media synergy, that's the game plan these days."

He walked across the street and stood in front of Brendan's house. On the cameraman's cue, he began, "The Chesapeake Bay University Police Department has released limited information about the murder of graduate student, Jennifer Biggio. Her body was found in a campus restroom on Tuesday morning. Police have zeroed in on Brendan Healy, a graduate student at CBU and Miss Biggio's boyfriend, as a person of interest in her murder. Channel 5 has learned that Healy has an extensive criminal record in his home state of New Jersey and served time in a juvenile correctional facility. Healy is holed up in this house in the Jefferson Terrace neighborhood near the university. He is being watched by the police but they've refused to confirm that an arrest is imminent. This is Shane Alvarez, reporting for Channel 5 Action News."

After he finished shooting Shane, the cameraman shot several seconds of footage of the police car to the annoyance of the plain clothes officer inside.

As Shane and the cameraman packed up, to their dismay I walked up to door and knocked. Someone looked through the bent plastic blinds and a few seconds later the door opened to Shane Alvarez's consternation. "Dr. Stanard, what are you doing here?" asked Dave Chen, another of the department's doctoral students.

"I need to see Brendan."

"Sorry I didn't open the door at first; reporters have been pestering us all afternoon. One pushy woman came in the back door."

"Did she have red hair?"

"Yeah, I was in the kitchen in my boxers when she barged in. I'd like to get a piece of her but I've heard Dr. Sanders is already boning her."

I laughed at Amanda Saltzman being thwarted in her attempt to interview Brendan.

"Brendan!" Dave yelled in the direction of the stairs.

A few seconds later Brendan emerged from his room and came down the stairs wearing a pair of black pants and a half buttoned white dress shirt clutching his cell phone in his right hand. He looked relieved that I was the one here to see him and not the police.

"I need to talk with Brendan in private."

"I'll go to my room," Dave replied.

Brendan showed me to a couch in the living room; he put his cell phone down on the coffee table and took a seat across from me.

"I was directed to give you this letter; please sign the receipt."

When I handed him the letter, he nervously dropped it on the floor.

"Are they lowering the boom on me?"

I nodded affirmatively. Brendan picked a pen off the coffee table and signed the receipt attached to the letter. He handed it back to me.

"Is this in response to the *Register's* web site?"

"It was initiated earlier in the day."

Doug Clayton had started the ball rolling after the meeting; it took several hours to draft the letter and have it vetted by the parties involved. I wasn't going to tell Brendan that the President ordered his suspension.

Brendan took a small pocket knife from his pocket and slit the envelope open. His face flushed with anger as he read the letter. He crumpled the letter into a ball and threw it into the empty fireplace.

"Nothing I've done in the last ten years to redeem myself counts for anything. It's as if they tattooed me on the chest with a scarlet "C" for being a criminal."

Brendan grabbed a soda can off the coffee table and hurled it against the opposite wall; it bounced off and clattered across the uncarpeted wood floor. Fortunately it was empty. Dave came out of his bedroom to see what happened.

"What was that?"

"They've just suspended me from the university."

"Sorry dude." Dave looked at me and wisely retreated back to his room.

"This is the second piece of bad news I've received in the last ten minutes. I was scheduled to work at the hotel tonight; the banquet manager just called and told me I wasn't needed."

"You think he saw the story?"

"The bastard won't admit he read it! I'm screwed! I don't have a job now! What do they want me to do? Sell my fucking blood in order to survive?"

Brendan stared down at the floor and played with his hands for several seconds. "I'm sorry I unloaded on you. I know you didn't have anything to do with the suspension; you're the only person I can trust. Do you believe in dreams?"

I found Brendan's question rather strange; I found New Age mysticism a bunch of hokum. "Not really."

"This summer I dreamed I was in a prison cell but the guards refused to tell me why I was locked up. I woke Jenny up when I screamed. It was a moment of reckoning; I had to come clean to her."

"My relationship with Jenny started out like all the others; she was just another conquest. But instead I fell in love with her. Jenny knew something was troubling me. I told her everything that night about my past and would understand if she left me. She didn't leave me; she wanted to help me. I'd always feared I'd turn out like my father; he was a real scumbag. I now realize that I'd deliberately avoided becoming emotionally involved with women because of what he'd done to my mother."

I saw tears welling in Brendan's eyes. His ramblings about his father and women didn't make any sense. Why would Jenny have left him because of his petty teenage crimes?

"I never told anyone about my past because I was so ashamed of what I'd done. Over the years I hid my life in Kearny behind a façade until I met Jenny."

Brendan got out of the chair and walked over to the window. He stared out in the direction of the police car for several seconds and turned to me.

"I'm sorry I've lied to you too. Everything will be out by tomorrow; it's not going to take too much digging in Kearny to find out I'm a killer."

Brendan's confession hit me like a gut punch. "You murdered that drug dealer?"

"No, I killed my father," he said almost inaudibly.

"Jesus Christ," I blurted out. It felt like I'd taken a second hit to the gut.

"I see your reaction; it's written all over your face. Anyone who would kill their own father is capable of anything."

"So that's why you were incarcerated?"

"My incarceration at Mountainview was unrelated to his death. I went out of control after that; a shrink might see a correlation between the two events."

I was having difficulty reconciling his previous statements with what he'd just told me. "So your father never abandoned your family."

"He ran out on my mother several times; the problem was he always came back. Alcohol fueled his demons. My mother is a devout Catholic; she tried hard to keep their marriage going as they say for the sake of the children. Instead it was a vicious cycle; my sisters and I were in the middle of his drunken rages."

"He abused your mother?"

"I don't know how she took it. She ended up in the emergency room a couple times. For some reason my father never hurt my sisters, thank God for that. Instead he targeted me; he broke my arm when I was fourteen."

"His drinking increased and my mother threw him out for good after he broke my arm. She got a restraining order against him and filed for divorce."

"How did you kill him?"

"With my fists,' said Brendan. He leaned back against the wall and stared at the ceiling

"What happened?"

"After my mother threw him out of house, my father shacked up with a dancer from his favorite bar. He never paid the child support he owed; my mother struggled to keep things together. His drinking spiraled out of control and his girlfriend threw him out too. One night he knocked on the door and Meghan foolishly let him in. She was only nine; we hadn't seen him in over six weeks. My sister Amy was spending the night at a friend's house; she was spared what happened. As usual he was drunk out of his skull; my mom told him to get lost. She would've called the police but our phone had been cut off because she couldn't pay the bill."

"My father didn't care we were standing there; he grabbed hold of my mother and dragged her to the couch trying to rip her clothes off. She grabbed hold of a lamp and it smashed into pieces on the floor. Despite being drunk he overpowered her; he just kept hitting her. She cried for my help; Meghan was screaming, hysterical with fright. Even today everything is a blur. I tackled my father and knocked him to the floor. My father was punching me; I was punching back. At one point he threw me against the wall cracking the drywall."

"How old were you?"

"Fifteen."

"Somehow my mom managed to get free and grabbed Meghan; they ran upstairs to her room and locked the door. My father beat the crap out of me; taunting me, laughing the whole time. He went upstairs after my mother and started kicking her door in. I pulled myself up and got up the stairs. I jumped on him, the next thing I knew he was tumbling down the stairs. There wasn't much room on the landing. His head hit the wall at the bottom and he broke his neck; he was dead by the time the paramedics arrived."

"Were you charged with any crime that night?"

"No, they never charged me but I'm the one who killed him. You don't know how hard it was to tell Jenny. She understood my guilt over killing my father. We drove up to Jersey the next weekend for Jenny to meet my mother and sisters."

"Did you tell any of this to the police when you were interrogated?"

"No; I'm too ashamed about killing my own father."

"You had no choice."

"Everything was so confusing that night; I replay it over and over in my mind. What could I have done differently? What if my mother had run to a neighbor's house instead of upstairs? Why did Meghan have to open the damn door?"

"Don't keep torturing yourself. Did you ever have any counseling?"

"We had some family counseling; it only made things worst. Amy blamed me for his death despite everything the bastard did to us. She was really close to him; she was his favorite. Not being home that night; she never understood what happened. After his death, I started getting into trouble with the law."

"The New Jersey police must have told the investigators here about it."

"Chief Simpson never asked me; he had all the details about everything else I did back in Jersey."

It was strange that Harley never questioned him about it unless he was waiting to spring it on him at an inopportune time. Or was he still having trouble like I was trying to make sense of the contradictions that made up Brendan Healy's personality.

"Did it make the newspapers up there?"

"No, but everybody in Kearny knows about it. It wouldn't take a whole lot of digging to put two and two together."

"It wasn't in the *Register's* story this afternoon."

"I'm sure Milkowski has tipped off that reporter; he always had it in for me. I can see the headline; 'He Killed His Dad; Did He Kill His Girlfriend Too?'"

Brendan sat down in a chair and buried his head in his hands. "It's too late; everything I've accomplished is now destroyed."

"You're surrendering without a fight."

Brendan glared at me. "I don't need John Wayne to give me a pep talk; this isn't *The Sands of Iwo Jima.*"

He looked out again at the parked police car. "Why don't they arrest me and get it over with it?" Looking down he spotted the soda can and gave it a kick that sent it sailing into the kitchen where it smashed into an avocado colored stove left over from the 1970's. Dave remained in the safety of his room out of the line of fire.

Hopefully Brendan's temper would not get the better of him in front of an unforgiving audience like Harley Simpson. His explosive outbursts in front of me gave credence to the police's theory he lost his temper and strangled Jenny. I wouldn't put it past Harley and his investigators to deliberately try to provoke him and get it on tape.

"I'm sorry I lost my temper sir; it's the one genetic trait I inherited from my father. It's unnerving; my shadow is sitting across the street, waiting for the order to arrest me."

The pressure of being under constant surveillance was wearing Brendan down.

"They have no evidence to arrest you; you're innocent."

"The prosecutor will twist every piece of evidence to point the finger at me. He'll have a field day with me killing my father."

"His death was an accident."

"Was it? The son of a bitch heaped most of his abuse on me. I wanted him dead."

Brendan's posture and facial expression indicated otherwise; his father's death still haunted him. Like most alcoholics, his father had battered the entire family. I almost wished I was a psychologist instead of a historian. Despite his professed hatred of his father, Brendan was clearly racked with guilt over his death. Suppressing his emotions all these years had not helped him overcome that tragic night.

"It's imperative you go to the police before this snowballs out of control."

"Nothing I say or do is going to help. When I was incarcerated at Mountainview, one of the other boys from Kearny spread the word that I'd killed my father. Everyone gave me a wide berth; the other inmates figured anyone who killed their own father was a taco short of a combination plate. If that's how they reacted, a jury is going to freak out."

Ever since Sophocles penned the play *Oedipus the King*, the crime of patricide has sent shivers down the spine of theatergoers. Skillfully manipulated by a prosecutor, the death of his father could turn jurors against Brendan before they heard his protestations of innocence.

"All the evidence is going to point to me."

"What do you mean?"

Brendan looked around the room and sighed. "We made love on Monday afternoon; my DNA will be all over Jenny. That alone will be enough to convict me."

Sergeant Ramsey's had speculated correctly the day before about Brendan grabbing a little afternoon delight as he called it. Television shows featuring police units solving crimes with DNA evidence made Brendan's fear understandable; the police would be able to prove he'd been in intimate contact with Jenny hours before her death and draw the wrong conclusion.

"You said Jenny went to the library after you left her apartment; somebody must've seen her there. You were at work when she was murdered; you have an alibi."

"The library is a big building; who'd remember seeing her? We don't even know how she ended up in Jordan Hall or if she even made it to the library."

I didn't want to add to Brendan's anxiety but he had a point. Even if she went to the library, staffing was thin at night. It was likely she passed through unnoticed unless she requested assistance from a staff member. The security guard stationed near the entrance to deter the homeless from camping out in the library was often more interested in reading a magazine than keeping an eye on the comings and goings of the library's patrons. Jordan Hall had seven entrances including one that connected to the second floor to the parking garage. No one monitored the entrances although there was supposed to be a camera in the parking garage elevator. Classes were held in the building from eight in the morning until ten at night; thousands of students passed through the building each day. Trying to determine when Jenny arrived in Jordan Hall would be worst than trying to find a needle in a haystack.

"The police are trying to find out what happened to Jenny."

Brendan snickered. "They're looking for proof I'm the murderer; I'm in their crosshairs and they're itching to pull the trigger."

Nothing I said was going to convince Brendan to trust the police; his past brushes with the law made him wary of cooperating with them. He needed a lawyer to sort through the mess he was in but like most graduate students he was living hand to mouth and couldn't afford one.

Brendan slumped into one of the arm chairs. "Unless my alibi holds up, I'm fucked."

CHAPTER XIV

SHANE ALVAREZ WAS GONE WHEN I went outside; it seemed strange to be in the middle of a news story instead of being a spectator on the sidelines. Brendan's behavior perplexed me. At times he seemed resigned to being arrested; at other points his anger boiled over. The life he'd so carefully built since leaving Kearny now lay in ruins. Everyone has something hidden in their past; Brendan believed his secret was safely interred under six feet of dirt in New Jersey. Its resurrection could prove fatal as he fought to clear himself of the accusations swirling around him.

Crossing the street, I noticed the officer jotting something down in his notebook, most likely the time I left. No doubt I'd be hearing from Harley in the morning about my visit.

"You're just in time for the six o'clock news," Laura greeted me as I came into the kitchen from the garage.

"Being omniscient I can tell you the lead story, 'Chesapeake Bay University suspends student at the center of the investigation of young coed.'"

"How do you know that?"

"I just delivered the letter to Brendan informing him of his suspension under Policy 157."

"We tried for months to get Dean Noble to invoke Policy 157 against that creepy student who hung around the library pestering women; that pervert exposed himself to one of the shelvers and they finally banned him from campus."

"It only took them one day in Brendan's case but there's no evidence to justify suspending him."

"Why were you selected to be the bearer of glad tidings?"

"They figured I was expendable if Brendan went psycho when he received the letter."

Laura looked at me with alarm. "Is Brendan coming unhinged?"

"Doug Clayton just wanted to cover the university's ass and invoked Policy 157."

"The university appears to have ample grounds considering what happened."

Laura's skepticism about Brendan's innocence was understandable. Most women would have the same reaction. "Brendan doesn't pose a threat; they're suspending him on the basis of his teenage criminal record. Dick Torelli figured some reporter would break the story today; he wanted to counter the bad publicity and change the focus. Now the public will perceive CBU as tough and decisive."

"At least Brendan will have a hearing to clear himself."

"So did Marie Antoinette."

I noticed James lurking in the doorway to the kitchen and decided to wait until after dinner to tell Laura about Brendan's disclosure to me this afternoon.

"Dinner will be ready after the local news. Why don't you open one of the bottles of Merlot we bought at the wine festival two weeks ago?"

"What are we having?"

"Meatloaf."

"I guess Merlot goes with meatloaf."

After opening the wine and pouring a glass, I settled into my leather chair and watched the final minutes of an MTV program with James and Robert. The police had begun their search of Brendan's room just before I'd left the house yesterday. They seemed interested in retrieving the clothing he wore on Monday leading to his fears about seemingly innocent DNA evidence linking him to Jenny's murder. If they found anything else incriminating, he never mentioned it. Or was he withholding something from me again? His fear of imminent arrest had to be based on something more than the DNA evidence from his afternoon lovemaking. Did the police had the goods on him and it was only of time before their tests confirmed his guilt? My faith in Brendan might be misplaced.

Laura entered the room and settled into the chair next to me. "Which channel shall we watch?"

"I was chatting with Shane Alvarez from Channel 5 when he was staking out Brendan's house; he was annoyed that Amanda Saltzman was going to be a guest reporter on Channel 12's newscast."

"You're such a name dropper; will you be having lunch tomorrow with Katie Couric?"

"No, I have a department chairs meeting with Tollie at noon; I had to scratch lunch with Katie."

"Shouldn't we watch Channel 5 if you're going to be on it?" asked James.

"We need to watch Channel 12; Amanda Saltzman seems to have the inside scoop on the murder investigation."

"I'm going to watch Channel 5 up in my room and see if dad made the news," replied James as he got off the couch.

"Amanda Saltzman tried to sneak in Brendan's house through the back door catching Dave Chen, one of Brendan's housemates, in his underwear."

"Considering what Barry Sanders looks like, that must have been a treat for her," laughed Laura.

With his plump cheeks and red beard, Sanders resembled an overgrown chipmunk. I hated to imagine what he looked like clad only in his boxer shorts.

Laura clicked the remote to change to Channel12; electronic theme music played over a montage of aerial shots of Eastern Virginia. "Channel 12, the station that covers the seven city metro-area with Sky 12, the only news helicopter in the Old Dominion, brings you the News at Six with Ryan Chandler and Kendra Warren." The camera closed in on Ryan Chandler.

"Good evening; there have been dramatic new revelations today in the murder investigation of Chesapeake Bay University coed, Jennifer Biggio. She was found strangled Tuesday morning in a restroom in Jordan Hall, the university's high rise classroom building. We begin our team coverage with Amanda Saltzman, a reporter with our sister newspaper, the *Norfolk Register*. She's live in their newsroom."

The camera cut to Amanda Saltzman standing next to a desk in the paper's newsroom; the other reporters pretended to be busy in the background. She was wearing a different outfit than the one she wore to my office in the morning; her blouse exposed a substantial amount of cleavage for the viewers at home. A split screen appeared with a photo of Jenny in the left frame and Amanda on the right hand side of the screen.

"Good evening Ryan. CBU campus police have zeroed in on Brendan Healy as a person of interest in the murder of Jenny Biggio." A photo of Brendan downloaded without permission from the History Department website replaced Jenny in the left hand screen. "Healy had been dating her for the past several months; their relationship has been described by friends as stormy. Healy, a CBU graduate student, is employed as a teaching assistant in the History Department where Miss Biggio's body was found on Tuesday morning."

Amanda Saltzman cleverly linked Brendan to the murder through his employment in the History Department; a jury might see it as strong circumstantial evidence of his guilt. More disturbing was who described Brendan and Jenny's relationship as stormy. The times I'd seen them together I'd noticed nothing amiss in their relationship. Did I have the whole picture? Was there a darker side to Brendan's personality? Had he been truthful with me about what happened the night his father died? I only had his version of events to judge him.

"Why have the police focused their investigation on Healy?" asked Ryan.

"I talked this afternoon with Melinda Kroger, Miss Biggio's roommate. She revealed that when police searched Jenny's room, they found a pregnancy test kit. CBU police wouldn't confirm or deny that she was pregnant; no autopsy findings have been released to the media."

"Sadly hundreds of pregnant women are killed in the U. S. each year by their boyfriends or husbands," interrupted Kendra Warren as she replaced Brendan in the left hand screen.

"If Jenny was pregnant, Healy has a strong motive for her murder. That's why police have focused their attention on him so early in their investigation of this senseless murder."

"What else have you uncovered about Mr. Healy?" asked Kendra.

"Brendan Healy is a native of Kearny, New Jersey. I talked by phone this afternoon with Sergeant Vincent Milkowski of the Kearny Police Department; he indicated that Mr. Healy had an extensive criminal record as a juvenile and served several months at the Mountainview Youth Correctional Facility in Annandale, New Jersey."

Brendan's old mug shot taken by the Kearny Police Department replaced Kendra Warren on the left hand side of the screen. A second mug shot of Brendan with his head shaved taken when he was incarcerated filled the right hand screen. Staring out from the wide screen television, he looked menacing, a totally different person from the one I knew. Laura looked at the two images intently; they reinforced her negative perception of Brendan. The screen returned to the split between the Channel 12 newsroom and Amanda Saltzman.

"The Kearny Police still consider him a person of interest in the brutal murder of a drug dealer eleven years ago. Healy disappeared from the police's radar when he joined the Marines and left New Jersey. His resurfacing has led the Kearny Police to reopen that cold case; they're hopeful that new DNA techniques will enable them to make an arrest."

"How was he able to join the Marines with a criminal record?" asked Kendra.

"The military services frequently grant waivers to individuals with criminal records during periods when they are having trouble meeting recruiting goals."

"Did he ever do any time in the brig during his enlistment in the Marines?" asked Ryan.

"I've been unable to confirm any details about his military service."

"If he was working on a Ph.D., it sounds like he turned his life around," commented Ryan.

It was the first positive comment about Brendan in the whole story.

"I posed a similar question to Sergeant Milkowski. He replied a leopard never changes its spots."

"What is Mr. Healy's response to these revelations?"

"He's holed up in a house that he shares with three other CBU students in the Jefferson Terrace neighborhood near the campus. Healy declined our request for an interview."

"Thank you Amanda for your report. After a commercial break, we'll switch to Chesapeake Bay University where Felicia Wright is standing by with breaking news."

We were forced to sit through a local car dealer's wretched commercial featuring a third rate James Brown impersonator. The screen switched to Dick Torelli standing behind a lectern in front of the Old Main Building flanked by Harley Simpson and Dean Noble. "During the Chesapeake Bay University investigation into the murder of Jennifer Biggio, it came to light that a student acquainted with Miss Biggio, Brendan Healy, failed to disclose his prior criminal convictions when he applied for admission to the university. In light of this fact, the university has suspended Mr. Healy until we can conduct a review. University administration took this step to ensure a safe learning environment for our students. You will find in your briefing packet, a copy of Policy 157 and an information sheet that should answer your questions about the suspension process."

"Is Mr. Healy a suspect in Miss Biggio's murder?" asked Felicia.

"I'm unable to answer any questions at this time about the investigation other than to say every resource has been made available to the campus police to bring it to a swift and successful conclusion," replied Dick Torelli.

"Dick, I have a question."

"Go ahead Shane."

"On my way over, I downloaded CBU's admission application; nowhere on the application did it ask for any information on criminal convictions. How can Mr. Healy be suspended for concealing something he was never asked about?"

Felicia Wright, sitting next to Shane, looked annoyed due to Shane shoehorning himself into Channel 12's broadcast.

Dick Torrelli stared acidly at Shane and replied, "I'm sorry, the Family Educational Rights and Privacy Act prevents me from divulging any further details about Mr. Healy."

I chuckled; Shane's question caught Dick Torelli off guard but he managed to parry the blow. Unlike Felicia Wright, Shane didn't accept everything foisted on him by Dick Torelli. He seemed willing to question the inconsistencies in the case being made against Brendan.

Although a lawyer would advise against it, Brendan needed to go on the offensive instead of being holed up in his house like Hitler in the Reich Chancellery bunker. Norfolk is a blue collar town; it was highly unlikely to find a dozen individuals who disdained television like Tollie Monroe. Unless he countered the barrage of negative publicity, a jury's opinion of him would be biased before the trial started. Brendan's situation was further complicated by the proliferation of local news programs on cable television that aired anything without regard to quality or veracity to fill the broadcast time. Should Brendan grant an interview to Shane Alvarez to counter Amanda Saltzman?

"We next go to Mike Napier with our affiliated station in Cleveland, Ohio, Channel 9, for a special report on the life of Jennifer Biggio."

"Jennifer Biggio grew up in Shaker Heights, a suburb of Cleveland. Her father worked at the local Ford assembly plant; her mother is a nurse at the world renowned Cleveland Clinic. She graduated near the top of her high school class here in Shaker Heights and played on the field hockey team."

A photo of Jenny playing field hockey probably taken from her high school yearbook appeared on the screen to be replaced seconds later by a photo of her in her cap and gown with a gold National Honor Society sash across her chest.

"At Kent State University she majored in economics, graduating magna cum laude. Earlier today I talked with Brad Biggio, Jennifer's cousin, when he emerged from her parent's house."

Brad appeared to be in his mid-twenties; he sported a close clipped goatee and was dressed in khakis and a polo shirt. I recognized him from some of the pictures taken at the beach I'd perused in Brendan's living room.

"My aunt and uncle are very distressed; Jenny was their only child. We're a close knit Italian family; we spent all our holidays together. She was always a lot of fun to be with; she was so full of life."

"When did you last see your cousin?"

"I took my vacation in Virginia Beach in August; I spent a lot of time with Jenny and her boyfriend. She seemed very happy; it's upsetting to find out that Healy is suspected of killing her."

"Jennifer Biggio's funeral will be held on Saturday morning at 11 AM in the Church of St. Dominic in Shaker Heights. This is Mike Napier reporting for Channel 9 Eyewitness News."

Jenny's cousin Brad let the cat out of the bag; Brendan was suspected of killing Jenny. Everyone else had referred to him as a person of interest; although few were fooled by the semantic gymnastics.

Laura looked over at me with a smug smile on her face; the news reports had substantiated her suspicions about Brendan. I took a long sip of my wine as James bounded down from his room as Channel 12 switched to a commercial from a local chiropractor.

"You didn't make Channel 5; they only showed Brendan's house," said James.

"Your student had gangsta written all over him in his old mug shots; he didn't look like the wimps I usually see hanging around your office," said Robert.

"I'm sure Brendan will be honored that you've placed him in the ranks of Tupac Shapur and 50 Cent."

Unless Brendan was reinstated by the panel, his academic career was over. Even if he was never charged with Jenny's murder, his reputation had been irreparably shredded. He'd have a cloud hanging over him for rest of his life. Academia is a small world; everyone in a department is part of the higher education tapestry. Threads run from schools attended through previous places of employment to professional societies. All it takes is an email to former colleague to get the lowdown on a job candidate. He'd be lucky to be hired for a one year appointment at a community college in Alaska or some other institution at the bottom of the academic food chain.

Laura announced dinner when the weather segment came on; all of the local stations were engaged in a contest over who had the most powerful weather radar. To boost ratings, Channel 12 moved their weather broadcast to the streets, broadcasting each night from different locations in the metro area. During the summer months, the station scored ratings points by broadcasting from local beaches nightly with the assistance of bikini clad young women. With the onset of fall, the ratings sagged as the broadcast moved to other venues like soccer matches, shopping malls and church suppers where scantily clad females were in short supply. Tonight the weather was done in front of the Student Union, either to tie in with the murder story or because one of their satellite trucks was already on campus. Several Kappa Deltas with matching hoodies emblazoned with Greek letters across the chest showed up to provide the desired pulchritude.

When we sat down at the table, Robert speared a piece of meat loaf with his knife.

"Use the serving fork next time," Laura corrected him.

"Your table manners show that you would've been right at home at a medieval banquet," I added.

"That's doubtful; pizza and bacon cheeseburgers hadn't been invented yet. I think that's why historians refer to that era as the Dark Ages," Robert replied.

"I don't recall from my reading in graduate school that civilization didn't advance until the fast food drive thru was invented."

"Just don't toss your bones on the floor when you're through chewing on them," reminded Laura.

"The Middle Ages would have been ideal for me. As the eldest son, I'd be in line to inherit everything. Primogeniture as I recall from honors history," said James.

"Primo asshole is more like it," replied Robert.

"Enough!" I admonished Robert.

"You need to be more pious; as the second son you'd be packed off to the monastery. There you'd lead a celibate life praying all day while I chase after the local wenches," said James in a holier than thou tone.

"As lord of the manor, you'd be too busy dealing with plagues, famine and war to have time for the young ladies," I suggested.

"Since Lori ditched you in August, you're the one with the celibate life style," laughed Robert.

After dinner, I suggested to Laura that we take a walk. With the sun down, the temperature had dropped and a slight chill filled the air as we walked the streets along the river. It was a full moon and the water sloshed against the bulkhead. Our neighbors were out walking their dogs; the larger the dog, the better it seemed in our neighborhood.

"I need to tell you something in confidence about Brendan; I don't want you blindsided when it comes out."

"You mean there's more than what was on news tonight?" asked Laura.

"This afternoon Brendan told me that he killed his father."

Laura stopped. "Didn't I read that play in high school?"

"Everybody did; that's the problem."

"Is that why they sent him to that youth correctional center?"

"Brendan said he was never charged in his father's death."

"What happened?"

"Brendan's father drank heavily and his mother threw him out. One night his father returned home and attacked his mother; Brendan had no choice but to protect her. When they were fighting, his father fell down the stairs and broke his neck."

"Do you really believe that crock?"

"If you were there and heard him, you'd see the guilt he's suffered over his father's death."

"He should feel guilty; he killed his own father for God's sake."

"Why don't you believe him?"

"I would view anything Brendan Healy told me with a great deal of skepticism. His girlfriend died violently as did his father; connect the dots. The police certainly will."

"You think he murdered Jenny?"

"Let's just say for now, I'm not convinced he's innocent."

I'd thought Laura would react more sympathetically to my account of Brendan's father's death. After all, Brendan was the same age as James when his father died. It failed to stir Laura's maternal instincts. Instead she saw it as additional proof of Brendan's violent tendencies and his culpability in Jenny's murder.

"Why didn't Amanda Saltzman say anything about Brendan's father's death?" asked Laura.

"She may be saving it for tomorrow's paper. Since Brendan was never charged in his father's death, she has to tread lightly. The *Register's* attorneys would have to vet any story."

"You're in over your head. Brendan Healy may be some kind of psychopath. Wasn't Ted Bundy in law school when he murdered all those women?"

CHAPTER XV

When the alarm rang on Thursday morning, I wondered if the *Register* contained any new revelations. It seemed like a week had passed since I'd found Jenny's body even though less than 48 hours had transpired. James and Robert were awake and getting ready to leave; their high school started classes a half hour earlier than CBU.

I retrieved the newspaper from the front steps and put on the coffee maker. Unrolling the paper, I found Brendan's mug shot staring back at me from the front page. When the photo had flashed on the television, it didn't have the same impact as when it appeared in print. James was right; Brendan looked like a cheap thug. Being a teenager when the picture was taken, he'd failed to realize the picture might come back to haunt him years later. Without thinking, he'd sneered at the photographer resulting in a menacing snarl the moment the photo was snapped.

While the coffee brewed, I read Amanda Saltzman's article. Her piece was rather anti-climatic; most of it, with the exception of Brendan's suspension, had already appeared on the *Register's* website. During her television appearance, she'd milked the story for all it was worth. No wonder readers were deserting newspapers in droves.

There was nothing about Brendan's involvement in his father's death. Amanda Saltzman was a savvy journalist; she may have been holding back that portion of the story in order to plant her byline on the front page another morning.

I sipped my coffee and pondered Brendan's situation. The suspension made him appear guilty of Jenny's murder even though he'd not been arrested. Even Harley Simpson admitted the police only had circumstantial evidence linking him to the murder; not enough to make an arrest stick. Despite his purported alibi, the police needed to delve further into the background of Felton Snyder, the homeless man who supposedly found Jenny's wallet in the alley. It seemed too pat that Snyder picked up the wallet and conveniently found Antonio McKinney at the nearby MacDonald's willing to take the credit card off his hands. My bet was that Snyder was behind many of the missing purses and laptops on campus. McKinney served as his fence for disposing of the bountiful harvest gleaned from careless students.

Harley had indicated that Snyder had done time in North Carolina for stabbing a man in a barroom brawl. What other crimes lurked in his background? He'd been hanging around the campus for almost a year. Where had Snyder been before he'd arrived in Norfolk? He had a history of violence to boot; it was not a stretch of the imagination to see him strangling Jenny.

"Morning dear," said Laura as she shuffled half awake into the kitchen. She went over to the coffee maker and filled her mug. Our morning routine never changed; despite having over 20 mugs in the cabinet, I drank my coffee from a mug I'd purchased during a vacation stop at the FDR Presidential Library while Laura used her UNC – Chapel Hill School of Library Science mug. "Are the boys ready to leave for school yet?"

"Robert is ready; James is still in the shower."

"They're cutting it close again," sighed Laura.

"James is not a morning person."

"In order to get to school on time; James is going to have to drive like a speed demon."

"It'll be good training if he wants to pursue a career in NASCAR."

"The way James drives, the demolition derby is more like it. He was playing that blasted computer game last night; he woke me up when he used the bathroom before going to bed at 1:00 AM."

I was same way when I was a teenager; I stayed up to all hours reading. At least I spent my time profitably instead of playing some mindless computer game. A professor in the College of Education praised computer games saying they promoted hand and eye coordination. Tollie Monroe denounced the professor as a blithering idiot; for once I had to agree with Tollie. Half of the students in my freshmen survey classes couldn't string together two coherent sentences or spell common five letter words; their grammatical problems could be traced to not reading enough. I hated to think where we'll be when the second generation of computer kids is loosed on the world; we might slide into another Dark Age with everyone glued to their computers, oblivious to the world around them.

"One of the things that the police have downplayed is the woman who tried to use Jenny's credit card at Wal-Mart. There's no mention of her in Amanda Saltzman's story this morning."

"It was in the paper yesterday. What about it?"'

"Does Felton Snyder, the homeless man who found Jenny's wallet, hang around the library?"

"There are dozens of community patrons who infest the library especially since the public library downtown now closes at 5:00 PM due to the city's budget cuts."

A community patron was the library's euphemism for the homeless. As my mother observed when she was growing up in the 1930's, homeless people were called bums. The term homeless people implied lacking a home was their only problem. Instead it masked more serious issues; many of the homeless are alcoholics, drug addicts, sociopaths or schizophrenics. At a minimum, Snyder had a drinking problem; could he also have been hearing voices the night Jenny was killed? It was a disturbing possibility that could explain the randomness of Jenny's murder.

"The Ark Church runs their soup and prayer dinner on Monday, Wednesday and Friday evenings starting at 6:30 PM. Reverend Franklin even has an old school bus that he sends downtown to pick the homeless up."

Reverend Franklin had taken over a boarded up Woolco Discount Store on the border of Jefferson Terrace and Braxton Homes several years earlier and built a thriving evangelical church that ministered to the people of the two communities. He also established an outreach to the homeless with disastrous consequences for the university's library.

"After dinner, they hang out in the library until we close at midnight. We have air conditioning in the summer and plenty of heat in the winter plus comfortable arm chairs and couches unlike the downtown library with its rock hard chairs and benches. What more could they want?"

"Showers and hot coffee would be nice."

"They already use our bathrooms for bathing. The library is like a resort for them. Since we opened the coffee lounge on the first floor in the old microfilm room, they can sip lattes all night. Last month, a student went into the ladies room on the third floor and found two of them having sex in one of the stalls. Our custodians find liquor bottles in the trash all the time."

"I think Harley Simpson dismissed Felton Snyder as a suspect in his headlong rush to arrest Brendan for Jenny's murder. During his briefing for Doug Clayton, he indicated Snyder had done time down in North Carolina."

"What did he do?"

"Harley said he stabbed someone in a bar fight in High Point back in the 70's; he was sentenced to two years in prison."

"That confirms some of our suspicions about our community patrons. His name means nothing to me; we only know them by sight. What does he look like?"

"He resembles Whit Tanner; he's short with a long scraggily beard; he always wears a baseball cap."

"Is he missing his two front teeth?"

"Yes."

"That's how we tell him apart from Dr. Tanner. I've dealt with some squirrelly professors over the years, whoever heard of wearing a tie with a bowling shirt?"

I laughed; Whit was CBU's most eccentric professor. "Homeless people move from city to city; Snyder could be a one man crime wave, moving on when the police get suspicious of him."

"He's on our watch list; we've been suspicious of him for a while. The problem is we don't have enough staff at night to monitor all the floors. We only have two security guards at night; one watches the front door while the other one walks the floors. Some of the guards do a better job than others; it's hard to catch them in the act."

"What do you mean?"

"Many of the library's community patrons use our computers to access porn websites; most of it is pretty hardcore stuff. You can only imagine what else those creeps do."

"Is Harley Simpson aware of what's going on?"

"He's had meetings with Dean Whitman; libraries all over the country have the same problems with these perverts."

I'd initially seen Felton Snyder as a harmless wino who hung around campus bumming quarters and fishing cigarettes from the trash. Laura raised the possibility that Snyder could be a sex offender, a potentially violent one at that. His story about finding Jenny's wallet behind Grave's Market sounded fishy; yet Harley accepted it at face value.

"Until you told me his name, I didn't know Snyder's identity. About two weeks ago he was in the reference room using one of the computers; he sent a rather graphic pornographic image to the printer. It really freaked out Henrietta when she found it on the printer; that sicko just sat there with a big grin on his face."

Henrietta Sealy had been a librarian at the university for over thirty years. With three ex-husbands lurking in her past, the picture must have been rather graphic to shock her.

"Did it get reported to Harley?"

"Henrietta filed an incident report; the problem was a student sent something to the printer at the same time. It's a networked printer; it could have come from any of the 64 computers in the reference room. That's why it's impossible to prove with complete certainty he did it; otherwise we could get him interdicted from the library."

At this point nothing but a thin plastic card connected Snyder to Jenny's murder. His background raised a lot of questions but I had no hard facts, only speculation, to bring to Harley.

"Don't you think Harley thoroughly investigated Snyder?"

"Harley sees the issue of Jenny's stolen credit card as a speed bump in the road to arresting Brendan."

"As much as I would like to run that pervert out of the library, there's been only one murder on campus."

"Snyder didn't run into Antonio McKinney by accident at the MacDonald's. He knew who would take the hot credit card off his hands."

"That's a sideshow; you don't need to murder someone to steal a purse."

"What if Snyder was trying to sexually assault Jenny?"

"You're making a pretty big leap."

"All I'm saying is Harley needs to take a second look at Mr. Snyder. Was Henrietta on duty in the reference room on Monday night?"

"I'd have to check the schedule. Why?"

"Brendan said Jenny was heading to the library after they parted on Monday afternoon. I'm wondering if Snyder crossed paths with her in the library later that night."

"Henrietta is keeping a sharp eye out for that creep; if she catches him in the act, she's going to whack him with her ruler."

I didn't ask Laura where.

***

Jordan Hall seemed back to normal when I pulled into the parking lot; at least no television broadcast trucks were parked in front of the building. While I waited for one of Jordan Hall's interminably slow elevators, I was ambushed from behind.

"Andy!" Emily Worthington hailed me from across the lobby as the elevator door opened.

Stepping into the elevator, I debated whether to push the open door or close door button. Why delay the inevitable? She'd be in my office in a matter of minutes.

"Bon jour Emily." She dashed into the elevator elbowing aside two students not trained in the ways of the New York subway like someone who'd earned her B.A. at Hunter College and her M.A. and Ph.D. at Columbia. The elevator door closed and the car shuddered as it began its ascent to the sixth floor.

"Greeting me in French is not going to placate me. Why didn't you tell me I no longer have a graduate assistant? If Julia hadn't watched the 11 o'clock news and called me, I'd be completely in the dark."

"It wasn't my decision to suspend Brendan."

"Am I going to get a replacement for him?"

"His suspension may only be temporary; he'll have a hearing next week."

"I'd put my money on the French restoring the Bourbons to the throne before I'd bet on Brendan being reinstated by the review panel."

"We owe Brendan the chance to clear himself."

"I owe him nothing; he's supposed to be grading my mid-terms."

"If the panel fails to reinstate him; I'll assign a new teaching assistant to finish out the semester."

"Do you even know where my mid-terms are?"

"What do you mean?"

"I gave them to him on Monday to grade; are they locked in the graduate assistant's office or at that wretched hovel he shares with Dave Chen and company?"

"I'll call Brendan this morning; if the police still have the office locked up, we'll have to wait."

"Did you ever investigate whether Brendan was harassing that student?"

"Your memo is on my desk; I was rather busy yesterday and didn't have a chance to get to it."

"One way or the other, he'll be out of here next week. Start looking for a replacement for me."

The elevator door opened and Emily headed to her office. Emily was right; unless some evidence surfaced to clear him, Brendan might be arrested before he ever had his hearing.

***

Janet was still not back from her daughter's in North Carolina so the department office was empty when I unlocked the door. I had a few minutes to check my emails before heading to my class at 8:00 AM; the students would be taking the mid-term delayed by the events of Tuesday. I'd have 90 minutes to myself while they took the exam and decided to spend it profitably investigating the background of Felton Snyder. After distributing the exams, I went back to my office and clicked open Google. I typed "Felton Snyder;" on the first page of results was a link to a police arrest log in *The Florida Times-Union* in Jacksonville, Florida indicating that Felton Snyder, age 55, had been arrested for drinking in public during the first week of February 2005. It appeared he'd headed south for the winter that year. I could find nothing further on him after searching the newspaper's website. A few clicks later, I found an article in *The Daytona Beach News-Journal* that Fred Snyder, same age, had been arrested for public intoxication in Daytona Beach two months later. Were Fred and Felton, one and the same?

I found an obituary in the *Roanoke-Chowan News-Herald* for Verna Atkins Snyder, age 97, of Murfreesboro, North Carolina who died in 2006. The obituary listed among her numerous survivors her son, Felton R. Snyder. Unlike his two brothers and five sisters, who were scattered across North Carolina, no location was noted for Felton. Her family was either unaware of their black sheep's whereabouts or didn't want to know where he was residing.

Murfreesboro in eastern North Carolina was about a 90 minute drive from Norfolk. Many from the region headed to Norfolk and Newport News for employment in the shipyards during World War II. After passing through Murfreesboro to a less than warn reception from his family, it was not hard to see Snyder ending up in Norfolk, the nearest metropolitan area.

Clicking through 30 pages of results that overwhelmed me with information on Dee Snyder of Twisted Sister, I found nothing further on Felton Snyder.

Taking a chance, I typed in "Snyder, Felton" and found a police log in the Charleston, South Carolina *Post and Courier* indicating he'd been arrested for shoplifting on May 5, 2003. Again no further details were available. Harley had more information available through the FBI's national crime reporting network. My search was running into a dead end; I had nothing concrete to bring to Harley other than my suspicions.

His conviction for assault didn't come up in Google since it occurred back in the 1970's; most newspapers only had digital content online dating back to the advent of the digital age in the mid-1990s. The morgues of most newspapers had indexes to their back issues stored on microfilm; they often permitted public and college libraries access to assist researchers.

I picked up the phone and called Laura. "Good morning dear, how's it going?"

"It's been quiet; the students must be sleeping late. What's up with you?"

"I've been researching Felton Snyder's background without much luck."

"Did you ever think to ask a professional librarian for assistance?"

"That's why I'm calling."

"How can the reference department assist you today?"

Laura was active in the American Library Association; I decided to play a hunch. "Do you know anyone through ALA down in High Point?"

"I ran into a classmate from Chapel Hill, Denise Stroud, at the ALA Mid-Winter meeting in Chicago last year; she'd recently taken a position with the High Point Public Library. She gave me her card. Public libraries usually open by ten in the morning; I'll send Denise an email."

"From what Harley Simpson indicated, Snyder was convicted sometime in the late 70's. He might also go by the name Fred Snyder."

"Librarians have started with less information than that."

***

To my surprise, Janet Hodges, the department secretary poked her head in my door.

"You're back from North Carolina; I wasn't expecting you until tomorrow."

"My daughter's in-laws arrived last night from Georgia; it was time for me to leave. They're staying for a week; I'll go back after they go home. It's only a four hour drive down to Cary."

"How's the baby doing?"

"Zachary David is doing wonderful; all nine pounds, two ounces of him."

"Do you have pictures?"

"I'm downloading them to my computer now."

University computers were not supposed to be used for personal purposes but I was not going to interfere with her joy over her first grandchild. "You've missed all the excitement here."

"Maureen called on Tuesday afternoon and filled me in." Maureen Lawson was the Economics Department's secretary and Janet's frequent companion for lunch and coffee breaks.

"My daughter has a computer; I followed all the developments on the *Register's* website. You could have knocked me over with a feather when I read that Brendan and Jenny were getting married."

"Jenny's pregnancy precipitated him asking the question."

"You and I come from different backgrounds; I understand someone like Brendan, you don't. Although I'm twenty-five years older than Brendan, we're both Irish working class kids. My old neighborhood in south Philly was full of guys like him. My first husband was a Marine like Brendan. Marines are only interested in getting drunk and getting laid; Brendan had no intention of marrying Jenny."

"It doesn't mean he murdered her."

"Maureen overheard Brendan on Monday morning shouting in Jenny's office; it was no lover's quarrel."

"What do you mean?"

"It was a really violent argument; at one point Brendan screamed, 'How could you have been so stupid? I can't afford to support a baby!' Maureen said Jenny started sobbing."

All of the floors were set up the same; the graduate student offices were down the hall from the departmental office. Either Maureen had very good hearing or she was standing right outside the door to Jenny's office.

"Maureen told all this to the police?" I asked.

"Yes, everyone in the econ department overheard them too."

No wonder the police pegged Brendan as Jenny's killer from the start. It seemed unlikely Maureen exaggerated what happened on Monday morning when she was questioned by the police. Was Laura right that I was closing my eyes to the possibility that Brendan murdered Jenny? Was Janet right that I didn't know Brendan? What had Sergeant Milkowski said? A leopard never changes his spots.

***

Janet handed me my morning mail and I leafed through a catalog from the Oxford University Press to kill time until the exam was over. My phone rang and Caller ID indicated it was Laura.

"I didn't expect a response so fast from High Point."

"Denise hasn't replied yet; I'm on the reference desk till 9:30, meet me in the library's coffee shop after your exam is over."

"You can't talk now."

"Exactly."

Something was happening at the library. I went downstairs to the classroom and found half the class still writing in their blue books. With students from the next class milling restlessly in the hallway, I had no choice but to indicate time was up. After they passed in their bluebooks, I put them in my brief case and walked across the parking lot to the library. Laura was waiting for me in the coffee shop with two cups of coffee on the table.

"What's up?"

"The police were here this morning with a subpoena for Jenny Biggio's library record."

"They already know she'd checked out the pregnancy books."

"Even though the books were found in her room, they need to confirm she checked them out."

"They're fixated that Brendan killed Jenny because she was pregnant to the exclusion of any other suspects."

"When circulation ran her record, something weird popped up. Jenny returned two books this morning she'd checked out last week."

"Dead people don't return library books."

"The books were in the overnight book drop when we opened; someone put them in there after the library closed last night."

"What did the police have to say?"

"Sergeant Ramsey was confounded to say the least; he took the books to have them dusted for fingerprints. The circulation staff has to report to the campus police station to be fingerprinted."

"When I found Jenny in the restroom, she had nothing with her. Her purse and wallet were found that morning; her messenger bag containing her laptop is still missing."

"Do you think the books were in her bag?"

"It's possible."

"I doubt whoever took her bag returned the books; it's more likely that someone in the Economics Department saw them in her cubicle and put them in the book drop. Brendan might have returned them; she could have left them at his house."

"He's banned from setting foot on campus; the police are watching him around the clock. Brendan knows they're itching for a pretext to arrest him."

"Maybe her roommate returned them."

"I guess that's possible."

"The murderer certainly didn't return them; that violates every tenet of library science."

I laughed. There was no logical reason that I could fathom for Jenny's murderer to return the books. If Felton Snyder was the murderer, he wouldn't have bothered with the books. He would've just pitched them in the bushes after emptying Jenny's bag of anything of value. Perhaps a Good Samaritan found the books and returned them to the library not knowing their connection to the crime. If Snyder's fingerprints were on the books that would further link him to Jenny's murder.

"Henrietta Sealy talked to Sergeant Ramsey this morning."

"Did she tell them about Snyder?"

"No, but she saw Jenny on Monday night in the library."

"When?"

"Right after she came back from her dinner break, she went up to the second floor to help a student find a journal in the periodicals room."

"What time was that?"

"Henrietta was scheduled to go on break at five; it must have been just after six."

"Why did she wait to talk to the police until today?"

"She didn't realize it was Jenny until she looked at the *Register* this morning; one of her cats was sick earlier in the week and she didn't have time to look at the paper or television while nursing it back to health."

"Here she comes now," whispered Laura.

I turned around to find Henrietta strolling into the coffee shop.

"Good morning Andrew."

"Good morning Henrietta," I greeted her.

"Laura was telling me you might have been the last person other than the killer to see Jenny Biggio alive."

Henrietta settled into one of the empty chairs at the table. She was clearly excited to be the center of attention. "I told Sergeant Ramsey I was up in the periodicals room helping a student find a discontinued journal in the compact shelving and I saw this young woman sitting at one of the tables staring out the window. Something was upsetting her; she slammed the journal she'd been reading down on the table and shouted, 'That no good lying bastard; I can't believe he's cheating on me!' I told her that was not the way we treated library materials. When I was in elementary school we were taught to respect library books. They don't teach that in the schools anymore; it's this whole era of permissiveness that started back in the 1960's."

"When I was in elementary school in the 1960's; Miss Stanhope made us wash our hands before we entered her library." Laura kicked my leg under the table signaling me not to get Henrietta going.

"That's a sound hygienic practice for school libraries; elementary school children are covered with filth from the playground."

"Are you sure Jenny said, 'That no good lying bastard; I can't believe he's cheating on me!'

"I had my hearing tested last year; I know what I heard," replied Henrietta.

"You're sure it was Jenny Biggio."

"I might wear glasses but I'm not blind; her picture was on the front page of the *Register* this morning. Incidentally it was an economics journal she slammed down on the table; I checked to make sure the spine wasn't damaged."

CHAPTER XVI

AFTER FINISHING MY COFFEE, I walked back to my office. Henrietta's sighting of Jenny in the library shortly after six o'clock gave the police their first fix on Jenny's whereabouts after she left her apartment. Jenny's utterance as reported by Henrietta could only apply to Brendan. It was damming that Henrietta caught Jenny in a fit of anger after she looked out the window and caught him with another woman. What else could explain Jenny becoming so enraged that she threw the journal down on the table?

There was no reason to doubt Henrietta's veracity; her reaction to Jenny abusing the journal was typical behavior for her. She severely reprimanded a colleague of mine for putting an open book face down on the table.

I needed to talk with Brendan; he'd better have a good explanation as to his whereabouts on Monday night. Who was he with that Jenny thought he was cheating on her?

When I reached my office, Janet handed me a message from Emily Worthington reminding me about her exams. Janet was showing Maureen the pictures of her grandson in a slide show, all two hundred of them. Since digital cameras needed no film and there was no cost to develop the photos, people now snapped inordinate amounts of pictures. In the past, when someone had a grandchild, you only had to sit through twenty-four pictures, now you were held prisoner for eons.

"The police found Jenny's car in the parking garage this morning; Dr. Ruiz said they were all over the car taking fingerprints," said Maureen.

"I didn't realize her car was missing."

"Apparently the police didn't spot it when they searched the garage on Tuesday; a lot of the kids in the dorms park their cars in the garage due to all the break-ins in the parking lots late at night."

Were the police following standard procedure dusting the car for prints or did the car have a connection to Jenny's murder?

I passed the rest of the morning grading mid-terms. Just before noon I picked up the phone and called Brendan on his cell phone. He didn't answer and I left a message. A few minutes later he called me.

"Good morning sir; I'm sorry I didn't answer. Somehow that bitch from the *Register* found out my cell phone number and she's been calling every twenty minutes."

Brendan's vituperative emphasis on the word bitch surprised me; I wasn't sure if he was frustrated by Amanda Saltzman's reporting about him or it showed something more sinister in his personality.

"Dr. Worthington is concerned about her mid-terms; do you know where they are?"

"I have them in my backpack; I graded them last night in order to keep from going crazy."

"I'm heading to lunch in a few minutes; I'll swing by your house to pick them up."

"My police shadow is still out front as well as an SUV from Channel 12; I'm practically a prisoner in my own house."

When I pulled up in front of Brendan's house, the plain clothes police officer looked me over suspiciously and wrote down my license plate number. The reporter and his camera man were eating hamburgers. They were staking out the house figuring an arrest was imminent and wanted footage for the evening news. Before I could knock on the front door, Brendan opened it and ushered me in.

"The police have a second officer watching the alley in case I try to slip out the back door. I should be honored they think I'm so dangerous."

"Were you aware that the econ department's secretary overheard your argument with Jenny on Monday morning?" Brendan looked as if I'd just slugged him in the jaw; he looked around the room avoiding eye contact with me.

"Jenny asked me to come up to her office and then told me she was pregnant. Coming out of the blue like that I just lost it and yelled at her. At that moment I had only $350 in my bank account; you can't support a baby on that. I'm living on the edge as you can see."

"I was just like my scumbag father; he always yelled at my mother. Once I cooled off, I was ashamed at how I'd reacted. I went to her apartment and begged her forgiveness. We worked everything out and made plans to get married at Christmas so the baby wouldn't be born out of wedlock. That was important for Jenny; I saw too many guys in Kearny get a girl pregnant and dump her. My mother raised me to do the right thing."

It must have been a whirlwind afternoon; Brendan and Jenny resolved their difficulties and made plans for their wedding with enough time left over to make love. No wonder the police were skeptical of his story.

"Henrietta Sealy from the Reference Department saw Jenny around six o'clock up in the periodicals room."

"Who's Henrietta Sealy?"

"She's a reference librarian; she wears her hair in a bun."

"I've had a few run-ins with her. What about it? Jenny headed to the library after I left her apartment."

"Henrietta said Jenny was looking out the window and suddenly exclaimed, 'That no good lying bastard; I can't believe he's cheating on me!' She slammed the journal she was reading on the table."

"Is she sure it was Jenny?"

"She saw her picture in the paper."

"That doesn't sound like Jenny at all."

"Did Jenny look out the window and see you with another woman?"

"I wasn't on campus at that time!"

"Henrietta talked to the police this morning."

"You must believe me; I didn't return to campus until later. I never cheated on Jenny!"

Henrietta's eccentricities were well documented but I'd never heard she hallucinated. I wanted to believe Brendan but nothing else seemed to explain Jenny's outburst. Combined with Maureen Lawson's account of Jenny and Brendan's argument earlier in the day, the police would paint a picture of an abusive relationship.

"I need to ask a favor."

"What?" I asked hesitantly.

"I want to attend Jenny's memorial service tomorrow but I'm barred from campus. Can you intervene with Dean Noble?"

"I'll try but it's out of his hands."

"Who's calling the shots?"

"President Clayton."

"The police won't let me leave the state. What does it matter? I don't even have the money to fly to Cleveland for her funeral anyway. Her memorial service is the only way I'll have to say goodbye to Jenny." Brendan lost his composure; he buried his face in his hands and began sobbing.

***

After leaving Brendan's house, I decided to grab a bite to eat at the McDonald's across from campus. After ordering a Big Mac and Coke, I patted myself on the back for being virtuous and not ordering French fries. I took a table in the back of the restaurant away from the noise up front so I could read *The Economist* while eating.

"Can I take your tray?"

I looked up from my magazine and saw Alan Melton, one of the department's majors holding a stack of trays. "I didn't realize you worked here."

"It's not glamorous but they give me enough hours so I can make ends meet. If I worked at Starbucks, I'd barely get twenty hours a week."

"Do you ever work nights?"

"We have a lot of turnover on the night shift; they call me in when they're in a bind. I can always use the extra money."

"Do you know Antonio McKinney?"

Alan looked around the restaurant as if to see it was safe to talk. "He seemed a bit shifty to me; I always thought he had something going on the side. Last week he showed up with a new set of rims on his car, a real expensive set. He couldn't afford them on what he makes here."

"Did you ever see him with a homeless man?"

"Normally we try to keep the homeless from loitering inside; they buy one cup of coffee and think they can hang out here all day. Antonio seemed rather friendly with one of them; he often slipped him free food."

"Is he short with a long, scraggily beard?" I asked.

"That's the one."

"Last week I went behind the restaurant to smoke a cigarette on my break; Antonio was in the back of the parking lot by his car talking with him. The homeless guy handed Antonio something that he locked in the trunk of his car. That part of the parking lot isn't well lit; it was hard to tell what was going on. The next day Antonio offered me a laptop for a $100."

"Did he explain how he obtained the laptop?"

"He gave me a cock and bull story about a friend who repaired computers and had one the owner never claimed. It didn't surprise me when they arrested him."

"Did you work on Monday night?"

"No, I was off. Why do you ask?"

Trying to help Brendan, I decided to bring Alan into my confidence to see if he had any further information. "The police think Brendan Healy murdered Jenny Biggio."

"I saw that in the newspaper. He's a cool dude; it's hard to believe he had anything to do with it."

"My theory is Mr. McKinney's homeless friend, Felton Snyder, murdered Jenny."

"Why would he murder her?" asked Alan.

"Snyder sold Jenny's credit card to McKinney as well as other items; I think Snyder is behind the purse snatchings and laptop thefts in the library and Jordan Hall."

"It explains why Antonio was always helping that wino; he didn't want the goose that laid the golden egg to starve."

"The problem is I don't have any hard evidence other than the credit card to link Snyder to her murder."

"Jenny caught Snyder trying to steal her laptop; they struggled and he killed her?" asked Alan.

"That's my guess."

"I'll keep my ears open to see if I can pick up anything."

***

After finishing my lunch I returned to campus and gleefully delivered the mid-terms Brendan graded to Emily Worthington.

Once I settled into my office, I picked up the phone.

"Good afternoon, Dean of Students' office," answered a perky voice on the other end.

It was probably a student worker and I decided to sound authoritarian. "This is Professor Stanard, Chair of the History Department, can I speak to Dean Noble please."

"Certainly sir."

A few seconds later, Dean Noble came on the line. "What can I do for you Dr. Stanard?"

"I'm forwarding a request from my graduate student, Brendan Healy. He wants to attend the memorial service for Jenny Biggio tomorrow afternoon."

Several seconds of silence followed before Noble finally answered. "Mr. Healy is barred from the campus until his hearing."

"I think you can make an exception; he can't afford to fly to Cleveland for her funeral."

"It's my perception he wouldn't be welcome there either."

"In the rush to find Brendan guilty, everyone seems to forget that he hasn't even been arrested."

"Doug Clayton wants the memorial service to put an end to all the negative publicity; Mr. Healy attending the service would create a media feeding frenzy."

"For God's sake give him a break; his girlfriend was murdered. He deserves to bid her farewell."

Dean Noble sighed. "I'm going to have to run it past the president. You'll owe me for this one."

During my almost twenty years with the university, I'd built up my share of chits; I knew how to cash them in when needed. Harold Noble had only arrived at the university the year before and I had nothing in the bank with him. "That's fair enough."

**

I went back to grading mid-terms; Janet brought in a supply requisition for me to approve.

"How's Brendan doing?" she asked.

"He's holding up; the media is still besieging his house. The administration doesn't want him to attend Jenny's memorial service tomorrow."

"It would be best for him to stay away; everyone is going to be staring at him."

My phone rang and I noticed it was Laura. "What's up?"

"Denise called from High Point; she only found three articles in *The High Point Enterprise*. A barroom stabbing hardly qualifies as the crime of the century."

"It's a start."

"She's converting the articles from microfilm to a digital format and will email them to me shortly. I gave her your email address too."

"I knew I could count on my local librarian."

"That's what we're here for," she laughed.

Every few minutes I anxiously checked my emails. Finally the email from Laura's library school classmate arrived. I opened the first file and found page 22 from *The High Point Enterprise* dated July 16, 1979; I enlarged the image to make it easier to read. A brief two paragraph article at the bottom of the page indicated that Felton Snyder of High Point had been arrested after a late night fight two days earlier at the Joker's Wild Tavern. Willis McCabe of Greensboro sustained a knife wound to his abdomen and was in critical condition in High Point Regional Hospital. Snyder was arrested attempting to flee the scene on his motorcycle and was being held without bail in the Guilford County Jail. Sergeant Jefferson Chambliss of the High Point police was investigating the melee that led to McCabe's stabbing.

The second file contained page 17 from *The High Point Enterprise* dated July 31, 1979. A brief one paragraph article stated Snyder had been bound over for trial by the grand jury. The victim was still hospitalized; his condition had been upgraded to serious.

My hopes that the final article would shed further light on Felton Snyder were dashed when I opened the final file dated January 24, 1980. After a two day trial, Snyder was convicted of malicious wounding and sentenced to five years in the North Carolina State Penitentiary; he was given credit for the time spent in jail awaiting trial. Willis McCabe, the victim, bumped into Snyder causing him to spill his beer. Snyder punched and kicked McCabe and stabbed him when the victim fought back. The jury rejected Snyder's claim of self defense and found him guilty.

So far, I'd found nothing in Snyder's past that would cause Harley to focus on him as the prime suspect; the stabbing, though vicious; bore little similarity to the circumstances of Jenny's murder. Was I following a false lead by pursuing Snyder?

Or was I not digging deep enough? If I were grading my research efforts like I graded my student's papers, I'd be flunked for relying solely on a handful of newspaper articles. Where were my primary sources? I scanned the web page of the High Point Police Department and quickly dialed my telephone.

"High Point Police Department, how may I direct your call?"

"Detective Jefferson Chambliss please."

"May I ask whose calling?"

"Dr. Andrew Stanard; I'm calling long distance from Norfolk, Virginia." Putting doctor in front of my name often opened doors; people thought I was a physician until I identified myself as a historian. Hopefully I wouldn't be put on hold or directed to his voice mail.

"Detective Chambliss; what can I do for you doc?" he drawled when he picked up his phone.

"I'm Chair of the History Department at Chesapeake Bay University."

"Your basketball team beat High Point University by two points at the buzzer last year; I'm looking forward to the rematch in December;" he interrupted me. Most colleges and universities were known around the country by the prowess of their athletic teams rather than their academic programs; it often served as an ice breaker in conversations.

"An article in *The High Point Enterprise* indicated you investigated a stabbing at the Joker's Wild Tavern in 1979; I'm researching the background of Felton Snyder."

"It's good you got a hold of me; I'm retiring at the end of the month. Beginning November I, I'm a professional golfer."

Historical research often hinges on lucky breaks; historians have made their reputations by finding a previously unknown document in a dusty box in an archive or a packet of family letters in an old lady's attic. My long shot had paid off.

"Why is a historian interested in a low life like Felton Snyder? To be honest he dropped off my radar over fifteen years ago when he moved down to Florida. I'm surprised that dirt bag is still alive; a liver can only take so much abuse."

Clearly Detective Chambliss held a high opinion of Snyder; I sensed I was ready to strike gold. "He's homeless and living off the largess of several churches that aid people in his situation. For the past year, he's been hanging around the CBU campus fishing half-smoked cigarettes out of the ashtrays outside the buildings."

"It doesn't surprise me; he started drinking heavily and abusing drugs in the early 70's when he was a Marine in Nam."

"On Monday, a graduate student was murdered at the university; a cleaning lady and I found her body down the hall from my office."

"I'm sorry to hear that."

"The campus police have focused on one of my graduate students, her boyfriend, as the prime suspect.

"You can't fault them for that; in over 95% of murders, the killer is a relative or close friend of the victim."

"I think they're barking up the wrong tree; on the night of the murder, Snyder sold her credit card to a local fence for $10. He claims he found her wallet in an alley; there have been a lot of thefts of purses and laptops from the library where he passes the time."

"Hmmm. Are your campus police aware of his criminal record?"

"During a briefing, Chief Simpson said Snyder had an extensive rap sheet."

"That's an understatement," laughed Chambliss.

"I've done some checking through the internet but found only newspaper accounts of arrests for petty offenses like drunk in public and shoplifting down in Florida and South Carolina. My wife is a librarian and had a colleague at the High Point Public Library dig up the articles about his arrest for the stabbing at the Joker's Wild Tavern in 1979; I thought you might shed further light on Snyder's past."

"The best thing that ever happened in High Point was when the Joker's Wild Tavern burned down in 1984." Detective Chambliss emitted a hearty laugh. "The bar was the headquarters for the Devil's Disciples biker gang; it was a center of drug dealing, prostitution and the fencing of stolen items."

"Snyder was a member of the gang?"

"Until he wore out his welcome; after he was released from prison, his substance abuse problems spiraled out of control. The gang no longer trusted him and cut him out of their illicit enterprises; the stabbing had turned a spotlight on the gang's activities."

"So you'd describe him as a career criminal?"

"When he first arrived in High Point he worked as a mechanic at his brother-in-law's gas station. His family disowned him; they're decent church going people. They were disgusted by his boozing, drugging and pimping."

"Snyder and, I come from similar backgrounds. I'm from a small town in eastern North Carolina, Williamston, just down the road from Murfreesboro where Snyder hails from. I served in Viet Nam as well. Snyder is a vicious dog; we were only able to pin the stabbing on him. He served as the gang's enforcer; we suspected him of two murders but we never had enough evidence to arrest him."

"Everyone seems to think he's a hapless homeless person," I replied somewhat stunned by what Chambliss had just revealed.

"I'm warning you not to cross Snyder. We had one member of the Devil's Disciples on the ropes facing long prison time; he was negotiating to cut a deal. He disappeared one night; hunters found his bones seven months later out in the woods. His hands had been bound behind his back; the coroner found a dozen cut marks on his bones, probably from a large buck knife. We'll never know how many times the knife hit only soft tissue."

"Geez!"

"I'm not clearing your student of his girlfriend's murder; Snyder might have been in the wrong place at the wrong time."

"Brendan is not a murderer."

"I'm curious; tell me more about him."

"Brendan is finishing his Ph.D. He had some trouble in his past; he did time in a juvenile correctional facility in New Jersey. After that he joined the Marines and straightened out his life."

"There were a lot of guys in Nam who were given the option of jail or the military; I always wonder if anyone opted for jail instead of the jungles of Vietnam." Chambliss laughed heartily again.

"Since enrolling at CBU, he's completed his Bachelors and Masters degrees."

"I sense you're holding something back."

Chambliss' long years as detective taught him to home in on voice inflections and body language while interviewing a witness or interrogating a suspect; he'd immediately noted the hesitancy in my voice. There was no point in deceiving him; he'd been fairly open in sharing information on Snyder with me. "His girlfriend, Jenny, told him she was pregnant the day she was killed."

"Bingo!"

The police automatically saw Brendan as the murderer since his girlfriend was pregnant. It was going to be difficult to make them focus on other possible suspects.

"Give me the phone number of your campus police chief; I'll brief him on what's missing from Felton Snyder's rap sheet."

CHAPTER XVII

Just before 4 o'clock my phone rang. "Dr. Stanard," I answered.

"You were ordered to keep out of my investigation," replied Harley Simpson.

"So you've talked with Detective Chambliss of the High Point Police Department?"

"Our conversation was enlightening but bears no relevance to Jenny Biggio's murder; Brendan Healy is still my prime suspect. You're not a detective; I don't want you fouling up my investigation!"

Harley's tone of voice indicated I'd crossed the line and he was furious that I'd called Detective Chambliss. I quickly defended myself. "You're missing the point on Snyder."

"I know who I'm dealing with. Snyder is a bad actor but he's not Jenny Biggio's murderer. His alibi checks out for the time of her death; he was at the prayer supper at the Ark Church."

"One of my students is employed at the McDonald's across from campus; Snyder frequently visited McKinney there. McKinney slipped Snyder free food; McDonald's usually rousts the homeless to keep them from becoming a nuisance."

"We know all about McKinney and Snyder's little racket; McKinney's ex- girlfriend squealed on him to save her pretty little ass from going to jail. That's old news you're trying to peddle."

Harley seemed rather emphatic that Snyder's alibi cleared him of Jenny's murder. Something just didn't jibe. It would seem Brendan's alibi would put him in the clear as well. He was downtown working at the Convention Center at the time of the prayer supper and Jenny's murder.

"Can you send me the articles from *The High Point Enterprise* you mentioned to Detective Chambliss? I'd like them for the case file."

Hopefully Harley would realize he made a mistake and take a second look at Snyder. "I'll email them to you in a few minutes."

"President Clayton called me about Healy's request to attend the memorial service tomorrow. He can attend if he agrees to certain restrictions."

"What are you requiring?"

"Mr. Healy will be escorted by one of my plain clothes officers and remain in his presence at all times. He will sit in the back of the auditorium and not talk with the media."

I was somewhat surprised President Clayton agreed to let Brendan attend the service; however barring him outright from attending would make the university look heartless. I saw Dick Torelli's hand behind this maneuver. Torelli hoped that Brendan would find the conditions unacceptable and not attend of his own volition. They underestimated his love for Jenny; he'd be there if they forced him to attend in handcuffs.

"My officer will meet him at his house at 3:30 PM tomorrow; he has until 5 o'clock today to accept the conditions under which he can attend. He has my number."

I sensed Harley's frustration; he was under tremendous pressure to make an arrest before the memorial service. Permitting Brendan to attend was an admission that the police still had no evidence linking him to the murder. "I'll relay your message."

After I hung up with Harley, I called Brendan's cell phone.

"Good afternoon sir."

"I just got off the phone with Chief Simpson. They're allowing you to attend Jenny's service tomorrow with certain restrictions."

"What do the bastards want now?"

"You'll be escorted by a campus police officer to the service; he'll remain at your side the whole time. You're to sit at the rear of the auditorium and not talk with the media."

"It's another humiliation!" Brendan pounding his fist on the wall came through the telephone.

"Right after you left the police picked me up and took me downtown. The terms of my New Jersey probation require me to cooperate fully with any police investigation or be jailed; the police even had a copy of the agreement I signed courtesy of that asshole Milkowski. After taking a blood sample from me for DNA testing, they required me to strip down and the evidence technician clipped a clump of my pubic hairs. Next I was photographed from head to toe to document any scratches on my body; they took several pictures of my tattoo. They even stuck a cotton swab up my penis for God knows what purpose. There were five people in the room looking me over; I felt like crawling under the linoleum."

Brendan sighed. "I'm sorry I unloaded on you; you're one of the few people who believe I had nothing to do with Jenny's murder. The police are really tightening the screws on me."

By continuing to pressure him, the police were hoping that Brendan would eventually crack. "You need to call Chief Simpson by 5 o'clock to accept his terms."

"I have his card. Thanks for sticking your neck out for me sir."

Marie Antoinette stuck her neck out too I thought as I hung up the phone.

A few minutes later Janet poked her head in the door. "Tammie McMillan needs to see you."

Tollie Monroe's secretary stood behind Janet with a yellow legal pad in hand. I motioned for her to come in. She looked rather harried. "Good afternoon Dr. Stanard. Dean Monroe tasked me with organizing a reception in the atrium of the Fine Arts Building after the memorial service. Due to the budget cuts this year, we don't have any funds to have a reception catered. Can Mrs. Stanard bake something?"

"I think we could bring a tray of brownies." Even though Laura would do all the work, I took partial credit for the brownies.

"Thank you."

"I'll make some deviled eggs when I get home," said Janet.

"Maureen is canvassing the econ department. This is not going to be as hard as I feared, everyone has been so helpful," replied Tammie.

"Let's go down the hall and see Dr. Worthington; she likes to bake."

Janet and Tammie went off in search of Emily. Since I'd committed Laura to baking a pan of brownies, it would be a good idea to alert her in case we didn't have a box of brownie mix in the house. Before I could pick up the phone it rang; Caller ID indicated it was Laura.

"You must be telepathic," I answered.

"Were you looking at the *Register's* webpage too?"

"Should I?"

"Hot off the presses, the lead headline of the 4 o'clock update is *'Murder Suspect Killed His Father.'*"

I clicked open the *Register's* website and quickly scanned Amanda Saltzman's article. Brendan's fears had come true; the article branded him with the crime of patricide.

"Brendan Healy, the chief suspect in the murder of Chesapeake Bay University graduate student Jenny Biggio, killed his father fifteen years ago in a violent altercation in their Kearny, New Jersey home. Healy was fifteen at the time his father, Mike Healy, died after a furious fist fight late one evening."

"Ida O'Reilly, a neighbor of the Healy family, said that Healy long had a troubled relationship with his father. 'Mike was a strict disciplinarian. Colleen Healy frequently intervened in her son's behalf; he was her favorite. His father favored the two girls more; Brendan always resented that.'"

"According to Mrs. O'Reilly, Brendan was a troubled teenager. 'He ran with a bad crowd and smoked marijuana. I wouldn't let my grandson, Sean, play with him.' Later Healy was sentenced to a New Jersey youth correctional facility according to the Kearny Police."

"Brendan blamed his father for the breakup of his parent's marriage according to Mrs. O'Reilly. 'They were a happy family until Colleen Healy filed for divorce; too many families split up over nothing these days.'"

"Healy's father had returned to the family's home one evening after the couple had separated according to Sergeant Vincent Milkowski of the Kearny Police Department. Brendan stepped in between his mother and father and a fight ensued. Mr. Healy fell down a flight of stairs, breaking his neck. Alcohol may have been a contributing factor."

"Healy was never charged in his father's death, the police ruled it an act of self defense. Sergeant Milkowski states, 'We accepted Mrs. Healy's version of what happened that night; it appeared that Brendan had come to his mother's aid during a fight with his father. Healy's youngest sister, present at the altercation, was too young to be a reliable witness."

Superficially researching the events of that tragic night and relying on a second hand report from an elderly neighbor, Amanda Saltzman's article downplayed Brendan's father's alcoholism and the effects on his family. Mrs. O'Reilly put the blame for Brendan's uneasy relationship with his father squarely on him; surely she was aware of the physical abuse Brendan suffered at the hands of his father. She portrayed Mike Healy as a doting father ignoring how he battered his wife and deserted his children.

Sergeant Milkowski crudely hinted that Mr. Healy's death now appeared suspicious by implying that Brendan and his mother lied about the events of that evening.

"What do you think?" asked Laura.

"Amanda Saltzman deserves a Pulitzer Hatchet Prize."

"Did you see the second article?"

Scrolling down the web page, I found the second article with Amanda Saltzman's byline, *"Marines Taught to Kill by Snapping the Neck."* I opened the article; it detailed how Marines are taught in basic training to kill with their bare hands. As a former Marine, Brendan was well versed in how to kill someone by snapping their neck according to the retired Marine Corps drill instructor consulted. The drill instructor also noted that unlike a civilian, a former Marine like Brendan was not squeamish about killing. "Amanda Saltzman is not going to stop until they strap Brendan to a gurney and stick the needle in him."

"You have to admit the evidence is beginning to pile up," replied Laura.

"It's not evidence; it's all hearsay and conjecture. She found some old marine drinking at the VFW who pronounces Brendan a trained killer between beers. This gives yellow journalism a bad name."

"I have to admit the articles were rather sensational; they would be more at home in the *New York Post* rather than the *Register.*"

"At least President Clayton relented and is letting Brendan attend the memorial service tomorrow."

"If I were Brendan, I'd be too ashamed to show my face. All eyes will be on him during the service."

"That's why they're making him sit in the back of the auditorium; hopefully everyone will be too polite to crane their necks. Tollie is holding a reception after the service; I put you down for a tray of brownies."

"Is Tollie holding a bake sale next month to cover faculty salaries?" laughed Laura.

"I've heard Doug Clayton is scheduling one to buy books for the library."

"These budget cuts are the worst the library has ever experienced; we won't be able to buy any new books after January."

"I'll pick you up at five in front of the library."

"See you then dear."

***

With the chicken and rice casserole baking in the oven, Laura sat down at six o'clock to watch the evening news with me. "I'll bake the brownies after dinner. Should I bake two pans?"

"If a lot of students attend the reception they'll be like a plague of locusts devouring everything in sight."

I clicked on the televisions as the last strains of the Channel 12's News opening theme faded out. "There have been dramatic new developments in the murder of Chesapeake Bay University student, Jennifer Biggio.

Channel 12's writers must have been suffering from writer's block; there had been dramatic new developments the day before. They figured most viewers had short term memory problems and wouldn't remember the phrase was used every night.

"We turn to Amanda Saltzman from the *Norfolk Register* for details. Amanda flew to New Jersey this morning to investigate the background of the prime suspect in Jenny Biggio's murder, Brendan Healy. She just arrived at our studio."

Amanda, with a smug look on her face, came on the screen. "Brendan Healy grew up in Kearny, New Jersey, a gritty suburb of Newark. This morning I visited his old neighborhood with cameraman Charles Woods. Healy was fifteen when his father fell to his death down a flight of stairs in this house where Healy's mother still lives with one of his sisters."

The camera zoomed in on a modest Cape Cod house that had been churned out on an assembly line with its neighbors. Brendan's former neighborhood looked like it had been on a downward slide since it was built in the 1950's.

"His mother and sister declined to be interviewed. A next door neighbor, Ida O'Reilly, the grandmother of his childhood friend Sean was kind enough to talk with me."

The frame shifted to Amanda Saltzman and Mrs. O'Reilly sitting on lawn chairs on a concrete patio. Mrs. O'Reilly's snow white hair and deeply lined face marked her as being in her early eighties. "Brendan always had a wild streak; I had to stop my grandson Sean from playing with him," said Mrs. O'Reilly in her thick New Jersey accent.

Brendan's drug dealing buddy, Sean, ended up riddled with bullets in the trunk of his car. It seemed more than a coincidence that Mrs. O'Reilly's grandson was named Sean too.

"Mike Healy was no saint; sometimes he drank too much for his own good. Brendan inherited his father's temper. Mike and Brendan had a terrible fight that night; Brendan knocked his father down the stairs, killing him."

"How old was Brendan when he killed his father?" asked Amanda Saltzman.

"Brendan and Sean were in high school. Mike turned mean when he was drinking but it didn't give Brendan the right to kill him."

Taking advantage of an elderly woman, Amanda Saltzman had cleverly manipulated the interview. The interview had a strange disjointed quality; it appeared to have been heavily edited and spliced together to make Mrs. O'Reilly's rambling reminiscences seem coherent.

"With his father gone, Colleen couldn't control him. He was sentenced to Mountainview for several months."

"Mountainview is the correctional facility in northern New Jersey where Healy spent several months as a teenager," interrupted Amanda in a voiceover.

"I haven't seen Brendan since he joined the Marines."

"Do you think Brendan strangled his girlfriend?"

"A boy who killed his own father is capable of anything."

Saltzman never asked Mrs. O'Reilly any questions about Mike Healy's drinking problem and temper. Living next door, Mrs. O'Reilly must have known about Healy's abuse of his wife and the restraining order she had against him.

"Did your student really murder his father?" asked James.

"It was an accident; his father was drunk and was beating up his mother. Brendan came to her defense. During the fight, his father fell down the stairs and broke his neck. The reporter deliberately distorted everything that happened to sensationalize her story," I said.

"I wonder if Brendan celebrates Father's Day," interrupted Robert.

Robert's impertinent remark did raise a disturbing point. A jury member might ask the same question as well as asking how Brendan planned to celebrate Valentine's Day.

Next the screen switched to Amanda talking with a tall white haired man wearing a stylish pair of silver wire rimmed glasses outside a brick building; the camera panned a sign over the entrance that read Kearny Police Department. "Sergeant Vincent Milkowski is a thirty-five year veteran of the Kearny Police Department," read Saltzman in a voiceover.

"Healy had several run-ins with our department as a teenager; he was sentenced to a year at the Mountainview Correctional Center. I'd hoped that he turned his life around when he joined the Marines but it doesn't appear to be the case."

"Is Healy still a suspect in the savage beating death of a drug dealer that occurred shortly before he left New Jersey for boot camp?" asked Saltzman.

"Our department doesn't consider that murder a cold case," replied Sergeant Milkowski adroitly side stepping the question.

"Why was Healy never charged in his father's death?"

Milkowski paused and parsed his words carefully. "Healy's mother backed his account of what happened that night. Although he had a troubled relationship with his father; we didn't have any evidence to support a murder charge."

"Are you reopening the investigation of his father's death in light of Ms. Biggio's murder?"

Looking straight at the camera, Sergeant Milkowski delivered a perfect ten second sound bite. "Healy's loved ones all seem to die unnatural deaths; it's a strange coincidence that his father died in a fall and his girlfriend was strangled to death."

The screen switched to the studio where Amanda was seated between the two anchors. "I understand that you will be appearing tonight on Crime TV cable network," said Kendra Warren, the co-anchor.

"Crime TV has invited me to give an update on the investigation into Jenny Biggio's murder on their *National Crime Roundup* at 9:00 PM," replied Amanda.

"That's exciting!" replied Kendra.

"Jenny's murder was so senseless; that's why this case has attracted so much attention."

Dick Torelli's blood pressure must have hit 250/130 by now. Chesapeake Bay University had to fight to get media coverage beyond the confines of Norfolk; now Dick Torelli was getting the national media exposure that he craved for CBU. The *National Crime Roundup* specialized in lurid murders and other sensational cases often involving celebrities, sports figures and politicians.

After dinner I settled into my study to finish grading exams when phone rang just before 8 o'clock. I ignored it figuring it was Laura's mother calling as she did most nights after dinner.

"Dad! It's for you!" screamed James from the kitchen.

I went out to the kitchen and picked up the portable phone. "Dr. Stanard," I answered.

"Good evening sir. Can we meet at Nick's for a cup of coffee in fifteen minutes?"

I hesitated; ordinarily I was not that chummy with my students.

Brendan sensed my reluctance to meet with him. "Saltzman really bashed me tonight on the news; everyone thinks I'm a homicidal monster now. Besides my mother you're the only person I trust."

There was a tone of desperation in Brendan's voice. Nick's was less than a ten minute drive from the house. "I'll meet you there."

"Where are you going?" asked Laura as she walked into the kitchen.

"Brendan asked me to meet him at Nick's for a cup of coffee."

"Why?"

"He sounded upset."

"Be careful. You're in over your head."

When I arrived at Nick's, the aroma of Philly cheese steak subs, French fries and bacon cheeseburgers hung thick in the air. The restaurant was crowded; everyone seemed in a festive mood getting an early start on the weekend. I found an empty booth in the back of the restaurant. About thirty seconds later Brendan entered the restaurant with Officer Benton in civilian clothes trailing behind him. Her burgundy and gold CBU windbreaker discreetly covered the bulge of the gun she was wearing in a holster strapped to her waist. She took a seat at a small table near the entrance where she could watch the entire restaurant; she put her walkie talkie on the table and watched Brendan like a hawk as her made his way to the booth.

"You made good time on your bike," I greeted him.

"Officer Benton generously offered me a ride when I told her I was going to ride my bike to Nick's. I took her up on the offer; the officer following me this morning almost ran me over when I biked to the grocery store."

I looked across the restaurant at Officer Benton; she was clearly a regular at Nick's; the waitress had already brought her a cup of coffee without her placing an order.

When the waitress stepped over to our table, Brendan asked for a cup of coffee. I ordered coffee and a piece of apple crumb pie since the brownies baking at home had provoked a yearning for dessert.

"You should have seen Dave Chen's reaction when the newscast implied I murdered my father. He was afraid I was going to whack him next."

"He hadn't seen the *Register* article before hand?"

"He'd just come in from the gym."

Our waitress put two cups on the table and poured our coffee; she went back to the counter for my pie. When she returned, she looked Brendan over and recognized him from the media coverage of the murder. Brendan realized she'd made the connection; he quietly seethed till she was out of earshot.

"In a few years she'll tell her grandchildren she served cherry pie and coffee to the infamous CBU strangler," said Brendan bitterly.

I watched the waitress go over to Officer Benton to give her a refill although I doubted she had time to take more than a few sips. They talked for about thirty seconds; the whole time the waitress kept looking over at Brendan.

"Eyewitnesses to history are often confused about what they saw," I remarked.

"Even if I'm not arrested for Jenny's murder, I'll have the stain of my father's death tainting me for the rest of my life. Anytime someone does a Google search on me; that bitch's articles will pop up."

"Things look momentarily bleak; you'll be cleared."

"Besides my mother and sisters, you're the only one who believes that."

I noticed four sorority girls sitting at a nearby table; one pointed Brendan out to her companion.

"The two other guys I share the house with came home a little while ago; I heard Dave talking with them in a low voice down in the kitchen. I'm going to be voted off the island while I'm here."

I took a forkful of pie and chewed on it. "They'll come around after the initial shock wears off."

"I doubt it; I have no future, no job and now no place to live. I'd run away if I could; reenlisting in the Marines is suddenly an appealing option."

"Have you considered the French Foreign Legion?"

For the first time Brendan laughed. "Would they mind that I took German for my foreign language requirement?"

"The Legion takes in all nationalities; I understand they turn a blind eye to recruits on the run from the law."

"Just what I need in case things go south," laughed Brendan.

"Why is Sergeant Milkowski carrying out a vendetta against you?"

Brendan nervously looked around the restaurant. "Other than the fact I screwed his daughter, I can't imagine why he'd hold a grudge against me."

Milkowski saw Jenny Biggio as a substitute for his daughter. He wanted Brendan locked up and wasn't going to mince words to do so.

"It would've been smarter to screw someone else."

"Looking back I did a lot of dumb things as a teenager. Sally and I hooked up just after I was released from Mountainwiew; I was like forbidden fruit to her."

Brendan the bad boy seduces Sally the good girl. Somehow I'd seen this movie before starring Jean-Paul Belmondo and Jean Sebring.

"After being locked up for seven months, my teenage libido was out of control. We were foolish and took a lot of chances."

No wonder Milkowski saw parallels between his daughter and Jenny Biggio. It dawned on me, "Did you get her pregnant too?"

"No, I always used condoms. Sally's mother would've hit the roof if she'd asked to go on the pill. It was bad enough when Milkowski found out she'd been seeing me; he would've come after me with a shotgun if he knew we were making love."

"You stole the Lexus to impress Sally?"

Brendan laughed. "It was pretty stupid of me to steal a car to impress a policeman's daughter."

"Are you still in contact with her?"

"Sally did her patriotic duty and sent me a couple postcards from the shore when I was in boot camp; she went off to Marymount College up in Tarrytown and I never heard from her after that. My mom saw in the newspaper that she married a West Point graduate after college."

"Did Milkowski have a hand in your enlisting in the Marines?"

"He didn't raise any objections to the judge; he figured the Marines would send me far away from his daughter."

"Was your drug dealing friend Sean, Mrs. O'Reilly's grandson?"

"His grandmother raised him; Sean's mother flitted in and out of his life. She didn't have a clue who was Sean's father; she lived to party and saw Sean as an inconvenience. To support her coke habit, she worked as a lap dancer down in Atlantic City. Her drug abuse ruined her looks and she was reduced to working the street corners in Newark. Sean was twelve when she died of an overdose. When Sean and I were sentenced to Mountainview, his grandmother blamed me for corrupting him. That was a laugh; she was never able to control him."

"I saw the interview with Mrs. O'Reilly; it had a strange disjointed quality."

"My mom says she has Alzheimer's. The poor woman thinks Sean and his mother are still alive; she sets places for them every night on the kitchen table."

That confirmed my worst fears about Amanda Saltzman's lack of ethics. If she had no qualms about taking advantage of an old woman suffering from dementia, she would distort the truth to suit her own ends.

"I need to ask a favor of you; could you and Mrs. Stanard put my mother up at your house on Friday night? She's driving down from Jersey to attend Jenny's memorial service. All of the hotels in Norfolk are booked for the weekend due to the football game; I don't want her driving out to the oceanfront to find a hotel. She'll leave early on Saturday morning since she has to be back at the hospital on Sunday. My place isn't suitable; I might even be staying at the YMCA after tonight."

It would be a lot to ask of Laura; she was not the type who took in stray cats. "Let me check."

I took my cell phone out of my coat pocket and pushed the button to call home. "What's up dear?" asked Laura.

"Brendan asked if we can put his mother up in our guest room tomorrow night. She's coming down for the memorial service."

Laura sighed. "You'll have to straighten up the guest room when you get home."

"I owe you one." I closed my phone and put it back in my pocket. "Your mother can stay at our house."

"Thanks for helping me out; having my mother at the memorial service means a lot to me. She always stood by me when I was trouble."

Brendan finished his coffee; I told him I'd take care of the check. He walked over to Officer Benton's table and they left the restaurant together. The police practically had him under house arrest.

As I was paying the check at the cash register, I overheard our waitress talking to a co-worker. "I hope they arrest that bastard soon for strangling that girl; I wanted to empty the coffee pot on his head."

I went out to my car in the parking lot behind the restaurant; in the shadows near the dumpster, I could have sworn I saw Felton Snyder sharing a bottle in a brown paper bag with one of his buddies. Either that, or Whitfield Tanner, eminent professor of philosophy, was out for a night cap.

CHAPTER XVIII

"You'll need to put the sheets on the bed in the guest room; I got them out of the linen closet," greeted Laura when I returned.

"I want to watch the *National Crime Roundup* first; it will be on in a few minutes."

"You're a glutton for punishment. How's Brendan doing?"

"He's afraid that his roommates are going to kick him out of the house."

"That's understandable; it would creep me out to sleep under the same roof as someone accused of murder."

"Brendan hasn't been charged with anything yet." It was doubtful that Dave Chen was scared of sleeping under the same roof with Brendan. According to Janet he was more active under the sheets than Brendan had been; he was more concerned that the bad publicity surrounding Brendan would negatively impact his sex life.

In the family room, James and Robert were playing a video game. "Don't you have homework?"

"I did it in study hall," replied James.

"You did all your homework in under an hour?"

"We have effective time management skills," said Robert.

I strongly doubted that. "Can you end the video game and play on the television up in your room? *The National Crime Roundup* is on at 9 o'clock."

"We'd prefer the big screen television; the one upstairs is so ghetto," replied James.

"I bought the big screen television; possession is 9/10ths of the law."

"They're not going to devote much time to Brendan; they arrested XTC last night at a strip club in Brooklyn," said Robert.

"Who is XTC?" I asked showing my ignorance of what passed for popular culture these days.

"He's a rapper."

"What did he do to rate all the media attention?"

"There was a shootout between him and a football player over one of dancers at a strip club in Brooklyn."

Dick Torelli's prayers had been answered by the patron saint of spin doctors. A story involving gunshots, a rapper, a football player and a stripper had more media appeal than the murder of a graduate student at an obscure southern university. Jenny's murder would be buried at the end of the hour or squeezed out all together.

The theme music for the *National Crime Roundup* blared from the television; it sounded like it had been plagiarized from *Dragnet*. The blond haired anchor, every hair of his spiky metrosexual hairstyle set precisely in place with hair gel, opened the show from its home base in Los Angeles. "Good evening, this is Nate Elster. Gunshots rang out at the La Galleria Dance Club near the Brooklyn Bridge early this morning when Rapper XTC and his posse traded gunfire with NFL wide receiver Delmar Jackson."

"Sources indicated that Jackson became enraged when one of the dancers, known by her stage name Sateen, rejected his advances despite Jackson putting a $500 tip in her G-string. Jackson opened fire with his Glock on XTC's stretch limo after she accepted a ride home. XTC and his entourage returned fire with weapons from the limo's arsenal. Manuela Fernandez is live in Brooklyn outside the La Galleria Dance Club with more details."

Sateen had recently been featured in a photo spread in *Maxim* magazine and those shots were alternated with footage of Jackson on the gridiron and clips from XTC's music videos.

"Gunshots shattered the windows of nearby storefronts and parked cars …."

Footage of the bullet riddled limousine was displayed along with mug shots of Jackson, XTC, his limo driver and his two bodyguards. "No one was injured in the melee; all of the perpetrators were released on bail this afternoon. A spokesman for the NFL Commissioner's office declined comment," said Manuela before the show cut to a string of commercials.

Helen of Troy had the face that launched a thousand ships. I had to admit Sateen cut an attractive figure but it was hard to see Delmar Jackson and XTC as Menelaus and Paris.

The next story featured an actress with a history of drug and alcohol abuse who crashed her Mercedes in Laurel Canyon.

The first two stories had taken up almost a half hour. I resisted the urge to change to another channel during the second barrage of commercials. "Now we turn our attention down south to the tragic murder of a young coed at Chesapeake Bay University in Virginia." Amanda Saltzman was standing in a studio with a large photo of Jenny projected behind her. Jenny was dressed in a pair of jeans and a sheer white silk blouse sitting on a sand dune with the ocean in the background; she was far more attractive than the young starlet featured in the previous story. "Our special correspondent, Amanda Saltzman, is reporting from Norfolk, Virginia."

"Jennifer Biggio was a Ph.D. student in economics at Chesapeake Bay University. She was found brutally strangled in a campus building on Tuesday morning." The screen switched to a helicopter sweep of the campus. "Police have focused their investigation on her boyfriend, fellow graduate student Brendan Healy, whom she began dating about six months ago." A photo of Jenny and Brendan in their swimsuits on the beach filled the screen. Gradually the camera zoomed in on Brendan."

"How did Saltzman get a hold of that photo?" I'd seen it at Brendan's house when I rummaged through his photos.

"They were on Jenny's *Facebook* page," replied James. "You need to fast forward from the 1950's."

Brendan next appeared on the screen in his teenage mug shot that put him in league with XTC and his fellow thugs. "Unknown to CBU officials when he enrolled, Healy is an ex-convict who served time in a New Jersey juvenile correctional facility. According to Jenny's relatives, she was unaware of Brendan's criminal past. Healy's father was killed during a fight with him when he was a teenager but he was never charged in his death."

"Sergeant Vincent Milkowski of the Kearny, New Jersey Police arrested Healy as a juvenile offender."

"Healy's loved ones all seem to die unnatural deaths; it's a strange coincidence that his father died in a fall and his girlfriend was strangled to death."

I was so furious that she used that sound bite again I picked up the remote and clicked off the television. Thanks to Amanda Saltzman, Brendan had been elevated to public enemy number one. All that was needed was for J. Edgar Hoover to appear with Brendan's wanted poster like he did at the end of *The FBI* back in the 1960's.

The telephone rang a few seconds later and I recognized Tollie's number on the Caller ID. "Hi Tollie."

"Were you watching the *National Crime Roundup*?"

"I was so angry I shut off the television."

Tollie laughed. "Where did that reporter graduate from? I'm going to call the dean of the journalism school and get her degree revoked!"

"She's portraying Brendan as the second coming of the Son of Sam."

"I tried for six months to get *The Chronicle* to do an article on our revamped first year writing program and they wouldn't budge off their asses. Dick Torelli just called; they're sending down a reporter from Washington tomorrow to do a story on Ms. Biggio's murder."

The Chronicle of Higher Education is a weekly newspaper that covers higher education. It spiced up its often turgid issues by reveling in the misdeeds and felonies of professors and administrators.

"We're being smeared in the media; Doug Clayton will be calling any minute. He's going to want blood if Healy is not arrested soon."

"So you're going to throw me to the wolves."

"I'll hold Clayton off as long as I can."

"Brendan hasn't been charged with any crime yet."

"You're still convinced he's innocent?"

"I still think the police need to concentrate their investigation on Felton Snyder."

"That wino who looks likes Whit Tanner?"

"I did some checking up on him today; Laura tracked down some articles about him through a colleague down in High Point. The articles led me to a police detective who filled me in on Snyder. He was a member of the Devil's Disciples motorcycle gang; the police suspected him of brutally murdering an informer."

"The Devil's Disciples were active when I was teaching at the University of South Carolina; they're nothing but a bunch of thugs and drug pushers. But what's the connection to Jenny Biggio's murder?"

"I find it hard to believe this guy had his hands on Jenny's credit card but had nothing to do with her murder."

"It sounds suspicious to me too. What did Harley Simpson say?"

"He told me to butt out; Snyder has an alibi for the time of Jenny's death."

"Woody Farrell called me tonight."

"Complaining about the restroom again?"

"No, when he finished his graduate seminar at 8:30, the police were poking around the sixth floor again."

"What were they looking for?"

"Woody asked the same question; the police told him to pack up and go home."

"I bet he took umbrage at that suggestion."

"Harley Simpson personally escorted him from the building."

I laughed. All Harley needed was a run-in with Emily Worthington to see what I faced daily as department chair. It was troubling that the police were searching the history department again. What were they looking for? The answer pointed straight at Brendan.

Even more puzzling was how Felton Snyder managed to get out of jail so quickly. Who paid his bail? Detective Chambliss indicated his family had cut their ties with him back in the 1970's. It seemed unlikely a judge would release someone like him on his own recognizance. His involvement in the sale of Jenny's credit card and the thefts on campus should've kept him in jail until he came to trial.

***

"Did you want to invite Brendan and his mother to have dinner with us after the memorial service?" asked Laura at breakfast.

"Are we having pizza like most Friday nights?"

"James asked last night if Peter could eat dinner with us; the boys are going to a movie at the mall after dinner. It's either pizza or tacos."

"Pizza is a safe choice since Brendan is a vegetarian. Vito's makes a great veggie pizza; we can order sausage and pepperoni for the boys."

"Are you sure Brendan is not a vegan? They don't eat cheese."

"I've seen him eat pizza before."

Laura's gesture surprised me; I doubted she would've invited Brendan to eat with us if she still believed he was guilty of Jenny's murder. Hopefully the hysteria was dying down and cooler heads would prevail.

"Do you know anything about Brendan's mother?"

"Brendan said she studied nursing at a community college after his father died and is now an RN."

"It sounds like she got her life together after that tragedy. I'm sure she's not happy about her husband's death being dredged up again."

"How would we feel if one of our sons were being dragged through the media like Brendan?"

"Inviting Mrs. Healy to dinner is the least we could do to help her. I know I wouldn't be able to sleep if I were in her shoes."

Women were always sympathetic to their sisters in trouble.

"Can you sit near the back at the memorial service? I'm going to have to slip in at the last minute; we're short staffed today since two of my staff will be attending a meeting at the State Library."

"I'm planning to sit there anyway. The police are requiring Brendan to sit in the rear of the auditorium; Dick Torelli is hoping that the media wouldn't spot him there."

"Fat chance; they'll be all over Brendan like flies on a dead carcass."

***

I dropped Laura at the library and parked the car at Jordan Hall.

"Morning Andy," greeted Mitch Blackwell, a journalism professor, as I got out of my car. Mitch had worked as a newspaper reporter for several years before going back to school and getting his Ph.D. He still freelanced for the *Journal-Register* and other newspapers and magazines.

"How are things in the English Department these days?"

"Three of my colleagues are testing the waters and applying elsewhere due to the salary freeze."

"Is anybody hiring? Most state universities are in the same boat we are, sinking fast."

Mitch laughed. "It's not an opportune time; the state schools have had their budgets slashed and private school endowments are in the toilet."

"Have you been following the coverage of Jenny Biggio's murder?"

"Al Carruthers has given Amanda Saltzman free rein after she broke the story on bid rigging on school construction projects. The education beat is seen by most reporters as dead end, you can't milk much out of a story on teacher of the year."

"She's out to crucify Brendan."

"A group of us old timers get together on Thursdays at Finnerty's across from the *Register* building; she's rubbed a lot of people the wrong way. I saw the interview she did with the senile old lady up in Jersey; I heard she rushed it on the air before the producer at Channel 12 could get a look at it. As long as Saltzman has Carruthers's ear, her editor has no choice but to go along."

"The newspaper business isn't the same as when I started out in the 70's. Carruthers and all the other newspaper owners are under tremendous pressure these days. Circulation is down, advertising revenue is down and expenses keep escalating. He sees Saltzman's brand of journalism as the savior of the *Register*."

"I thought the *Register* had standards? They've won all those Pulitzer Prizes."

"They won three Pulitzer Prizes between 1930 and 1964; old man Carruthers was willing to stand up to the political brokers that ran this state during that period. His son is trading on the *Register*'s past glory."

"Saltzman is going to skin your student alive to move up the ladder; her goal is the *LA Times* in two years. She was working for a paper down in Alabama when the *Register* recruited her two years ago. There was one small problem; she was married to the paper's editor. She didn't have the courtesy to give Ben Saltzman two weeks' notice; she handed him her resignation letter and the divorce papers at the same time."

"It sounds like Barry Sanders is getting screwed in more ways than one."

***

"Tiffany Finley is here to see you," said Janet as she poked her head into my office shortly after my ten o'clock class ended.

"Can you ask Dr. Worthington to join us? I'd like her present. Thanks."

"Tammy said to thank Mrs. Stanard for the brownies. Everyone came through on short notice; Dr. Farrell brought in some of his wife's bourbon balls."

I feared we'd all need a stiff drink after the memorial service. Since alcohol was banned at most campus events, Varina's bourbon balls were the closest we'd come to getting one at the reception. Varina's mother, a member of the Daughters of the Confederacy, named her eldest daughter in honor of Jefferson Davis's wife, Varina.

A few minutes later Janet ushered in Miss Finley and Emily. Tiffany Finley wore her bleached hair long and her jeans skin tight. Her taut black t-shirt proclaimed her loyalty to Abercrombie & Fitch. Emily arched her eyebrow with appropriate feminist disdain at Tiffany's provocative attire. I motioned for her and Emily to sit down.

Janet closed the door. "Thank you for coming Ms. Finley. I wanted to talk with you about the possibility that one of our graduate teaching assistants interacted inappropriately with you on Monday morning."

"Do you mean Brendan Healy?" asked Tiffany.

"Yes," I replied.

"Why is everybody making a federal case of this?"

Caught off guard by Tiffany's response, Emily gave me a quizzical look. I had to admit I was equally puzzled. "What do you mean?"

"A campus police investigator came by my room last night and asked me all sorts of questions. I admit I got carried away and gave Brendan a hug on Monday after I found out I passed the mid-term. It's just the way I am. Why does everyone think I'm having an affair with him?"

"No one thinks that; we were just concerned that Mr. Healy may not have treated you with proper decorum. Male instructors, on occasion, have tried to take advantage of vulnerable female students," replied Emily.

"After the mid-term on Friday, I thought I'd failed. It upset me all weekend; I couldn't eat. I even woke up in the middle of the night on Sunday. When Brendan told me I'd passed, I was just so relieved!"

"What grade did you receive?"

"A C+, Brendan said I missed a B by one point."

"I'm sure you'll do better on the final in December," said Emily in an almost sisterly tone.

"You said the police visited you last night."

"Sergeant Ramsey insisted I spent Monday afternoon with Brendan. He said I was spotted with him around six o'clock in front of the library. That's crazy; I was in my biology lab all afternoon. Then I was at sorority rush; the Kappa Deltas invited me to their house for pizza. It started at six; I walked over with two other girls from my dorm. I think I'm going to get a bid from them."

The sorority houses were on the other side of campus; it seemed unlikely that Tiffany was near the library when Henrietta Sealy observed Jenny's outburst. The police were spending an inordinate amount of time and effort trying to track down the mystery woman that might have been with Brendan the night Jenny was murdered. Jenny must've mistaken someone else for Brendan in the twilight since he was bicycling to work at the time. The police had not released the time of Jenny's death to the media, Harley had implied that Jenny was murdered sometime between six and seven o'clock. Henrietta's encounter with Jenny, after she returned from her dinner break, confirmed that Jenny was still alive at six o'clock, if not fifteen to twenty minutes later.

"Thank you for coming," I said to end the interview.

"I didn't say anything to the police about this," said Emily after the door closed.

"Was anyone else near the elevator?"

"There's always a queue waiting for the elevators in this building. Elevators in the Third World are more reliable; one is always out of order in this building. I had to use the service elevator yesterday."

"Did Brendan show her any favoritism in the grade he assigned?"

"When I checked the exam; there was a one point difference between me and Brendan on the essay question. I would've given her the B-."

"You've trained Brendan well."

Emily smiled. In an era of rampant grade inflation, she was the toughest grader in the department. Her high standards rubbing off on Brendan was a testament to her mentorship.

"I'm sorry; I had to be sure there was nothing untold going on in my class," Emily admitted.

"It raised red flags with me too. No student ever hugged me when I was a teaching assistant." There were some things one had to keep secret; I wouldn't admit to Emily or my wife my past indiscretions as a graduate student.

"You're not as good looking as Brendan plus your sarcastic demeanor makes students afraid to approach you."

It was always helpful to have Emily detail my shortcomings; no wonder Tollie ended her term as chair two years early.

Although Brendan had been cleared of sexual harassment, the police were going to continue chasing after Brendan's phantom lover in their effort to tie Jenny's murder around his neck. If Emily didn't report the incident to the police, who did? Did someone have an ulterior motive?

Memorial Service for Jennifer Biggio

Welcome - Dr. Joaquin Ruiz — Chair of the Economics Department

Opening Prayer - Father Anthony Novello, Catholic Chaplain

How Great Thou Art - Carl Gustav Boberg/Stuart K. Hine
Chesapeake Bay University Concert Choir

Reminiscences - Bradley Biggio — Cousin of Jennifer Biggio

No Fear to Die - Ralph Waldo Emerson
Reverend Deidra Livingston-Bailey, Unitarian Chaplain

Psalm 23 - Reverend Charles Franklin, Pastor of the Ark Evangelical
Church

John 11: 17- 27 - Father Anthony Novello

Eulogy - Father Anthony Novello

Meditation - *Ave Maria* — Johann Sebastian Bach
Dr. Li Yang - Music Department - Harp Solo

One equal light - John Donne
Dr. Taliaferro Monroe - Professor of English and Dean of the
College of Arts, Social Sciences and Humanities

Closing Prayer - *An Instrument of Peace* - St. Francis of Assisi
Bradley Biggio

Hymn to Joy - Henry J. van Dyke/Ludwig van Beethoven
Chesapeake Bay University Concert Choir

A reception will follow the service in the atrium.

CHAPTER XIX

At two-thirty I walked over to the Fine Arts Building; the imposing structure was designed to be the crowning glory of the reign of Doug Clayton's predecessor, Harlan Baines. President Baines frequently criticized the Stalinist-style buildings that were put up on campuses across America during the 60's and 70's to serve the baby boomers. He proclaimed that universities needed to build monumental buildings just as the Catholic Church built magnificent cathedrals in the Middle Ages to proclaim its power over heaven and earth.

Faculty critics diagnosed Baines as suffering from an edifice complex. Built during a period of miniscule faculty salary increases, the atrium of the Fine Arts Building featured crystal chandeliers and Italian marble floors. No expense was spared in the auditorium; plush maroon seats, a Wurlitzer pipe organ salvaged from a 1920's movie palace and superb acoustics made it a first-class venue for plays and concerts. Whether it was necessary was another question. The Board of Trustees sacked Harlan Baines before the ribbon cutting and he was unable to bask in the limelight of his triumphal building.

I passed the satellite trucks from the three local stations setting up shop in a parking lot adjacent to the building. Amanda Saltzman sat in her car talking furiously on the cell phone; the car's windows were rolled up and I was unable to catch any of her conversation. Tollie Monroe and Dick Torelli were smoking at the front entrance and looking over a sheet of paper.

"Afternoon Tollie, Dick," I said as I climbed the steps.

Tollie acknowledged my greeting with a nod. Torelli gave me a look as if I were an escaped leper. In his eyes, the sins of the student had been passed to his dissertation advisor.

"It's important the service stays on schedule. The Claytons and Ms. Biggio's cousin have a six o'clock plane to catch," said Torelli as I passed them.

"Jake Ruiz is on the same flight," said Tollie to Torelli's deaf ears.

It was about twenty minutes before the service was to start; Janet and the other secretaries from the college were busy arranging the tables for the reception in the atrium. A trim Navy ROTC cadet in his crisp dress uniform handed me a program as I passed into the auditorium.

"Hi Andy."

Turning around, I found Cynthia and Stan Wallach behind me. I had to admit I was jealous of Stan; even though we were about the same age, he looked ten years younger. A college tennis star at Duke, Stan kept in shape with frequent games at the university's tennis center, often thrashing much younger opponents. With his hefty six figure salary, Stan could afford weekly visits to a trendy men's salon to keep his hair dyed blond and styled. Rumors abounded on campus that he'd undergone cosmetic surgery when he came back from an extended vacation two years ago looking extremely refreshed and invigorated.

"Congratulations," I greeted him. Stan had recently been selected for an endowed chair in the Finance Department. I'd not crossed paths with him in several months.

"Thank you," he replied.

"Did you ever think that when we started out at CBU that you'd be Chair of the History Department, Laura would be Head of the Reference Department and Stan would be the Simon T. Grayson Endowed Professor in Finance," said Cynthia.

"You're not doing too badly either dear; you were finally promoted to professor last year," replied Stan in a condescending tone.

"I hope I can get through the service without crying," sighed Cynthia. "Thank god Jake told Art to take a flying leap off the top of Jordan Hall."

"What happened?" I laughed.

"When the department was planning the service, Art demanded a non-religious service; he went off on one of his atheistic rants not caring at all that Jenny was a devout Catholic. Jake also nixed Art's idea for an open mike at the end of the service."

"Art would use his turn at the microphone for one of his anti-globalization diatribes; we'd be here all night."

Stan and Cynthia laughed.

"Jenny's murder is so unnerving; the police shooed us out this afternoon while they conducted another search of the econ department."

"What were they looking for?" I asked.

"They wouldn't say; a policeman was up on a ladder lifting up ceiling tiles and looking around with a flashlight. All he did was stir up the asbestos above the ceiling tiles. Where's Laura?"

"As usual, she's arriving at the last minute; duty calls in the library. You can catch up with her at the reception."

"We'll have to get together for dinner soon and relive the good old days," said Cynthia.

Stan seemed strangely anxious to end the conversation. There'd been rumors circulating on campus last year that their marriage had hit a rocky patch. Stan supposedly moved into an apartment near campus for a few months while they worked things out.

I settled into a seat in the last row so that Laura wouldn't have any trouble finding me; I left two seats open for her and Henrietta Sealy. The University Concert Choir was assembling on the stage as the organist began playing softly to greet the mourners as they took their seats. Jake Ruiz and Jenny's cousin Brad were chatting with Father Novello near the stage.

The program featured a photo of Jenny on the cover and a montage of photos of her on the back. Inside was the order of the service and a brief biography of Jenny but it answered none of the questions rattling around my mind.

I knew next to nothing about Jenny. Did Jenny get along with her roommate? Did she have an ex-boyfriend who was upset she dumped him for Brendan? Did she have a rivalry with another graduate student?

Did someone else she knew have a motive for murdering her? Why did I have the sense that the police had not been asking the right questions?

Harley had focused on Brendan chiefly because the murderer is a close friend or relative of the victim in a large percentage of the cases. By concentrating on Brendan, the police were overlooking other possibilities. What if it had been a random murder? Had Jenny wandered into something illegal going on in Jordan Hall and was permanently silenced for her discovery? Maybe Harley was right that Felton Snyder had an alibi. There were almost a dozen other homeless individuals hanging around campus. Had the police investigated their backgrounds or even knew who they were?

The mugger who'd robbed the women in the stairwells earlier in the month had not been caught; the police described him as a short, African-American or possibly Hispanic male in his mid-twenties wearing a dark hooded sweatshirt. His description sounded like it came from central casting for a mugger. It amazed me that the police could watch Brendan 24/7 but apparently devoted no resources to catching the mugger.

Out of the corner of my eye I saw Amanda Saltzman and Felicia Wright from Channel 12 enter the auditorium from a side door and walked up behind me. The high seat back obscured me from their view.

"Have you spotted Healy?" asked Felicia.

"I doubt he'll show his face; he doesn't have the balls to come here today."

"Just in case, I'll stake out the front of the building."

"Good, I'll be up front with Barry; dating him has made me part of the exciting CBU community. If I go to one more women's basketball game I'll puke!"

"Do you really think this story is your ticket out of here?"

"Healy murdering his girlfriend was a Godsend. Once he's behind bars, I'll have my pick of offers."

"If it wasn't for you, the police wouldn't have known about Healy's misspent youth up in New Jersey."

"He murdered daddy dearest and thought he could get away with strangling Jenny too."

"Won't you miss Barry when you leave?" asked Felicia.

"A vibrator has more personality than Barry."

Felicia cackled.

"I don't want to sound like a heartless bitch but Barry was a pleasant interlude, nothing more. What else is there to do in this one horse town? My choices were bowling, bingo or Barry."

"Everything has been arranged for our affiliate in Cleveland to cover the funeral tomorrow."

"I wish the gumshoes would hurry up and arrest Healy; I don't have a headline for Sunday's paper yet. Her funeral isn't going to rate more than an inch or two in the middle of the paper," replied Amanda.

"Is that Jenny's cousin talking with the priest?"

"Maybe he knows something; he'll be good for a quote or two anyway." Saltzman hurried down the aisle to catch up with Brad Biggio.

The Economics Department was assembled in the front row; Father Novello chatted with Jake Ruiz while Tollie reached Brad Biggio ahead of Amanda Saltzman, thwarting her efforts. She clenched her fist and waited impatiently for Tollie to finish. I spotted Barry Sanders sitting near the front; he seemed surprised that Saltzman walked right past him without saying hello.

My neighbor, Julia Adams, was talking with a young woman in a sleeveless white blouse with short blond hair near the stage. I thought I saw a tattoo circling her upper right arm but it could have been the lighting playing tricks with my eyes. Was she Jenny's roommate?

"Do you mind if my mother and I join you sir," asked Brendan. I was accustomed to seeing Brendan casually dressed; today he was wearing a blue blazer and tan slacks; his white dress shirt was complemented by a red Marine Corps tie. Helped by his change of attire and sunglasses, he bore no resemblance to the cheap thug in his teenage mug shot. Somehow he'd managed to evade Felicia Wright staking out the front entrance with her film crew.

"Mom, this is Dr. Andrew Stanard, my dissertation advisor."

"I'm pleased to meet you." I stood up and extended my hand to shake hers.

Brendan's mother was younger than I expected; she must've been no more than twenty years older than her son. Tall and slender, she was stylishly dressed in a tan suit and brown silk blouse. Her long chestnut colored hair was tied up in a French knot; Brendan must've inherited his blue eyes from her. I'd expected her face to be lined after all she'd been through in her marriage and Brendan's brushes with the law as a juvenile. Even though her face was unlined, her eyes expressed the troubles she'd been through.

"I'm pleased to finally meet you Dr. Stanard; it was most gracious of you and your wife to allow me to stay with you this evening. Brendan has told me a lot about you over the years."

"It's sad that we're meeting under these circumstances."

Officer Benton, dressed in a dark blue pants suit, discreetly took the seat across the aisle. I noticed another plain clothes officer taking the seat at the other end of our aisle to block any potential escape by Brendan.

"It was nice of the police to give us an escort," remarked Mrs. Healy looking in the direction of Officer Benton.

Dave Chen and two other young men climbed over the officer at the end to sit next to Brendan.

"This is Hank Nielsen and Tom Craig; they share the house with us. They're both grad students in Electrical Engineering."

"Pleased to meet you," I replied.

Laura, accompanied by Henrietta Sealy, arrived a few minutes later.

"Hi dear," I stood up and kissed her.

Laura took the seat next to me and Mrs. Healy while Henrietta took the seat on the aisle after casting a disdainful glance in Brendan's direction.

"I'm Laura Stanard."

"Colleen Healy; pleased to meet you. Brendan has been telling me how you and your husband have helped him over the past few days."

"I hope you and Brendan will join our family for dinner tonight after the service; we have two teenage boys so we usually have pizza on Friday nights."

"That's so thoughtful; we'd love to join you," replied Colleen.

When had Laura become Brendan's supporter? She'd been ready to string him up only the day before. I was totally surprised by the turn of events.

The participants began taking their seats on the stage. It looked like over 500 people had come to the memorial service. Many appeared to be students from Jenny's classes during her time as a teaching assistant. I wondered how many of the morbidly curious had showed up after the unrelenting media coverage of the murder. President Clayton and his wife were seated near the stage along with other officials of the CBU hierarchy. I was surprised at the number of faculty that showed up on a Friday afternoon.

Jake Ruiz stepped to the podium. "Good afternoon, I would like to welcome you on behalf of the Economics Department. We've come together this afternoon to celebrate the life and to mourn the passing of our student and friend, Jennifer Biggio. Jenny came into our lives six years ago as a master's degree student and quickly won our hearts. Father Anthony Novello, the university's Catholic chaplain, will now lead us in prayer."

Father Novello, tall with curly white hair, took over the podium from Jake; he was not wearing any vestments, just a black suit and a Roman collar. "God, our Father in heaven, we invoke your name today on behalf of our sister Jenny."

I looked over at Brendan. He sat impassively, lost in his thoughts. At one point during Father Novello's invocation, his mother reached over and squeezed his hand. Brendan smiled back at her. I suddenly realized that Felicia Wright had planted herself in the back of the auditorium and was watching Brendan intently, no doubt to report back to Amanda Saltzman.

"The University Concert Choir under the direction of Dr. Ian Crosby will now sing, *How Great Thou Art,*" said Jake upon the completion of Father Novello's prayer.

The choir sang the song flawlessly; even a confirmed atheist like Art Campbell should have been touched by their performance. Art sat there fuming, irritated that he'd been unable to hijack the service to serve as a platform for his tiresome viewpoints.

"I would like to introduce Bradley Biggio of Shaker Heights, Ohio. Brad is Jenny's cousin and is representing her parents today. He is going to share some memories of Jenny," announced Jake.

Brad Biggio, an athletic looking young man in his early 20's, was dressed in a fitted, dark blue suit with a striped red shirt and matching tie. Jenny's cousin had the air of a banker or stockbroker; he stepped authoritatively to the microphone in the manner of a young man on the rise.

"My aunt and uncle will take great comfort in how many people came to remember Jenny. She was four years old when I was born. Jenny was an only child; I was the little brother she always dreamed of. I was the oldest child in my family; Jenny was the older sister I could go to when I needed help."

Brad's voice choked with emotion; he was momentarily unable to continue.

"I went to her a lot when I was a teenager; it seemed she was always bailing me out when my boat was sinking. She counseled me when I my first girlfriend dumped me and I thought it was the end of the world at age fifteen. When I was going to the junior prom, Jenny took one look at the tux I wanted to rent and saved me from a fashion disaster by telling me it was the most God awful thing she ever saw!"

A wave of laughter broke the somber mood in the auditorium; a smile filled Brendon's face for the first time.

"Jenny was always a whiz at math. I was having trouble learning my multiplication tables. She came over every day and drilled me with flash cards; without Jenny, I'd still be stuck in third grade. In high school even though Jenny was busy playing field hockey, captain of the swim team, president of the Science Club, member of the French Club, and president of the National Honor Society, she found time to tutor under-privileged children in math. Her skill in math was one of the gifts that God granted her. During college and graduate school she continued volunteering her time to tutor elementary and high school students. Before the service, Pastor Franklin of the Ark Church introduced me to the group of elementary school girls Jenny was helping at his church. I'm very excited that all of them are here today; their parents took time off from work to attend too."

Alarm bells went off in my head. Jenny was conducting tutoring sessions at the Ark Church while Felton Snyder was attending prayer suppers there; it seemed more than a coincidence that their paths had crossed at the church and her credit card passing through his felony prone hands. Had she attracted Snyder's attention at the church and he followed through with his warped fantasies when he encountered her in the empty hallways of the sixth floor of Jordan Hall on Monday night? Or had he followed her to the sixth floor from the library? Snyder's alibi was not as airtight as Harley suggested.

It was equally conceivable that Jenny had attracted the attention of one of the other homeless men who frequented the soup and prayer suppers at the Ark and also hung around campus? Had Harley bothered to delve into their criminal backgrounds? My sleuthing had dug up some interesting background information down in High Point on Felton Snyder. A little more digging might find the real killer.

I recalled a recent article in the *Register* about a Neighborhood Watch volunteer recognizing a convicted sex offender delivering flyers promoting a pizza chain to her neighborhood. The man had been hired by the pizza chain along with a dozen other homeless men from the Ark Church to deliver the flyers around the city. Were other sex offenders lurking around the church unknown to Pastor Franklin and the police?

"My aunt and uncle were very excited that she would be receiving her Ph.D. degree at the December commencement. Instead her life was tragically ended."

Once again Brad was unable to continue and he fought back tears. "I hope we will remember Jenny as a person who enriched the lives of many in her brief time on earth. Somehow I know that even though God has closed one door, he will open another to provide those girls with a new tutor." Everyone in the audience broke out in applause.

Jake Ruiz returned to the podium. "Reverend Deidra Livingston-Bailey, our Unitarian chaplain, will recite *No Fear to Die* by the great American essayist and philosopher, Ralph Waldo Emerson."

Deidra's hair, dyed a shade of red not found in nature, and her billowing purple caftan gave her a commanding presence on the stage as she recited the poem.

"That was beautiful Deidra; Reverend Charles Franklin, pastor of the Ark Evangelical Church will now read *Psalm 23*," said Jake.

Reverend Franklin, tall and sandy haired, presented a more conventional appearance after Deidra's flamboyant performance. In his soft Texas drawl, he reassuringly proclaimed:

> *The Lord is my shepherd, I shall not be in want.*
> *He makes me lie down in green pastures,*
> *he leads me beside quiet waters . . .*

"My brother in Christ, Father Anthony Novello will read from Chapter II of John's gospel and give the eulogy."

"Thank you Pastor Franklin," replied Father Novello.

On his arrival, Jesus found that Lazarus had already been in the tomb for four days ...

Jesus said to her, "I am the resurrection and the life. He who believes in me will live, even though he dies; and whoever lives and believes in me will never die. Do you believe this?" . . .

He paused for a moment before beginning the eulogy. "Monday is my day off; I went out to Virginia Beach and walked along the ocean. It was like the beautiful hymn we heard earlier, one could feel God's majesty amid the roar of the sea. When I arrived home late Monday, I found a message from Jenny on my telephone. She wanted to make an appointment to begin the preparation for the sacrament of marriage. I tried to return the call and received no answer. On Tuesday afternoon, the police came to my office and told me that Jenny was dead. Instead of helping Jenny and Brendan plan their wedding, I began assisting Jenny's friends with her memorial service."

Brad Biggio's jaw dropped. A murmur went through the audience; it hadn't been reported in the media that Brendan and Jenny were planning to get married. Harley Simpson was nowhere in sight; I would've loved to see his reaction to Father Novello's statement. I looked over at Officer Benton but she betrayed no emotion.

Father Novello had confirmed Brendan's statements that he and Jenny were engaged. It was the first time during the service that Brendan had been mentioned. Like a victim of the Stalinist purges, he'd been excised from all official photographs.

A smile crept over Mrs. Healy's face; she believed her son had been vindicated. Brendan sat there struggling to hold in his emotions; his eyes filled with tears. His mother squeezed his hand again.

"Are you all right?" she whispered to him.

"I'm okay," he replied.

"Nothing we do here today will bring our sister Jenny back to life; we have to take comfort in John's words, 'whoever lives and believes in me will never die.' Jenny will live forever in the perpetual light of Christ, our Lord and Savior."

After the eulogy, Dr. Yang of the Music Department took her place on the stage and played Bach's *Ave Maria* on her harp. Soothing and peaceful, it helped relieve the tension that permeated the auditorium. Brendan appeared to relax and leaned back in his chair.

"Dr. Taliaferro Monroe, Dean of the College of Arts, Social Sciences and Humanities will recite *One Equal Light* by the 16th century English poet, John Donne."

An unrepentant English professor, Tollie loved to recite poetry every chance he got. Unlike Art Campbell, Jake Ruiz couldn't refuse Tollie the opportunity to take the stage. Tollie's booming baritone voice rang out over the auditorium as he recited the stanzas of the poem.

"Thank you Dean Monroe; Brad Biggio will lead us in the closing prayer."

"My aunt Rita read to Jenny when she was a little girl the story of St. Francis of Assisi; she became fascinated with his life and philosophy. In her bedroom Jenny had a plaque on the wall with his famous prayer. It seems appropriate today for us to pray it together."

Everyone on the stage stepped forward and joined hands with Brad. Following their lead, the audience held hands too. I took hold of my wife's hand and Mrs. Healy's hand; I felt a slight trembling in Colleen's hand. Mrs. Healy turned and looked into her son's eyes.

Lord make me an instrument of your peace;
Where there is hatred, let me sow love;
Where there is injury, pardon;

At the conclusion of the prayer, the choir broke into the *Hymn of Joy*. Colleen Healy softly sobbed into a handkerchief before the choir finished. Brendan put his arm around his mother to comfort her. Despite his tough façade, I saw the other side of Brendan's personality. During the breakdown of her marriage, Brendan's mother relied on her son for emotional support. When she cried out for help the night her drunken husband returned home, Brendan came to his mother's rescue. It was a heavy burden for a young boy, especially one who'd been savaged emotionally for years by his abusive father. She instinctively realized the danger facing her son and knew she'd be unable to protect him from the storm that was about to engulf him.

CHAPTER XX

AFTER THE CHOIR FINISHED, EVERYONE filed out of the auditorium into the marble atrium. Fortunately not everyone who attended the service stayed for the reception otherwise Deidre Bailey-Livingston would've been called upon to repeat the miracle of the loaves and fishes. Brendan and his mother moved into a corner of the atrium; the two police officers watching him hovered discreetly nearby. He introduced his mother to his friends who stopped by to offer their condolences.

I poured cups of punch for Laura and me; Dave Chen brought a cup over to Mrs. Healy. My survey of the table found Varina's bourbon balls and I put several on a paper plate along with one of Janet's deviled eggs. A swarm of students blocked me from reaching the plate of Emily's oatmeal cookies before they were devoured.

"Does Varina know how to make any other dessert?" asked Laura as she picked a bourbon ball off my plate.

"The bourbon balls keep Woody pacified; it's best not to mess with a sure thing," I replied.

Art Campbell drifted over to the food table; he seemed annoyed that he'd been unable to hijack Jenny's memorial service for his own gratification.

"Hello Art," I hailed him.

Art didn't hear me or decided to ignore me; despite his quirks, he was usually friendly even when I chided him. He looked nervously around the atrium as he filled his plate as if someone was going to scold him for taking three deviled eggs and a stack of Emily's cookies.

Art looked resplendent in a pair of blue jeans, a black T-shirt emblazoned with a portrait of Che Guevara, ratty blue Keds and a corduroy sport coat badly in need of its leather elbow patches. After quickly devouring his plate of goodies as if he were a Russian on the brink of starvation in the 1930's, Art spotted his anti-globalization acolytes among the knot of econ students chatting. Swiftly he moved to the other side of the atrium and horned in on their conversation.

"Who's that talking with Brendan and his mother?" asked Laura.

She discreetly pointed to the blond woman I'd spotted chatting with Julia Adams before the service. From a distance what I thought was a sleeveless blouse was actually a man's sleeveless undershirt worn without the benefit of a bra. The undershirt exposed a large snake tattoo circling her upper right arm, a butterfly tattoo on the nape of her neck and a barbed wire tattoo circling her left arm. She finished off her outfit with skin tight black leather pants. A length of thick chain circled her right wrist as a crude bracelet.

Laura looked alarmingly at her fashion statement; she looked as if she were dressed for a night out at a biker bar rather than a memorial service. "She gives off a rather strong vibe."

"I think she's Jenny's roommate."

"Are you sure?"

I spotted Julia finishing off the last of the bourbon balls and hailed her. It surprised me that bourbon balls were part of a healthy vegetarian diet.

"Is that Jenny's roommate with Brendan?"

"That's Melinda Kroger. She's finishing her Ph.D. in botany; she already has a post-doc lined up at Texas A & M beginning next summer," Julia replied.

I'd not imagined Jenny sharing an apartment with a lesbian but it seemed unlikely it had any connection to Jenny's murder. It might be an avenue that needed to be explored.

Surveying the atrium I spotted Jake Ruiz introducing Brad Biggio to some of his faculty and their spouses near the entrance to the auditorium. Tollie chatted with Father Novello as they made their way down the table, filling their plates. Cynthia Wallach chatted with Mrs. Clayton who was working the crowd on behalf of her husband. President Clayton held court near the punch bowl talking with Stan Wallach, whom he regarded as one of the stars of the faculty. Stan's eyes were focused on a tall, blond coed serving punch whose tight black dress oozed cleavage.

"Watch it; Woody and Varina are heading this way," warned Laura.

"I hope they get the men's bathroom reopened soon," I muttered under my breath.

"You scumbag!"

I whirled around to find Brad Biggio rushing toward Brendan. Although he was twenty-five years younger than me, I stepped in front of him and blocked his advance but I knew I wouldn't be able to restrain him for long. Fortunately Jake Ruiz took hold of Brad too. Everyone in the atrium froze and turned their attention to Brad and Brendan.

The words to the Prayer of St. Francis buzzed in my head. *"Lord make me an instrument of your peace; Where there is hatred, let me sow love..."*

"Why is he here?"

The prayer appeared to have made little impact on Brad during the service. Brad's chest heaved furiously; only Jake and I kept him from venting his rage on Brendan.

"Where there is injury, pardon," I muttered under my breath.

"That sleazebag murdered Jenny!"

I would've made for a side door and quickly exited the building if I were in Brendan's shoes; instead he calmly walked over to Brad. "I had nothing to do with Jenny's death!"

Brendan's reply only served to enrage Brad even more. "Why don't you take off your shirt and show everyone your jailhouse tattoo? If Jenny had known you were an ex-con, she never would've dated you!"

"Jenny knew everything about my past. She accepted me for what I was."

"You got away with murdering your father but you're not going to get away with murdering Jenny. I'm going to make sure you rot in prison for the rest of your life!"

"I did things as a teenager that I'm not proud of but I didn't murder my father or Jenny!"

"You filthy liar!"

"I loved Jenny; we were going to get married!"

"You were playing her like all the other women you've conned."

"Jenny was going to have my child!"

Brendan's admission that he impregnated Jenny reignited Brad's fury. He escaped from my grasp; somehow Jake caught his right arm just before he would have launched his fist towards Brendan's face. I grabbed hold of his left arm again.

"Crawl back in your hole you slimy bastard!"

Brendan stood his ground in spite of Brad's taunts. His mother's tight grip on his right arm prevented him from throwing a punch that Brad richly deserved for being such a jerk.

Father Novello put himself between Brad and Brendan. "You're upset over Jenny's death but beating up Brendan is not going to bring her back!"

"I'm sorry Father; God will punish him soon enough."

Jake and I let go of Brad. I noticed President Clayton was standing next to me; Dick Torelli was behind him. Everyone in the atrium turned toward President Clayton. Tollie Monroe's ashen look told me I was in big trouble.

"You're no longer welcome here Mister Healy." President Clayton turned to Officer Benton, "Escort him out of the building and off the campus immediately!"

"Yes sir!"

Officer Benton cracked a smile as she grabbed hold of Brendan's right arm. "You heard the president, get moving."

She marched Brendan out the door. It was Brad who'd lost his temper yet the blame fell on Brendan. He'd done nothing to incite the altercation. I wasn't going to contradict Doug Clayton publically. I was in enough trouble already.

Colleen Healy stepped over to President Clayton and pointed her finger at him. "All of you are wrong about Brendan," she said in a shaky voice that betrayed her New Jersey accent.

Doug Clayton appeared shocked that anyone would dare defy him, his face reddened with anger. No one in the atrium moved, everyone's eyes were now focused on Brendan's mother.

"Brendan never lied to Jenny about his past; she was the only one he ever entrusted with his secrets. Jenny and I had a heart to heart talk when she came to visit. So what if Brendan was in trouble as a teenager! He atoned for those sins during his four years in the Marine Corps."

"My children and I suffered years of mental and physical cruelty at the hands of an alcoholic. Finally I could take it no more and filed for divorce; it was necessary to take out a restraining order against my husband. He came to the house one night drunk as a skunk and attacked me. Brendan stepped in to stop him; he was only fifteen. It took a lot of courage; his own father almost killed him. What Brendan did that night, he did only to protect me! Don't judge him!"

Brendan's mother started sobbing; Laura went over to Colleen and put her arm around her. Deidre Bailey-Livingston came over and they helped Mrs. Healy to the door. It must have been extremely difficult for Colleen Healy to bare her soul in front of an audience of total strangers. I suspected a lot of the faculty present wanted to elect her President of the Faculty Senate for standing up to Doug Clayton.

Out of the corner of my eye, I saw Amanda Saltzman holding a rather large purse at an odd angle. She'd secretly captured the whole confrontation on video tape. I wouldn't put it past her to have provoked Brad Biggio in hopes that a fight with Brendan would ensue.

I followed Mrs. Healy, Laura and Deidre out the door to the parking lot. Brendan was standing with Officer Benton by a Camry with New Jersey plates.

"It was about time somebody told that bully off," said Deidre to Mrs. Healy.

Deidre was still smarting from Doug Clayton's ire after last year's commencement. He wanted to fire her from her position as a part-time instructor but the university's general counsel warned him that it wasn't legally prudent for the president of a state supported university to make theological pronouncements; matters of dogma were best left to the Pope.

Brendan's mother handed him the car keys; she was too upset to drive. He helped her into the car.

"You're banned from the campus; get moving punk," ordered Officer Benton with heavy emphasis on the last word. She put her hand on her night stick to indicate her willingness to enforce her order.

Brendan's face flushed with anger but he ignored her provocation. I maneuvered between him and Officer Benton.

"Brad came down to the beach several times this summer; I thought he was my friend. He acted like a total dickhead in there," said Brendan as he shucked his tie and his blazer. Opening the back door of car, he laid them on the seat.

"Have you talked with Jenny's parents?" I asked.

"I left a message on their voice mail; but they haven't called back. Jenny and I went out to Cleveland for a long weekend at the end of summer school. She thought it best I sack out in their guest room; her parents thought she was still a virgin."

"Her dad did a stint in the Marines too. I really liked him; we had a lot in common. Although he was a bit taken aback when he found out I was a vegetarian. I helped her dad out in the yard and took my shirt off because it was a hot afternoon. He saw my tatt; I'm sure he figured it out. There were a lot more jarheads with jailhouse tattoos during the Viet Nam War."

"Hopefully when all this dies down, I can square things with her family."

Brendan climbed into the driver's seat. Colleen Healy rolled down the window. "Brendan and I need some time alone; we're going to go back to his house. We'll be at your house at six for dinner; thank you again for the invitation. All of you have been most kind."

They drove off with an unmarked police car tailing them.

We walked across campus to Jordan Hall; it was a warm autumn afternoon. It was too nice to go back to the office. "Shall we head for home?" I asked.

"No one is in the library this afternoon; the weather is too nice. I might as well call it a day."

"Colleen Healy was certainly brave to take on Doug Clayton," said Laura.

"I hope President Clayton won't retaliate against Brendan when he applies for reinstatement."

"She was only defending her son."

"I know you'd do the same for our boys."

"Hopefully our boys won't get involved in a murder like Brendan."

"We need to stop by my office; I left a book on my desk. I'd like to read it over the weekend if I have time."

Inside the lobby, a police officer was guarding the elevator. "Where are you headed?"

"To my office on the sixth floor," I replied as I reached for my wallet to get out my ID card.

"The tower is closed for the rest of the day."

"Why?" I asked even though I knew the answer.

"Police business," he replied.

After we exited the building, Laura asked, "What's going on?"

"Before the reception, Cynthia said the police were searching the eighth floor this afternoon. Last night they kicked Woody Farrell out; they must not have found what they were looking for."

The boys were shooting baskets in the driveway with their friend Pete Redmond when we returned home. Tall and blond, from a distance Pete vaguely resembled Brendan.

"What time are we ordering the pizza?" asked James.

"Brendan and his mother are coming at six; we'll probably sit down to eat about a half hour after that."

"Our movie is at eight."

Laura and I went inside; she set the dining room table and I picked up the downstairs.

"Can you put towels in the guest room for Ms. Healy?"

"Sure."

The boys burst into the kitchen and grabbed some sodas out of the refrigerator before heading back out to play basketball.

"Do you want to watch the news at five?" asked Laura as silence reigned again.

"We're probably going to be on it?" I replied.

"What?"

"Amanda Saltzman captured Brad Biggio attacking Brendan with a concealed camera; my bet is she goaded him knowing fisticuffs would erupt." I related the conversation I overheard between Amanda and Felicia Wright.

"What a manipulative bitch!"

"And women wonder why throughout history they've been burned at the stake," I noted.

"I'm going to report you to Emily Worthington."

By now the boys had taken over the family room and were playing a video game.

"We need to watch Channel 12 in a few minutes," I said.

"Is Brendan going to be the lead story again?" asked James.

"Please watch what you say in front of Brendan and his mother when they're here for dinner."

"Your father and I were right in the middle of a fight between Brendan and Jenny's cousin," said Laura.

Channel 12's news theme blared from the television. "This is Ryan Chandler; Kendra Warren has the night off. The Chesapeake Bay University community came together this afternoon to bid farewell to murdered graduate student, Jennifer Biggio. Over 500 people gathered in the Fine Arts Auditorium for her memorial service. The somber occasion was marred by an altercation at the reception following the service. Jennifer Saltzman, our special correspondent from the *Register*, has the details."

"Thank you Ryan. Bradley Biggio, Jennifer's cousin, gave a heart breaking eulogy during the memorial service. He became upset when he spotted Brendan Healy, Jenny's boyfriend and the prime suspect in her murder, during the reception afterwards. Healy was ordered removed from the Fine Arts Building by CBU President, Doug Clayton."

Saltzman had the whole confrontation on tape. As I suspected, she'd instigated the verbal brawl between Brad and Brendan. Dick Torelli wanted the service to repair the damage to CBU's image; the last thing he wanted was Brad Biggio punching out Brendan's lights on television.

"That was a good block dad; have you thought of going out for the CBU football team next year?" asked James.

"I'll talk to Sparky Wilson about trying out the next time I see him."

"The game should be good tomorrow night; my dad and I have tickets," said Pete.

Doug Clayton's biggest accomplishment so far as president had been to hire Rendell "Sparky" Wilson to start CBU's football team.

With the team off to a 6-1 start, football fever had swept the campus and the city.

The screen switched to Amanda Saltzman standing in front of the Fine Arts Building. "Aren't most murders solved by the police within the first 48 hours?" asked Ryan.

"Jenny's friends and relatives are distressed that no one has been arrested almost four days after her murder," replied Amanda.

Dick Torelli must have been furious; the entire story about the memorial service was devoted to the altercation afterwards.

"Felicia Wright has the next story in our team coverage of Jenny Biggio's murder."

A photo of Brendan showing off his tattoo as he clowned with Brad Biggio on the beach filled the screen.

"I found this photo on Jenny's Facebook page; I was curious about Brendan Healy's tattoo and the meaning of the Chinese characters. Healy was tattooed when he was incarcerated as teenager in New Jersey. According to the Chinese language expert I consulted, the two characters mean killer in Mandarin," said Felicia pointing to an enlargement of the tattoo.

"It seems strange that Healy was tattooed with the word killer shortly after his father's death," remarked Ryan.

I turned to Laura. "I bet the linguistic expert she consulted was the waiter at the Chinese restaurant where she ate lunch today."

***

I called Vito's, a pizza shop near the campus and ordered one sausage, one pepperoni, one cheese and a veggie pizza for delivery. With three teenage boys at the table, I doubted more than a few slices would be left for the boys' breakfast in the morning.

A few minutes later, the doorbell announced the arrival of Brendan and his mother. "Good evening sir," said Brendan when I opened the door. He'd changed into a pair of jeans and a maroon CBU sweatshirt identical to Pete's sweatshirt. Colleen Healy was casually dressed in a pair of black slacks and red sweater. Brendan carried in his mother's suitcase and put it down next to the door. Parked up the street from our house was the police car that had followed Brendan and his mother after the memorial service. The boys came to the living room out of curiosity about our dinner guests; it was the first time we'd invited a murder suspect to dinner.

"Welcome, I like you to meet our sons, James and Robert," Laura greeted Mrs. Healy.

"I'm James." He extended his hand to shake Mrs. Healy's.

"Robert."

"Peter Redmond, I'm a friend of the family," he said with a bow.

"I'm pleased to meet all three of you," she said.

"They're going to be out in the family room playing a video game until dinner; we'll sit in the living room."

Laura and I took seats on the sofa while Brendan and his mother settled into the wing chairs on the other side of the coffee table.

"Would you like a glass of merlot?" asked Laura.

"Thank you," said Mrs. Healy.

"What about you Brendan?"

"Can I have a Coke Mrs. Stanard? I don't drink alcohol."

Brendan's response caught me off guard. I'd never noticed before that Brendan didn't drink alcohol. His response caused Laura to raise an eyebrow.

"Alcoholism runs in families; I didn't want to take the chance of becoming one like my father. I swore off alcohol when I enlisted. That was tough; drinking is a favorite pastime in the Marines."

"It's the favorite pastime of a lot of academics too," I remarked as I went out to the kitchen to help Laura.

Out in the kitchen, Laura whispered, "What else don't you know about him?"

Laura was right; I didn't know Brendan as well as I thought I did. She feared it could come back to haunt me later. I put together a platter of tortilla chips and black bean salsa and carried it out to the living room while Laura brought in the drinks. A glass or two of wine would help me relax. After the events of the day, I was looking forward to a peaceful evening.

"You have a lovely home," said Colleen.

"Let me show you where you'll be staying." Laura spotted Robert coming into the living room to grab some chips. "Can you carry Mrs. Healy's bag upstairs?"

"Sure mom."

"I guess there's no hope for me being reinstated," said Brendan after his mother left the room.

"Your case will be heard on its merits," I replied even though I knew otherwise. President Clayton made his position clear this afternoon; no one on the panel would dare oppose him. The hearing would be a sham although a façade of due process would cover the preordained decision. Everyone who'd reviewed his dissertation believed it would rank among the best produced in the department. Under Emily's tutelage, he was developing into a fine teacher. Just as everything was coming together for Brendan, his career was going to be flushed down the toilet.

"Is Felicia Wright correct about the meaning of your tattoo?"

"I never would have gotten myself tattooed if I thought it would be flashed across television screens years later. A Chinese dude from Jersey City tattooed me at Mountainview; he told me the characters meant tough guy."

"What does Dave Chen say?"

Brendan laughed. "Dave grew up in Knoxville, Tennessee; his grandparents came to the US before World War II; he doesn't know a word of Chinese."

"Since you were in the Marines, do you want to join us playing *Call of Duty 4*?" asked Robert when he came downstairs.

"Sure," replied Brendan. He followed Robert back to the family room.

"Where's Brendan?" asked his mother when she and Laura returned from their tour of the house.

"He's out in the family room playing a video game."

"I wanted to talk to you without Brendan present. He was so excited when he called Monday night to tell me he and Jenny were getting married. After going through the disintegration of my marriage, I was afraid he was too emotionally scarred to ever trust his heart to someone. The press has misrepresented what happened the night his father died.

Please don't turn your back on Brendan; you're the only person he trusts besides me."

The doorbell rang announcing the arrival of the pizza; like most of Vito's employees, the deliveryman had too many tattoos and piercings to count. From his anti-globalization T-shirt, I recognized him as one of Art Campbell's acolytes. Brendan returned to the living room to retrieve his glass and grab some chips; he eyed the delivery driver suspiciously. After paying the driver, I handed the pizza boxes to James to carry to the dining room.

"That driver delivered the pizza to Jenny's apartment on Monday afternoon. Jenny told me he'd stalked a student in one of her classes last year; the student filed a complaint and he was suspended by the disciplinary committee. When Jenny was paying him, he said, 'I didn't know you lived here; you'll have to order pizza more often.' His cheesy remark really unnerved her."

"Did he see you?"

"I was still in the bedroom; I hadn't gotten dressed yet."

"Do you know his name?"

"I don't think Jenny mentioned it."

"Did you tell what happened to the police?"

"Jenny's murder pushed it out of my mind; it didn't register with me until now."

Only the week before, the *Chronicle of Higher Education* reported an alarming rise in the number of stalking incidents on college campuses facilitated by *Facebook* and other social media. The stalker's job as a pizza delivery driver should raise a red flag with the campus police; it gave him access to the apartments and dorm rooms of female students.

Laura lined up the pizza boxes on the sideboard and restrained the boys until Mrs. Healy selected a couple slices.

"Vito is from South Orange; he makes pizza the Jersey way. When I was stationed at Camp Lejeune you couldn't find a decent pizza in that end of North Carolina," said Brendan to his mother.

"What did you do in the Marines?" asked Pete.

"If you're a Marine, you're an infantryman first; I also drove a deuce and half."

"Deuce and half?" asked Laura.

"A deuce and half is Marine vernacular for a two and half ton truck," replied Brendan.

"Were you a sniper?" asked James.

"I was a pretty good shot but never that good."

"I'm thinking about doing Navy ROTC in college; I want to be a Marine Corps officer after graduation," said Pete.

"I have no complaints about my time in the Marines; they sent me to California and Okinawa. That was pretty good considering the farthest I ever got from Jersey was visiting my grandmother in Brooklyn."

Brendan regaled the boys with stories from his Marine Corps days. Laura thought I'd ordered one pizza too many but the sausage and pepperoni pizzas quickly disappeared under the withering assault of three ravenous teenage boys. I noticed Brendan had three slices; two vegetable and one cheese. His mother had whispered to Laura that he'd not eaten much since Jenny's death; she was glad his appetite had returned.

The dinner passed without incident until Robert directed a question at Brendan. "What was it like in prison?"

Almost immediately all conversation at the table ceased. Everyone looked at Robert then at Brendan. After briefing the boys before dinner, I couldn't believe Robert would embarrass our guests.

"Robert, that was inappropriate; please apologize to Brendan," I said.

"No apology is necessary Dr. Stanard; it's a fair question. They sent me to the Mountainview Youth Correctional Facility; it's up in the mountains in northern Jersey. I went to school in the morning and worked on the dairy farm in the afternoon. We lived in stone cottages on the grounds; fortunately I was only in a cell during my evaluation period. My buddy Sean was there too although we lived in different cottages."

"It sounds almost bucolic," said Laura.

"Believe me, it was still a prison. You woke up when they rang the bell, you ate when they told you to eat, you showered when they told you to shower and you went to bed when they turned the lights off. If you followed orders and kept out of trouble, the guards left you alone. Take it from someone who's been there; stick to the straight and narrow and you'll avoid places like Mountainview."

I looked over at Brendan's mother; she seemed surprised that Brendan talked openly about his incarceration. For the first time he was able to get that weight off his chest.

"My sentence was for a year but they released me after seven months due to good behavior. Being incarcerated made twelve weeks of boot camp seem like breeze; unlike the other recruits, I didn't complain about the food, my bunk or taking orders," he laughed.

I went out to the kitchen and put on a pot of coffee to go with the brownies Laura had saved from the batch she baked for the memorial service.

Pete challenged Brendan to play the video game again; while playing the game, Brendan seemed like a kid without a care in the world. Our boys drifted out to the family room to watch the duel.

"What time are you leaving?" asked Laura.

"We need to leave around 7:30 to make the 8 o'clock show; Pete is driving," replied James.

"You have about twenty minutes; see if Pete wants some milk with his brownies."

Everyone returned to the table for the brownies; the adults sipped coffee while the boys gulped milk with their brownies. Pete seemed slightly annoyed that Brendan had beaten him every time they played tonight. Laura and Colleen chatted at their end of the table about her career as a labor and delivery nurse; a topic of no interest to the men and boys around the table.

After polishing off the last of the brownies, the boys bid adieu and headed out to Pete's car. About a minute after the phone rang; it was Robert's cell phone according to caller ID.

"Dad!" Robert sounded frantic. "Police officers have stopped Pete's car; they have guns pointed at us."

"What?" I screamed.

"Drop it!" I heard over the phone. I could hear shouting in the background but nothing intelligible. Robert must have dropped his cell phone on the seat of the car.

"What's going on?" asked Laura as she watched distress creep over my face.

"Police have surrounded Pete's car; they have guns drawn."

I thought Laura was about to faint; fortunately Colleen was a nurse. She grabbed hold of Laura and helped her to a chair. In the darkness, the police saw a tall blond male wearing a maroon sweatshirt get into the car and must have thought Pete was Brendan attempting to flee. Brendan and I looked out the window of the dining room and thought I saw two figures moving around in the shadows.

"They're here to arrest me," Brendan said as if resigned to his fate.

Colleen Healy could no longer maintain her composure and started sobbing. I went to the front porch to see what was happening to the boys. Julia Adams and my other neighbors were on their porches watching the flashing lights up the street. I wanted to rescue the boys but I knew I wouldn't get through the cordon of police surrounding Pete's car. A squawk from a walkie talkie alerted me to a police officer jumping out of my hedge with his gun drawn.

"What are you doing to my sons? You didn't need to pull guns on them!"

Another officer with his gun drawn came around the other side of the house. "They stopped the wrong car; it was three teenagers. Healy has escaped." He suddenly realized I was standing on the porch.

"If you're looking for Brendan Healy, he's inside waiting for you!"

The two officers brushed past me; I followed them into the house. Brendan's mother had her head buried in Brendan's chest muffling her sobs; he had his right arm wrapped around his mother to comfort her. They pointed their guns at Brendan.

"Put your hands behind your head Healy! You're under arrest."

Brendan released his mother and slowly raised his arms behind his head. Laura sat frozen in her chair; stunned that gun toting police had invaded her dining room. I went over to her and put my arms on her shoulders. One of the officers walked over to Brendan and pointed his gun at his face.

"You've been arrested before so you know how to assume the position. Turn around slowly; put your hands on the wall and spread your legs. Don't make any sudden movements or I'll splatter your brains all over the wall."

That remark did little for Laura's nerves especially since James and Robert had painted the dining room over the summer. Brendan complied and the other officer holstered his gun; stepping over to Brendan he slowly patted him down. Reaching into Brendan's front right pocket, he seemed disappointed as he pulled out a ring of keys and tossed them on the table. From his left pocket, he grabbed his cell phone. Next he pulled Brendan's wallet out of his back pocket and quickly inspected its meager contents. He tossed them into a plastic evidence bag handed him by his partner.

Brendan flinched when the officer put his hand between his legs and started patting down his left leg. "Careful with the family jewels!"

"Shut up punk!"

When he finished patting Brendan down, the officer took a pair of handcuffs off his belt and unlocked them. He roughly grabbed Brendan's right arm and twisted it down behind his back. The cuff quickly closed around Brendan's wrist with a sharp metallic snap. A few seconds later his left wrist was joined to his right by the handcuffs. Brendan grimaced as the stainless steel cuffs bit into his wrists.

I suddenly realized Harley Simpson was standing in my dining room. "You should be more careful about who you invite to your dinner parties."

"Your officers should be more careful about pulling your guns on three teenage boys," I replied.

"The driver was wearing a maroon sweat shirt like Healy."

"So are a thousand other kids tonight."

Out of the corner of my eyes I was relieved to see the boys were safe in the living room with Officer Benson. After the police left, I'd need to call Pete's father and explain what happened.

Harley stepped over to Brendan and pulled a card out of his pocket. "Brendan Healy, you're under arrest for the murder of Jennifer Biggio. "You have the right to remain silent …"

I'd heard the Miranda warning enough times during police dramas on television; I never thought I'd hear it in my own dining room. After Harley finished, he grabbed hold of Brendan's arm and directed him to move out. Mrs. Healy moved to hug Brendan but one of the officers blocked her.

"Can I at least speak to my mother?"

"No." Harley jerked Brendan's arm to move him away from his mother.

"All of you are wrong! He had nothing to do with Jenny's murder" sobbed Brendan's mother as the police hustled him out the front door.

I stood at the front door and watched Harley shove Brendan into the backseat of a police cruiser and slam the door shut. A second later the electric lock clicked to imprison Brendan in the car; he sat there impassively lit by the car's interior lamp as Harley gave orders to the driver. Brendan turned and bravely flashed a smile to his mother as the car lurched from the curb and sped off.

Mrs. Healy turned to one of the officers remaining on the lawn. "What's going to happen to my son?"

"He's being taken to the police operations center downtown for interrogation; he'll be transferred to the jail later for booking. They'll arraign him on Monday."

"Will I be able to see him in the morning?"

"Friday nights are pretty busy with all the bar fights and gang shootings; he might not be transferred to the jail until Saturday afternoon."

Doug Clayton had his wish; he'd be able to tell Jenny's parents at the wake that their daughter's killer was behind bars. I'm sure Harley called him on his cell phone as soon as the handcuffs were clapped around Brendan's wrists.

CHAPTER XXI

"ARE YOU ALL RIGHT?" ASKED Laura as she hugged James and Robert.

"It was scary; all of sudden two police cars cut Pete off at the intersection and another one pulled up behind us. The next thing we knew, police surrounded the car pointing guns at us. They screamed at us to get out of the car and lay down on the ground," said James.

"They thought I was Brendan; one officer handcuffed my arms behind my back. The shit really hit the fan when a female police officer showed up. She called them every name in the book when she realized they'd arrested me instead of Brendan. Excuse me," said Pete when he realized he'd used inappropriate language in front of Laura and Colleen.

Officer Benton cursing like a sailor would've been funny at another time but I was in no mood to laugh after what happened; a trigger happy officer could've accidently shot one of the boys. What prompted the police to act so recklessly?

"Have you called your parents yet Pete?" I asked.

"I dropped my cell phone on the seat," he replied.

"Mine fell on the floor of the car when the police pulled me out but I managed to snap a couple of pictures," said Robert.

"Good work, you have evidence for a police brutality suit," said Laura.

"Where's your car?"

"It's still in the middle of the street;" replied Pete.

I tossed Pete my cell phone. "Call your parents; then let's go move your car."

"I'm sorry your family and Peter were put in danger; I should probably go stay in a motel," said Mrs. Healy.

"Absolutely not; you're still in shock," said Laura. She helped Mrs. Healy over to the couch.

"My parents will be right over," said Pete.

Pete's parents were rather overprotective of their only child forgetting that he was seventeen years old and six feet tall. They weren't going to take what happened lightly. In a few minutes, the media would be descending on our street in search of a story for the eleven o'clock newscasts. Why had the police moved so suddenly to arrest Brendan? If they merely wanted to appease Doug Clayton, they could've arrested him before the memorial service and forestalled the confrontation with Brad Biggio. What new evidence did the police have?

"Dr. Stanard; your phone is ringing," said Pete as he handed it to me.

"This is Andy Chen; the police are ransacking the house! Brendan is not answering his phone."

"They arrested him a few minutes ago."

"Geez! I was in bed with my girlfriend; the next thing I knew the police burst through the front door. Talk about coitus interruptus."

Somehow I restrained myself from laughing. The police had already searched Brendan's room and confiscated the clothing he'd worn on Monday. What were they searching for now? Tonight's search seemed to reinforce my opinion that the evidence against Brendan was flimsy at best. "Let me know if they find anything."

The doorbell rang and James went to the door to find Julia Adams standing on our front porch; she marched past James into the living room. "I thought all of you needed some Chinese herbal tea; this variety soothes the nerves and relaxes you. I'm Dr. Julia Adams," she said as she extended her hand to Colleen Healy.

"Are you a physician?" Colleen asked.

"No, I'm a botanist. I special order this tea from San Francisco; it's not available in stores."

Colleen was somewhat taken aback by the indomitable Julia's response.

"Julia taught at CBU for over thirty years," said Laura as if that would allay Colleen's bewilderment.

"We're going to retrieve Pete's car." I said, leaving Laura to deal with Julia. Also I wanted to alert Tollie Monroe about Brendan's arrest without upsetting Colleen.

The police had stopped the car at the end of our block; half of the neighborhood surrounded the car. Everyone was speculating why the police had stormed my house and drew their guns on the three boys. Teenagers were taking pictures with their cell phones and sending them to friends; it would be old news by the eleven o'clock broadcasts. Basking in their newfound status as celebrities, Pete and James climbed in the car and turned it around to go back to the house.

I punched in the number of Tollie's cell phone. "Dr. Monroe," he answered.

In the background I could hear Bizet's *Carmen* playing before Tollie silenced it.

"Tollie, this is Andy. Brendan Healy was just arrested at my house."

"It doesn't surprise me. After the debacle this afternoon, Harley Simpson was under tremendous pressure from Doug Clayton."

"It wasn't Brendan's fault that Brad Biggio came spoiling for a fight."

"For someone who's on the verge of getting his Ph.D., Healy isn't too bright. He should've slipped out the side door after the service and avoided her cousin. Better yet that slimeball should've stayed home altogether."

I was surprised that Tollie used a word not sanctioned by the *Oxford English Dictionary*. He was feeling the effects of the glass or two of port he purportedly enjoyed every evening.

"Brendan has nothing to hide; if he'd skipped the memorial service that would've been seen as an admission of guilt."

"Now that Healy has been arrested for Ms. Biggio's murder, I can't afford for you to publicly support him. What in the hell was he doing at your house anyway?"

"I invited Brendan and his mother to have dinner with us; his mother is staying with us tonight."

"Have you lost your mind?" screamed Tollie.

"It was the Christian thing to do."

"Doug Clayton is going to come down on me like a ton of bricks when he finds out; fortunately he's still at the funeral home with Jenny's parents. I can see Amanda Saltzman's headline, *Murder Suspect Arrested at Professor's Dinner Party*."

"It wasn't a dinner party; we ordered pizza from Vito's."

"At least Laura didn't serve pâté or some other decadent intellectual dish; Saltzman would've had a field day with that."

"As a card carrying member of the ACLU, I expected better than a knee jerk reaction from you."

"Defending freedom of expression is one thing; murder is another. You must distance yourself from Healy immediately." Tollie clicked off his phone.

Laura carried a tray with a teapot and mugs into the living room as I returned home. Julia attempted to console Colleen Healy but what can one say to a mother when her son has just been arrested and is facing the prospect of spending the rest of his life behind bars.

"I'm to blame for what happened to Brendan; if only I'd been stronger and left Mike. Being the oldest child, Brendan was the one most affected by Mike's drinking."

"You can't blame yourself," said Laura as she handed Colleen a mug of Julia's herbal tea.

"I'd met his father at the shore the summer after I finished my LPN training. Mike was blond and blue eyed like Brendan; he'd just moved to Jersey from Brooklyn. I should've realized he was drinking too much but everybody did in the 70's."

Colleen paused and took a sip of her tea. "I was twenty when I had Brendan; we hadn't even been married a year. Things started going downhill shortly after that. Foolishly I stuck it out hoping things would get better."

Julia's herbal tea did seem to possess some medicinal qualities; my heart, beating rapidly since Robert's phone call, had returned to its normal rhythm. Having another empathetic listener took some of the burden off Laura and me.

"Everything came home to roost the night Mike died; Brendan is not a murderer like they're making him out to be. I tried to get him into counseling but he was too headstrong. It was hard for Brendan to walk around Kearny; everyone pointed at him and whispered that's the boy who killed his father."

Colleen broke down and started sobbing again. Julia put her arm around her.

"My father got him into the Marine Corps; if he'd stayed in Kearny he would've ended up dead like Sean O'Reilly. Maybe he kept that part of his life secret from all of you but Brendan told Jenny everything about what happened when he was a teenager. When they came to see me over Labor Day weekend; he even drove her up to Mountainview."

"Did you tell any of this to the police?" I asked.

"No one from the police has even talked with me."

The door bell rang and Robert let in Pete's parents. "Where's Peter?" cried his mother looking around the room frantically.

"He's in the family room playing a video game with James; he's all right," said Laura as she led Pete's mother to the back of the house.

"What happened?" demanded Pete's father.

"The police were staking out our house because my graduate student was here for dinner. When the boys left to go to the movies, the police mistook Pete for Brendan since they were wearing the same sweatshirt. They stopped his car down the street with guns drawn."

"You showed incredibly poor judgment! It was all over the newspaper this week that your student had murdered his girlfriend."

"Your son is lucky to have you for a father; Brendan's father was an abusive alcoholic," said Colleen.

"I'm sorry; I was so upset when I heard that Pete had been manhandled by the police. Your son is presumed innocent. As a lawyer, I should know better," apologized Tom Redmond.

"You're a lawyer?" asked Colleen.

"My specialty is taxation not criminal defense; I'd be ill advised to help your son."

"Will Brendan be assigned a lawyer by a court?"

"He'll be assigned a public defender; unfortunately they all have huge caseloads. At the last bar association meeting I heard that some of them are juggling over a hundred clients. Due to the low pay, many of them are fresh out of law school. This is turning out to be a high profile case; the Commonwealth's Attorney will no doubt assign its most experienced prosecutor. You need to hire a good criminal defense attorney for your son."

"Putting Brendan's two sisters through college depleted my savings."

"Nick Papadakis is the best defense attorney in town; he got Tandi Brooks off the hook with the raccoon defense," said Tom.

Colleen had a puzzled look on her face. "What's the raccoon defense?"

"Tandi was a former exotic dancer who married a local businessman; he was thirty years older than her. She shot her husband late one night in the garage by accident with one of his hunting rifles; she thought a rabid raccoon was rummaging around. It was a brilliant ploy; somehow the jurors never asked how she mistook a 275 pound man for a raccoon."

Julia shook her head. "There must have been a lot of dumb city slickers on that jury. I'm a country girl from Georgia; folks down home know that coons usually weigh about 15 to 20 pounds. A 275 pound coon would be like Godzilla!"

We laughed heartily bringing some levity to the wake taking place in our living room. There was hope for Brendan; a good defense attorney might be able to poke holes in the prosecution's case and persuade a jury of his innocence. However a sharp prosecutor could easily sway a jury in the other direction despite the lack of evidence.

Nick Papadakis lived high and didn't come cheap; even if Colleen Healy took out a second mortgage she'd be unable to afford him. Brendan appeared to have no other choice but to take his chances with the public defender's office; he'd being playing Russian roulette with his life.

"Dad! Channel 12's satellite truck just pulled up in front of the house," screamed Robert from his room.

"They probably picked up Brendan's arrest off the police scanners." I didn't know what was worse; having the police barge in my house or

Amanda Saltzman on my doorstep. A raccoons in my garage would be a more welcome guest than Amanda.

"We need to go home now," said Pete's mother when she emerged from the family room with her son.

"Mom, can I be on the *National Crime Roundup* tonight; they're out front," said Pete.

"You'll do no such thing Peter; you've been handcuffed and had guns pointed at you. That's quite enough for one day!"

Laura and I didn't have time to walk the Redmonds to the door before the doorbell rang. Opening the door, I found Amanda Saltzman standing on my porch.

"Good evening Dr. Stanard," she greeted me as the Redmonds pushed past her.

"I don't recall inviting you and Barry Sanders over this evening." Looking across the street I saw the telescoping pole with the satellite dish on top slowly extending upward from the truck. My neighbors were again out on the sidewalk to observe the latest intrusion in our normally peaceful neighborhood.

Amanda smiled. "I understand the police took Brendan Healy into custody less than thirty minutes ago."

"You missed the arrest of the century; I'm sure they're downtown by now." I hoped Amanda and her crew would pack up and leave; reporting from in front of police headquarters was always more dramatic than a broadcast from a quiet residential street.

"Can you explain why you were harboring Healy from the police?"

"Brendan and his mother shared pizza with my family; the police knew where he was the whole time. He didn't resist arrest."

"I see Mrs. Healy is still here; I'd like to interview her," said Amanda as she tried to force her stiletto heeled shoe through my doorway.

Colleen rose from the couch and walked over to the door. "Brendan told me about your interview with Ida O'Reilly; that poor woman is in the throes of dementia. You don't care who you hurt with your manipulative reporting."

I was glad to see Colleen's assertiveness returning after being in shock after Brendan's arrest.

"You're one to talk about manipulating people. How can you sleep at night after pulling your little puppet's strings to murder your husband for you? That was very clever; the police never figured it out. You were able to collect his life insurance plus social security benefits for your children. It must have been like winning the lottery!"

"You lying bitch!"

"Your scheme is unraveling after Brendan murdered Jenny; the police back in New Jersey will be looking at your unfortunate domestic squabble through a new lens."

I slammed the door on Amanda Saltzman; I might regret it later but it was clear she'd stop at nothing to make a national reputation for herself from a local murder case that wouldn't normally rate a mention in the national media. If she could dredge up the accidental death of Brendan's father and insinuate his mother directed Brendan to kill him, it put a whole new veneer on the story of Jenny's murder. With Kearny's proximity to the New York City, it would give her additional exposure in the country's largest media market.

"Why is she saying I directed Brendan to murder my husband?" said Colleen between sobs.

"In my research I studied plant parasites; Amanda Saltzman is a rather pernicious variety," said Julia.

"Mike never paid a dime of the child support that the court required; I was behind on the mortgage and other bills. All I received was $10,000 from a life insurance policy he had with the union; that was enough to keep the house from being foreclosed and pay off some of our debts. Sure I received social security benefits for the children; it was not a huge windfall like she implied."

It was not the windfall that Tandi Brooks received but for someone struggling to keep afloat, it was a lifeline. Spin the story the right way and Amanda had the sensational headline she needed.

"Did the police know all this?"

"Of course; they knew about the restraining order. I'd called the police the week before when Mike showed up drunk; they escorted him away instead of locking him up. His little chippie had also obtained a restraining order after she kicked his ass out."

"My ex-husband wasn't an alcoholic and it was still difficult when we divorced. I know it must have been a trying time for you," said Julia.

"Why is that reporter picking at the scab of that old wound? I worked hard to pull my family out of the wreckage left by Mike; I'd already gone back to the community college and started working on my associate's degree in nursing. Things improved for us when I became an RN. I blame myself for Brendan getting into trouble with the law when he was a teenager; working and going to school I wasn't around to keep an eye on him."

"We all did things as teenagers that we shudder at as adults," said Julia.

Knowing my own misdeeds as a teenager, I wondered what Julia had done as a teenager but that would have to be left for another day. Despite my initial skepticism about Julia's uninvited visit, she helped Colleen calm down after watching her son be arrested.

"Thank you for helping me tonight; I'm going to go upstairs and try to get some sleep. I want to go down to the jail in the morning; hopefully I can see Brendan before heading back to Jersey. Your tea was wonderful, Dr. Adams."

"You're welcome to the rest of the box."

"That's most kind of you."

I escorted Julia to the door; the broadcast crew had set up lights on the sidewalk for Amanda's broadcast in fifteen minutes; Oxford Place was going to be starring on the *National Crime Roundup* whether we wanted it to or not. As Julia crossed the street to get to her house, she was ambushed by Amanda Saltzman. She stiff armed Amanda and knocked her to the ground. Without pausing, Julia marched up the steps to her house while a chagrined Amanda Saltzman was being helped to her feet by her cameraman.

Laura cleared the coffee table and put the mugs on a tray. "I hope the boys are all right; I couldn't stop shaking until a few minutes ago."

"They've been calling and texting their friends; I doubt they'll be permanently traumatized by what happened tonight."

"This was worse than the night we hosted the dinner party for that visiting World War I historian. As drunk as he was, I'll never figure out how he managed to deliver the lecture afterwards."

"He held on to the podium for dear life; he gives that talk at least once a month so he had it memorized."

"I didn't know whether to laugh or cry when Varina brought bourbon balls for dessert that night," laughed Laura.

I carried the tray out to the kitchen and helped Laura load the dishwasher to kill the time until *The National Crime Roundup* came on. I didn't know whether we should watch the program on the television or out in front of the house. We opted for the safety of the family room; the boys watched the broadcast unfold from the window of Robert's room.

"We go to Norfolk, Virginia for breaking news in the murder investigation of Chesapeake Bay University coed Jennifer Biggio. Our special correspondent, Amanda Saltzman, has the details regarding the arrest of her killer," said Nate Elster to open the broadcast.

Amanda was standing in front of our house. "Good evening Nate. Police crashed a dinner party in Norfolk's fashionable University Terrace neighborhood and arrested the guest of honor, Brendan Healy, for the murder of Jenny Biggio. The party was hosted by Healy's mentor, Professor Andrew Stanard, Chairman of the Chesapeake Bay University History Department. According to neighbors, Healy was led away in handcuffs while his mother watched."

"Why was Professor Stanard hosting a dinner party for a murder suspect?" asked Nate.

"Intellectuals often adopt radical causes and support criminals in their quixotic quest for justice. In the 1960's, Leonard Bernstein hosted a reception for the Black Panthers at his New York apartment."

"Have police said what evidence led them to the arrest Healy this evening?" asked Nate.

"The police have been carefully building their case against Healy since Jenny's body was found on Tuesday morning."

A photo of Jenny flashed momentarily on the screen before returning to Amanda.

"It takes several days to process forensic evidence; the police may finally have DNA or fingerprints to link Healy to Jenny's murder. We have footage of Healy's arrival at Police Headquarters courtesy of WNFK, Channel 12."

A police car pulled into the parking lot of Police Headquarters. Due to his hands being handcuffed behind his back, Brendan awkwardly emerged from the back of the police car. He looked grim faced as a detective grabbed his arm and led him past the camera into the building.

"They plan to question Healy tonight before transferring him to the city jail in the morning for booking. There is also a report that the house Healy shares with three other CBU students was searched by police tonight and evidence taken away."

"I understand there was an incident at Jenny's memorial service this afternoon."

"To everyone's surprise, Healy attended her memorial service this afternoon. Jenny's cousin, Bradley Biggio, delivered a moving eulogy."

"… Her skill in math was one of the gifts that God granted her. During college and graduate school she continued volunteering her time to tutor to tutor under-privileged children in math."

"After the service, her cousin spotted Healy at the reception and confronted him."

Footage of Jake Ruiz and I restraining Brad Biggio flashed on the screen. "If Jenny had known you were an ex-con, she never would've dated you."

"Jenny was going to have my child!"

"Crawl back in your hole you slimy bastard!"

They'd cleverly edited the exchange to give Brad two potent sound bites that would be seared in viewers' minds; Brendan's words reinforced the police's theory that he killed Jenny in a fit of anger because she was pregnant.

"Police have not released the details of their investigation nor any autopsy results. We may not know anything until Healy's arraignment next week."

"Thank you Amanda for your update."

There was nothing in her reporting about the police's bungled stop of Pete's car and pulling their guns on three scared teenage boys; I was curious if that would be suppressed by the media. If my boys hadn't been in the car, it had a Keystone Cops aura to it. What else the police had missed in their slipshod investigation of Jenny's murder?

Thoroughly exhausted by the night's events, Laura decided to follow Colleen Healy's lead and turn in early. The boys took over the television for their video game and I retreated to my study. I pulled out a yellow legal pad and started sketching out my thoughts.

In the center of the page I drew a big box and wrote in Jenny. Next I drew a line connecting the box for Brendan and started writing the reasons why the police suspected him of the murder. There were two; Jenny was pregnant and he was cheating on her with Tiffany Finley. Except Brendan wasn't involved with Tiffany; someone falsely tipped off the police that he was cheating on Jenny.

Except for Sergeant Milkowski, Brendan seemed to have no enemies unless Kate Goodman, the library science graduate student, still held a grudge against him. Dropping a dime on Brendan and insinuating he was having an affair with Tiffany might be the way Kate settled her score with him. Someone witnessed Tiffany hugging Brendan and reported it to the police. Either that or someone else in Jordan Hall wanted to stab Brendan in the back. What was their motivation?

Communication with Brendan would be hampered by his incarceration and would likely be monitored by the police. Had Jenny dated anyone before Brendan? One thing that struck me was how quickly Jenny fell for Brendan. She was ready to marry Brendan despite knowing him a little over six months although her pregnancy may have accelerated their trip to the altar. Did she believe she had no other option besides marrying Brendan? Unlike in the 1950's, there was no stigma having a child born out of wedlock. One of our department's junior faculty members had two children sired by her live-in boyfriend and no one at the university gives it a second thought.

Maybe Cynthia Wallach or Jake Ruiz could fill me in on Jenny's background although they likely knew little about her personal life. Her parents as well as her cousin Brad would refuse to speak with me because of my close association with Brendan.

That left Jenny's roommate Melinda to shed light on Jenny's personality. I still found it a weird coincidence that Jenny shared an apartment with a lesbian; it was enough for me to put a large question mark by Melinda's name. Or was it just a marriage of convenience necessitated by the outrageous rents for the run down apartments near campus? My disquiet may be a sign of my prejudices from growing up in a less tolerant era. If Jenny had roomed with an African-American girl in the 1960's and been murdered, her roommate would've likely been added to my suspect list.

Brendan's remark about the pizza delivery driver gave me pause. I fished the receipt from Vito's out of my pocket; the delivery driver was listed as Leo. In addition to his first name, all I knew was he drove an aging red Toyota Camry. I had good rapport with Jake; he'd probably be willing to share the details of the stalking incident with me.

Jenny's tutoring at the Ark Church opened another avenue of inquiry; one I doubted the police had even considered. Who were the other homeless men who hung around the church and the university library? It might be worth paying a visit to Pastor Franklin next week and looking into their backgrounds.

Unless the police proved otherwise, my prime suspect was still Felton Snyder. He was no harmless drunk; Detective Chambliss down in High Point had indicated that Snyder had already murdered and gotten away with it. It troubled me that Snyder had been released from jail; someone with his criminal past would be adept at manipulating the police.

CHAPTER XXII

Just before seven o'clock the next morning, I heard Colleen Healy turn on the shower in the bathroom next to the guest room. Putting on a pair of jeans and a CBU sweatshirt I let Laura continue sleeping and went downstairs to prepare for our guest's departure. While the coffee brewed, I went into my study and turned on my computer.

The jail's website offered no hope for Colleen to see Brendan before she left. Visiting hours were noon to five on Saturday and Sunday and one to four on Wednesday; I printed off the information about the jail's canteen and mail requirements just as I heard her coming down the stairs.

"Would you like some coffee?" I greeted her.

"Please don't go to any trouble for me," Colleen replied.

"It's already made."

"Thank you; you and your wife have been so kind to me." She took a seat at the kitchen table.

I poured a mug for her and one for me. "We have English muffins; if you'd like a Southern breakfast, I can microwave a sausage biscuit for you."

"An English muffin is my usual morning fare. Thank you."

Laura came downstairs; smelling the coffee she shuffled over to the coffee maker where I was standing. I filled a mug and handed it to her.

"Did Andy offer you any breakfast?"

"Oh, yes."

"I have bad news; the jail doesn't allow visitors until noon." I handed Colleen the information sheet.

Colleen looked the paper over. "I feared as much; do you mind if I call the jail and see if they've transferred Brendan yet?"

"Would you like to use the phone in my study?"

"Thank you; I'd like to conserve my cell phone battery for the trip back to Jersey."

I showed her to my study off the kitchen and went out on the front porch to retrieve the newspaper. On the front page was a color picture of Brendan in handcuffs under the large headline "Boyfriend Charged in CBU Strangling." Quickly scanning Amanda Saltzman's article, it offered no insight on what led the police to arrest Brendan last night. Instead she served up a rehash of the half-truths and innuendos that had dogged Brendan all week.

On another day I might have found it amusing to be the focus of a front page article except she chose to smear me with her poisoned pen.

"Healy was the guest of honor at a dinner party hosted by his mentor, Professor Andrew Stanard, Chairman of the CBU History Department. He was taken out in handcuffs to the chagrin of the other dinner guests. His mother harangued the police for arresting her son."

"Dr. Stanard has emerged as the chief defender of Healy, an ex-con from New Jersey. Like many liberal professors, Stanard has chosen to side with the criminal element over law enforcement."

Amanda had not carried through with her threat to paint Colleen as the manipulative mother who directed her son to kill her husband for financial gain. That would likely come next week when she needed a lurid headline to keep the story on the front page.

A second article on the front page covered the memorial service or more accurately it detailed the near brawl between Brad Biggio and Brendan. Two short paragraphs describing the commemoration of Jenny's life were relegated to the continuation of the article on page five. It was a shame; Laura and I had found the service quite moving. For Jenny's friends, the service had started the healing process. Dick Torelli's plan for the service to repair CBU's tarnished image was drowned out by Brendan's arrest. No doubt Torrelli was furious that when Brendan was arrested he wore a sweatshirt with CBU emblazoned across his chest.

Colleen returned to the kitchen several minutes later. "Brendan is still undergoing questioning at police headquarters; they're not expecting him to be transferred until later in the morning."

It wasn't a good sign that the police were still questioning him; they were trying to take advantage of his exhausted state and extract a confession. Brendan was savvy; he knew his rights and wouldn't say anything without a lawyer present.

Colleen took a sip of her coffee. "I can't come down next weekend; my schedule requires me to work both next Saturday and Sunday. Can I impose on you again and ask you to visit Brendan during the week?"

I met the jail's requirement that a visitor be a relative or a positive influence in the inmate's life. "I'd be glad to go see him."

Laura gave me a look that indicated her plans for the week didn't include a trip downtown to the jail. The click of the toaster indicated Colleen's English muffin was finished; I put it on a plate and handed it to her and then dropped one in for Laura. Colleen spread some butter and marmalade on her muffins.

"There's no way I'll be able to come down for Brendan's arraignment."

"He knows your schedule and understands; your love and support is what's important," said Laura.

"When Brendan was at Mountainview, I tried to write a letter to him every night."

"If I don't have a class, I'll try to attend," I volunteered.

"Thank you." Colleen nibbled indifferently at her English muffin. "I'm sure that reporter will find some way to twist my absence just like she tried to distort Mike's death. I didn't even know Mike had any life insurance until the union's business agent came to see me after the funeral."

"I'm sure the insurance company thoroughly investigated your husband's death before they paid the claim," I replied.

"Who would have the records now; that was over fifteen years ago."

"It might take some digging but those records can be located. Insurance companies keep warehouses full of records to protect themselves; during my research I found polices from the 1850's insuring slaves for their owners," I replied.

"If only I'd had the courage to leave Mike sooner. Things might have turned out differently for Brendan."

"You did the best you could under some very trying circumstances," Laura replied.

Colleen finished her coffee. "I have a seven hour drive ahead of me; it's time to get on the road."

She'd left her suitcase in the hallway. When Colleen came downstairs, I carried it out to her car for her.

"Mike didn't even carry my suitcase on our honeymoon." She handed me an envelope. "I almost forgot. Here's $50 to put in Brendan's canteen account at the jail. When he was incarcerated at Mountainview being able to buy a candy bar broke the monotony of incarceration."

"That's not a problem."

"How come I never met someone like you when I was younger," she sighed as she climbed in her car.

***

Since we were up earlier than usual on a Saturday, Laura decided to beat the crowds and do the grocery shopping early. Since the boys were still asleep. I took advantage of the quiet in the house and graded midterms in my study. Finishing around ten o'clock, I decided to head to the Rec Center to swim before the crowds descended on the campus for the football game that evening. With the summer humidity banished until spring, I opted to ride my bike and burn off a few extra calories.

Expecting to find the faculty locker room deserted at that hour, I was surprised to find Harley Simpson coming out of the showers with a towel wrapped around his waist.

"We just finished questioning Healy; I didn't have time to go home and take a shower before getting started on the preparations for the game tonight. I won't get home until after midnight," he yawned.

"You owe me an explanation about what happened last night. Why did your officers pull their guns on my sons and their friend?"

Harley sat down on a bench. "Those weren't my men who stopped them. The crime lab had confirmed Healy's fingerprints on Ms. Biggio's wallet and credit card; that was the final piece of evidence we needed. We were getting ready to arrest him when a rookie city cop thought the blond kid was Healy and jumped the gun."

I doubted Harley realized his slip of the tongue. "Is that all the evidence you have against him? What about Brendan's alibi for the time of the murder?"

"His alibi doesn't hold water."

"He was at work when the murder occurred."

"You're wrong about that; we place the time of the murder between six-fifteen and six-thirty. The autopsy confirms that timeline. He didn't clock in at the convention center until six-fifty."

"There's no way he could ride his bike from campus to downtown in under twenty-five minutes."

"Healy didn't ride his bike; his fingerprints are all over the steering wheel of Ms. Biggio's car."

"Her car?"

"Biggio's parents gave her a dark blue Ford Focus station wagon two years ago. A security camera monitoring the front entrance of the convention center captured her car driving by around six forty on the night of the murder; it nailed him!"

"Are you certain it was Jenny's car? How can you be sure that Brendan was driving it?"

Harley ducked my question. Parking on the streets in the vicinity of the convention center was limited to one hour. Brendan would've needed to park in one of the garages downtown. He didn't have time to drive around looking for a parking space if he had to be at work at seven. Due to a spate of robberies and car thefts, the city had installed cameras to monitor the parking garages. One of the cameras should've captured Brendan entering one of the garages before he clocked in as well as leaving after he finished work.

The security camera captured a Ford Focus driving by the convention center. Whether Brendan was driving it was another question. Still it was troubling that his prints were on the steering wheel.

"According to Henrietta Sealy, Ms. Biggio spotted Healy on campus just after six o'clock when he walked by the library with Tiffany Finley. She'll break and spill the beans about her relationship with Healy."

Had Brendan been playing me all along? His fingerprints on Jenny's wallet and credit card were damning. Jenny's car being caught by the security camera downtown seemed to be another nail in Brendan's coffin. Tiffany Finley denied any relationship with Brendan during her meeting with me and Emily Worthington. Did she lie to protect him?

"I gave Healy every break possible but the evidence against him is incontrovertible. We found his Marine Corps ring under one of the cubicles in the graduate student's office; the ring he bestowed upon Ms. Biggio as a token of his affection just before murdering her," said Harley, his voice dripping with sarcasm.

"You found the ring in the graduate student's office?"

"He murdered her in the office; he came back after the Women's Studies seminar was over and carried her body across the hall to the bathroom. What else could he do? We found her messenger bag above the ceiling tiles in the hallway. Your boy wasn't too bright; he left his fingerprints all over everything. Having done time already, I thought Healy would've wiped everything clean."

Harley had strong circumstantial evidence against Brendan but it didn't conclusively prove his guilt. "An innocent person doesn't go around wiping off their fingerprints. If Brendan had the presence of mind to come back and drag the body over to the restroom; why didn't he take the time to obliterate all his fingerprints?"

"He'll have plenty of time behind bars to ponder that point. Anyhow I have a witness who saw Healy dump her wallet in the alley behind Tait's Market."

That was how Felton Snyder got out of jail! I should've smelled a rat when I saw him behind Nick's on Thursday night. "Do you really believe a wino like Felton Snyder is a reliable witness?"

Harley was taken aback that I figured out the identity of his star witness. He hesitated momentarily and parsed his words carefully. "When we questioned Snyder, he said a blond man on a bike dropped the wallet in the alley. He perfectly described Healy's bicycle; as you recall it has a Marine Corps bumper sticker on the frame. That's a key detail that ties Healy to the alley. Later Snyder identified Healy in a photo lineup. He'll testify against Antonio McKinney too."

"How can you trust a murderer like Snyder?"

"I've talked extensively with Detective Chambliss down in High Point. They couldn't make a murder charge stick thirty years ago; their cold case unit recently reopened the case at the request of the victim's family. The body had been out in the woods for months and scavenged by animals; there was no usable DNA evidence. The only witness who'd seen Snyder with the victim before he disappeared died of an overdose shortly after the body was discovered; she was an addict who turned tricks at the tavern that Snyder and his biker buddies frequented."

"So you've cut a deal with a thug like Snyder and let him go free."

"To put a murderer like Healy behind bars, I'd shake hands with the devil! As much as I'd like to put Snyder behind bars, whatever he may've done in North Carolina isn't admissible in court."

"You're making a big mistake."

"Don't be duped by Healy; he's a clever psychopath. Sergeant Milkowski told me about Healy serving as the enforcer for a drug dealer; I bet he never told you the Kearny Police suspected him of bashing in the skull of a competitor with a baseball bat. He kicked his old man down the stairs and killed the poor bastard!"

"His father was in a drunken rage threatening to harm his mother!"

"His father's blood alcohol limit indicated he was in a drunken stupor; he didn't have to kill him to protect his mother! Healy's mother lied to protect him."

"You've closed your eyes to other suspects."

"No other suspect has even surfaced; no one else has a motive. I'm your friend; I shouldn't even be telling you any of this but I wanted to prevent you from making a total ass of yourself. The Commonwealth's Attorney is considering charging Healy with first degree murder."

"What do you mean by first degree murder?" I asked without admitting that my knowledge of legal matters was limited to two semesters of Constitutional History.

"Biggio and Healy were overheard by the econ department secretary on Monday; it was no lover's quarrel. He was furious that she was pregnant. To buy time he strung her along and held out the prospect of marriage. Healy had no intention of getting married; his story that he and Ms. Biggio made love on Monday afternoon is a total fabrication. He was screwing Tiffany Finley; he couldn't resist her nubile charms."

"She already told your investigator she wasn't with him."

"Henrietta Sealy overheard Ms. Biggio in the library when she saw the two of them together. When she confronted him on Monday evening about cheating with Ms. Finley, he raped and strangled her. That's first degree murder in this state."

"That's preposterous. He didn't rape her."

"We found stains on the chair in his cubicle indicative of seminal fluid; once the DNA results come back from the lab, they'll confirm his guilt. The evidence all fell into place just as I thought it would when I interviewed him on Tuesday morning."

Harley turned away and stalked down the row to his locker at the other end of the room. A locker closed on the other side of the locker room; I wondered who'd been eavesdropping on our conversation. I went to my locker and changed into my swimsuit. At the pool, I handed my faculty ID card to the lethargic lifeguard on duty. He scratched his hairy chest and yawned; the red ink stamp on his hand betrayed his drowsiness was the result of spending Friday night at a popular bar across from campus. Art Campbell was the only other person in the pool; the rest of the campus appeared to be still snug in their beds.

My goal on Saturday and Sunday was to swim a mile; it usually wasn't possible to do a mile during my lunch hour. However I soon lost count of my laps because my mind was elsewhere.

I wondered why Harley shared with me about the case against Brendan; information he'd withheld from the press. He knew I was Brendan's chief defender; was it a pre-emptive strike to forestall my advocacy on his behalf. Harley admitted that he'd pegged Brendan as Jenny's killer when he first laid eyes on him; he never even bothered to investigate other suspects. That revelation troubled me.

Perhaps the most damning piece of evidence was the argument overheard by everyone in the econ department. The commonwealth's attorney would have several witnesses to bolster the theory that Brendan killed Jenny in a rage over her pregnancy. No one would've been present at their private reconciliation later in the day; the pizza delivery driver was unaware of his presence at Jenny's apartment. Brendan's reckless sex life made an affair with Tiffany Finley seem plausible even though Harley had no hard evidence that it ever progressed beyond Tiffany's hug in the elevator.

Henrietta Sealy's statement that she overheard Jenny exclaim, "That no good lying bastard; I can't believe he's cheating on me!" seemed to support Harley's assertion that Brendan was screwing Tiffany Finley. Yet Brendan denied being on campus at that hour. It was unlikely that Henrietta fabricated the incident in the library on Monday night. Jenny definitely saw something out the window that upset her. Did Jenny mistake someone else for Brendan in the twilight? Or was Henrietta somehow mistaken?

Harley's theory that Brendan raped and strangled Jenny was supported by the DNA evidence; no doubt his semen was on her body from their assignation earlier in the afternoon. Yet when Vivian and I found the body, Jenny was completely dressed. If Brendan had raped and murdered Jenny in a rage, it seemed strange that he'd put her clothes on afterwards. I knew little about criminal behavior but Harley with all his investigative experience should've seen that incongruity.

Finding Brendan's Marine Corps ring in the graduate students' office further connected him to Jenny's murder; the other five students who shared the office had no motive that I could fathom. Brendan admitted giving Jenny the ring on Monday afternoon after he apologized for his initial reaction to her pregnancy. Jenny was wearing the ring on a chain around her neck when she was strangled. During her struggle with her murderer, the chain broke and the ring rolled under one of the desks. Or was that what the killer wanted us to think?

It seemed too pat; the ring could have been planted after the fact. But who had access to the office besides Brendan and the other graduate students? Janet and I controlled the department's set of master keys; I doubted Emily still had one from her tenure as department chair. The Building and Grounds Department controlled all keys on campus. Could someone employed by Buildings and Grounds be involved in Jenny's murder? Buildings and Grounds had over 150 employees from plumbers to housekeeping workers. If someone from Buildings and Grounds was involved, it went a long way to explaining the seeming randomness of Jenny's murder.

Finding Jenny's messenger bag concealed in the ceiling further linked Brendan to Jenny's murder. But why did Brendan hide the bag in the ceiling? If he was laying false trails as Harley claimed, he wouldn't have been stupid enough to leave the bag where it would've pointed right back to him. He would have dumped it in the bushes like Jenny's purse or left it in the library to further muddy things. Again it appeared someone was trying to draw suspicion to Brendan.

Harley failed to mention if Jenny's laptop was in her messenger bag. If her laptop was missing that pointed right back to Felton Snyder. The police had pressed Snyder to implicate Brendan; Snyder was more than happy to oblige, realizing that Brendan was his ticket to get out of jail. Detective Chambliss had indicated that Snyder was a cold blooded killer; he'd have no qualms about sending another man to prison to save his own skin. The smoking area for Jordan Hall was next to the bike racks where Brendan locked up his bike; hanging around the building and fishing cigarette butts out of the ash trays when he couldn't afford to buy a pack, Snyder would've been familiar with Brendan and made the connection from watching the television news reports in the jail.

Snyder, flush with cash on Monday night according to Reverend Franklin, would've been too drunk and bleary eyed to see Brendan or whoever else dropped Jenny's wallet behind Tait's Market. Like a house of cards, Harley's case was propped up by a couple of Snyder's empty wine bottles.

Usually I felt exhilarated after finishing a mile swim; this morning I felt strangely empty. I retrieved my ID card from the lifeguard and took a quick shower. As I biked home, I passed the parking lots on campus beginning to fill with tailgaters planning an afternoon of partying before the game at six. One thing Harley was right about, I risked harming Brendan if I blundered trying to exonerate him. It would be best to leave it to his attorney to coordinate the investigation although it seemed unlikely a public defender would be able to devote much time to his case. Tollie had also warned me not to get involved in Brendan's defense or risk the ire of President Clayton.

An ally in the media would be helpful in publically shooting down Harley's theories and countering the tidal wave of negative publicity flowing from Amanda Saltzman. Mitch Blackwell and his wife, Maggie had seats next to ours at the stadium; with his contacts, he might be able to steer me to someone in the local media who might be willing to go against the tide and advocate Brendan's innocence.

⁂

We had an early dinner before walking over to the stadium for the game. The boys separated from us and went off in search of their friends. A cold front had moved in during the afternoon and the temperatures had plummeted. After settling into our seats, I got out my binoculars and scanned the stadium while waiting for the kick off. I spotted Woody Farrell and Colin McIntosh, the department's British Isles historian across the field. Colin sneaked a swig of scotch from a silver hip flask while Woody sipped bourbon from his flask to ward off the chill.

I focused my binoculars on the President's box; Doug Clayton had returned from Jenny's funeral in Cleveland. Harley Simpson and Dick Torelli flanked him; Harley appeared to be briefing him on Brendan's arrest and interrogation.

"You remind me of James Stewart in *Rear Window*," interrupted Mitch Blackwell as he took his seat.

"Take a look at the President's box," I laughed as I handed him my binoculars.

"It appears they're celebrating Healy's arrest," replied Mitch.

"Doug Clayton wanted an arrest by the time he met Jenny Biggio's parents. When he arrived at the funeral home last night, he was able to tell them her murderer was in custody."

"You still think Healy is being railroaded?"

"I ran into Harley Simpson at the Rec Center this morning; he outlined the case against Brendan. His star witness is that wino who hangs around Jordan Hall bumming cigarettes."

"The one who resembles Whit Tanner?" laughed Mitch.

"Felton Snyder is a former member of the Devil's Disciples motorcycle gang. I talked with a detective down in North Carolina; Snyder served time for a vicious stabbing plus he was a suspect in a murder."

"I covered the Devil's Disciples when I was a reporter starting out in Charlotte; they terrorized the Carolinas in the 70s and 80s. What's the connection to Jenny Biggio's murder?"

"Snyder found Jenny's credit card in the alley behind Tait's Market; he claims Brendan dropped her wallet there. He sold it to the fence behind all the laptop thefts on campus."

"So Snyder cut a deal and implicated Healy."

"You got it; the rest of the case is all wild supposition as far as I'm concerned."

"I heard that Healy was banging a freshman in one of the sections he taught while he was involved with Jenny Biggio."

"Who's spreading that rumor?" I asked.

"I ran into Barry Sanders at a tailgate party before the game."

"That's the whole problem; Amanda Saltzman is running around unchecked. Brendan won't get a fair trial. Someone in the media needs to poke some holes in her balloon and send it crashing to the ground."

"As long as she has Carruthers's ear, no one at the *Register* is going to challenge her even though they all hate her guts."

"Is there anyone in television news I can contact with my suspicions?"

"Carruthers owns Channel 12 through his Media National holding company; no one there has the guts to buck him."

"I guess Brendan is going to keep getting hammered."

"I'm a member of an informal group of journalists that meets at Finnerty's Pub on Thursday nights for a drink or two. Shane Alvarez from Channel 5 has been joining us. He's ambitious but he his head screwed on straight. On the five o'clock broadcast tonight, he showed the police mistakenly arresting your sons' friend. It was savvy reporting; he pulled the footage off *YouTube*. The other media outlets ignored it; the police wanted to suppress it but it had already gone viral."

"You think I could join you on Thursday?"

"I'll introduce you to Alvarez. He's not going to help Healy out of altruism; if there's a story, he'll run with it. If Healy is guilty, Shane will throw him to the sharks."

CHAPTER XXIII

SUNDAY MORNING'S *REGISTER* FEATURED BRENDAN'S latest mug shot front and center under the headline, *"Murder Suspect Cheated on Fiancée with Young Coed."* Dressed in a sleeveless undershirt, a weary Brendan stared grimly back at the camera. Gone was the tough guy smirk from his teenage mug shot. I wondered if Dick Torelli arranged to have his CBU sweatshirt removed before the mug shot was taken.

With Brendan behind bars, Amanda Saltzman saw no need to pull her punches. "Witnesses in the economics department related that Healy and Jenny Biggio had a violent argument on Monday morning when she told him that she was pregnant with his child; Healy stormed off leaving Miss Biggio in tears. Police have discovered that Healy spent Monday afternoon with a student he taught in his introductory history class; her name hasn't been released by the police. On Monday evening, Miss Biggio spotted Healy and the young woman together. She went to Healy's office and confronted Healy him; he raped and strangled her in a blind rage. Later he dumped her body in the restroom across the hall."

It seemed that Saltzman had a source in the police department who divulged the case against Brendan to her. Or had Dick Torelli thrown the Rottweiler a bone?

On the sports page; the *Register's* sports columnist saw the Neptunes' victory as proof that life at Chesapeake Bay University was returning to normal after the tragic murder earlier in the week; the game helped heal the grieving campus community. Gladiatorial games served the same role in Etruscan funeral rites and were later adopted by the

Romans. Fortunately no CBU players fought to the death like the slaves condemned in the games.

I became enraged when he stated at the end of his column, "The CBU football players embody the American values of fair play, hard work and competition. Brendan Healy had several brushes with the law as a juvenile; many coaches have used athletics to mold individuals like him into productive members of society. Healy's arrest lays open the sleazy underside of American academia that coddles criminals from a misguided perception that they were never given a fair break. These self-proclaimed intellectuals want to curtail college athletics as part of their misguided quest to reshape American universities to their leftist agenda."

If it hadn't been Sunday morning, I would have called the *Register's* circulation office and cancelled my subscription. That would have to wait until Monday.

At Mass, my mind wandered during Father Novello's sermon to my planned meeting with Brendan at the jail this afternoon. Leaving church, Father Novello greeted me. "Have you been in contact with Brendan since his arrest?"

"No, I plan to go see him this afternoon," I replied.

"Is his mother still in town?"

"She had to go back to New Jersey yesterday; she was due back at the hospital today."

"I'll try to visit him during the week. Jenny's call on Monday afternoon for information on marriage preparations surprised me; they'd been dating such a short time."

"The police seemed skeptical that Jenny and Brendan planned to marry."

"When they questioned me, they seemed disappointed that I corroborated Brendan's statement. Last spring Jenny seemed distracted; I thought she might be depressed."

"All graduate students get into a funk every now and then, wondering if all the sacrifice is worth it particularly when their friends from college are already established in their careers and starting families."

"Jenny's death is so tragic; it's hard to believe that Brendan is accused of murdering her." Father Novello turned his attention to an elderly woman patiently waiting to talk with him without explaining his comments further.

✿✿✿

Laura reminded me we had the Friends of the University Library Dinner that evening as I left for downtown after lunch. A long line of visitors waited to be admitted to the jail when I arrived; the guard said I'd have an hour wait before Brendan could be brought down to the visitors' room. I filled out the visitor's card and handed over my driver's license to the guard. Another guard reluctantly took the book I brought for Brendan and gave me a receipt for the money his mother entrusted to me for his canteen account.

I sat in the waiting area and perused a rival professor's book on the antebellum slave trade until my name was called. A guard directed me to booth twelve in a line of twenty booths; I noticed I was the only male visitor. The other visitors were women waiting to visit their sons, husbands and boyfriends. A thick sheet of Plexiglas separated me from Brendan; we'd have to communicate through a telephone.

A few minutes later, a guard escorted Brendan to the opposite cubicle. I was taken aback by his arms being handcuffed behind his back. He was wearing orange coveralls with Norfolk City Jail emblazoned on the back. His two day growth of beard added to my perception that he looked fatigued. Brendan attempted to smile as the guard unlocked his left cuff and locked it to a stanchion on the side of the cubicle. When the guard left, Brendan picked up the telephone with his free hand.

Instead of Brendan's voice, a recorded voice indicated that all conversations were monitored for security purposes.

"I was surprised when the guard told me I had a visitor. I didn't think anyone wanted to associate with me."

"How are you doing?"

"Dreams really do come true," Brendan replied recalling the nightmare he suffered over the summer.

"Your mother tried to see you yesterday before she left for home. She left $50 for your canteen account; I put in $20 too."

"Thanks, I'll be able to buy some deodorant now. If I'm lucky, I get to shower twice a week." Brendan noticed I shuddered at his comment.

"Don't worry, they ran me through the showers with the other new arrivals yesterday."

"Have you been assigned a lawyer yet?"

"From what I've heard, you get five minutes with a public defender before your arraignment. I had a bail hearing last night before the magistrate; he ordered me held without bail. My arraignment is not till Thursday."

"The police told your mother you'd be arraigned on Monday."

"It's being held Thursday afternoon to allow Jenny's parents to attend. I don't know how I'll be able to face them."

"You're innocent; hold your head up high."

"Everyone thinks I'm guilty."

"The case against you is weak."

"The police don't seem to think so; they think it's a slam dunk with all the DNA and fingerprint evidence. They interrogated me all night; I couldn't convince them of anything."

"I ran into Chief Simpson at the Rec Center yesterday morning; he claims you raped and strangled Jenny in your office."

Brendan leaned back in his chair and didn't say anything for several seconds. He looked around the walls of the cubicle as if to avoid looking at me. "They're misconstruing everything that happened; Jenny and I had sex in my office last Friday."

"What?" I couldn't believe what I was hearing.

A sheepish look came across Brendan's face. "Late Friday afternoon I was editing my dissertation after meeting with you, Jenny came to see me. Everyone had gone home for the day; one thing led to another and we had sex in the office. It was impossible to be alone at my house; Jenny tried to respect Melinda's space," replied Brendan.

I wondered what else my graduate students were doing behind my back. Tollie would have a fit if he found out that the graduate students were using their offices for afternoon trysts.

"So Harley's claim that he has DNA evidence is true?"

"But that was three days before Jenny was murdered!"

Brendan's assignation with Jenny made Harley Simpson's case against him seem even stronger. He practically handed Harley a conviction on a silver platter.

"Harley Simpson said your fingerprints were on Jenny's wallet and credit card. He also claims a witness saw you throw her wallet in the alley behind Tait's Market."

"Of course, my fingerprints are on Jenny's credit card. We drove up to Williamsburg on Sunday and rode our bikes on the Colonial Parkway. I gassed up her car on the trip home. She handed me her wallet while she used the restroom; I swiped her credit card on the pump."

"Did you drive her car on Sunday?"

"She was tired and asked me to drive back; I told all that to Chief Simpson."

"Did you ride your bike through the alley behind Tait's Market on Monday night?"

"Tait's Market is a three block detour from my normal route home. No one in their right mind even shops there; you run the risk of getting shot during the fights between the rival gangs."

"Harley says he has a witness who saw you there on Monday night."

"I thought they were bullshitting me again during my interrogation."

"Do you know Felton Snyder?"

"Who's he?"

"He's Harley Simpson's star witness; he's the wino who hangs around Jordan Hall fishing for cigarette butts."

"Is he Professor Tanner's twin brother?" laughed Brendan, momentarily breaking the grim tenor of our conversation.

"That's the one."

Brendan shook his head. "He bummed a buck off me once; playing on my sympathy because he'd been a Marine in Nam. After that he always tried to hit me up; the Marine Corps sticker on my bike always reminded him I might be an easy mark."

That confirmed my hunch that Snyder was familiar with Brendan and quickly made the connection when prompted by the police. I doubted that Snyder saw anyone in the alley that night; he astutely used Brendan to draw suspicion away from himself. Harley was so obsessed that Brendan was Jenny's killer that he failed to see that Snyder had lied to save his own skin.

"Were you with Tiffany Finley on Monday evening?"

"No, the police kept questioning me about her. I had nothing to do with that girl."

"Where were you after leaving Jenny's apartment?"

"I went home and took a shower; I left around six to go downtown."

"Did any of your roommates see you?"

"No, Andy was over at his girlfriend's apartment. Hank and Tom were at the Rec Center working out; I was originally supposed to lift weights with them but went instead to Jenny's to apologize."

"Did you drive Jenny's car downtown?"

"No, I rode my bike."

"The police say you didn't clock in till just before seven."

"After I got downtown, I sat for awhile in Town Point Park and watched the ships on the river; everything had happened so fast on Monday I needed time to think."

"Did anyone see you?"

"I doubt it."

"The police say they have you on video driving Jenny's car past the convention center."

"I locked my bike to a pipe on the loading dock of the convention center; there's a security guard there who checks everybody in. He can vouch for me."

"How did your ring and Jenny's messenger bag wind up in the graduate students' office?"

"When I left Jenny, she'd already put the ring on a chain around her neck. You got to believe me; someone is trying to frame me!"

Who was trying to frame Brendan? "Do you have any enemies who want to get even with you?"

"No!"

"What about the waitress from the convention center; is she upset you took up with Jenny?"

"She moved back to Michigan in June. It was a one night stand; I found out she used me to get even with her husband.

"What about her husband?"

"He was screwing another sailor on his ship; he's shacked up with her now."

With deployments lasting six months or longer, assigning female sailors to warships put additional strains on Navy marriages. My brother, a retired naval officer, asserted that with women now aboard Navy ships, many sailors acted like they were on the "Love Boat".

"What about someone from New Jersey?"

"When I joined the Marines I cut all ties with everyone including Sean."

If I'd hoped to make progress in solving Jenny's murder, all Brendan was able to do was poke a few small holes in Harley's scenario. The forensic evidence was problematic; Brendan's fingerprints were on Jenny's car, wallet and credit card. Would the crime lab be able to tell whether the prints were made on Sunday or Monday? Having sex with Jenny on Monday afternoon further muddied the evidence. It would be up to a jury to decide if they believed Brendan or the police's version of events.

"Do you have a cellmate?" I asked to change the topic.

"They assigned me to murderer's row; my cellmate caught his wife in bed with his neighbor and shot him. He's a deacon in his church and reads his *Bible* all day; he's not very talkative, not that I'm in the mood to talk to anyone."

I recalled reading about his cellmate's case the week before; he was a long distance truck driver who arrived home early. He carried a gun for protection and killed his former fishing buddy. An interesting parallel to Brendan; a normally mild mannered man kills in a moment of rage. Could Brendan have done the same thing?

"I guess they don't have a vegetarian menu."

Brendan laughed sardonically. "I'll eat what's served and keep my mouth shut. If the other inmates suspected I was a vegetarian that would be an invitation to a gang rape in the showers."

Vegetarians were ubiquitous in academia and no one gave them a second thought; other sectors of society perceived them differently. Having been locked up before Brendan knew the ropes and reacted by his instincts. In jail, it was likely his life would be threatened more than once; it would take all his wits to survive.

"Your time is up in two minutes," interrupted a recorded voice.

"A couple years ago at a used book sale, I picked up an abridged version of Gibbon's *Decline and Fall of the Roman Empire*. After it's searched for contraband, the guard said it would be delivered to your cell."

Brendan laughed again. "You shouldn't have bothered with an abridged edition. I'm going to be in prison for the rest of my life, I'll have time to read all three volumes."

At least he'd managed to hang on to his sense of humor; it might help him over a rough patch or two. "You'll be out of here soon."

"It's hard to be optimistic with everything I'm facing. Thanks for coming to see me today; your continued trust in me really means a lot."

"I'll call your mother and tell her you're all right."

"Thanks, although I doubt you'll fool her."

A burly guard stepped behind Brendan and ordered, "I don't have all day; it's time to go back to your cell."

"Yes sir." Resignedly Brendan hung up the phone; the guard unlocked Brendan's left wrist from the stanchion and quickly handcuffed his arms behind his back before leading him away.

On my way home, I detoured by Tait's Market again. No police car was monitoring the store and the drug dealers were out in force; they eyed me suspiciously as I slowed down and turned into the side street next to the market. I stopped and surveyed the alley behind the store. It was just wide enough to allow delivery trucks to park and unload; the rusty fence separating it from the houses bordering the alley was overgrown with vines and tall weeds. Broken bottles of Thunderbird and Schlitz Malt Liquor, the market's best selling items, littered the alley.

Other than a broken light hanging from the wall near the door, there were no other lights or security cameras that I could see in the alley. Most of the houses in the block were abandoned and boarded up, providing havens for the drug addicted prostitutes that plied their trade in front of the store. The house next to the alley had the plywood ripped off one of its windows; I suspected Felton Snyder could've bedded down there for the night with his bottles of wine. A bicycle rider wouldn't have made enough noise to arouse Snyder's suspicions; whoever dumped the wallet must have been driving a car. Brendan was right; no sane person would go there after dark or during the daytime. A leggy prostitute with bleached blond hair wearing tight jeans and a tube top three sizes too small sashayed across the street toward me; I put my car in gear and drove off.

***

"How's Brendan doing?" asked Laura when I arrived home.

"He tried hard to stay upbeat but he's understandably afraid; he hasn't even talked with a lawyer yet. His arraignment has been postponed till Thursday to allow Jenny's parents to attend."

"Too bad I can't be there; I'd like to see how he handles himself in front of them."

Perched in the courtroom would be the media vultures, hoping for a confrontation between Brendan and Jenny's parents. Hopefully they'd be less hot headed than their nephew.

"I'm going to try to call his mother before we leave for the dinner; she indicated her shift was seven to three today."

Just before five o'clock, I dialed her cellphone.

"Colleen Healy," she answered hesitantly.

"This is Andrew Stanard; I saw Brendan this afternoon. They'd interrogated him all night Friday but he's holding up. He's managed to hang on to his sense of humor."

I withheld from her that they brought Brendan to the visitors' room in handcuffs; if she went to see him, she wouldn't even be able to hug her son due to the Plexiglas barrier.

I heard a sigh of relief on the other end. "That's good to hear."

"I was able to put the funds in his canteen account."

"Thank you."

"Brendan's arraignment has been postponed till Thursday afternoon; Jenny's parents will be in attendance."

"Does he have a lawyer yet?"

"No."

"Colleen Healy broke down and started sobbing. "Brendan needs me there; I'm scheduled to work that day. I've never felt so hopeless in all my life."

"I'll be able to attend since the hearing is in the afternoon."

"I can't thank you enough for all your help."

***

The Friends of the University Library Dinner was the group's annual fund raising event. The committee usually picked an author who was entertaining and the audience was drawn for the most part from the university community except for the few true bibliophiles remaining in the city. Local librarians also turned out to support their colleagues at the university.

Doug Clayton stood by the entrance to the dining room with his wife and greeted guests. He looked at me again as if I had leprosy.

A cocktail hour proceeded the dinner; I paid the bartender for two glasses of merlot and left him a generous tip. He was one of my students and would likely brand me a cheapskate to his classmates if I hadn't. I brought the glass over to Laura who was chatting with her friend Sarah Whitaker, the head of the city's law library and a stylishly dressed woman with frosted blond hair.

"Andy, I'd like you to meet my friend, Carla Burnham. She's with the public defender's office," said Sarah.

"Pleased to meet you; what brings you to the dinner tonight?"

"Sarah dragooned me," replied Carla.

We all laughed. "How long have you been with the public defender's office?"

"I returned home to Norfolk last year after my divorce; fortunately there was an opening."

Our meeting appeared to be a lucky break; I needed someone to guide me through the maze of the public defender's office. "Have you been following the case of my graduate student?"

She laughed. "We were speculating in the office on Friday morning if Mr. Healy would be in need of our services."

"Brendan can't afford a lawyer; like all graduate students he's up to his neck in debt. Do you know who'll be assigned his case?"

"One of the senior defenders qualified to handle murder cases. Do you know when they've scheduled his arraignment?"

"Thursday afternoon."

"Why so late?"

"The victim's parents plan to attend."

Carla shook her head. "That will be a nasty confrontation."

"I'm trying to help Brendan; the police have botched the investigation of Jenny's death from the start."

"I hate to sound cynical but all our clients say the police have arrested the wrong man."

"Would it be possible for me to meet with Brendan's lawyer when he's assigned one? I've identified two possible suspects that someone needs to pursue."

"Everyone is pretty stressed for time in our office. I don't want to disillusion you but in most murder cases working out a plea bargain is the best course of action. With a plea bargain for second degree murder, he could be released in thirty years. From the stories in the paper, it looks like the commonwealth's attorney is angling for first degree murder. If Healy goes to trial, he gets a life sentence and dies in prison."

Thirty years for a murder he didn't commit was no bargain for Brendan. The public defenders were under pressure to clear their caseloads quickly; whether justice was served in the process was another question. "When I visited Brendan at the jail today, he said they were threatening to charge him with rape."

Carla took a sip of her wine. "They usually don't pursue a rape charge without solid DNA evidence; the commonwealth's attorney may be brandishing it as a bargaining chip."

Brendan's future had been reduced to a red plastic chip tossed down on the table during a poker game.

"Can I call you tomorrow to find out who's been assigned Brendan's case?"

She fished in her purse and handed me her business card. "Sure."

Sarah took Carla to meet some other friends. Out of the corner of my eye, I saw Tollie Monroe coming my way.

"I just met with Doug Clayton and Harley Simpson," he greeted me.

"I'm surprised I wasn't invited."

"You're too closely aligned with Healy; Simpson is afraid you're a conduit to his defense attorney."

"Brendan doesn't have an attorney yet."

"How do you know that?"

"I visited him at the jail this afternoon."

"I warned you to distance yourself from him! Healy is a psychopath; he raped that girl before strangling her."

"Harley Simpson is misinterpreting the evidence and drawing the wrong conclusions."

"Doug Clayton wants this whole affair off the front page quickly."

"You should be talking to Barry Sanders not me."

Tollie's face turned red. "You can best help the university by convincing Healy to accept a plea bargain."

CHAPTER XXIV

Monday morning I opened the *Register*. *Love Triangle Led to Murder* was the morning's headline. Inside on page four, the article featured a color photo of Brendan and Jenny at the beach. Clad only in their swimsuits, the photo showed off their buff bodies to perfection. Next to it was a photo of Tiffany Finley, courtesy of her *Facebook* page, clad in a tight red bikini looking every inch a temptress. Tossing journalistic ethics aside, Saltzman named Tiffany as the other woman who Brendan turned to for consolation as his relationship with Jenny soured.

My gut instinct told me that Barry Sanders served as the conduit for the lead on Tiffany. But someone else tipped Sanders off. Who was behind the effort to smear Brendan? Or was Tiffany Finley actually the object of the smear campaign? Young women were often vicious toward their rivals; I wouldn't put it past a competitor for a coveted spot in a sorority to make Tiffany the target of a venomous attack. It might be worth paying Barry a visit and try to smoke him out.

After my class, I called Carla Burnham. Her voice mail message indicated she was in court and wouldn't return until the afternoon. I went upstairs to chat with Jake Ruiz about the stalking incident that Brendan had mentioned.

"I'm sorry to hear about what happened on Friday night," Jake greeted me.

"We only invited Brendan and his mother for pizza. Before the night was over, my family ended up with guns in our faces. What can you tell me about the stalking incident in your department last year?"

He hesitated for a moment. I'd feared that he wouldn't be able to tell me much due to the confidentiality of student disciplinary actions. "Why do you ask?" Jake replied.

"Just before he was arrested, Brendan told me the stalker delivered a pizza to Jenny's apartment on Monday afternoon and made a cheap remark to her. Jenny indicated that he'd been a student in her class as well as the girl he'd been stalking."

"A freshman in Jenny's macro class last fall began receiving erotic text messages from an unknown individual. She reported them to the campus police. The poor girl became frightened out of her wits when a florist delivered flowers to her dorm room. Shortly afterwards the stalker sent her a photo of his genitals just like that quarterback. It took the police two months to track him down; all the time he sat behind her in Jenny's class."

"What is the stalker's name?"

"Leo Plaskett. Why do you think he's connected to Jenny's murder?"

"It seems a weird coincidence he delivers a pizza to Jenny's apartment and two hours later she's dead."

Jake nodded in agreement. "I've been so distraught over Jenny's death I'd put the stalking incident out of my mind."

"How did he get out of jail so quickly?"

"He received a suspended sentence in a plea agreement that requires him to undergo counseling. The university expelled him; he's not permitted to set foot on campus."

"Did the police think he was capable of murder?"

"The young man has an inferiority complex related to his short stature. Chief Simpson never warned us he had violent tendencies."

Harley Simpson was familiar with Plaskett; the fact that he was at Jenny's apartment on the day of the murder should give him pause.

"When he delivered the pizza to my house on Friday night; I noticed he was wearing one of Art Campbell's anti-globalization T-shirts."

"Plaskett went with Art's group to Washington to demonstrate at last year's IMF meeting. Art saw Plaskett's arrest as a conspiracy led by Doug Clayton to muzzle his little band of protesters."

"We should be so lucky!"

Jake laughed.

I went down the hall to Art Campbell's office hoping he could shed more light on Leo Plaskett. His door was open and I appraised his new oriental rug. As Cynthia Wallach had indicated, it was a definite improvement over the multi-colored shag rug that had festered in his office for over twenty years.

"Nice rug, I didn't know you were an oriental carpet aficionado."

"What can I do for you?" Art put down the journal he was reading; he seemed annoyed by my presence. Normally he took my ribbing good naturedly; I decided not to chide him about buying the rug at Wal-Mart.

"Jake told me Leo Plaskett is a member of your anti-globalization group."

"What about it?"

"Confidentially, Plaskett may have knowledge of Jenny Biggio's murder. He delivered a pizza to her apartment shortly before she was killed; Brendan overheard him make a crude remark to her."

Art ran his hand through his graying beard. "They crucified Leo because he stood up for the rights of workers around the world; Doug Clayton wants to silence me in order to court favor with the military-industrial complex that runs this state. All he's concerned about is getting research dollars out of the Department of Defense."

I suppressed laughing at Art linking the arrest of Plaskett to the university's strategic plan for increasing research funding; that was typical of his rants.

"The student he stalked was in Jenny's class."

"Only Healy has a motive for Jenny's murder; he knocked up her and wouldn't take responsibility for it. I overheard their argument on Monday morning; Maureen told Healy to leave or she'd call the campus police. Don't try to pin it on Leo!"

Knowing nothing about stalkers, I realized I might be making a big leap regarding Plaskett's involvement in Jenny's murder. Plaskett had sent sexually explicit text messages to the girl he stalked. Sitting in Jenny's class all semester; was it possible he secretly desired Jenny too? Did everything come together for Plaskett the night he delivered the pizza to her apartment? Other than a pizza long since eaten, I had no physical evidence to link him to the murder.

Could Plaskett have followed Jenny to the library and lay in wait for her? Everything hinged on what Jenny saw outside the library that night when she looked out the window. If Henrietta Sealy was right, something infuriated Jenny that made her storm out of the library. Did Plaskett follow her to Jordan Hall when she mistakenly went to confront Brendan? Instead Jenny reached the sixth floor only to find it deserted. When she turned to leave, did she find Plaskett standing there?

If the graduate students' office had been left unlocked, Plaskett could have forced Jenny into the room and strangled her. Harley's scenario stated Brendan strangled Jenny and moved her body across the hall to the women's restroom after ten o'clock. Otherwise her body would've been discovered when the seminar's participants took a bathroom break. Plaskett could easily fill Brendan's shoes in Harley's scenario except I couldn't figure out why he'd bother to move the body to the restroom later unless he'd been trapped in the office by the arrival of the seminar's participants.

After my noon swim, I had a yen for pizza and walked to the run-down strip mall across from campus that in addition to Vito's Pizzeria featured a tattoo parlor, a laundromat, a used bookstore, a tanning salon, and a copy shop. The University Plaza was a thorn in the side of Doug Clayton's beautification efforts; he wanted to turn the area across the street into Norfolk's version of Harvard Square with chic boutiques and trendy restaurants. Unlike Harvard, most CBU students were from middle class backgrounds and didn't have money to burn; a pizza from Vito's was a splurge for most of them.

I put in my order for two slices of pizza topped with anchovies and sat at a battered table by the window to read my magazine. Sipping my root beer, I scanned the restaurant for Leo Plaskett; he must've been out on a delivery. Just as my number was called by the counterman, Leo elbowed past me to pick up a stack of delivery tickets by the oven; he sorted through them and put them in order. He sipped from a water bottle and chatted with the cashier while waiting for the pizzas to finish cooking.

Plaskett was rather short; no more than five feet, five inches tall. As Jake had mentioned, his height, or lack of it, was the source of his psychological problems. I pretended to read my magazine while observing him. Despite his short stature, he was well muscled, he looked like he could've been a wrestler in high school. He would've had no trouble over powering Jenny Biggio. I counted three piercings in his right ear and two in his left. A Celtic tribal tattoo circled his left arm above the elbow; his right arm was engulfed in tattooed flames from elbow to his wrist. His T-shirt appeared to be strategically ripped to allow the ring piercing his right nipple to poke out. Vito handed Plaskett several pizza boxes and two hoagies; as Plaskett walked out the door, he looked me over and tried to place me. As he backed out of the parking space, I nonchalantly wrote down the number of the license plate of his aging Toyota in the margin of my magazine. Most likely it was a hand-me-down from his parents who also paid for the lawyer to keep him out of jail.

After finishing my lunch, I went back to my office and typed up my observations on Plaskett. It was too early to pay him a visit and rattle his cage; I didn't want to tip him off that I considered him a "person of interest" (to use the police euphemism) in Jenny's murder. If he wasn't the murderer, I didn't want to alienate him since he could confirm Brendan's presence in Jenny's apartment on Monday afternoon.

In mid-afternoon, I picked up the phone and called Ms. Burnham again.

"Carla Burnham," she answered on the third ring.

"This is Andrew Stanard; do you know who's been assigned to defend Brendan Healy?"

"When I returned from court this afternoon, I found I'd been assigned his case."

"I thought his case would be assigned to someone more senior in your office."

She laughed. "I was a bit disingenuous last night; I didn't mention that I'm one of the senior public defenders. Although I've been with the Norfolk office a little over a year, I handled numerous murder cases during my tenure with the public defender's office in Richmond."

"My apologies; I was wondering if we could meet to discuss Brendan's case."

"I'm meeting with him tomorrow morning to discuss his arraignment; I'm booked the rest of the day."

"Could I meet you for lunch?"

Carla paused for a minute. "If Mr. Healy objects to my discussing his case with you, the meeting is off. I have a preliminary hearing scheduled in Circuit Court at 1:30; we can meet at 12:30 at the Courthouse Pub downtown."

"I'll be there."

"I haven't had much time to review Mr. Healy's file. From what I've so far, it's not hard to see why the police zeroed in on him as a suspect. When a pregnant woman is killed; it's usually the boyfriend who did it."

"That's why we need to meet."

After finishing with Carla Burnham, I called the Biology Department, "Melinda Kroger please."

"I'll transfer you."

"Botany lab, Melinda speaking."

"I'm Dr. Stanard from the History Department, Julia Adams's neighbor. I was wondering if I could meet with you. I'm trying to help Brendan Healy." I held my breath; I wasn't sure how she'd react. Someone aiding the accused killer might be the last person she wanted to talk with.

"I'm not sure there's much more I could tell you," she replied.

"Whatever you tell me will be kept confidential."

"I'll be home from my yoga session around 5:30. Can you stop by my apartment?"

Normally I would've preferred to meet her in my office or a neutral location like the Student Union but I wanted to see the apartment since it was where Jenny and Brendan were last together. "Where is your apartment?"

"It's over in Jefferson Terrace, 1321 79th Street, second floor."

"Dave Chen would like to speak with you," said Janet as she poked her head in the door.

"Sure," I replied.

Dave came in carrying several library books; he settled his lanky frame in a chair after I motioned for him to sit down. "I heard you visited Brendan. How's he doing?"

"What do you think?"

"It must be pretty grim even for an ex-con. I found these books in his room; I thought you could turn them over to your wife so she can clear his record."

"Brendan could get an additional ten years for being a library scofflaw."

Dave laughed. Locked in his cell, I doubted Brendan found anything to laugh about.

"Brendan's share of the rent is only paid through the end of the month. Hank has a friend who needs a place to live."

Halloween was next week. My efforts could take months to uncover the evidence necessary to free him. It might even come down to convincing a jury that reasonable doubt exists. As much as I hated to admit it, there appeared little chance of Brendan being home by Christmas or even Easter. "He'll understand."

"The police carted off a lot of his belongings on Friday night; they even took his bike and computer. We're going to put what remains under the eaves."

"I'm planning to go see him on Wednesday; I'll tell him."

"Thanks."

***

Jenny's former apartment was located several blocks from Brendan's house; the block was showing signs of gentrification chiefly because it dead ended at an inlet of the Elizabeth River. The houses situated on the inlet had been renovated by developers hoping to flip them and make a quick profit. Her apartment was in a post World War I house that had likely been divided into apartments during Norfolk's World War II housing shortage. I rang the door bell and a few seconds later Melinda, still dressed for yoga in sweat pants and a T-shirt, came down the stairs and let me in. Melinda's low cut, sleeveless shirt allowed a full viewing of her tattoos. At the memorial service I'd missed a second butterfly that spanned her cleavage.

"I've already told everything to the police. They asked me not to speak to the media; that pesky reporter has been here twice trying to get in and look over the apartment," said Melinda as I followed her upstairs.

Jenny and Melinda's apartment was tidier than the house Brendan shared with his three friends. They'd made an effort to decorate the combined living and dining room in a style Laura's magazines described as second hand chic. Several plants added to the room's warmth.

Melinda picked up a bottle of water and took a sip before sitting down on the couch. I took an arm chair across from her.

"I'm trying to help clear Brendan but I know very little about Jenny; I thought you could give me a fresh perspective. Something that seems insignificant may be a key to solving her murder. The police may be overlooking important evidence."

"I find it hard to believe Brendan murdered Jenny. She fell hard for him; it was a mutual attraction. Jenny took him home to meet her parents; she never did that with any of her other boyfriends."

"She had other boyfriends?"

"Jenny's boyfriends all came from the same mold; they were tall, athletic, blond, and blue eyed. At Kent State she dated a soccer player named Paul for almost two years; shortly after we started rooming together he came to Virginia Beach for a long weekend. Jenny said the sex was great but she now found him a little vapid; he must have headed the ball a few times too many."

I chuckled.

"Lance Mattingly was almost a clone of Paul; he was a grad student in electrical engineering. He was a surfer from Virginia Beach; I'd never seen anyone so tanned in my life. Jenny always joked he left sand on the sheets when he slept over."

"Where is he now?" Jenny and Melissa appeared to be close friends for Jenny to have shared the details of her love life.

"After he graduated, he moved out to San Diego."

"In search of the perfect wave?"

Melinda laughed. "Next she dated Tomasz Podolski, a Polish graduate student, for over two years. After he finished his doctorate in econ, he took a job with a bank in New York."

"What ended the relationship?"

"Jenny ended it when she found out Tomasz was screwing a Polish girl at Pratt Institute. She put a lot into that relationship and was hoping to marry him; he was just interested in the fringe benefits."

"Do you know anyone who would be jealous that she started dating Brendan?"

"No, although there was a strange incident in February that I forgot to mention to the police; it didn't seem relevant at the time."

"What happened?" This was about the same time as the stalking incident; could it be connected?

"My yoga session was cancelled and I came home earlier than usual. The door to Jenny's bedroom was closed; she was definitely in bed with someone. A few minutes later she came out and pretended she'd been taking a nap. Jenny and I always respected each other's privacy so I didn't press her about it. Her friend didn't want to be seen; he remained in the bedroom."

"Was that unusual?"

"Jenny was never shy about her sex life; Tomasz often spent the night here. So did Brendan; she complained his house was like making love in the middle of Grand Central Terminal."

"What happened next?"

"I took a shower; it had been a long day. When I was in the bathroom, I heard the door close. I looked out the bathroom window and saw a blond guy drive away in a BMW."

"A BMW, are you sure?"

"I'd noticed it earlier when I drove up; a brand new car like that sticks out on our block. It was a dark blue sedan. A graduate student can't afford a $60,000 car."

"Nor can many college professors. Did you ever see the car again?"

"No."

"Did you recognize him?"

"I only saw the back of him as he climbed in the car."

Who was Jenny's visitor? Was he another potential suspect?

"Did it seem out of character for Jenny?"

Melinda took a swig of water. "Jenny never pretended to be a virgin nor was she the type to be a notch on someone's bedpost either."

"Father Novello mentioned yesterday that Jenny seemed distracted last spring."

"She was upset after breaking up with Tomasz; she'd invested a lot in that relationship. Most of her friends from high school and college were married; one friend already had two little girls. Jenny definitely felt her biological clock was ticking away."

Melinda's statement might lead the police to conclude that Jenny became pregnant to trap Brendan into marriage lending credence to their theory he killed her in a rage.

"Was Brendan ever abusive to Jenny?"

"Never in my presence," replied Melinda.

"I'm curious, how did you and Jenny come to share an apartment?"

"She posted the apartment with the Off-Campus Housing Office; I responded to the listing. She was cool with me being a lesbian. Brendan too, we even had sex once."

Melinda's casual admission hit me like a ton of bricks. She smiled at my bewilderment.

"It's complicated; I stray from the faith occasionally."

"Did Jenny know?" I blurted out.

"I never told her; neither did Brendan. We'd hooked up two years ago before he'd started dating Jenny; I wasn't living with Jenny at the time. My girlfriend had shipped out on a six month Med cruise. I was feeling lonely and met Brendan at a party; one thing led to another and I bedded him."

"Did Brendan know you were a lesbian?"

"He's not blind. Brendan was nothing more than a big blond vibrator. If I'd cheated with another woman; it would've gotten back to Jesse. Our relationship is complicated enough."

"Don't ask; don't tell?"

"The Navy is on a witch hunt against lesbians. Jesse and I can't live together; we have to be careful when we're together in public since she's an officer."

I suddenly thought of Amanda Saltzman digging around the fringes of Jenny and Brendan's lives in search of a new angle to keep the story in play. "Did anyone see you leave the party together?"

"Who'd remember something that happened over two years ago?"

"People have long memories." It sounded like parties from my graduate student days. The couplings of Friday and Saturday nights were bantered around till the next round of parties the following weekend. If anyone recalled the events of that evening, it would be further trouble for Brendan. His one night stand with Melinda reinforced the police's contention that he killed Jenny because she was pregnant and their forced marriage would've hampered his pursuit of other women.

"Brendan said he spent Monday afternoon here with Jenny."

"I spent Monday night at Jesse's apartment; her ship went out for two weeks of training exercises the next morning."

"That's why you didn't sound the alarm when Jenny failed to come home on Monday night."

Melinda nodded. "After leaving Jesse's, I went straight to campus. The police tracked me down later in the morning to inform me of Jenny's murder and asked for permission to search the apartment. They went through everything."

"Did the police find Jenny's laptop in the apartment?"

"The police asked me if I knew where it was. Apparently it's still missing."

"Interesting," I muttered.

"Jenny's parents are coming at the end of the week to pack her things up and take them back to Ohio."

"That will be hard for them."

Melinda began sobbing. "With her things still here, it seems like she only went out for the evening. Jenny accepted me for who I was; she never judged me. Everything is unraveling; I'm afraid that Jesse could be dragged into this mess."

"Why would your girlfriend be involved?"

"The detective asked where I was on Monday night. I told him I spent the night with my boyfriend; he was going out to sea for two weeks. My heart dropped when he asked what ship he was on and I misled him."

"How?"

"I told him my boyfriend, Lieutenant Jesse Brooks, is assigned to the *Truman*; I never bothered to set the record straight that Jesse is a woman."

"With Brendan behind bars, it seems doubtful that the police will dig any further."

"Jesse is close to getting discharged from the Navy; she's coming to Texas A & M with me and going back to school for her MBA. They'll take away her veteran's benefits if she's dishonorably discharged."

At this point the police had no interest in where she spent Monday night. However Amanda Saltzman still posed a threat to Melinda and Jesse.

I thanked Melinda for talking with me and headed for home. Since it was close to six o'clock, I took a detour and stopped by the Ark Church. Sitting in the parking lot, I watched the homeless men and women lining up for the soup and prayer supper. At the back of the line, Felton Snyder talked with another man.

Melinda confirmed that Jenny's laptop was missing; that pointed to Snyder. He had lied to implicate Brendan as the one who left Jenny's wallet in the alley. Snyder sold the credit card to Antonio McKinney, why not the laptop too? If Snyder didn't take Jenny's laptop, then who did?

CHAPTER XXV

I'D FAILED TO FOLLOW THROUGH with my threat on Sunday to cancel my subscription to the *Register* so the newspaper was on my front porch on Tuesday morning as usual. "NJ Police Reopen Investigation of CBU Murder Suspect" read the large headline. Amanda Saltzman managed to keep her byline on the front page for the seventh straight day. With Brendan's arraignment set for Thursday, she was shooting to extend her streak through Friday.

"Police in Kearny, New Jersey are taking a second look into the death of Brendan Healy's father. Arrested for the strangulation murder of CBU coed Jennifer Biggio, Healy killed his father fourteen years ago during a fight. Allegedly Healy's father forced his way into the house and attempted to assault his wife. Healy came to his mother's defense and knocked his father down the stairs in the ensuing scuffle, claiming he'd no other choice. Kearny Police investigated the incident and decided not to press charges against Healy considering his father's history of domestic violence."

"'We had no reason to doubt his mother's version of the events of that evening,' stated Sergeant Vincent Milkowski of the Kearny Police Department. 'The toxicology tests from Mike Healy's autopsy confirmed that he had a high blood alcohol limit the night he died.'"

"According to a neighbor, Ida O'Reilly, Healy long had a turbulent relationship with his father. Brendan hated his father for deserting the family and shacking up with a topless dancer."

"Colleen Healy received a financial windfall after her husband's death; she was the beneficiary of his union life insurance policy and also received his social security benefits. Mike Healy was in arrears on his child support payments; he was worth more to her dead than alive."

"'We're looking into the possibility that Healy goaded his father into a fight. A muscular fifteen year old like Brendan would've been able to manhandle a drunk and kick him down the stairs,' speculated Sergeant Milkowski."

"'Brendan was always closer to his mother. Colleen always stepped in to protect him from his father. He didn't shed any tears at his father's funeral,' said Mrs. O'Reilly."

Amanda Saltzman cunningly linked her interviews with Sergeant Milkowski and Ida O'Reilly to insinuate that Brendan was manipulated by his mother to murder his father. Ida O'Reilly's reminisces were likely total fabrications. It was convenient that she was suffering from Alzheimer's disease; she was too disoriented to cry foul if she believed she'd been misquoted.

"What's in the paper?" Laura yawned as she plodded into the kitchen.

"According to Amanda Saltzman, Colleen Healy manipulated Brendan to kill his father."

I handed Laura the paper; she quickly read the story and laughed. Not quite the reaction I expected.

"As the mother of two teenage boys, I can't get either of them to take out the trash. Motherly influence ends when boys turn ten; any mother reading that story will find it utterly preposterous that Brendan's mother directed him to murder his father."

"Sergeant Milkowski is taking it seriously."

"I'm sure it's distressing for Colleen; her husband is coming back from the grave to haunt her. His abusive behavior must've been documented in the restraining order."

For each person like Laura who laughed at the story, there was another person who'd believe it. Even if Mike Healy's death was not admissible as evidence, the story would've already poisoned the subconscious of potential jurors.

***

Distracted by my upcoming lunch with Brendan's lawyer, I made a classic teaching mistake and returned the mid-term exams at the start of class. Dismayed by their low grades and pondering the prospect of flunking the semester, the class tuned out my lecture.

After class, I told Janet I had a lunch appointment downtown. I found a parking space on a side street near the courthouse and fed the meter. The Courthouse Pub was already crowded with jurors wearing ID badges and lawyers in dark blue suits talking on their cell phones. At Laura's urging, I'd worn my pin striped suit again so I would look like I belonged at the courthouse. Carla Burnham hadn't arrived yet and I took a table near the door so she could spot me.

Looking out the window, I spotted a dark blue BMW parked in front of the courthouse. Finding the man who Melinda Kroger had seen leaving her apartment wouldn't be easy; it appeared that he'd no connection to the university by the car he drove. My gut instinct told me he didn't want to be seen because he was married. Where had Jenny met him?

The usual places where someone met a member of the opposite sex no longer applied today. After breaking up with Tomasz, she could have started a cyber romance in a chat room. Jenny was too smart to use her university email account for such activities; it was more likely she used an anonymous email account for her liaisons. Harley Simpson could easily retrieve her email messages from her university account and probably had already reviewed them. With her laptop still missing it would be almost impossible for the police to find and access her other email accounts.

The liaison may have run its course; she ended it and took up with Brendan. Her ex-lover, angered at being dumped, could have watched Jenny and Brendan's relationship from afar and waited to take his revenge. Jenny's missing laptop supported the theory that an ex-lover was responsible for her murder. He kept Jenny's laptop or destroyed to prevent any incriminating files, photos or email messages falling into the hands of the police.

"Good afternoon Dr. Stanard," said Carla Burnham as she took the seat across from me and picked up the menu. Her taut navy blue suit showed off her figure, the end product of many hours of hard work in the gym. She looked at her reflection in the window and ran her fingers through her frosted hair in an effort to neaten it up.

"How did your meeting with Brendan go?"

"The commonwealth's attorney is playing hardball; she's arraigning him for rape and first degree murder on Thursday. If he'll plead guilty, she'll recommend a 40 year sentence to the judge. A jury is likely to give him a life sentence without parole."

"What's the difference?"

Carla looked up from the menu. "With time off for good behavior, he'd be out by the time he turns sixty-three if he accepts the plea bargain. He dies in prison with a life sentence. It's the best deal he's going to get under the circumstances."

Carla Burnham seemed too eager to accept the commonwealth attorney's offer.

"May I take you order?" interrupted the waitress.

"I'll have the chicken salad on a croissant and a cup of coffee," replied Carla.

"I'll have the Philly cheese steak and ice tea."

"What did Brendan think about the deal?" I asked after the waitress left.

"He refused to consider it; I warned him it's only going to be on the table for a short period of time."

"They have no evidence; their star witness, Felton Snyder, is a wino who lied to save his own skin." I passed Carla copies of the articles I'd collected on Snyder; she quickly scanned them.

"That's helpful to attack Snyder's credibility; but it doesn't clear Healy."

"What if I told you Snyder was a suspect in a brutal murder twenty years ago down in High Point?"

"It's not admissible in court. The police claim they have strong forensic evidence proving Brendan's guilt; Snyder isn't vital to their case."

"What if I told you there was a connection between Jenny Biggio and Snyder? He may've have killed her."

Carla sighed wearily. "Do you have any evidence linking him to the killing?"

"His fingerprints are on Jenny's credit card."

"So are Healy's fingerprints."

"Snyder's story about seeing Brendan dump the wallet in the alley is a total fabrication. I went by the alley yesterday; the only light in the alley looked like it had been broken for years. There was no way Snyder could've seen Brendan ride by on a bicycle; I doubt he was even sober at the time."

"Why do you think Snyder killed Jenny?"

"Jenny tutored students at the Ark Church; Snyder took advantage of Pastor Franklin's soup and prayer suppers. He saw her there and …"

"Good afternoon Carla."

I recognized Nick Papadakis from his television commercials. Despite being close to sixty, his jet black hair was complemented by an unlined face thanks to his plastic surgeon. Carla Burnham looked like she'd rather have a raccoon rummaging around in her garage. Papadakis eyed me suspiciously; my pin striped suit made him believe I was an out of town lawyer muscling in on his turf.

"Good afternoon Nick, this is Dr. Andrew Stanard, chairman of the CBU history department. Nick extended his hand. "I'm pleased to meet you." From the expression on his face, I doubted it.

"I'm defending Dr. Stanard's graduate student, the one accused of murder."

"I've been following the case in the newspaper; it looks like you're defending another loser. My offer is still on the table; I have several lucrative personal injury cases coming up and can use a good trial lawyer like you."

"As I said before, I'm happy in the public defender's office."

"That I doubt," Papadakis said as he turned and walked away.

"Unfortunately Brendan doesn't have a nice pair of tits like Tandi Brooks; otherwise Nick might have been interested in taking his case."

"He was screwing the grieving widow?"

"Nick has a couch in his office; he gives all his female clients a discount on their bills for services rendered. After her acquittal, Tandi dumped Nick. She's now living in Miami with a bronzed Adonis she plucked off a South Beach lifeguard stand."

"What does Nick's wife think about his pro bono work?" Mrs. Papadakis was a high profile real estate agent in Virginia Beach.

Carla laughed. "She's banging the thirty-something tennis pro at the country club. Women with money, like Tandi Brooks and Leona Papadakis, don't have to play by the rules."

The waitress put our plates on the table.

"Nick only wants me to join his firm so he can get in my panties; being divorced, he figures I'm easy prey."

Carla's frankness surprised me; I took a bite of my sandwich figuring that was the safer course of action. "Do you see Brendan's case as a losing effort like Nick Papadakis?"

"The rape charge is going to be hard to knock down; Brendan handed the commonwealth's attorney his DNA evidence on a silver platter."

She reached into her briefcase on the chair next to her and pulled out a file. "In addition to Brendan's semen and pubic hairs being found on Jenny; the police found skin under her fingernails. Before his arrest, the police photographed these scratches on his neck and back."

I took the file from Carla. The police had photographed Brendan stripped to his boxers; they took several close up shots of the scratches on his back. Another set of photos focused on his jailhouse tattoo.

"Was Brendan's skin under her fingernails?"

"DNA testing of the skin, hair and fluid samples will take several weeks."

"If Brendan raped Jenny in his office, why would he have undressed? It suggests Jenny scratched his back when they had sex at her apartment earlier in the afternoon."

"You have a point; rapists usually don't get undressed. They drop their pants at most."

"I've found a witness that could prove that Brendan spent Monday afternoon in Jenny's apartment. There's one problem; he might be the killer."

Carla put down her croissant. "What?"

"Leo Plaskett delivered a pizza to Jenny's apartment on Monday afternoon."

"Did Plaskett see Brendan?"

"No, Brendan was still in the bedroom."

"That might be enough to undermine the rape charge; Brendan wouldn't have known that Plaskett delivered the pizza if he hadn't been there. Jenny's autopsy would confirm she ate pizza just before she died. What merits Mr. Plaskett being added to your suspect list?"

"He'd been convicted of stalking a student in Jenny's class last year. Brendan said Plaskett made a sexually suggestive remark to Jenny. He could have followed her to campus after Brendan left"

Carla rubbed her chin. "Stalkers often harbor violent sexual fantasies. It might be worth subpoenaing Plaskett as a witness; the police will have to release his criminal record. "

"His plea deal required him to undergo psychiatric evaluation."

"I'll subpoena his counselor's files; they'll make interesting reading. Like you, I find it disturbing that the police failed to investigate other suspects."

"Melinda Kroger, Jenny's roommate, told me Jenny had a liaison with a visitor in March who went to great lengths not to be seen. He hid in Jenny's bedroom until Melinda took a shower."

"No doubt a married man, was she screwing Brendan at that time?"

"That was about two months before Jenny became involved with Brendan."

"What makes you think Jenny ended that relationship when she became involved with Brendan?"

Carla Burnham made a point I hadn't considered. Melinda said Jenny fell hard for Brendan; it didn't necessarily mean the other relationship had run its course. Father Novello said Jenny seemed troubled during the spring; her relationship with a married man may have bothered her conscience. Who put an end to the affair?

"If Jenny told her married friend to get lost, he may not have taken it well and killed her."

"It cuts both ways. If the police discover she was two-timing Brendan, it bolsters their theory he killed her in a rage. During the autopsy, they tested the DNA of the fetus. If it comes back that Brendan is not the father, being cuckolded is a strong motive for Brendan killing Jenny."

Even if I discovered the identity of the mystery man, there was a possibility it might hurt Brendan rather than help him. It might be better if he wasn't found.

"Was Brendan aware of Jenny's gentleman caller?" asked Carla.

"Melinda saw him at a distance getting into his car and briefly at that."

"Did she get a good look at the car?"

"No, it was a dark blue BMW like that one." I pointed to the one across the street from the restaurant.

Carla laughed. "Half the lawyers in Norfolk drive that model. Did she mention it to the police?"

"I don't think so."

"Maybe a nosy neighbor saw your mystery man coming and going from Jenny's apartment. I doubt the police canvassed Jenny's neighborhood since the murder was committed on campus."

"A BMW like that would stick out in Jefferson Terrace."

"It looks like Jenny had a sugar daddy."

"Whoever killed Jenny still has her laptop."

"If he murdered her to cover up his extra-marital affair he would have ditched it in the Elizabeth River by now. How well do you know Brendan?"

"He's been my student for almost six years now."

"You never realized he was conning you about his past?"

"Why?"

"Like anyone who's done time; Healy is good at manipulating people. I'll be candid with you; I'm not 100% convinced he's innocent. You've put some possible suspects on the table but you've produced no compelling evidence that would cause a jury to have reasonable doubt about Brendan's guilt. Sure, something smells about the deal Felton Snyder cut with the police; all plea deals stink. But that's not enough to derail the commonwealth attorney's case; I've seen people convicted with a lot less evidence than the police have produced so far. I'll see you at the arraignment on Thursday."

With Carla due in court in ten minutes, we settled our bills with the waitress. I watched her long legs carry her across the street in several quick strides to the entrance of the courthouse. It disturbed me that

Carla was skeptical of Brendan's innocence and didn't believe it was her job to find Jenny's killer.

I had nothing pressing waiting for me in the office so I decided to walk over to the convention center.

"Can I help you?" asked the African-American security guard seated behind a desk at the loading dock entrance. His crisply pressed uniform and close cropped gray hair suggested he'd spent time in the military; no one was going to slip past him and enter the building.

For what it was worth, I handed him my business card. He seemed surprised I wasn't a salesman. "I'm a friend of Brendan Healy."

"I'm Cal Norton." He extended his hand to shake mine. "I'm an ex-Marine like Brendan; I spent thirty years in the Corps."

"This is your retirement job?"

"After my wife passed away two years ago; I was bored sitting around the house and playing golf."

"Were you on duty last Monday night?"

"Why do you ask?"

"The police claim Brendan drove Jenny's car to work that night. I figured someone saw he rode his bike that night as he always did."

"Brendan chains his bike to that standpipe." He pointed to the end of the loading dock.

"Would you be willing to talk to the police?"

"I already have; a detective stopped by last Wednesday. He talked to the banquet manager and searched Brendan's locker; the maintenance man cut the lock off. Last Monday was my night off; a temp guard filled in."

"Did he see Brendan chain up his bike?"

"It's doubtful." Cal bent his elbow to simulate taking a drink.

Even if the boozing guard remembered anything; he wasn't a reliable witness to challenge to the police's theory that Brendan drove Jenny's car to the convention center the night of the murder.

"Can you give me a call if you hear anything? You have my card."

"Sure thing, Brendan talked all the time about that girl. There was no way he murdered her."

Leaving downtown I was stopped at a traffic light and noticed a dark blue BMW like the one Melinda described parked two blocks up the street. A tall blond haired man walked up to the car; a turning truck momentarily blocked my view as he disappeared into the car. Despite only getting a brief glimpse of his back; he looked vaguely familiar. I caught up with the BMW at the next traffic light but the car's tinted windows shielded the driver from my view. My curiosity aroused, I decided to follow the car to get a better look at the driver on the off chance that he was Jenny's mysterious visitor.

Movies always make it look easy to tail a car; however it was hard to keep up with the car in the heavy traffic as well as not tipping off the driver that he was being followed. Luckily the car headed in the general direction of the university and I was on my home turf. Unexpectedly the car turned into Jefferson Terrace; was the driver trying to lose me? Five blocks later the BMW pulled into the parking lot of the Ark Church stopping in the space reserved for Pastor Franklin. The door opened and the sandy haired minister stepped out.

He looked in my direction; my car was all alone on the street across from the church's empty parking lot. I doubted he recognized me; we'd only exchanged a brief handshake at the reception following the memorial service. I grabbed my cell phone and pretended to make a call to allay his suspicions while I wrote down his license number. Even though several months had passed, Melinda might remember more details about the car she observed.

Although he knew Jenny from her tutoring at the church, Pastor Franklin was the last person I would've suspected of being her secretive visitor. It also explained why he didn't want to be seen.

Even though he was probably fifteen years older than Jenny, he was over six feet tall with an athletic build and sported a stylish goatee. At the memorial service, he'd worn a fitted Italian suit. It was easy to see why Jenny may've been attracted to him despite their age difference and the fact that he was married with three sons as I recalled from a feature story I'd read in the *Register*.

I had to tread carefully before I accused a respected member of the clergy of adultery much less murder. Nothing linked him to Jenny's murder; as Carla noted there were dozens of dark blue BMWs in Norfolk. The location of the murder suggested the killer was somehow connected to Jordan Hall and that seemed to rule out Pastor Franklin. Or did it?

***

Back at the office, I retrieved the article from the *Register's* website that ran on Father's Day about Pastor Franklin and the difficulties of his teenage sons growing up as preacher's kids. Charles Franklin had built his multi-racial congregation in an abandoned shopping center and tried to tackle the problems of Jefferson Terrace. He'd grown up the son of a wealthy businessman in Texas and found God while a student at Princeton; I speculated a trust fund paid for the BMW and his Italian suits. My gut instinct told me he was not the type who'd have an affair; however I'd seen too many colleagues during my career in academia involved in extra-marital entanglements and they never seemed like the type either.

Playing a hunch, I went to the university's web site. On the faculty roster for the Philosophy and Religious Studies Department, I found Dr. Charles S. Franklin, listed as an adjunct faculty member teaching World Religions. Philosophy was one floor below History in Jordan Hall! Reverend Franklin would've been familiar with the layout of Jordan Hall.

"There's a student to see you," interrupted Janet as she poked her head into my office.

"What's it in reference to? If it's another problem with a mid-term grade, refer them to their professor."

"He wouldn't say."

"Okay, show him in." Reverend Franklin would have to wait.

A few seconds later Leo Plaskett entered my office; he declined my offer to sit down and stood in front of my desk. If he'd been taller, I might have felt threatened by his hostile stance. "What are you trying to pull Dr. Stanard? I saw you watching me yesterday at Vito's."

"I eat lunch at Vito's at least once a week."

"Dr. Campbell said you're trying to pin Miss Biggio's murder on me."

"You may've been the last person to see her alive."

Plaskett glared at me. "How do you know that?"

"Brendan Healy was in the bedroom when you delivered the pizza to her apartment; he overheard the crude remark you made to her. What would your probation officer say about that? I don't think Vito would be too pleased about you propositioning his customers."

Plaskett's face reddened. "Who'd believe a murderer like Healy?"

"It would be in your best interest to go to the police and tell them you delivered a pizza to Jenny's apartment; otherwise Brendan's lawyer will have to call you as a witness at his trial. You don't want to be dragged through the media."

"I was delivering pizzas in Jefferson Terrace when she was murdered. Vito gives the dorm deliveries to the other drivers because I'm banned from campus."

"What are you doing here now?"

"Look, I sent a few emails to a girl and got expelled because she was a stuck up bitch who couldn't take a joke. So what if I delivered a pizza to that apartment; after I was convicted on that trumped up charge that was the only job I could get!" Plaskett stormed out of my office.

A few seconds Janet came into my office. "What was that all about?"

"He delivered a pizza to Jenny's apartment the afternoon she was murdered; Brendan said he made a sexually suggestive remark to her. Jake Ruiz indicated he'd been expelled for cyber stalking a student in one of Jenny's classes."

"Maureen told me all about that little pervert. Do you think he murdered Jenny?" asked Janet.

I should've figured that Maureen had briefed Janet; my trip upstairs to see Jake had been unnecessary.

"It's an odd coincidence that someone with Plaskett's history visited Jenny's apartment and an hour later she was murdered. Art Campbell had tipped Plaskett off about my suspicions."

"If Plaskett is a follower of Art Campbell, he definitely has a screw loose," laughed Janet.

I'd shown my hand too soon and needlessly antagonized a witness that could potentially clear Brendan. Or was Plaskett enraged because I was getting too close to the truth?

CHAPTER XXVI

"How was your lunch with Carla Burnham?" greeted Laura when I arrived home. She barely concealed her annoyance that I'd lunched with a woman other than herself.

"Nick Papadakis stopped by our table; he declared Brendan's case a losing effort."

"Carla needs to pull a raccoon out of her hat like Papadakis did to get Tandi Brooks acquitted," she laughed.

"It's going to take something like that to save Brendan from going to prison for the rest of his life." I decided not to take Laura into my confidence about my suspicions regarding Reverend Franklin until I had more conclusive evidence. If I had time after visiting Brendan on Wednesday afternoon, I planned to pay a call on the esteemed reverend.

"Why don't we watch the news; the casserole will be ready in about a half hour."

"Boeuf Bourguignon," I asked jokingly.

"You'd better head to Emily Worthington's house for dinner."

I poured two glasses of wine and turned on the television. Whoever had been watching the television last had left it on Channel 12; there was the omnipresent Amanda Saltzman standing in front of Jordan Hall. "Brendan Healy stands accused of strangling his pregnant girlfriend, Jenny Biggio. While involved with Miss Biggio, Healy simultaneously carried on an affair with Tiffany Finley, who was a student in the freshman history class he taught. Earlier this afternoon I confronted Miss Finley about her involvement with Jenny Biggio's killer."

The screen switched to Tiffany Finley striding across campus and Amanda Saltzman struggling to keep up with her long legged prey. Tiffany's skin tight jeans and painted on red sweater made her look every inch a temptress to the viewers at home; men have killed for less. "Miss Finley, the police have indicated that you spent Monday afternoon at Brendan Healy's apartment."

Tiffany kept on walking, ignoring Amanda Saltzman's calculated taunts. Her silence made it appear that she had something to hide.

"Brendan murdered Jenny Biggio. Can you tell me why you're protecting him?"

Suddenly Tiffany dissolved into tears. Another girl appeared on the screen, mostly likely a friend of Tiffany's, grabbed hold of her arm and pulled her into a side door at Jordan Hall and slammed the door in the pit bull's face.

The camera cut back to Amanda Saltzman live in front of Jordan Hall. "It disturbs me that Miss Finley is willing to shield a killer."

Barry Sanders and Art Campbell were chatting in the background as the camera panned the crowd standing behind Saltzman. Barry, who shared Art's left wing views, was a card carrying member of his anti-globalization cabal. I suspected that Art Campbell may've overheard my conversation with Harley Simpson in the locker room on Saturday morning. Either that or he'd observed Tiffany's exuberant hug of Brendan. Art, like everyone on campus, knew that Barry passed information to Amanda. He just had to tell Barry about Tiffany Finley and it would be in the *Register* the next day.

Art was such a contrarian it was always hard to fathom his motives; he may've merely been caught up in the excitement of the murder investigation that gripped CBU when he gossiped with Barry. Doug Clayton made no secret that Art's anti-globalization activities irked him and at one point told Tollie Monroe he wanted Art gone; although there was fat chance of that happening since Art had tenure as he enjoyed reminding Tollie at every opportunity. Jenny's murder was a major crisis for Doug Clayton. Art would perversely enjoy poking his finger in the president's eye by helping Amanda keep the story alive in the media. I doubted that Art bore any animosity toward Brendan; it was unlikely their paths had ever crossed. Getting back at Doug Clayton through Brendan made no sense except to someone as petty as Art who wore his grievances on his sleeve.

One thing was certain; Art was not Jenny's mystery lover. He drove a stolid Volvo manufactured by the good socialists in Sweden not a sleek BMW. At one Faculty Senate meeting when he railed against reserved parking spaces for senior university administrators, Art enumerated that gangsters, pimps, drug dealers, bankers and blood sucking academic bureaucrats drove BMWs.

"You need another glass of wine," said Laura as she picked up my empty glass and headed to the kitchen.

***

After my class on Wednesday morning, I reviewed the files of the finalists the search committee recommended for the department's vacancy in Asian history. I tried to read between the lines of the letters of recommendation to see if the committee had missed anything. One applicant looked quite impressive on paper due to his pedigree of a Ph.D. from a top flight program but the stilted English in his cover letter suggested he might have trouble communicating in the classroom. I made a note for the committee and recommended they delve further with his dissertation advisor.

"Chief Simpson is on line one," said Janet as she poked her head into my office.

"Good morning Harley."

"Look, I warned you to stay out of my investigation," Harley thundered.

"Excuse me, but what do you mean?"

"Leo Plaskett was just here; he claims you're harassing him and trying to make him the fall guy for Jenny Biggio's murder."

"I only stopped at Vito's on Monday for lunch."

"Don't try to blow smoke and obscure the facts; Healy murdered Jenny Biggio!"

"I think you have the facts all wrong; let me set you straight. Leo Plaskett delivered the pizzas to my house on Friday night. Your own surveillance team will confirm that. Brendan recognized Plaskett as the deliveryman who delivered more than a pizza to Jenny's apartment on Monday afternoon; Plaskett tried to hit on her."

"Healy wasn't in Biggio's apartment on Monday afternoon; he was screwing Tiffany Finley."

"If that's the case, how did Brendan know Plaskett delivered the pizza to Jenny's apartment?

"None of the pizza chains will risk delivering to Jefferson Terrace; Healy knows that only Vito's delivers in that neighborhood."

"Answer me how Brendan knew that Jenny snacked on pizza shortly before her death?"

There was a long silence; Harley knew that Jenny's last meal hadn't been divulged to the press. "A lucky guess, Plaskett never saw Healy."

"He was still in the bedroom!"

"Butt naked or not, if someone was hitting on my girlfriend, I would've come charging out of that bedroom and punched the bastard's lights out."

"It doesn't give you pause that a sex offender like Plaskett was in Jenny's apartment on Monday just an hour before she was strangled."

"Plaskett's lawyer arranged a plea bargain; he's not even on the sex offender registry. When we searched Jenny's apartment; we found the pizza box. We've already checked Plaskett out and dismissed him as a suspect. He was delivering pizzas in Jefferson Terrace at the time of Jenny's murder; Vito confirmed that. There's no evidence that Healy was in Biggio's apartment that afternoon; we even canvassed the neighbors."

"No one in Jefferson Terrace has ever seen anything during your investigations."

Harley chuckled. "The block Biggio lived on is a little different from the rest of JT; it's pretty much gentrified. One of the neighbors is a professor in the English department; Dr. Dealy was home that afternoon grading papers and never saw Healy. It's a dead end street; you notice people coming and going more so than on a through street."

"Brendan was on his bike; he wouldn't have been as noisy as a car."
From my visit to Vito's, Plaskett's battered Toyota sounded like a B-17

coming in for a crash landing. Harley didn't mention that Dr. Dealy had seen Plaskett.

"Dr. Dealy's study looks out at Jenny's front door; Healy had two chances to be spotted by her. If you count Plaskett not seeing him, it's three strikes against Healy."

I hung up in frustration; Harley refused to admit the obvious. There was no other way Brendan could've known that Plaskett delivered the pizza unless he'd been in Jenny's apartment that afternoon.

**

After lunch, I headed downtown to visit Brendan. The jail's waiting area was less crowded than on the weekend and I only had to wait fifteen minutes before Brendan was escorted in handcuffs to the visiting room. He still looked haggard and hadn't shaved since his incarceration. Hopefully he'd be allowed to shave before his arraignment; his scraggily beard made him look like a cheap thug.

"Thanks for coming," he greeted me when he picked up the phone after being handcuffed to the stanchion.

"Are you making any progress reading *The Decline and Fall of the Roman Empire?*" I really didn't know what else to say; visiting someone in jail is almost like trying to be upbeat in a cancer ward.

"Father Novello stopped by yesterday and left me a copy of *The Imitation of Christ.* I decided to read it first since I'm about to be crucified."

I laughed at Brendan's stab at gallows humor but immediately got down to business. "I'm not making any headway in my efforts to clear you; the pizza deliveryman, Leo Plaskett, proved to be a dead end."

Brendan sighed. "Yeah, I feared as much."

"It's time for me to be blunt. Nothing about Jenny's murder makes any sense. At first I thought her killing was random; it now seems likely that Jenny knew her killer. Could she have been cheating on you with someone else?"

I watched Brendan's right fist clench and his face instantly flushed with anger. He pushed his chair back as if he wanted to leave but his handcuffed left arm prevented it. "What in the hell are you talking about?"

I still sensed Brendan was withholding something; I hated to do it but I had to provoke him to get to the truth. "Jenny screwed other guys before you; isn't it possible that she was still involved with one of them?"

"Jenny wasn't like that!"

Father Novello's comment on Sunday that Jenny seemed distressed by something during the spring buttressed Melinda's tale of Jenny's mystery visitor. "What about a married man?"

"Why are you asking these questions?" Brendan clenched his fist again; he looked like he wanted to punch me through the thick glass barrier.

"Melinda said she came home in February and heard Jenny making love in her bedroom. Her visitor went to great lengths not to be seen; Melinda saw him slink off in a BMW when she went into the bathroom to take a shower."

Sighing heavily, Brendan looked like he'd just been kicked in the gut. If Jenny had been cheating on him, he was either clueless or a damn good liar. "If there was another guy, do you think he killed her?" he asked.

"It could be just another dead end like Leo Plaskett; it's going to be hard to pick up any trail seven months later." I didn't feel comfortable divulging my suspicions regarding Reverend Franklin.

"Most graduate assistants can barely afford a car much less a BMW; it doesn't sound like anyone she knew from the university."

After dating penniless graduate students like Tomasz and Lance, had Jenny succumbed to the allure of a wealthy suitor? Brendan would've noticed Reverend Franklin driving around Jefferson Terrace in his BMW; if he'd made the connection to Jenny, he wasn't sharing it with me.

"Last night I managed to sleep a couple hours. Why did you have to tell me this? I'm sick to my stomach now. Jenny never cheated on me; you didn't know her. I loved Jenny!"

Brendan stared off into space; he wouldn't look me in the eye. Even though we had a few minutes left, it was best I ended my visit. I hated doing what I'd just done but it was better that he heard it from me rather than being caught off guard by the police. "I'll be at your arraignment tomorrow."

"At least someone there won't be part of the lynch mob."

***

Reverend Franklin's freshly washed and polished BMW was sitting in its reserved parking space when I pulled into the Ark Church's parking lot.

"Can I help you?" asked the attractive blond receptionist when I entered the church's office. I'd expected to be greeted by a middle aged woman or older. Was the receptionist a sign that Reverend Franklin suffered from a weakness of the flesh?

I handed her my card. "I'm Professor Stanard; is Dr. Franklin in?"

"He's working on his sermon for tonight's service; I'll check if he can see you." She got up from her desk and knocked on his office door before entering. A few seconds later she emerged. "Pastor Franklin will see you now Dr. Stanard."

She showed me into his wood paneled study, one wall lined with books. "We met at Jenny Biggio's memorial service," I said as I shook his hand. The mention of Jenny's name failed to get a reaction from Reverend Franklin.

"What can I do for you?" Reverend Franklin motioned for me to take one of the two leather arm chairs across from his desk; a massive leather bound *Bible* sat on a small table between the chairs. It looked more for display than reading; one would need a forklift to raise it.

"Brendan Healy is my graduate student; I'm trying to help clear him of Jenny's murder."

"Shouldn't the investigation be left to the police?"

"The police are only interested in proving that Brendan murdered Jenny; they've overlooked several things that will bring the real killer to justice."

Reverend Franklin sat there impassively as if carved out of marble.

"I believe there may be a connection between Jenny's murder and your church."

"My church? How?" He had a slightly puzzled look on his face but betrayed no other emotion. By now I expected him to be sweating profusely but he sat there coolly knowing he'd covered his tracks well and figured I was only fishing around.

"Jenny tutored students here; Felton Snyder attended your suppers for the homeless. Snyder claimed he found Jenny's wallet in the alley behind Tait's Market. I believe he was involved in her murder and falsely implicated Brendan."

Reverend Franklin leaned back in his chair; my allegation that Snyder murdered Jenny failed to get a reaction from him. I passed him copies of the articles from the High Point newspaper.

"It's easy to demonize the homeless," he replied after quickly scanning the articles. "I founded this church to reach out to those in despair; I was not called to minister to the wealthy out in Virginia Beach."

Despite my natural cynicism; I believed Reverend Franklin was genuine and not feeding me a line. If my suspicions about him were true, it would make it a great tragedy. "I talked with a detective down in High Point; he said that Felton Snyder was suspected of brutally stabbing to death an informant on the motorcycle gang's activities."

"And was he ever charged?"

"No, the only witness who could link him to the murder died of an overdose. Did Jenny ever cross paths with Felton Snyder?"

"The tutoring program was usually over by five o'clock; we usually send the bus downtown to pick up the homeless around five-thirty. Some of the homeless who hang around Jefferson Terrace and CBU may arrive earlier. Jenny had no involvement with our outreach program to the homeless."

"Do any of the other homeless you help have criminal records?"

"Our ministry gives assistance to those in need without asking any questions; I'm well aware that many of the homeless we help here have substance abuse problems. We sponsor Alcoholics Anonymous and Narcotics Anonymous groups to help them break their addictions."

"How well do you know Snyder?"

"I've counseled him on several occasions. War does terrible things to people; he joined that motorcycle gang when he came home from Viet Nam. His sister down in Murfreesboro told me he was raised in a good Christian home. The devil turned him away from his faith and led him into the darkness; our mission is to bring him back into the light."

"The police believe Jenny was killed around six-thirty on Monday night. Snyder claimed he was here at the time."

"Yes, I've already told the police that Felton attended our prayer supper," he replied.

It dawned on me that Reverend Franklin may've hired Felton Snyder to do his dirty work. Who would contradict him about Snyder's whereabouts on Monday night? A room full of homeless people whose brains had been eroded by years of booze and drugs would hardly make ideal witnesses. Throw in a schizophrenic or two and Snyder could've easily slipped away and killed Jenny without anyone noticing.

But I still lacked proof that Reverend Franklin and Jenny even had an affair. If an affair had occurred and became public knowledge, Reverend Franklin would likely lose everything. He had every reason to permanently silence her. As for Jenny, she had no reason to expose the affair; or did she?

What if Brendan wasn't the father of Jenny's baby? Bedding down with both Brendan and the good parson, who sired her child? Even after twenty years of marriage, Laura's feminine intuition still surprised me; Jenny would've known the father of her baby.

Reverend Franklin examined his well manicured fingernails while I attempted to put the pieces together.

Did Jenny turn to Brendan only after Reverend Franklin spurned her? Was Jenny really in love with Reverend Franklin and not Brendan? Had Brendan not been playing straight with me again? His initial anger at Jenny's pregnancy might've been more than the shock of becoming a father. Out of love for Jenny, did he offer to step in and raise another man's child?

"Thank you for taking the time to speak with me; I appreciate it," I said to end the meeting.

"I'm sorry I couldn't help Brendan; next time I'm down at the jail, I'll visit him."

"I was in prison and you came to me."

Reverend Franklin ushered me to the door. "I see you're familiar with Matthew Chapter 25, Verse 36."

I refrained from asking if he'd read the Seventh Commandment recently.

***

"Alan Melton would like to see you; however he's on Dr. Worthington's advising list. Do you want me to have him wait and meet with her," said Janet moments after I returned to the office.

"No, that's okay; I'll see him."

Janet eyed me suspiciously; she'd overheard my exchange with Leo Plaskett and her friend Maureen had reported on my visit to Art Campbell. I could tell she was annoyed that I'd not brought her into my confidence.

"I wanted to pass something on to you," said Alan when he entered my office.

"What's up?" I asked in the vernacular of my students. I've found over the years if you talk like them, it puts them at ease.

"That homeless guy you asked me about has been hanging around the restaurant; he's no longer bumming cigarettes. I was working the register at lunch and he pulled a large wad of cash out of his pocket and paid for his meal."

"Are you sure it wasn't Professor Tanner?"

Alan laughed. "Professor Tanner isn't missing his two front teeth."

"How much money do you think he had?"

"He peeled a twenty off the top; there was another one underneath it. It looked like he had at least a dozen more bills."

"Even if the rest of the bills had been ones, that's a lot of money for a homeless person." Forty dollars was a windfall; if the other bills were tens or twenties, Felton Snyder was sitting on a small fortune. Where did it come from? Did his sister in Murfreesboro send money to Reverend Franklin to pass on to him? Hadn't Detective Chambliss indicated his family had cut all ties with him; it was doubtful they'd send him money knowing he'd just blow it on bottles of Thunderbird. Nor was it likely the police paid Snyder for serving as an informant; they'd already been quite generous releasing him from jail and giving him immunity for his testimony against Brendan.

Someone was paying Snyder off. He'd murdered before; he'd have no qualms about blackmailing Jenny's killer. Either that or he was being paid to incriminate Brendan. I was beginning to see a light at the end of the tunnel.

"Call me the next time you see him at McDonald's." I wrote my cell phone number on my card and handed it to Alan. It would be safer to talk with Snyder in a public place like the McDonald's rather than the poorly lit alley behind Tait's Market. I was not going to take any chances with a killer like Snyder.

"I'll be glad to."

CHAPTER XXVII

After a quick lunch at my desk, I headed downtown for Brendan's one o'clock arraignment. At the other end of the third floor hallway of the courthouse, I saw a coffle of five prisoners, dressed in their orange jail coveralls, escorted by two armed sheriff's deputies. Brendan was in the center, the only white prisoner in the group. His arms were handcuffed behind his back and leg irons locked around his ankles; a chain attached to his handcuffs shackled him to the four other prisoners.

Although I'd seen Brendan taken away from my house in handcuffs, I'd not been prepared to see him in the middle of chain gang like in a scene from *Cool Hand Luke*. As the prisoners shuffled listlessly toward me, their progress slowed by their leg irons, I noticed Brendan's coveralls were faded and frayed from numerous trips through the jail's laundry but at least he'd been allowed to shower and shave for his arraignment. Normally Brendan walked with a confident swagger earned through four hard years in the Marine Corps but his pained expression betrayed the humiliation he was suffering as he was publicly paraded like the convicts in *Les Misérables*. Brendan looked down at the floor, trying to avoid the stares of the good burghers of Norfolk milling outside the courtrooms. When he recognized me, he flashed a tight lipped smile in my direction.

"No talking," ordered one of the sheriff's deputies guarding the coffle. He shoved his nightstick in Brendan's ribs to enforce his directive.

According to the docket posted on the door of Courtroom Five, a number of arraignments were scheduled for the afternoon Circuit Court session. I took a seat on one of the rock hard wooden benches reserved for spectators; I'd arrived almost a half hour early and brought a book to kill time till Brendan's arraignment. Built in the early 1960's, the courtroom's light blue cinderblock walls had become a dingy gray; the wall behind the judge's bench was wood paneled and featured oil portraits of the circuit court judges who had served over the years.

The defendant's side of the courtroom was beginning to fill with relatives of the accused; several defense attorneys sat reviewing folders and scribbling notes on yellow legal pads. Carla Burnham was nowhere in sight.

To my surprise, Brendan's mother entered the courtroom with a willowy young woman with strawberry blond hair. Her facial features greatly resembled Brendan's.

"I didn't think you'd be able to make it," I greeted her.

"I was able to switch days with one of my co-workers. We left Jersey this morning at five o'clock to get here; we're driving back immediately after the hearing."

"Hi, I'm Brendan's sister Amy." She flashed a blinding white smile that reflected an investment in orthodontic care by her mother.

"Pleased to meet you," I said as I shook her hand.

"Have you seen Brendan yet?" Amy asked.

"When I passed him in the hall about ten minutes ago; they wouldn't allow him to speak to me."

Brendan's mother sighed. "I hoped we'd be able to talk with him, especially after driving all this way."

"You might want to check with the sergeant standing by that door; he seems to be in charge." Colleen and her daughter went over to him; he appeared to nod sympathetically to their request. I scanned the courtroom and noticed Dick Torelli had arrived with Jake Ruiz in tow. Torelli stopped to chat with Amanda Saltzman and the other reporters seated behind the Commonwealth Attorney's table.

Colleen and Amy returned about five minutes later. As Colleen settled into her seat she dabbed her eyes with a balled handkerchief. I noticed his sister appeared to have been crying too. "The deputy let us have a few minutes with him," sobbed his mother.

"It was hard seeing Brendan in handcuffs," said Amy.

"What is Sergeant Milkowski doing here?"

Colleen asked as she pointed to the tall white haired man in a blue blazer chatting with Harley Simpson. I recognized him from his interview with Amanda Saltzman; they both had smug looks on their faces.

Dave Chen and Tom Craig arrived and took seats next to us; Brendan's supporters now numbered five. A buzz went through the courtroom as Brad Biggio escorted Jenny's parents to their seats across the aisle from us. Jenny's mother looked like she might just crumple up and blow away; she held tight to her husband for support. The Commonwealth's Attorney went over to greet them as did Amanda Saltzman who was summarily repulsed by Brad Biggio. Just before the courtroom clock hit one o'clock, Carla Burnham rushed in and signed in with the clerk. She took a seat in the front row behind the defendant's table. I introduced her to Brendan's mother and sister.

"This session of the Circuit Court is now in session, the Honorable Alva T. Warren presiding. All rise," announced the bailiff as the judge entered from a side door.

Judge Warren, wearing an orange and blue striped bow tie, took his place on the bench. In almost an assembly line fashion, handcuffed and shackled defendants were brought out to the courtroom by a deputy from the holding cell. Judge Warren arraigned the first seven defendants on drug and weapons charges; after they pleaded not guilty, he set the date for their preliminary hearings. Deputies quickly whisked each prisoner from the courtroom when finished.

"Brendan R. Healy!" called the bailiff.

Like the other defendants, due to his leg shackles, Brendan shuffled into the courtroom escorted by two deputies and took his place at the defendant's table next to Carla Burnham; has hands were still manacled behind him. He flashed a smile in the direction of his mother and sister but avoided the stares of the Biggio clan. Mrs. Biggio dabbed at her watery eyes with a handkerchief in her right hand while her left hand squeezed her husband's hand tightly. Brad Biggio still looked eager to

Daniel P. Hennelly

punch Brendan's lights out; he restrained himself due to the presence of his aunt and uncle, and the armed deputies in the court room.

Judge Warren quickly leafed through a sheaf of papers. "A defendant should be arraigned the day after being arrested; if arrested over weekend, the next day the court is in session. Why wasn't this defendant arraigned on Monday?" directed Judge Warren to the prosecution.

"Your honor, the victim's parents indicated their desire to be present at the arraignment," replied the Commonwealth's Attorney.

"Be mindful of the provisions of the speedy trial statute."

"We're aware of our responsibilities and this defendant will be brought to trial within the specified period."

Carla Burnham scribbled a note on her yellow legal pad. I couldn't tell whether this was a legal technicality or something actually helpful to Brendan.

"Brendan Ryan Healy you are charged with first degree murder in the death of Jennifer Marie Biggio and her unborn child. How do you plead?" asked the judge.

Before Brendan could reply, Mrs. Biggio began sobbing softly. Her husband put his arm around her and patted her on the shoulder.

"Not guilty sir," barked Brendan as if still in the Marines.

"Brendan Ryan Healy you are charged also with the rape of Jennifer Marie Biggio. How do you plead?"

"Not guilty sir."

"A preliminary hearing is scheduled for 10 AM on November 15. The defendant is remanded to the custody of the sheriff."

Brendan turned in the direction of Jenny's parents. "I didn't kill Jenny; I loved your daughter!"

Brad Biggio jumped to his feet; Jenny's father blocked him from charging Brendan. Trembling, Jenny's mother stood up. "You heartless liar! How can you stand there and say that? You strangled our daughter and murdered your own child!" Her husband grabbed hold of her as she lapsed into trembling incoherence.

"Please believe me!"

Judge Warren pounded his gavel. "Remove the defendant! Decorum will be observed in my courtroom at all times. Is that clear?"

The deputies grabbed hold of Brendan and hustled him toward the exit; with his legs shackled, he almost tripped. His mother and sister sobbed softly into their handkerchiefs.

With Brendan's arraignment over; his supporters exited the courtroom and gathered at the end of the corridor. It was like a wake; no one immediately spoke. Dave put his arm around Amy to console her although I suspected he had ulterior motives. Sitting in jail, Brendan had enough on his plate without having to worry about his sister succumbing to Dave's oily charm.

The arraignment had been a disaster; Brendan's innocent plea had been drowned out by Mrs. Biggio's grief stricken denunciation of him. Cameras had been barred from the courtroom and there would be no clip on the evening news although I was certain Amanda Saltzman would exploit the melodramatic aspects of the confrontation in the morning paper.

"Will you visit Brendan this weekend?" asked Colleen to break the uneasy silence.

"I'll probably see him on Sunday."

She handed me an envelope. "Could you put another $25 in his canteen account?"

"No problem," I replied.

"My next weekend off is after Election Day; I'm planning to come to Norfolk to see him."

"We need to head back to Jersey," said Amy, impatient to get on the road.

After a quick exchange of farewells, I escorted Colleen and her daughter to the elevator. The doors opened at the second floor; Mr. and Mrs. Biggio entered the elevator with their nephew. They didn't immediately notice Colleen standing behind me until after the doors closed; when the Biggios recognized her, a palpable tension filled the confined space. It was as if the Capulet and Montague families had just encountered each other, only the swords were missing.

"I'm sorry that we've had to meet under these circumstances; I enjoyed meeting Jenny when she visited me over Labor Day weekend," said Colleen Healy. She extended her hand to Mrs. Biggio.

Jenny's mother stared down at Colleen's hand as though she was being greeted by Typhoid Mary. Brad Biggio recognized me from the altercation at the memorial service; he looked rather eager to pounce on me since Brendan was unavailable to serve as a punching bag.

"Your son murdered our daughter," said Jenny's father. The doors opened and the Biggio clan left the elevator without uttering another word.

***

Just before 4 o'clock, Janet came into my office and handed me a business card. "Sergeant Vincent Milkowski from Kearny, New Jersey would like to have a word with you."

"No doubt about Brendan," I replied.

"I thought you may've been involved in an armored car robbery," laughed Janet.

Unconcerned for his health, Sergeant Milkowski shook my hand and settled into one of the chairs in front of my desk. "Chief Simpson indicated that you're Brendan Healy's advisor." Although not a linguist, I detected traces of Brooklyn in Milkowski's New Jersey accent.

"I'm the chair of his dissertation committee," I corrected him. "Are you here to view the crime scene?"

"Chief Simpson showed me around last night; he told me you're Healy's most vocal defender."

"He's innocent of Jenny Biggio's murder."

"Why do all you intellectuals think you know more than the police?"

"The police have overlooked evidence in their rush to make a quick arrest; Harley settled on Brendan as the suspect within minutes of Jenny's body being discovered."

"You know Healy as one of your students; I know him from when he served as Sean O'Reilly's enforcer."

"He told me all about his days as juvenile delinquent and his stint at Mountainview."

"Juvenile delinquent is such a quaint term; teenage sociopath would be a better way to describe Brendan. Sean was only five feet six; he needed Brendan's muscle. Brendan enjoyed beating punks to a pulp, or doing whatever other dirty chores Sean assigned him. Did he ever tell you what happened to Sean?"

When Brendan revealed his past to me, I detected that he wasn't totally ashamed of his partnership with Sean. But was he a sociopath as Sergeant Milkowski claimed? "He said a rival drug dealer pumped Sean full of bullets."

"Brendan was a lot smarter than Sean; he realized the Dominicans were muscling in on the drug trade in Kearny. He jumped at Judge Meehan's deal and joined the Marines. The Dominicans were angry that Brendan bashed in the skull of one of their boys with a baseball bat. Without his goon to protect him, it was only a matter of time before Sean met his maker."

"Brendan said he had nothing to do with that murder."

"A blood covered aluminum bat was found at the scene; Brendan always brandished a bat when backing up Sean."

"Were Brendan's fingerprints found on that bat?" I asked skeptically.

"Most likely he wore gloves," replied Sergeant Milkowski as he deftly dodged the question. "Here are a few photos of the victim; take a good look at them."

Sergeant Milkowski handed me a folder with several 8 by 10 grisly color photos of the victim. I looked at the photos of a man lying face down in an asphalt parking lot; his arms were bound behind his back with duct tape. An irregular pool of blood surrounded his head and was bisected by the yellow lines of the parking lot. The head had been smashed to an unrecognizable blood covered pulp.

I handed the folder back to him. "If you had any evidence, you would've arrested Brendan by now."

"There have been a lot of advances in DNA testing in the last ten years; it might prove worthwhile to reopen this case. You have influence with Healy; the Commonwealth's Attorney has offered him a generous plea bargain. Convince him to take it; otherwise the wheels are in motion. No one really cares about a dead spic; I can easily drop this case if Brendan plays ball and pleads guilty to Ms. Biggio's murder."

"Why are the New Jersey police interested in a Virginia murder?"

"When Healy joined the Marines, I figured he'd end up in the brig. I should've put Brendan behind bars when I had the chance; Ms. Biggio would be alive today."

"Instead he thrived in the Marines and ended up here at CBU working on his Ph.D.; so much for your crystal ball." Sergeant Milkowski glared at me but didn't take the bait. "According to the newspaper, you're supposed to be reopening your investigation into the death of Brendan's father."

"Mike Healy was nothing but a scumbag; as they always say, the apple didn't fall far from tree. That reporter's theory that he conspired with his mother to kill that rotten son of a bitch is an interesting angle. Brendan was a juvenile when his father met his unfortunate demise; charging him now would serve no purpose."

"Aren't you taking this personally just because Brendan dated your daughter?" I patted myself on the back for not saying Brendan screwed his daughter.

Milkowski stiffened; I'd obviously touched a still raw nerve. "Do you have any daughters Dr. Stanard?"

"Only two sons," I said pointing to the picture of my sons on the credenza.

"If you had a daughter, you wouldn't want Healy within a hundred yards of her. Fortunately my daughter wised up and forgot about him when she went off to Marymount College. Jenny Biggio wasn't so lucky."

"You came down from New Jersey just to get me to pressure Brendan to accept a plea bargain, is that it?"

"I came down to serve a warrant on Healy for violating the terms of his probation; if Virginia ever releases him, he'll be spending two years in Rahway."

Obviously, there was a concerted effort to put pressure on Brendan to plead guilty and accept the plea deal to avoid going to trial.

"Liberals are supposed to be compassionate. You were in the courtroom today; Mrs. Biggio is distraught over her daughter's death. That poor woman won't survive the ordeal of a trial. Have a heart; persuade Healy to accept the deal that's on the table."

"They're offering him nothing," I replied.

"After living the cushy lifestyle of a graduate student, do you think Brendan could survive in a maximum security prison? Maybe as part of a plea bargain, it can be arranged for him to be assigned to a medium security prison with tofu on the menu."

"The evidence against Brendan is flimsy at best."

"In my thirty years in law enforcement, I've never seen a more rock solid case. I always thought people with a Ph.D. were smarter than the rest of us; you really are a dumb smuck if you believe Healy is innocent." He got up and left my office, angry that he failed to sway me.

Milkowski's visit was an ominous development. The Commonwealth's Attorney knew that the case against Brendan was circumstantial and; there was a good chance that Carla Burnham would expose those flaws to a jury.

***

Julia Adams hailed me from her front porch as I got out of my car. "I helped Melinda at the lab today; her apartment was broken into yesterday."

"When did it happen?"

"The thief broke in during the afternoon when she was in the lab. No one on her block was home at the time."

"What about Dr. Dealy?"

"Alicia had a graduate seminar that afternoon."

It would seem that Alicia Dealy's house would be a more tempting target for burglars than an apartment shared by two penniless graduate students. "Do the police think the burglary is related to Jenny's murder?"

"There have been several break-ins in Jefferson Terrace over the last couple weeks; the time of the day makes the police think high school kids are behind the robberies."

"Why do they think that?"

"In the other burglaries, they targeted the houses where CBU students live in search of laptops and video game systems. During one of the burglaries, a CBU student came home and surprised the burglars."

"Did they take anything?"

"Melissa had her laptop at school; the burglar ransacked the apartment but nothing appeared to be missing,"

"How did the burglar get in?"

"Melissa said he smashed in a window on the back door with a brick and then unlocked it; the police told Melissa that the other break-ins were similar."

It seemed a strange coincidence that Jenny's former apartment was turned upside down by a burglar. Could Reverend Franklin be behind the burglary? Was he trying to retrieve a piece of jewelry or an inscribed book he'd given Jenny? Or was he searching for an incriminating love letter? Jenny may've kept a journal. Someone desperately needed to remove something from the apartment before Jenny's parents stumbled upon it while packing up her belongings for the sad trip back to Ohio. What had the police overlooked when they searched the apartment? Once they found the pregnancy test kit, they believed they'd struck gold and probably searched no further. Once again they'd failed in their investigation when they missed the obvious link between the burglary and Jenny's murder.

Now that I'd possibly identified Jenny's mystery lover, I needed to pay another visit to Melinda to see if she remembered any further details that would confirm my suspicions.

***

I turned on Channel 12 when I arrived home to find Amanda Saltzman standing in front of the courthouse broadcasting the opening segment live. "The suspect in the strangulation murder of CBU coed, Jenny Biggio, was arraigned this afternoon in Norfolk." On the screen flashed Brendan being marched from the jail to a rear entrance of the courthouse chained to his fellow inmates; the images of Brendan in his jail overalls and shackles would reinforce the viewer's perception of his guilt. Brendan wisely refused to respond to the questions peppered at him by Saltzman; although some viewers would likely take his silence as an admission of guilt. "Present at the arraignment was Jenny Biggio's parents who came from Ohio to confront their daughter's killer." The screen switched to the Commonwealth Attorney escorting Jenny's parents and cousin to the front entrance of the courthouse past the scrum of reporters and television cameramen staking it out. Since she was facing reelection in five days, the Commonwealth's Attorney saw no need to bring them into the courthouse by a side entrance and waste the free media exposure. No doubt she also allowed the media access to the normally secure rear entrance of the courthouse to capture Brendan's arrival.

"During the arraignment, Healy was confronted by Jenny's heart broken mother." Even though cameras were banned from the courtroom, somehow Saltzman or a confederate had smuggled in a miniature camera and clandestinely recorded the exchange between Brendan and Mrs. Healy. The concealed camera's angle gave the clash a cinéma vérité aura; if one was scoring it like a boxing match, Mrs. Biggio's tearful retort enabled her to score a knockout victory over Brendan.

After dinner I headed downtown to meet Mitch Blackwell and his journalist friends. Finnerty's Pub had started out catering to longshoreman due to its location near the docks. As the number of longshoreman declined due to the rise of container ships, the bar became a neighborhood hangout in the 70's. Its décor, if one could call it that, had changed little since it opened in the early 1950's. The knotty pine bar was complemented by a black and red linoleum floor; several large and dust covered trophy fish caught by the former owner and mounted on the cinderblock walls were the only decorations. Booths ran along the wall across from the bar; at the end of the long narrow room was a larger space with several tables surrounding a pool table.

Mitch was holding court near the pool table; I recognized Shane Alvarez and a couple other faces from local television stations. The rest were unfamiliar since only columnists rated a picture along with their byline in the *Register*. "Welcome to the weekly meeting of the Al Carruthers fan club," Mitch greeted me. He introduced me to everyone around the table.

I took a seat between Mitch and Shane Alvarez. "How's the slumlord business," Shane greeted me.

"I'm sorry I had to deceive you; I didn't know who I could trust."

"Who says you can trust me?" Shane laughed and took a sip of his Corona.

"I'm Tom Maguire," said a tall white haired man who extended his hand to me.

"You're the retired editor of the *Register*," I replied.

"Fired editor is more accurate; the *Register* didn't report that Al Carruthers canned me when I resisted his plan to gut the paper. There were ways to cut costs and still put out a quality paper."

"What can I get you?" asked the olive skinned waitress as she tossed her long black hair. Despite the chilly weather she wore a pair of tight cut-off jeans that revealed the tail of a sea horse inked on her derrière. Her low cut blouse exposed stars tattooed on her plump breasts.

"A Corona," I replied.

She got orders for refills from the others and returned to the bar. Most of the well lubricated conversation around the table revolved around the decline of the newspaper business. Besides taking frequent potshots at the publisher of the *Register*, those around the table also viciously skewered Amanda Saltzman. Mitch enjoyed his role as the group's informal moderator.

"Al Warren isn't going to be all that happy that Saltzman smuggled a camera into his courtroom," said Maguire.

"The rest of us followed the rules; hopefully he'll cite her for contempt of court and slap her sweet little ass in jail," said one of the television reporters.

"There are some old bull dykes down at the jail who'd love to get their hands on sweet little Amanda," laughed Maguire.

"The talk around the courthouse this afternoon was that Healy is guilty as sin; you're the only one besides his mother who thinks otherwise," said Shane.

"There are a lot of angles that no one has pursued."

"Like what?"

"The police maintain that Brendan spent Monday afternoon with one of the students in his class."

"Ah yes, the nubile Miss Finley; I'd like to jump in the sack with her," blurted out Shane.

"She was in her chemistry lab all afternoon; then she was at a rush party that evening. There was no way she could've been spotted with

Brendan in front of the library. That shoots a big hole in the police's chain of events."

"Why did she avoid Amanda?"

"What would you do if you had Saltzman nipping at your heels?" asked Tom Maguire.

"She could nip a little higher on me," replied Shane, obviously feeling no pain.

The boys around the table laughed again. Hard drinking by nature, they'd all consumed several more beers than me.

"Even if that's true, the police still have DNA evidence that Healy raped Biggio before strangling her. They claim it's a slam dunk case."

"He's never denied having sex with Jenny during the afternoon; he even told that to Harley Simpson when he interviewed him the morning they discovered her body."

"You're not offering me much to go on; unlike Amanda Saltzman, I have to justify every story to my editor."

"Jenny's apartment was broken into yesterday afternoon."

"There are half a dozen burglaries in Jefferson Terrace every day. It's not even newsworthy," said Maguire.

"I think the murderer was trying to retrieve something incriminating from her apartment before her parents found it."

Shane took a swig of his beer. "Or it could be a crack addict just trying to finance his next score."

At this point I had no hard evidence to link Reverend Franklin to Jenny; it was too early to voice my suspicions about him to this group.

"The whole case against Brendan is based on the testimony of a homeless wino that supposedly found Jenny's wallet and sold her credit card to a fence; he was granted immunity from prosecution for testifying against Brendan."

"I'm getting a whiff of a ten day old dead fish," said Shane.

"Here's some background on Felton Snyder." I handed Shane copies of what I'd dug up on Snyder; he quickly perused it.

"He's a real unsavory character. Is he still connected to the Devil's Disciples?"

"I doubt he's been on a motorcycle in years. One of my students works at the McDonald's near campus; Snyder was in yesterday and flashed a wad of money."

"We've been pursuing a story that the gang has been reconstituted and established a chapter in the area around Camp Lejeune; supposedly they're cooking up meth in the woods and running it up to Norfolk," said Shane.

"What does that have to do with Jenny's murder?" I asked.

"It could explain why Snyder is so suddenly flush with cash. Nor can you overlook the fact that Healy was once stationed at Camp Lejeune. Jacksonville is a pretty rough burg; no telling what he was involved in down there not to mention his prior involvement with the drug scene in New Jersey," conjectured Maguire.

"Jenny may've been collateral damage if someone from his past came looking to settle a score," said Mitch

I immediately defended Brendan. "He cleaned up his act when he left New Jersey and joined the Marines."

"It's odd that Snyder is smack dab in the middle of this case and the police are willing to deal with him. It might be worth taking a second look at him. Where can he be found?" asked Shane.

"Since the murder he's been making himself scarce. I've seen him at the Ark Church; another night he was hanging out behind Nick's."

"Can I get you another Corona?" The waitress leaned over and picked up my empty beer bottle exposing both of her ample charms to view.

"Definitely, I'll have another." I finally seemed to be making headway in convincing others that Brendan was innocent; a celebratory beer was definitely in order.

The waitress stepped over to Shane; he discretely slipped her a note with his empty bottle and she winked back at him. Shane wouldn't be burning the midnight oil pursuing the lead on Felton Snyder; it would have to wait till morning.

CHAPTER XXVIII

AFTER MY CLASS ON FRIDAY morning, I started writing the pre-tenure review for one of the department's assistant professors. Dr. Victoria Paget's pedigree included degrees from Stanford, the University of Pennsylvania and Johns Hopkins. Her first two years at the university had gone relatively well. She was making good progress toward finishing her book, *The Manipulation of American Women by Advertisers from 1920 – 1959*. Reviewing her class evaluations from spring semester; however, I noticed a disturbing trend among the student comments. She appeared to have trouble relating to her students. Several students described her as condescending and aloof; one even described her as rude. I sent her an email requesting she meet with me on Monday to discuss her evaluations.

My cell phone rang; I didn't recognize the number. "Dr. Stanard," I answered.

"This is Alan Melton; I'm working the lunch shift today. That homeless guy just came in. He paid for his meal with a twenty; I saw another twenty on the top of his wad."

Forty bucks was a king's ransom for someone like Felton Snyder. What was the source of his money? Was he actually selling meth for his former buddies in the Devil's Disciples as Maguire speculated? Or was someone buying his silence?

"I got to get back to my register; just thought you wanna know."

"Thanks for calling." I decided to head to McDonald's; hopefully Snyder would still be there when I arrived. As I walked the two blocks,

I went over in my mind what I'd ask Snyder when I confronted him. For the end of October, it was fairly chilly for Norfolk and I wished I had put on more than my tweed sport coat when I left the house this morning. Pulling open the side door at McDonald's, I bumped into Leo Plaskett on his way out. He glared at me but didn't say a word.

I spotted Snyder right off sitting in a booth at the front of the crowded restaurant; he stared blankly out the window at the passing traffic. Strangely no one was seated in the booths on either side of him. I went to the counter and ordered a cup of coffee from Alan. "Did he meet with anyone?"

"We've been slammed since eleven-thirty; with all the customers in line, I can't see the dining area that well."

"Be ready to call the police if necessary. Thanks for your help."

Alan patted the bulge of his cell phone in his pants pocket; I paid him for the coffee. The coffee cup shook in my hand as I walked over to Snyder. His Big Mac box and fries bag sat empty on his tray; he was taking his time finishing his supersized drink, he was in no hurry to go back out into the cold.

"Do you mind if I join you?" I took the seat across from him before he had time to answer. Then I realized why the other patrons had given him a wide berth. It was unlikely Snyder had taken a shower since being released from jail. His long salt and pepper beard was matted and sprinkled with debris from his meal.

"What do you want?"

Even across the table, Snyder's stale breath reeked heavily of cheap red wine.

"My grandfather was a New York City policeman and he always warned me not to flash my money. I understand you've been showing off a quite a wad."

"And what's it to you?"

"You know, I find it odd that someone who's down on his luck is carrying around such a large stash."

"Who in the hell are you?" Snyder squinted at me through his rheumy eyes.

"I'm Dr. Andrew Stanard." I handed Snyder my business card. "Brendan Healy's lawyer will find your sudden windfall rather interesting; don't you think the police will too?"

"Look, my sister sent me the money; if that's any of your business."

"Or is Jenny Biggio's killer paying you to lie about Brendan Healy?"

"I'm just sitting here eating my lunch. Leave me alone!"

"Brendan was never in that alley the night you found Jenny's wallet. In time the police will figure it out, can't you see that?"

"Get lost!" Snyder let out a loud belch that drew stares from nearby diners.

"Who dropped the wallet in the alley that night?"

"Screw you!"

"What were you trying to steal from Jenny Biggio's apartment yesterday?"

"Huh? I don't know what you're talking about!" With some difficulty, Snyder got to his feet and staggered toward the side door almost bowling over a young mother and her twin daughters in his haste to escape. Being a good citizen, I picked up Snyder's tray and emptied it in the trash. Out of the corner of my eye, I noticed Art Campbell standing in line waiting to order. I couldn't pass up the chance to tweak Art's nose.

"Good afternoon Art; I didn't realize that a Big Mac and fries were part of a healthy socialist diet."

"I'm actually having a salad; I'll leave the burgers for you meat eating fascists."

"You forget that der Fuhrer was a vegetarian." Although I'd read that Hitler was supposedly unable to resist Bavarian liver dumplings prepared by his friend and photographer, Heinrich Hoffmann.

"What were you and Whit Tanner discussing over lunch?" asked Art.

I laughed. "Felton Snyder found Jenny's wallet in the alley behind Tait's Market and sold her credit card to a fence. He lied to save his own skin and falsely implicated Brendan."

"Look, just because he's a downtrodden reject of our capitalist society doesn't mean he's automatically a liar."

"Here's your salad sir," said Alan as he handed Art his tray. "What can I get for you Dr. Stanard?"

"I'll have a Big Mac and fries to go. Thanks."

"Face it Andy, you're going to end up on a slab in the morgue like Rick Hanson," chided Art.

I took another sip of my coffee. I hated being lectured to by self-righteous vegetarians; most of them suffered from chronic logorrhea, probably from eating too many beans.

"I thought Leo Plaskett was your suspect de jure earlier in the week?" asked Art with a smug smile.

"The way I see it, the police quickly arrested Brendan, ignoring all the shady individuals on the periphery of Jenny's murder. There are still a lot of unanswered questions. Plaskett just left here; I wonder if he was meeting with Snyder."

"You believe a great miscarriage of justice has occurred but just ask Jake or Cynthia if they think Healy is guilty. He's nothing but a petty thug who's behind bars where he belongs."

Having delivered his verdict, Art walked away and took a seat.

"Here's your order sir," said Alan handing me my bag. "You wanna know something; Dr. Campbell is a sanctimonious fraud. I've sold him plenty of Big Macs; he only ordered a salad because you were here."

I chuckled at Art's double life being exposed.

Alan brought over the coffee pot. "Let me top off your coffee sir."

There were some advantages to being a department chair. Back at the office, I ate my lunch and made several notes about my encounter with Felton Snyder. His reaction to my questions only served to confirm my suspicion but was it possible that his sister sent him the money? Although I doubted it, I needed to check it out before going to the police. I picked up my phone and called the Ark Church; I'd also rattle Reverend Franklin's cage again.

"Pastor Franklin please," I asked the receptionist who answered.

"I'll put you through. Have a blessed day."

"Reverend Franklin," the now familiar and chilly voice answered.

"This is Dr. Stanard. Felton Snyder seems to have come into a large amount of cash recently. Do you know if his family has sent him any money recently?"

"Snyder's sister Ida sent me fifty dollars for him last Christmas. Why do you want to know?"

"My hunch is that Jenny Biggio's killer is paying him off."

"Shouldn't you go to the police?" His voice betrayed nothing to indicate he was perturbed by my inquiries; either that or Reverend Franklin was a very good liar. Was his suggestion that I go to the police an attempt to throw suspicion away from him?

"I'd like to speak with his sister to confirm some details before I do. Do you happen to have her phone number?"

"Mrs. Tolbert lives down in Murfreesboro; she's listed as his emergency contact in our records. I'll get it for you." A few minutes later he came back on the line and gave me her number. His cool demeanor still showed no cracks.

I dialed Mrs. Tolbert's number. "Good afternoon," answered a woman's voice steeped in rural North Carolina.

"Ida Tolbert please; this is Dr. Andrew Stanard calling."

"Are you that doctor who'll be removing my gall bladder next week?" She sounded like she was looking forward to it.

"No, I'm the Chair of the History Department at Chesapeake Bay University. One of my students was arrested and charged with murder last week based on testimony from your brother Felton."

"I've been following that on the news; I just love that cute little reporter." With a good antenna, the residents of Eastern North Carolina could receive the Norfolk television channels. "You say Felton is involved."

"Yes, he sold Jenny Biggio's credit card to a fence and claimed my student threw her wallet in the alley."

"Exactly, why are you calling me?"

"The last couple days, your brother has been seen with a large amount of money for someone in his reduced circumstances."

"Ha! That's a polite way of putting it," she laughed.

"Reverend Franklin of the Ark Church said you sent Felton money last Christmas."

"I was in the Christmas spirit when the reverend called; too much eggnog I guess." No doubt flavored with a little bourbon I speculated.

"Did you send him any money recently?"

"Heavens no!"

"Did anyone else in your family send him money?"

"My brother burned his bridges with all of us; none of us had heard from him in years until he popped up six months after momma died looking for his share of her estate. Fortunately Parker Judson wrote an iron clad will for momma. Mr. Judson made sure Felton didn't get a dime; he would've just wasted it on booze anyway."

"I think the real killer is paying him to keep silent."

"Felton was the smartest one of all of us but he never did use his God given talents except to further his no good criminal activities. He broke my parent's hearts and disgraced our family; my daddy was a deacon and momma was in the Eastern Star. Buying a bus ticket to Norfolk and getting him out of Murfreesboro was just about the smartest thing I ever did. Leonard, my husband, gave him a bottle of bourbon to sweeten the deal."

"Thanks for talking with me." Snyder was lying as I'd suspected; no one in his family would lift a finger to help him. His sister also confirmed he was clever enough to frame Brendan.

"I'll have to call my sister Ota and tell her to watch the news tonight," Ida Tolbert exclaimed. "She loves that TV reporter too!" It was disturbing that Amanda Saltzman had a fan club.

I dialed the High Point Police in hope of catching Detective Chambliss on his last day of work. "Jeff Chambliss," he answered.

"This is Dr. Stanard from Chesapeake Bay University."

"What can I do for you doc? I just finished cleaning out my desk."

"I need some more information on Felton Snyder."

"I've been following your student's case on the *National Crime Report*. Are you still convinced he innocent?"

"I'm working to clear him; he doesn't deserve to rot in jail for a crime he didn't commit."

"Just keep in mind I'm not going to undermine another police department's investigation."

"I understand completely. Over the last couple days, Snyder has been seen with a lot of cash."

"That's odd for a homeless bum. How much are we talking about?"

"Today he had over $40; yesterday he had at least $25 to $35."

"What are you thinking?"

"Snyder claims he saw Brendan dump Jenny's wallet in an alley; I believe Jenny Biggio's killer is paying him to implicate Brendan."

"The more logical explanation is Snyder's family sent him money."

"Nope, I just got off the phone with his sister in Murfreesboro; she sent him $50 last Christmas in a moment of weakness. According to her, none of his family wants anything to do with him."

Chambliss laughed. "I can't say that I blame them."

"I met with some reporters last night and one of them threw out a possibility that Snyder is involved with the Devil's Disciples again."

"I think you'll find that most of his associates are either in prison or dead; motorcycle gang members usually don't live to a ripe old age."

"The reporter indicated that the Disciples have established a chapter in the Camp Lejeune area and are running meth up to Norfolk."

"Do you know what they teach in the schools in eastern North Carolina?"

"No." I didn't see the connection between my inquiry and the educational system in the Tar Heel State.

"They teach the three Rs — reading, 'riting and the road to Norfolk."

I laughed at his joke; a lot of North Carolinians had migrated to Norfolk during World War II to take jobs in the shipyards and military bases. After the war, the migration continued as the agricultural economy in eastern North Carolina declined.

"The Devil's Disciples is like kudzu; every time you think you've eradicated it, a new patch springs up down the road. I've heard some of the younger members are active in the vicinity of both Camp Lejeune and Fort Bragg. Your source is right about them cooking meth; through their chapters they've got the network to distribute it. What's the connection to Snyder?"

"The reporter speculated Snyder might be dealing meth for them, thus explaining his sudden affluence."

"It's unlikely they'd trust someone as unreliable as Felton Snyder."

"Could he be blackmailing someone over that unsolved murder you mentioned?"

"I doubt it. The head of the High Point chapter at the time of the murder died in the Federal prison in Atlanta six years ago of lung cancer; he's the only one Snyder could've threatened with that murder."

"Thanks for your help."

"Don't take any chances with Snyder. He'll react like a vicious dog when cornered; even though his teeth are yellow and rotting, he can still bite. The last time we talked I told you that the only witness in that murder case died of a drug overdose; I failed to tell you that I always suspected it wasn't accidental."

Suddenly I got a sick feeling in the pit of my stomach; I'd foolishly given Snyder my business card even though it was unlikely he was going to call and confess.

"Take my advice doc, leave the investigation to Chief Simpson; if your student is innocent, it will all come out in the wash."

***

Friday was Halloween as well as the start of homecoming weekend. After I finished with Detective Chambliss, I went downstairs at three o'clock to watch the 20th Annual Pumpkin Plunge, the first event of homecoming. A crowd had gathered on the plaza to watch engineering students drop dozens of pumpkins from the top of Jordan Hall and see if they survived the ten story fall by landing in the ingenious devices the students built to cushion the landing. I saw Laura chatting with Cynthia Wallach and went over to them.

"Hello dear," she greeted me.

"I'm surprised the library could spare you."

"All of the students have started their weekend partying early; I thought I could slip away for a while." The Pumpkin Plunge was always a lot of fun; when the boys were younger we had brought them to enjoy the festivities. Watching a pumpkin fall from the roof of a ten story building and crash land always thrilled young boys and also men reliving their boyhoods. It looked like most of the faculty from Jordan Hall had joined the festivities. Tollie Monroe was chatting with the

Dean of the College of Engineering; the College of Arts, Social Sciences and Humanities graciously loaned its building for the Pumpkin Plunge since the Engineering Hall was a squat, two story building. A couple of Art Campbell's anti-globalization acolytes were working the crowd, attempting to get signatures on yet another petition. Also out of the corner of my eye, I spotted Reverend Franklin with two of his tow headed sons.

"Everyone please keep behind the ropes; if a ten pound pumpkin lands on you, it would crush your skull," announced Professor Gupta of Civil Engineering, the master of ceremonies.

A group of Navy ROTC students brought out a stack of decaying mattresses scavenged from the streets of Jefferson Terrace ahead of the trash trucks. Professor Gupta using a walkie-talkie gave the signal to a team of students on the roof to let the first victim drop. Breathlessly the crowd watched as a pumpkin the size of a basketball plunged into the middle of the top mattress, sending a mushroom cloud of dust into the air. One of the students triumphantly picked up the intact pumpkin off the mattress and held it aloft to applause from the crowd.

Next a group of civil engineering students brought out a wooden frame holding a net. A gust of wind blew across the courtyard as the pumpkin was dropped; it landed slightly off target hitting one of the posts instead of the net and shattered into pieces, spewing pumpkin pulp and seeds over a wide area. A second pumpkin was dropped and landed dead center but the pumpkin tore through the thin net, plunging to a painful death.

Julia Adams came over and joined us. "I thought a botanist would find it too traumatic to watch pumpkins being slaughtered."

She laughed. "I saw you coming out of McDonald's today; you really need to change your diet."

"Actually I went over to McDonald's to meet with Felton Snyder."

The mention of Snyder's name drew a puzzled look on Julia's face. "Who's Felton Snyder?"

"He's the homeless man who claims he saw Brendan throw Jenny's wallet in the alley behind Tait's Market; Snyder resembles Whit Tanner."

"Oh, I've encountered him on campus; he smells like moldy old cheese, the same way Whit smells."

Laura and Cynthia laughed. Over the years, Julia and Whit had locked horns in the Faculty Senate on numerous occasions; there had never been any love lost between them.

"How are you doing in your efforts to clear Brendan?" asked Stan Wallach, Cynthia's husband, who arrived to join our merry group.

"I'm finally making some headway. One of my students works at McDonald's. He reported that Snyder has suddenly come into a lot of cash; my suspicion is Jenny's murderer is buying his silence. I met with Shane Alvarez of Channel 5 last night and he's willing to take a second look at things and possibly do a story."

A group of frat boys in purple T-shirts brought out a stack of ten layers of empty beer cans held together in a card board frame. They got a big laugh from the crowd when their spokesman indicated they'd pulled an all-nighter assembling their entry. To my surprise and to the crowds as well, when the pumpkin landed it crushed the beer cans and survived the ten story fall without a scratch.

"So Snyder knows who killed Jenny?" asked Cynthia.

"I believe he lied to implicate Brendan; he's the lynch pin in the Commonwealth Attorney's case against Brendan. Pull out his testimony and their case collapses."

I'd never been a believer in a sixth sense but I suddenly had a strange sensation that someone was watching me. I looked around but didn't see anyone behind me that I recognized. Detective Chambliss' warning about Felton Snyder had unnerved me and I chalked it up to that.

A sorority, whose members all seemed to possess blond hair and snow white teeth, brought out a device constructed of several layers of Styrofoam cups and cardboard. As the rotund pumpkin crashed into the cups, they didn't quite absorb the impact as well as the beer cans, causing the pumpkin to shatter after it flattened the cups and hit the bricks of the courtyard.

The hilarious competition went on for almost an hour. For the grand finale, more than a dozen pumpkins were slaughtered, dropped from the roof with nothing put in place to cushion their landing; the poor pumpkins hit the ground with crushing thuds and were smashed to smithereens. As the crowd dispersed, I said goodbye to Laura and went into the lobby to take the elevator up to my office. When the elevator doors opened, Art Campbell stepped out of the car.

"You're too late for the Pumpkin Plunge," I greeted him.

"What a horrendous waste of food! The Native Americans could feed a family for a week from a single pumpkin. The university should've canceled this annual atrocity ages ago," said Art as he brushed past me.

As usual, Art didn't mince words. If I was grading his paper, I would've given him two points of extra credit for effectively using alliteration to make his point.

Janet had still not returned and when I opened the door to the department office, I found a folded piece of loose leaf paper on the floor with only my last name crudely scrawled on it. I opened the paper and read the message, *Meet me at the statute at 5:30. Snyder.*

Statute? I laughed. He must mean the bust of President Jordan in the courtyard behind Jordan Hall; that was the only statue nearby. Along with the pigeons, Snyder and the other homeless men often hung out on the benches near President Jordan's bust bumming cigarettes. The message seemed genuine; the misspelling of statue was indicative of Snyder's inebriated state. Snyder could've slipped in the building unnoticed while everyone was downstairs at the Pumpkin Plunge and delivered his note. It wasn't my first choice for a meeting place but it was public enough that I didn't perceive that I'd be in any danger. Even though it would be early evening, people would still be coming and going from Jordan Hall and the library on the other side of the courtyard. I wondered if Snyder was willing to admit anything or was planning to shake me down for cash in exchange for some bogus information. My first inclination was to call Harley Simpson but he'd likely whisk Snyder away before I even had a chance to speak with him.

I went back to work on my review of Dr. Paget but I was having a hard time concentrating, thinking ahead to my meeting with Snyder. Instead I sorted through the information I'd already collected on the case and tried to organize it. Since Snyder was already soused at noon, I doubted he'd be able to give me any sort of coherent answer but it might be my only chance to break the case wide open.

***

At five-twenty I shut down my computer; I re-read the note Snyder had written me and put it in the folder with the other information I'd developed on Jenny's murder. I locked the folder in my desk and closed up the office for the weekend. Taking the elevator down to the lobby, I found it deserted. Even on a Friday there were usually students hanging around the computer lab. Snyder was nowhere in sight when I stepped out into the courtyard; I suspected he was hiding in the building's shadow waiting for me to make my appearance. With the end of Daylight Savings Time, the sun was already down and a chill was in the air. A stiff wind blowing down from Canada was supposed to drop the temperature down to freezing overnight. My tweed sport coat did little to keep me warm.

I stood next to the bronze bust of President Jordan that was mounted on a block of black granite and waited for Snyder. The courtyard was eerily empty; two young men wearing CBU hoodies sitting on a bench and smoking cigarettes were the only other people around. In the grove of trees near the library, I thought I saw someone move and took a step forward to get a better look. Suddenly I heard a strange whistling noise and felt a rush of air behind me. I jumped as an object impacted on the pavement with a loud thump at my heels. Something jagged and orange flew over my head and landed some twenty feet in front of me; my coat was splattered with something wet and slimy. Dazed, I feared my head had been split open and my brains were slowly oozing out. To my relief, I found my head intact when I ran my hands through my thinning hair.

"Dude, did you see that! That pumpkin missed him by inches," screamed one of the students as they rushed over to me.

"Get the hell out of here!" I ran for the safety of the lobby fearing the fall of another pumpkin. The two students followed after me. Once I caught my breath, I reached inside my coat pocket and pulled out my cell phone. I dialed the emergency number for campus police and when the dispatcher answered, I tried to sound as calm as possible, "Someone just tried to kill me in the courtyard behind Jordan Hall!"

"Exactly how did they try to kill you?" asked the female dispatcher in a dispassionate voice.

"He dropped a large pumpkin from the top of Jordan Hall. Fortunately it missed me."

"Excuse me, have you been drinking sir?"

"No!"

"I'll send an officer over right away."

About two minutes later, I saw the blue flashing lights of the police car pull up in front of Jordan Hall. Officer Benton got out of the car and walked over to the remains of the errant murder weapon. She poked at one of the pieces with the toe of her shoe. I came out of the building with the two students in tow.

"Were you the one who called about someone trying to kill you?" Her voice was edged with a tone of obvious skepticism.

"Yes."

"Looks like a Howden Field to me."

"What is a Howden Field?"

"The Howden Field is known for its thick walls and dark orange color. It's been the industry standard for the last twenty years; I'm a master gardener."

Was Officer Benton here to investigate a murder attempt or give me a horticultural lesson?

"You're Dr. Stanard?"

"That's right."

"That pumpkin must have been left on the roof from the Pumpkin Plunge."

"It would take hurricane force winds to blow a ten pound pumpkin off a roof. Look, they saw it hit." I pointed to the two students and tried to damp down my rising anger.

"You're right; it looks like it was at least a fifteen pounder maybe closer to twenty. What kind of moron tries to kill someone with a pumpkin? It would've been much easier to use a gun or knife." She nudged another pumpkin shard with her shoe as if inspecting the tires on a used car. "You witnessed the attack?" she asked the students.

The two students nodded. Officer Benton took their names and phone numbers; she asked them to have a seat in the lobby.

"Why were you out here?" she asked me.

"I was waiting to meet someone."

"Who?"

"Felton Snyder."

"Stay here." Officer Benton got inside her car and talked on her radio. I took advantage of her absence to call Laura and told her to meet me in the lobby of Jordan Hall. A few minutes later Harley Simpson's car arrived; he got out and walked over to the pumpkin pieces, inspecting them with the toe of his shoe as had Officer Benton. They huddled over one of the larger shards, discussing the attempt on my life. They came into the lobby and Harley walked over to the two students.

"You two saw it happen?"

"Yes sir," answered one of the students.

"What were you doing out there?"

"We'd just finished in the computer lab and were having a smoke and shooting the breeze before heading over to the dining hall."

"Cigarettes or something stronger?" A fair question I thought, the two of them looked rather scruffy; I would've pegged them as potheads if they sat in one of my classes.

"Cigarettes." He nervously looked over at his partner.

"Did you two notice anything out of the ordinary?"

"No sir."

Harley turned to Officer Benton. "Did you get their contact info?

"Yes sir."

"You two can go now. We'll call you if we have any more questions."

The students got up and left. Within fifteen minutes, the story of the attack of the killer pumpkin would be all over the dining hall.

"Get one of the detectives to check the remains of the pumpkin for fingerprints; I doubt we'll find any in the condition it's in." He turned to me, "I told you not to meddle in my investigation. What were you doing meeting with Snyder?"

I hated to admit it but Harley had me dead to rights; however Snyder's attempt to kill me supported my thesis that somebody other than Brendan murdered Jenny. "One of my students reported that Snyder has been showing up at McDonald's with a lot of cash in his pocket; I went over at lunch time and asked Snyder where he'd gotten his money.

He wouldn't answer me and ran off. Follow the money; somebody is buying Snyder's silence."

"That's bullshit! Snyder's family probably sent him money."

"I talked with his sister in North Carolina this afternoon; in a weak moment, she sent him fifty bucks last year at Christmas. His brothers and sisters cut him off years ago. So where is the money coming from?"

"Felton Snyder is a habitual criminal."

"Does his plea bargain give him free rein to engage in illicit activities?"

Harley glared back at me. "Why were you standing by the statue?"

"Snyder shoved a note under my office door when I was watching the Pumpkin Plunge this afternoon asking me to meet him at five-thirty."

"Let's see the note," demanded Harley.

"It's up in my office."

Just then Laura walked into the lobby. "What happened to you?" She walked over to me and attempted to brush the pumpkin mush and seeds off the back of my coat.

"I just had a close encounter with a falling pumpkin."

"Who would do a sick prank like that?"

"It was no prank; someone was trying to kill me."

"I don't have all night; let's go up to your office," interrupted Harley.

We took the elevator to the sixth floor; immediately I noticed the door to the department office was wide open and the lights were on. I'd locked everything up before I'd left. Harley instinctively pulled out his gun and motioned for Laura and me to remain where we were. He silently crept into the office.

"No one is in here!" he called out a few seconds later.

I walked past Janet's desk into my office; the papers and folders on the top of my desk had been strewn on the floor. Whoever broke into the office had attempted to jimmy the lock on my desk with my letter opener. The tip of the letter opener remained in the lock; the haft lay on the floor where the intruder had dropped it. No doubt he'd heard the elevator and took off down the stairwell. Jordan Hall had eight exits on the ground floor plus the second floor walkway to the parking garage; there was no way Harley could seal the building.

"How did he get in?" I asked as I stared at the wide open door. Laura looked at me apprehensively; she realized the danger I was in.

"When they built this place in the late 1960's, the builder used the cheapest locks he could find. For two years I've been after Building and Grounds to replace them; you can force them open with a student ID card."

An office break-in was a piece of cake for someone like Snyder with an impressive list of criminal talents on his vita. "I'd locked the note in my desk."

Harley pulled the piece of the letter opener out of the lock. "Looks like an amateur job," he muttered.

I inserted my key and unlocked my desk. I handed my file to Harley; he pulled a pair of disposable gloves out of his pocket and put them on. Gingerly he picked up the note by the edges and looked it over suspiciously.

"Do you have a campus mail envelope?"

I handed him one off my credenza.

"I'll get this checked for fingerprints," he said as he slipped the note in the envelope.

I put the file in my briefcase; deciding it would be safer at home.

"I ought to have you arrested for tampering with a witness; Snyder is probably going to bolt now that you've poked your nose where you had no business going."

"The attempt on my life proves your star witness is nothing but a star liar!"

"We knew all about Snyder's background when we made the deal with him. Sure, he's no choir boy. You had no right to harass him with your bumbling inquiry."

"Someone is paying Snyder off."

"Who's paying him off? Give me a name!"

Harley was right. Other than my gut feeling that Reverend Franklin was Jenny's mystery lover, I had nothing that I was able to share with him.

"What was your theory earlier in the week? The pizza delivery driver killed Jenny."

I reached down to pick up some files off the floor.

"Don't be touching anything; I'm going to have my men go over your office tonight and see if we can find any fingerprints."

"Can I straighten up my office in the morning?"

"We'll be finished tonight. No doubt Healy's attorney is going to attempt to discredit Snyder with this. I'm warning you for the last time; stay out of my investigation!"

"Chief." Officer Benton poked her head in my office.

"What is it?" Harley growled.

"The hatch to the roof is padlocked; whoever dropped the pumpkin did from a window inside the building."

"Check all the offices on this side of the building. Before you do that, call that professor in charge this afternoon and make sure he removed all the damn pumpkins from the roof!"

Laura and I took the elevator down to the lobby. Out on the courtyard, Sergeant Ramsey was photographing the remains of the murderous pumpkin; another police officer was using a measuring tape to record the distance one of the errant shards flew. When we reached the car, Laura tried again to brush the drying pumpkin seeds off the back of my sport coat.

"Harley Simpson is right," she said through clenched teeth. "You're blundering around oblivious to the danger you're putting yourself in. What if Snyder comes after me or the boys? Did you ever think about us?"

"I'm sorry; I didn't realize the risks I've been taking."

"Snyder is not going to sleep easy as long as he knows you're still on his trail; don't you think it's possible he's going to try to kill you again. Next time, he's going to use something more accurate than a pumpkin."

With all the alcohol he'd consumed today, I strongly doubted that Snyder would have any trouble sleeping. Laura was right; I'd blundered and failed to see the obvious. Whoever wrote the note, deliberately misspelled statue to make me think a drunken Snyder wrote it. Then he desperately turned my office upside down to try to retrieve the forged note after his attack failed. My attacker cleverly tried to take advantage of the Pumpkin Plunge to make it look like an accident. As drunk as Snyder was at noon, he wouldn't have missed me by a matter of inches. He couldn't have landed the pumpkin within ten feet of me. No, someone very sober and quite cunning was behind the attempt on my life.

Snyder was telling the truth when he said he knew nothing about the burglary of Jenny's apartment. He'd killed a witness previously to protect his ass and would've had no qualms about torching Jenny's apartment to destroy any evidence. Subtlety was not one of Snyder's strong points; he wouldn't have tried to kill me with pumpkin. A buck knife was his preferred weapon.

Jenny's killer took a huge risk breaking into Jenny's apartment on Wednesday. He was getting desperate; there must have been something that linked him to her murder that he needed to retrieve. Taking a bigger gamble, he tried to eliminate me fearing I'm on the right track to finding him. The only problem was I didn't know what train I was on.

Laura hugged me and ran her hand down my back. "I'm not sure your coat can be dry cleaned. How old is it anyway?"

CHAPTER XXIX

THE BOYS WERE PLAYING A video game when we walked in the family room. James paused playing the game when he saw my ruined sport coat draped over my arm. "What happened?"

"Someone tried to kill your father by dropping a pumpkin from the top of Jordan Hall; it missed him by a matter of inches," Laura answered for me.

"Are you joking me?" James asked.

"I wish I were," she replied.

"Who wants to kill a history professor? It's not like you're a drug dealer over in JT," said Robert.

"Couldn't he have used a .44 magnum? No one is going to believe that someone tried to kill you with a pumpkin," said James.

"If he'd used a .44 magnum, I'd be dead."

"You know what I mean."

The doorbell rang and Laura went to the front door to distribute chocolate bars to two boys in vampire costumes swarming around the neighborhood in search of Halloween candy.

After surviving the attempt on my life, I thought a celebratory dinner was in order. Visions of filet mignon, lobster tails or lamb chops with mint jelly danced in my head. There was only one problem; it was Friday night and the boys had different expectations for dinner. My plans dashed, I called Vito's and ordered two pizzas, one with pepperoni and one with onions and peppers.

I opened a bottle of merlot and poured glasses for Laura and me. Laura sat in the living room trying to take her mind off what happened by thumbing through the latest *Smithsonian*.

"I'm not going to be able to sleep until they arrest that creep," she said as she took her glass from me.

"I don't think we have anything to fear from Snyder."

"He tried to kill you tonight!"

"When I saw Snyder at noon, he was already three sheets to the wind. Even if he had a Norden bombsight, he couldn't have hit the broad side of a barn."

"Then who tried to kill you?"

"Snyder is blackmailing Jenny's killer; I overplayed my hand when I confronted Snyder this afternoon and provoked the killer instead."

Laura leaned forward in her chair. "You know who killed Jenny."

"He thinks I'm closing in on him."

"Are you?"

"I've got threads of evidence when I need a tapestry."

"Who are your suspects?"

"I found it a strange coincidence that I ran into Leo Plaskett coming out of McDonald's at noon. It's quite possible he'd just met with Snyder and left when he saw me coming."

"Is Plaskett the pervert that harassed Jenny's student?"

"Yes."

"A pizza delivery driver doesn't have the cash to pay off a blackmailer."

"I don't think Snyder has high expectations; he just wants enough to buy a couple bottles of Wild Irish Rose and a meal at McDonalds."

"That would bleed someone like Plaskett dry," speculated Laura.

"Definitely."

"How did Plaskett get into an office to drop the pumpkin?"

"Harley said the locks are easy to force; Plaskett looks industrious enough to figure that out. One thing troubles me; Jenny's apartment was broken into on Wednesday. The killer needed to retrieve something incriminating and I think that points to Reverend Franklin."

"Reverend Franklin killed Jenny?"

"Melinda, Jenny's roommate, said she came home early in February and heard Jenny in bed with someone. Jenny came out and pretended like nothing happened; her mystery lover stayed in the bedroom not wanting to be seen."

"Do you have any proof it was Reverend Franklin?"

"Melinda was in the bathroom and looked out the window. She saw a blond haired man get into a dark blue BMW and drive off. I saw Reverend Franklin driving a BMW on Tuesday."

"That's a rather slender thread to hang an accusation on, don't you think?"

"Franklin was at the Pumpkin Plunge this afternoon; he's also an adjunct professor in Philosophy and knows his way around Jordan Hall. He also knows Snyder and would be a far wealthier target for blackmail."

"Still, I can't imagine Jenny boinking Reverend Franklin. He's at least fifteen years older than her."

I was somewhat surprised by Laura's use of the boys' slang. "Melinda said Jenny's lovers were all cut from the same bolt of cloth; tall, blond haired and blue eyed."

"Maybe you're looking in the wrong direction."

"No one else appears to have a motive."

Just then the doorbell rang. I went to the door and found the delivery driver from Vito's with the pizzas. Frank had been in one of my classes the year before. "I thought Leo Plaskett usually covered this neighborhood."

Frank looked at me as if Leo Plaskett was none of my business. "Leo up and quit this morning; he told Vito he was leaving this burg."

"Where's he headed?"

"Back to Munchkin Land, he's hitting the yellow brick road next week." Frank laughed heartily at his own joke about Plaskett's height. "He's been acting strangely the last couple weeks, not to speak ill of the dear departed."

I paid him for the pizzas and gave him a generous tip for the information on Plaskett. Where was Plaskett headed? More importantly what prompted his sudden departure? Jenny had been dead less than two weeks; roughly the start of Plaskett's odd behavior according to Frank.

***

After dinner, the phone rang. "Dad! Dean Monroe wants to speak to you," yelled Robert.

I went into my study to take the call. "Hi Tollie."

"How are you doing? Harley Simpson briefed me about the attempt on your life."

I was almost touched by Tollie's solicitousness until I realized that he was afraid that if anything happened to me, Emily Worthington was the only one willing to assume the duties of department chair. "I'm all right although my sport coat is a goner according to Laura."

Tollie laughed. "The drunk who tried to kill you dropped Homer from the reception area outside my office; the window screen was lying on the floor."

"Homer?"

"Tammie painted a face on a pumpkin she bought at the farmer's market and named it Homer; women do things like that. It was an eighteen pounder; Harley said it would've crushed your skull if his aim was better."

When I'd been up to Tollie's office earlier in the week, I'd seen the lethal pumpkin perched on a table in the reception area. Tammie loved to decorate for whatever holiday was approaching. It also suggested that whoever tried to kill me knew the pumpkin was sitting there, waiting to be used.

"By any chance was Reverend Franklin in your office this week?"

"I met with him, Rabbi Rubin, Father Novello and Whit Tanner on the Interfaith Understanding Conference that the Philosophy and Religious Studies Department is sponsoring next week. Why do you ask?"

"I thought I saw him getting on the elevator on the tenth floor," I said as nonchalantly as possible.

"My hunch is that the police are focusing on the wrong suspect."

What did Tollie know?

"I bet the wicked witch of the History Department tried to do you in. Right now, she's out flying around on her broom." Tollie chuckled; he could never resist the opportunity to take a poke at Emily.

***

After Tollie's call I went out to gas up the car and pick up a gallon of milk. As I was inserting my credit card in the pump, I had the sense again that someone was watching me. I jerked around and saw Jenny's father standing at the opposite pump next to a dark blue station wagon, the car Brendan supposedly used on the night of the murder. The interior was filled with boxes for the trip back to Ohio. I felt uncomfortable as he walked over to me.

"You're Brendan's professor, aren't you?" he asked.

"Andrew Stanard," I replied as I extended my hand. "I'm very sorry about the loss of your daughter."

Mr. Biggio looked down at my hand but couldn't bring himself to shake it. "Why do you believe that Brendan is innocent? That I don't understand."

Against my better judgment I took the bait. "Harley Simpson zeroed in on Brendan within minutes of finding Jenny; the chief witness against Brendan is a wino with an extensive criminal record."

"The police often have to make deals with unsavory individuals; they also have forensic evidence that links Brendan to Jenny's murder."

"Over the last couple days, things have happened that prove Brendan is innocent."

"Like what?"

"The break-in at Jenny's apartment proves that her killer is still at large."

"According to the police it was a random burglary and totally unconnected to Jenny's murder."

"I'm curious what did the burglar take?"

"Jenny's roommate said he tossed things around but nothing was taken. He rummaged through Jenny's desk and bookcase; Melinda thought Jenny's backup hard drive was gone but she wasn't 100% certain. My wife was relieved that he missed the pearl ring we gave Jenny when she graduated from Kent State."

It was interesting that the thief concentrated his efforts on Jenny's desk and bookcase. But what was he looking for? "Don't you find it odd that the thief wasn't interested in jewelry?"

Her father paused for a minute. "Chief Simpson thinks the burglar was a kid; he simply got scared and ran off."

The kids who inhabited Jefferson Terrace never impressed me as the type that scared all that easily. "Felton Snyder, the wino I mentioned earlier, has been awash in cash the last couple days."

"So what?"

"I've never believed in pennies from heaven. My suspicion is he's been blackmailing Jenny's killer."

"You're pulling all this out of thin air."

"When I confronted Snyder this afternoon he ran off; later I found a note under my office door requesting a meeting but instead Jenny's killer tried to silence me permanently with a pumpkin dropped from the tenth floor of Jordan Hall."

"Are you sure it wasn't a bunch of fraternity boys pulling a prank? They missed you, didn't they?"

There was no point in asking Jenny's father if she'd been involved with Reverend Franklin. "Did Jenny ever mention if anyone was stalking her or if a relationship with an old boyfriend had gone sour?"

"Why are you asking me all these questions?" Jenny's father stiffened; he stared silently at a billboard for a local car dealer across the street. "I liked Brendan when Jenny brought him home to meet us this summer; he'd served in the Marines like me. No offense, I always feared Jenny would marry some wimpy intellectual. But if I'd known that Brendan had done time; I wouldn't have allowed him near my daughter. As far as I'm concerned, the police have arrested the right man. Don't reopen this wound; my wife has been barely able to function since they told us Jenny had been murdered." He got in his car and drove off.

***

I awoke early on Saturday; my plan was to straighten up the mess left from yesterday's ransacking of my office before heading to Tollie Monroe's tailgate party at noon. With the kickoff for the Homecoming Game scheduled for two o'clock and the parade starting at ten; I needed to ride my bike to campus since all the parking lots would be reserved for pre-game tailgating.

After filling a thermos with coffee, I kissed a still sleeping Laura goodbye. Biking across campus to Jordan Hall, I noticed several police cars parked near the pond between the library and the engineering building. In no particular hurry, I detoured to get a closer look and came upon Harley Simpson and Dick Torelli arguing loudly next to a black, windowless van.

"The homecoming parade starts in two hours; you need to clear out of here quickly. I don't want alumni getting the impression that this campus is unsafe because some old wino falls into the pond and drowns because he's too drunk to swim," said Torelli.

The pond had been dug to aid drainage on campus and add a picturesque setting to the campus; a Japanese style bridge crossed the figure eight shaped pond where it narrowed in the center. Around the edges it was only three or four feet deep before gently sloping to about ten feet deep in the center; I found it hard to believe anyone would drown if they stumbled in. Having overheard that a wino had drowned, I was willing to bet even money that it was Felton Snyder's body that two police divers were retrieving from the murky green waters near the bridge.

"I don't need you interfering with my investigation," replied Harley.

"Do I need to call Doug?" If anyone had President Clayton's ear, it was Dick Torelli and he was always quick to invoke the president's name to get what he wanted.

"What happened?" Both turned around in dismay; they'd been arguing so intently, they'd been unaware of my presence.

"A jogger saw the body shortly after seven and called it in on the emergency call box over there; somehow the body drifted under the bridge and is lodged under the pilings," replied Harley.

One of the divers, a young man in his twenties with close cropped hair, walked over to Harley. His wetsuit was zipped open to reveal a Celtic tattoo in the center of his chest. "Tell me, why do murderers always wait to dump their victims in water until cold weather comes along?"

"He was murdered? Are you sure of that?" asked Harley.

"The coroner is examining the body now; it looks like someone bashed in the victim's skull with a rock. His backpack weighted him down," replied the diver. To make the pond more scenic, its banks had been lined with imported rocks and boulders providing the murderer with a handy array of weapons.

Harley and the diver walked over to the coroner leaving me alone with Dick Torelli; he seemed infuriated by the diver's pronouncement. "What in the hell is going on? A second murder in less than two weeks," he muttered as he went over to a nearby tree and called someone on his cell phone, most likely breaking the news to Doug Clayton.

I decided to stick around and see what I could find out since none of the officers had made an attempt to force me to leave. Harley talked with the coroner for several minutes before the body was zipped up in a black plastic body bag and loaded it into the black van.

"You said that you had a phone conversation with Felton Snyder's sister yesterday; can you give me her phone number?" asked Harley.

"It's back at my office. So, that was Snyder floating out there?"

Harley paused before answering. "Someone cracked his skull open before dumping him in the pond."

"He was killed with a rock?"

"That was the diver's speculation. But he's only a rookie; he'd been a diver in the Navy. Rocks are generally a poor choice for a weapon; I'd put my money on a pipe or in Snyder's case, a vodka bottle."

"A vodka bottle?"

"A filled 750 milliliter liquor bottle will make a nasty indentation on someone's skull; it also fits that one of Snyder's wino pals saw the wad of cash you caught a glimpse of and beaned him for it."

"Snyder's murder confirms that Jenny Biggio's killer is still at large."

"Nuts! Jenny Biggio's murderer is sitting in a cell on the fifth floor of the city jail reading *The Decline and Fall of the Roman Empire*. Snyder's death is totally unrelated to her murder. You forget that Snyder double crossed Antonio McKinney and his associates; I'm going to bring McKinney in for questioning. His motorcycle gang buddies also have reason to see him dead; the fact that he's now a snitch violates their code of silence. It's a point of honor with bikers; you don't make deals with the police.

Besides Snyder knew too much; they were concerned he'd turn on them the next time he was in trouble. Those are more plausible scenarios than your half-baked theory."

"Snyder's death does put a big hole in your case against Brendan."

Harley laughed. "Don't think for a minute that Healy is going to get off the hook; even without Snyder, we have more than enough evidence to convict him. Besides we took the precaution of videotaping Snyder's statement in case his liver didn't last until the trial."

"You have one problem to explain; Snyder didn't try to kill me last night. Jenny's murderer made it look like Snyder tried to kill me. If you check Snyder's blood alcohol level and his time of death; there was no way he could've carried out the attempt to kill me."

"Okay, it's time for you to leave; I have a murder investigation to conduct here." Harley motioned for one of his officers to come and escort me away from the crime scene.

"The Alumni Association picnic is going to be held by the end of the bridge after the parade; you need to get this mess cleaned up before the caterer arrives," demanded Torelli.

"If you don't get out of my face, you're going to end up floating in the pond like the corpse we've just removed," replied Harley.

***

As I locked my bike to the rack, I observed the orange stain on the bricks where the pumpkin had spilled its guts in its failed kamikaze attack that is if one believed Harley's rationalization that the pumpkin fell from the tenth floor without human intervention. Otherwise how could he fail to see the connection between the two murders and the attempt on my life?

Up in my office, I began picking up the papers off the floor and putting my desk back in order. Around nine o'clock I decided to take a chance and see if Brendan's lawyer was working on Saturday.

"Carla Burnham." She sounded weary.

"This is Andrew Standard; there have been some developments that I thought you should be aware of."

"What happened?"

"Felton Snyder was found floating in a pond on campus. Someone bashed his skull in."

"Damn it! No doubt they have his statement on tape; the Commonwealth's Attorney will move to have it admitted into evidence. I could've torn Snyder to shreds on the witness stand and totally undermined his credibility."

"Can't you have the tape excluded?"

"Judge Warren is a former Commonwealth's Attorney; his rulings generally favor the prosecution. But it definitely would be an issue on appeal."

I was trying to free Brendan now; not get him off on a technicality years later. "Someone broke into Jenny's apartment on Wednesday; my hunch is her murderer needed to remove something incriminating."

"Like what?" Her voice was edged with a tone of exasperation.

"I ran into Jenny's father last night; he said the burglar left behind a pearl ring, instead he ransacked Jenny's bookcase and desk."

"Interesting but its only speculation; I can't begin to tell you how many Jefferson Terrace burglary defendants this office represents. Burglary is a cottage industry in that neighborhood."

"My suspicion is that Felton Snyder was blackmailing Jenny's killer; he was seen carrying a large roll of cash the last two days."

"How much are we talking about?"

"He had at least $40, maybe $50 according to my witness."

"That seems like a piddling sum for a blackmailer."

"You're talking about someone who was scrounging cigarette butts. I confronted Snyder on Friday afternoon and that evening someone tries to eliminate me by dropping a pumpkin from ten stories up."

"You've got to be kidding me! No jury is going to believe Jenny's killer is still at large and attempted to kill you with a pumpkin; I'll be laughed out of the Bar Association."

I failed to see what everyone found so funny; if the pumpkin had crushed my skull, I would've been just as dead as if a bullet had pierced my heart. "Snyder was my best shot at finding Jenny's killer. Now that he's dead, my chance may be slipping away."

Carla sighed. "Nothing in this case is adding up."

After finishing with her, I dialed directory assistance in North Carolina. "Do you have a listing for a Jefferson Chambliss in High Point?"

"Let me check." A cloying recorded voice gave me the number and I dialed it.

"Good morning. This is Andrew Stanard."

"What can I do for you doc?" he asked in a slightly annoyed tone of voice.

"The campus police just fished Felton Snyder out of a pond this morning; someone cracked his skull open."

"Well, I can't say that I'm going to send a wreath to his funeral."

"Chief Simpson thinks it possible the Devil's Disciples did him in."

"Nah, the Devil's Disciples are too smart to leave a body for the police to find. If you cross them, you're going to end up deep in the piney woods. We lucked out, if you can call it that, when a hunter's dogs found the bones of Snyder's murder victim. I have a ten o'clock tee time so it was good talking to you doc."

"Enjoy your retirement."

I picked up Harley's Simpson's card off my desk and dialed his cell phone.

"Chief Simpson," he replied.

"This is Andrew Stanard. I can't find the phone number for Snyder's sister; the slip of paper must've been lost when my office was ransacked. Reverend Franklin had previously been in contact with Ida Tolbert; I got her phone number from him."

"Thanks, I'll give him a call."

I looked at the pad of paper with Ida Tolbert's number jotted down on it. Rather than making things easier for Harley Simpson, I decided it might be a bit disconcerting for Reverend Franklin to have the police call him so soon after Snyder's body was discovered.

***

The caterers were busy setting up the tables and chairs for the Alumni Association picnic when I stopped by the pond on the way home. The sun had come out and it felt warmer than fifty degrees; there was no hint that a murder had occurred a little over twelve hours earlier. It appeared that Dick Torelli had prevailed over Harley Simpson; after all it was only a homeless wino that had been murdered. There was no need to disrupt the homecoming festivities. Why upset the well-heeled members of the Alumni Association just before Doug Clayton was going to put the squeeze on them for a donation to the football team.

I surveyed the pond; despite being in the middle of a busy campus, it was a secluded location, perfect for a murder. On Friday night, the library closed at six o'clock and no one could've observed the murder from its windows. Opposite the library was the Engineering Building; by nightfall on Friday, it was deserted too. The Jordan Hall parking garage anchored the west end of the pond; on the east end, the Health Sciences Building was under renovation. Trees along the banks, including several weeping willows, provided needed privacy for amorous students in balmier weather and a murderer last night.

I took a seat on one of several teak benches strung out along the banks. As in Jenny's murder and my attack, Snyder's murder pointed to the fact that the perpetrator was more than familiar with the campus. The killer set up the meeting with Snyder fearing that he was no longer to be trusted. Snyder was likely dozing from a drinking binge on one of the benches when the murderer crept up behind him and caved in his skull. A chill ran down my spine; I nervously turned around and saw no one in sight.

With his back against the wall after being implicated by Antonio McKinney's girlfriend, Snyder had few options. The police, anxious to make a case against Brendan, presented him with a way out of jail. At the time of his arrest, he probably didn't know the identity of the person who dumped the wallet in the alley but he knew enough details about Brendan to fake a plausible story that duped the investigators.

Snyder saw something in the alley that night that led him to Jenny's killer. Surely he'd seen the BMW in Reverend Franklin's reserved space from his visits to the Ark Church's soup kitchen. If he'd recognized Reverend Franklin's car, why didn't he turn him over to the police instead of Brendan? Or had it been his intent to blackmail Reverend Franklin all along? Mrs. Tolbert indicated that Felton had always been the cleverest member of the family; playing both sides against the middle would be within his talents. But with booze dulling his wits, he overplayed his hand and provoked Jenny's killer.

Snyder's murder troubled me. I could see Reverend Franklin killing Jenny in a momentary fit of rage but it was harder to fathom a man of God trying to kill me and then murdering Felton Snyder in cold blood. Was I looking at the wrong suspect or merely underestimating Reverend Franklin's capacity for homicide?

CHAPTER XXX

BEFORE HEADING TO TOLLIE'S TAILGATE party, I dialed the cell phone number listed on Shane Alvarez's business card.

"Alvarez," he answered on the fifth ring. He seemed out of breath as if he'd just come in from a jog.

"This is Andrew Stanard."

"What can I do for you?" he asked in voice tinged with barely concealed annoyance.

"Felton Snyder met his maker last night."

"There were no murders on the police scanner last night; for a Friday night in Norfolk it was dead quiet. We had no blood to lead the eleven o'clock news." His tone of voice shifted. In the background I could hear the rustling of sheets and the unmistakable creaking of an aged box spring.

"Who is it baby?" asked a squeaky female voice.

"It's work; roll over and I'll be back in a minute," he attempted to whisper to his companion. "What happened?"

"Someone cracked his skull open."

"How did you find that out?"

"I was there when the campus police fished his body out of a drainage pond early this morning."

"What do the police think?"

"Chief Simpson immediately declared there was no connection to Jenny Biggio's murder."

"He's still fixated on Healy?"

"He won't budge. Snyder's murder is only the tip of the iceberg; someone attempted to kill me last night."

"How?"

"My attacker dropped a pumpkin from the top of Jordan Hall."

"Sounds like the Headless Horseman is after Ichabod Crane again," Shane laughed. I filled him in on what I'd discovered about Snyder and how I'd been set up. His tone turned serious again. "I'm sticking it to Amanda Saltzman tonight; I interviewed Tiffany Finley yesterday afternoon."

"Hey, I thought you were spending the night with me again!" I recognized the voice as belonging to the waitress at Finnerty's.

"It's a journalism term; you're the only one I'm ..." It sounded like he dropped his cell phone on a wooden floor and I heard nothing for several seconds. "Catch the six o'clock news tonight." Then the call abruptly ended. Either the phone's battery died or his companion had other plans for the few minutes that remained of the morning.

***

Surprisingly for an unreconstructed poet, Tollie Monroe had been caught up in the football mania sweeping the campus with the inaugural season of Chesapeake Bay University's football team. He'd invited the faculty and their spouses (or significant others in some cases) to his house near the campus for a tailgate party before the game. By the time Laura and I arrived, Tollie's backyard was jammed. I surveyed the gathering for members of the History department. Due to their mutual antagonism, I figured Emily declined Tollie's invitation. She regarded football as little more than a modern version of the gladiatorial games put on by the emperors to pacify the Roman mobs.

I grabbed a Corona from an ice filled plastic tub and handed another to Laura. Tollie was holding court near his enormous gas grill; he'd hired a long haired graduate student from the English department to man the grill and pass out hot dogs and bratwurst.

"You look no worse for wear and tear," Tollie greeted me.

"I'm doing a lot better than Felton Snyder; Harley Simpson found him murdered this morning in the pond behind the library."

"You mean the wino who tried to kill you?"

"That's what Jenny Biggio's murderer wanted everyone to think."

"Good afternoon Dr. Stanard," interrupted Amanda Saltzman. She had a Bud Light in one hand and Barry Sanders in the other. Like her taste in beer, she preferred her men to be lightweights too. "Out with it, who helped you stage your little charade last night? Did one of Healy's buddies drop the pumpkin, perhaps Dave Chen?"

"There were two eye witnesses," I replied.

"Two stoners, I wouldn't deem them as reliable witnesses."

"You have some nerve accusing my husband; someone killed Felton Snyder last night to silence him," said Laura before I could respond.

Saltzman laughed. "You and your husband are so naïve. Only one person had a reason to silence Felton Snyder. The police know that Brendan Healy was left alone with his mother and sister for several minutes before his arraignment on Thursday, plenty of time to make arrangements with his little sister to contact one of his pals from New Jersey to take care of Snyder."

"You're incredible!" Laura pointed her finger in Saltzman's face. "Did you study journalism under Joseph Goebbels?"

Not wanting his party turned into a brawl, Tollie diplomatically stepped in. "Amanda, I understand from Barry, the interns from our journalism program are thrilled to be working at the *Register*. Such real world experience is invaluable for them."

Tollie's intervention allowed us to make our escape. "Are they training those students at the *Register* to be vipers like its star reporter?" asked Laura when we were out of earshot.

As word of the attempt on my life spread through the party, I basked in the glow of my new found celebrity status. Fortunately Amanda Saltzman and Barry Sanders stayed on the other side of the yard until they left.

After Tollie's party broke up, we met up with the boys at the stadium. By half-time, CBU had rolled to a 28 to 0 lead much to the delight of the sold out stadium.

"We now introduce the members of the homecoming court," announced the master of ceremonies standing at mid-field. Standing next to him was President Clayton, Dick Torelli and the Dean of Students plus the five young women elected to the court by the student body. "Sabine Crawford, a senior nursing major from Williamsburg, Virginia is the first member of our court. Next is Donna Nelson, a junior elementary education major from Vienna, Virginia. The third member of the court is Cassandra Hayes, a senior biology major from Cherry Hill, New Jersey. Helena Barton, a junior history major from Seaford, Delaware, is the fourth member of the court. Tara Jenkins, a senior sociology major from Danville, Virginia, is the final member of the homecoming court."

I trained my binoculars on President Clayton chatting with Dick Torelli. He was smiling broadly; after all everything was going his way. Brendan Healy was in jail and the headlines about Jenny's murder would be replaced by stories in Sunday's paper about a lopsided football victory. The murder of Felton Snyder would be buried in the back pages of the local news section of the *Register*; no one cared about a dead wino. President Clayton had another reason to smile; he'd soon be planting a kiss on the homecoming queen.

"Andrea McGowan, president of the Accounting Majors Association, will reveal the winner of the on-line voting conducted this week," said the announcer as he handed the microphone to a leggy brunette. Andrea, attractive as any member of the homecoming court, didn't fit the stereotype for the accounting profession.

"It gives me great pleasure to announce that the students of Chesapeake Bay University have elected Tara Jenkins as your homecoming queen!" Dean Noble presented Tara with a bouquet of carnations dyed burgundy and gold to the applause from the crowd.

"President Clayton will now congratulate the winner," read the announcer from the prepared script.

Tara looked like she was suffering from indigestion after wolfing down a couple of greasy chili dogs as Doug Clayton wrapped her in a big bear hug.

***

At home after CBU's homecoming victory, I turned on Channel Five. Shane was anchoring the broadcast since it was a Saturday and the regular anchor had the night off. He looked no worse for the wear from Saturday morning.

"Good evening, there have been new developments in the investigation of the murder of Chesapeake Bay University coed, Jenny Biggio. One of the key witnesses against her accused boyfriend, Brendan Healy, was found dead in a pond on the CBU campus early this morning. Campus police have released few details about the death of Felton Snyder, a homeless wino, who panhandled at the university."

The screen switched to Harley Simpson standing outside the campus police station, taped earlier in the afternoon. "We're treating Mr. Snyder's death as a homicide; at this time we don't believe there's any connection to Ms. Biggio's murder. It's likely he died during a dispute with another homeless individual, probably over drugs or alcohol."

"And what about the attempt to murder Professor Andrew Stanard, Brendan Healy's mentor last night?" asked Shane.

"Someone dropped a pumpkin from a window in Jordan Hall that landed near Dr. Stanard last night. I'm not sure if I would characterize it as a murder attempt; it may've been a prank," replied Harley.

"Wasn't Dr. Stanard supposed to be meeting with Mr. Snyder at the time of the attack?"

"Since this is an ongoing investigation, I'd rather not comment on specifics."

"Next, after a word from our sponsors, will be my interview with Tiffany Finley, the CBU coed accused of being Brendan Healy's lover."

After a string of drug commercials, Tiffany Finley appeared on the screen wearing an electric blue sweater that showed off her cleavage to the viewers at home and appeared tight enough to constrict her breathing. She and Shane were sitting on a bench by the pond where Felton Snyder had met his watery fate later that day. Laura looked askance at Tiffany's bleached blond hair and body-hugging sweater.

"Why doesn't her mother do something about her wardrobe?"

"Mom, all the girls dress like that," replied James.

"Tiffany Finley is a freshman nursing major from Danville, Virginia," said Shane to start the segment. "You've been accused by the police of spending Monday afternoon with Brendan Healy."

"That's simply not true! I was in my chemistry lab all afternoon."

"Do you have any proof of that?"

"We all have to swipe our ID card to check out the glassware and chemicals for the experiments. I told the police that; my lab instructor can verify I was there."

"How well do you know Mr. Healy?"

"He's the instructor of my history class."

"Have you ever dated him?"

"No!"

"Where were you on Monday night when Jenny Biggio was murdered?"

"I attended a sorority rush party at Kappa Delta."

"But why have the police insinuated that you're his lover?"

"It's a nightmare! That female reporter from Channel 12 has been hounding me day and night with her false accusations. I impetuously gave Mr. Healy a little hug when he told me I passed the quiz. That's all." Tiffany began sobbing and Shane gallantly gave her a monogrammed handkerchief to dab her eyes.

"Impetuously! Where in heaven did she learn to use such large words?" asked Laura.

"It's one of the SAT study words," said James.

The interview served its purpose. Coupled with Felton Snyder's murder and the attack on me, the police's case against Brendan was rapidly fraying.

***

After church on Sunday, I headed downtown to visit Brendan. The guard checking in visitors now recognized me as one of the jail's regulars. Brendan was escorted to the visiting room about fifteen minutes later; the thick glass couldn't obscure the fact that he looked listless and depressed.

"Thanks for coming," he greeted me.

"I put the money your mother gave me in your canteen account."

He nodded. "Next time you talk with my mom, tell her to save her money. Things are tight for her; I can survive without it. I'm not her little boy up at Mountainview."

"Someone murdered Felton Snyder on Friday night."

"Chief Simpson was here this morning questioning me. He thinks I'm behind that bum's murder. Somehow I've contacted one of my gang pals in New Jersey to bump him off. Look, when I joined the Marines, I completely left that life behind me."

It was hard for me to see how Harley believed something that preposterous.

"He also thinks you and Dave Chen staged that attack on Friday night."

"What!" I was furious that Harley would even think to question my integrity. It worried me that I might be in over my head. Tollie had warned me that he couldn't protect me. Doug Clayton wanted Jenny's murder wrapped up and moved off the front page; my efforts were seen by Harley as unwarranted meddling and would be dealt with severely by the president. I needed to move fast to clear Brendan before the blade of Doug Clayton's guillotine descended on me.

"Simpson is trying to locate Dave. Unlike Tom and Hank, he hasn't come to see me here in the jail. Knowing him as I do, he's probably off banging some babe. Dave's parents want him to settle down and marry a nice Chinese girl but he's fixated on redheads," laughed Brendan interrupting my thoughts.

It was the first time he even cracked a smile but he quickly turned serious again. "You know I've only been in jail for a week but it feels like I've been here for years. I keep dredging up that nightmare I had this summer about being in prison again."

"The developments over the past few days will eventually clear you."

"Even if I'm cleared of Jenny's murder; I'm going to spend the rest of my life behind bars up in Jersey."

Brendan's statement alarmed me. "What do you mean by that?"

"When Milkowski visited me after my arraignment, he said they were going to run new DNA tests on the spic that was murdered before I shipped out to boot camp. It's going to implicate me. You see, Sean was my brother."

"He's your brother?"

"Half-brother to be exact; my father poked his pecker in some sorry ass women including Maura O'Reilly. He cheated on my mom from day one," said Brendan.

"When did you find out?"

"I began to suspect it at Mountainview when one of the guards asked if Sean was my younger brother. Ordinarily people wouldn't have noticed the resemblance. I have blond hair while Sean had brown hair; Sean was six inches shorter than me due to his mother being short. With our heads shaved, it accentuated our facial features and the guard picked up on it."

"Does your mother know?"

"She was in denial for years about my father's unfaithfulness. From what I heard later, the summer Sean's mother conceived him; she was drugging and drinking down at the shore. Blitzed out of her mind, she didn't care where, when or who she screwed including her best friend's husband."

"I thought that the drug dealer was killed in a turf war between rival gangs."

Brendan shrugged. "The spics have no compulsion about killing one of their own; they do it all the time. Sean swore he'd nothing to do with that murder but I was never 100% convinced of his innocence. He was doing some heavy drugs at the time and becoming more and more erratic. It will be bigger headlines for Milkowski to pin it on me; the other suspects are probably all dead now. The DNA evidence will be icing on the cake."

"I'm going to talk with Julia Adams; she may be able to shed some light on the subject or point me to a DNA expert other than Maury Povich."

Brendan laughed. "Thanks, you're the only other person I can trust now. I really appreciate your support."

When I returned to my car, I checked my cell phone since I couldn't bring it into the jail. I'd missed a call from Laura. I called her cell phone; she'd said she might go out shopping.

"Thank God you called. Sergeant Ramsey was just here. The police believe you staged the attack on yourself Friday night." After twenty-one years of marriage I could read the tone of Laura's voice like a book; she was frightened.

"Was the purpose of his visit to question me or to arrest me?"

"I don't know."

"Hold down the fort; I'm going to pay a visit to the Ark Church."

"What if he comes back?"

"Stall him."

"Do we need to call an attorney?"

"It might be a good idea."

"I'll see if Tom Redmond knows a good one."

*✻✻

A tan Volvo station wagon was in Reverend Franklin reserved parking space in front of the church when I arrived. A few church members were still milling around in the lobby sipping coffee even though the morning service had ended about thirty minutes earlier.

"What can I do for you brother?" asked an elderly man when he realized that I wasn't a member of the congregation.

"I'm here to see Reverend Franklin," I replied.

"Do you have an appointment?"

"No, I thought the pastor's door was always open."

"You seem troubled, do you need someone to pray with you."

"It's important that I talk directly with him; it's about Felton Snyder, the homeless man who was murdered. I'm Dr. Stanard."

He gave me a puzzled look before going down the hall to Reverend Franklin's study and returning a few minutes later. "The pastor will see you now."

Reverend Franklin was sitting behind his desk, his tie off, his suit coat draped on a chair. "I was just getting ready to head home for lunch." He was politely telling me to make it quick.

Knowing the purpose of my visit, I had to steel myself to confront him. "Were you able to get in touch with Mrs. Tolbert?"

"She was saddened by her brother's death but she'd always feared something like that would happen to him. It troubled Mrs. Tolbert that he never renounced Satan and accepted Christ as his Lord and Savior before he died. Once the coroner releases his body, he'll be cremated and the family will inter his ashes next to his parents in the family plot in Murfreesboro."

"I imagine with all the alcohol that he consumed over the years he should burn like a torch."

Reverend Franklin was unable to suppress a laugh. "You have a sardonic wit Dr. Stanard but I get the impression you didn't come here to discuss the eternal damnation of Felton Snyder, did you?"

I took a deep breath; it was time for the direct approach. "Did you have an affair with Jenny Biggio?"

In the tick of a second, his face reddened and he rose from his chair. He snarled, "I ought to throw you out of my office and kick your ass down the street. Now get out!"

His Texas accent, refined by a Massachusetts prep school and Princeton University, came through menacingly. Not quite the response I expected from a born again Christian who was supposed to turn the other cheek.

"Hear me out; if I came to this conclusion, the police may too."

Reverend Franklin sat back down in his chair and glared at me.

"Last March, Jenny's roommate came home early and heard Jenny in her bedroom with someone. When she realized her roommate was home, she came out and pretended that nothing was happening. Her gentleman caller remained in the bedroom not wanting to be seen. Normally Jenny was not that secretive about her lovers."

"And why do you think it was me?" he demanded, tapping a silver pen on his desk blotter.

"Melinda went to take a shower and the man left; she looked out the bathroom window and saw a tall blond haired man get into a dark blue BMW and drive off."

Reverend Franklin laughed. "You must've read too many Hardy Boys' mysteries in your misspent youth. I drive the twelve-year-old Volvo station wagon sitting out in front of the church. My sister and her husband were on a cruise and loaned me their BMW while my car was repainted; it saved me from having to rent a car for a week. My congregation gave me grief about it; they thought it was too highfalutin for a preacher to drive a BMW."

"Forgive me. I'm sorry I accused you."

"Apology accepted. Did you actually think I murdered Jenny?"

I looked past his shoulder at a picture of Jesus Christ on the wall. "I didn't know what to think. It seemed out of character for someone like you to have been involved with Jenny; I'm relieved it wasn't you."

"The scandals of Jim Bakker and Jimmy Swaggart have unfortunately tarred all ministers. Did you share your suspicions with anyone?"

"No." Other than telling Laura I hadn't.

"It seems like your student may be guilty after all."

"No, Felton Snyder's murder proves that someone else murdered Jenny. I tried to question Snyder on Friday at McDonald's; the killer must've seen me with him and panicked. He tried to kill me on Friday night."

"Kill you?"

"He dropped a pumpkin from the top of Jordan Hall and missed me by few inches."

Reverend Franklin laughed again. "Didn't Washington Irving write that story?"

"Jenny's killer strangled her in a moment of rage. To muddy the trail, he tossed Jenny's wallet in the alley behind Tait's Market but Snyder somehow recognized the killer and began blackmailing him. He murdered Snyder to silence him."

"You may never find Jenny's killer now," Reverend Franklin replied as he stroked his goatee. He got up from behind his desk and showed me out.

I was now down to one suspect; I needed to find Leo Plaskett if he hadn't already disappeared.

Outside in the parking lot a disheveled, bearded African-American man approached me. I recognized him as one of the many homeless men who infested the campus. It was hard to tell his age; his missing front teeth and scraggily gray beard made him look older than he probably was. "Can you spare a ten spot, sir?" I flinched at his olid breath that betrayed his recent imbibing of Richard's Wild Irish Rose. "I saw you with Freddy in McDonald's on Friday; you didn't need to murder him."

"I think you have the wrong person; move along."

"Somebody was paying Freddy a lot of money and that cheap bastard wouldn't share any of it with us. It wasn't right."

I'd used a twenty when I exited the parking garage at the jail; I fished in my pocket and gave him a five. "Tell me more and you might earn another five."

"After Freddy got out of jail he was acting strangely."

"Was Snyder afraid of someone? Were Antonio McKinney's friends threatening him?"

"The guy at McDonald's he sold the stolen computers to?" He suddenly realized he'd said too much. I handed him another five.

"No, he was a small time punk."

"What about Snyder's pals from the motorcycle gang?"

"He bragged a lot about his days in the gang running pot up from Texas and selling it in North Carolina and all the women he screwed but it was all talk, Freddy was nothing but talk."

I gave him the final five. "What was he doing this past week?"

"He just walked around the parking lots and garages at the university looking at cars."

"What type of car was he looking for? A BMW perhaps?"

He looked at me blankly. "You got me."

"Were you with him the night he found that wallet in the alley behind Tait's Market?"

The man sighed. "You know, I have trouble remembering things these days; I might have been there that night. We often stayed in a boarded up house behind the store. He didn't share the wallet with me."

"What's your name?"

"Forget it! I'm not going to end up floating face down in a lake like old Freddy; I'm leaving town tonight. Thanks for the money, kind sir." He turned and staggered away. Our conversation confirmed that Jenny's murderer was connected to CBU, but who had Snyder seen in the alley that night? The driver of the BMW was as elusive as ever. Or did I need to start looking for another car? But what car was I looking for?

It was almost two o'clock and I'd had nothing to eat since breakfast; I headed to Vito's for a late lunch. If the police were waiting for me at the house, it would be best to evade them for as long as possible so I could continue my search for Jenny's killer. My former student, Frank, was watching the Redskins game while waiting for a delivery order to finish baking. After placing my order for an Italian hoagie, I went over to him. "How are you doing?"

"Not bad, Sunday afternoon is usually busy due to the football games. Tips have been good; after a few beers guys suddenly become generous."

"Do you know where I can find Leo Plaskett?"

"He lives on 89th Street over in JT but as I said on Friday, he was clearing out. What do you want with that creep?"

Frank clearly held Plaskett in high regard. "The afternoon Jenny Biggio was murdered; he delivered a pizza to her apartment. I need to ask him a few questions."

"Be my guest; it's 6211, the upstairs apartment."

After hurriedly eating my sandwich, I drove to Plaskett's apartment; 89th street was the boundary between Jefferson Terrace and the Braxton Gardens housing project. Tait's Market was just two blocks away. The rundown frame house had been subdivided into four apartments long ago; the second floor screened sleeping porch sagged in the center above the front porch. His car was parked in the muddy side yard. It was certainly distinctive; its rear bumper and trunk was festooned with stickers proclaiming Plaskett's support for a variety of left wing causes as well as covering up rust spots. Was it the car that Felton Snyder had searched for in the CBU parking lots?

I knocked on the door to Plaskett's apartment. An elderly man sipping from a quart bottle of beer eyed me suspiciously from the porch of the house next door. Plaskett bounded down the stairs and jerked open the door. He was dressed only in a pair of jeans giving me an unwanted showing of his pierced nipples and the sunburst tattoo circling his navel. "Why are you here?" he growled.

"It's interesting that you're leaving town so soon after Jenny Biggio's murder."

"That's none of your business."

"Do you want it to be your neighbor's business?"

He looked over at his neighbor who'd moved his lawn chair to the end of the porch. "I'll give you two minutes. Come upstairs."

Several boxes were stacked near the top of the stairs confirming Plaskett's pending departure. Plaskett's living room was furnished bizarrely; a mini-van bench seat functioned as a couch flanked by two bucket seats taken from a car. Several hardcore pornographic magazines and five crushed Budweiser cans were scattered on a piece of plywood supported by four cinderblocks which served as a poor man's coffee table. He made no attempt to conceal a bong sitting on the edge of the table. Hanging on the walls were paper targets of human figures sporting several bullet holes in the area of their hearts even more disturbing was the targets had names of several CBU professors scrawled in magic marker across the top. Why bash Snyder's skull in with a rock when you could put six bullets in his heart?

"My roomie is a gun nut," Plaskett said when he realized that I was eyeing the targets intently. No one else appeared to be living in the squalid apartment. Who was he rooming with? Annie Oakley?

"Don't you think the police are going to find your imminent departure a bit suspicious after finding Felton Snyder's body floating in the pond behind the library yesterday morning?"

He gave me a puzzled look. "Who in the hell is Felton Snyder?"

"He's the homeless man who claimed Brendan ditched Jenny Biggio's wallet in the alley behind Tait's Market."

"So what, a lot of homeless guys hang around Vito's trying to get the pizza slices we throw out?" Either Plaskett was a very good actor or he had no clue who I was talking about.

"Why are you leaving Norfolk?"

"The truth is there's nothing for me here; CBU denied my request for readmission three weeks ago. A buddy runs a tattoo and piercing shop down in Miami; he's taking me on as an apprentice. I'm going to make a new start down in Florida."

"Good luck." Becoming a tattoo artist didn't sound like a wise career move.

"Look me up if you're ever in South Beach; I'll give you a discount on a tattoo," he laughed.

I'd struck out again. Plaskett was a troubled young man but was not involved in Jenny's murder. Even worse, I no longer had a suspect in focus.

CHAPTER XXXI

MY EFFORTS TO CLEAR BRENDAN had run into a dead end; I feared that I might never discover the identity of Jenny's killer. Before heading home, I threw caution to the wind and stopped by the campus police station to confront Harley Simpson. I was still furious that he believed I'd staged the attempt on my life.

"What can I help you with?" asked the plump, silver haired dispatcher when I entered the police station.

"I'm here to see Chief Simpson." I handed her my card.

A few minutes later, I was escorted into Harley's wood paneled office by another dispatcher.

"Your investigator had no right to insinuate that I staged that attack on myself Friday night," I said coming quickly to the point.

"Just standard police procedure to rule out all the possibilities," he replied.

"I haven't even seen Dave Chen since Wednesday; he had nothing to do with that attack."

Harley drummed his fingers on his desk. "My investigator caught up with Mr. Chen a few minutes ago. It seems he's just returned from spending the weekend with a young lady at her parent's beach house. According to a credit card receipt he produced, he bought two six packs of Heineken at the BrewThru in Nags Head about fifteen minutes before you called dispatch on Friday night."

Dave didn't spend the chilly first weekend of November surfing. "Was he with a redhead?"

Harley laughed. "I should've arrested him for violating the Mann Act."

Nags Head, just over the North Carolina border from Norfolk, was a favorite destination for CBU students in search of a sun, sand and sex during warmer weather. "You'd have to arrest most of our male students."

Harley laughed again.

"So you're admitting now that Jenny's killer was behind the attack."

"Let me say it again that the incident on Friday night is unrelated to Jenny Biggio's murder."

"Then who tried to kill me?"

"Look, I wouldn't even classify it as a murder attempt. Some disgruntled student dropping that pumpkin is a more plausible explanation than your phantom murder attempt."

"Jenny's murderer was paying Felton Snyder off and he's afraid I'm getting too close to the truth. My visit to the Ark Church this afternoon confirmed that."

"Just give me a name!" Harley demanded.

"A homeless man accosted me in the parking lot; he'd seen me confronting Snyder on Friday at McDonald's. He confirmed Snyder's windfall."

"Snyder's wino buddies were angry because he wouldn't share the wealth; one of them murdered him for the cash. That's a more likely scenario."

"But it still doesn't explain where Snyder got the money."

"You and your wild conclusions; okay, come with me," ordered Harley.

He got up from his desk and led me through a doorway that connected his office to a conference room. Up on the cinderblock wall was a bulletin board with over thirty surveillance photos and mug shots of the homeless men and women who hung around the campus. "This is my war room; I've been trying for a year to get a handle on the homeless problem. Take a gander at my rogue's gallery and show me who you talked with at the Ark Church."

I studied the photos carefully. Their faces reflected the ravages of alcohol and drug abuse; most were missing a tooth or two. About two thirds of them were black men. One of the surveillance photos captured the man who confronted me earlier in the day. "Photo number twelve," I replied.

Harley picked up a binder off the conference table. "Number twelve is Horace Meekins; he's done time for burglary, drug possession and assault." He waved his hand at the gallery of photos. "Those four in the top row are probably schizophrenics. Of the rest, three of them have done time for murder; almost half have convictions for assault. Any one of these jokers would've killer Snyder over a ten spot without batting an eye."

"Meekins said that Snyder had been acting strangely the week before he died. He was walking around campus looking at cars. I think Snyder was looking for the car that dumped Jenny's wallet in the alley behind Tait's Market."

Harley shook his head. "Snyder was doing nothing more than looking in cars for something to steal. We had two cars with windows bashed in last week; the thief cleaned out the loose change left in the ash tray."

"Snyder had a lot more than pocket change according to Meekins."

"Tuesday night an instructor in the math department locked her purse in the trunk of her car before she went into the rec center for her yoga session. A thief had smashed her car window and popped her trunk from inside the car. Most likely he'd been watching her from the bushes and netted himself $200 for his efforts."

"And what makes you think it was Snyder?" I asked.

"It's a much more logical explanation for Snyder's wad than your crazy theory that Jenny's murderer was trying to buy his silence. Look, we took Healy's skin from under her fingernails. Once we get the DNA results back, we'll have all the evidence we need to convict Healy."

Harley's rebuff frustrated me. His refusal to see a connection between Jenny's murder, the break-in at her apartment and Snyder's murder was utterly baffling. That damned pumpkin made the attack on me seem like a silly farce. My son was right; if my attacker had taken a shot at me on Friday night, my suspicions would've been taken seriously. Of course, I might've been killed.

***

Julia Adams was raking leaves when I returned home. "Do you have a minute?" I asked.

"Sure," she replied leaning against her rake.

"I just visited Brendan at the jail. He's concerned he could be falsely implicated by DNA evidence. His half-brother may've murdered a drug dealer back in New Jersey."

"I thought Brendan only had two sisters."

"Sean, his partner in crime, was likely the product of one of his father's extra-marital relationships."

Coming from Puritan stock, Julia arched an eyebrow. "Having different mothers, I doubt there'd be a match since they only shared their father's DNA. Being half brothers, only 25% of the tested genes would likely be identical. I wonder when Watson and Crick discovered DNA if they ever imagined they that their discovery would be used to titillate the viewers of *The Maury Show*," she chuckled.

I was more than a little suspicious that in her retirement, Julia sneaked a peek at *The Maury Show* every now and then. "How long does it take to run DNA tests?" I asked.

"Testing has to be done in specialized laboratories; it takes weeks to get the results back."

Harley might be in for a rude awakening when the DNA tests came back on the skin found under Jenny's fingernails.

***

"Thank God you're home!" cried Laura and she hugged me as I came in the door. "I was afraid they'd arrested you. Where have you been?"

"I went to see Harley Simpson after I confronted Reverend Franklin."

"And did Reverend Franklin have an affair with Jenny?"

"I was barking up the wrong tree. At this point, I don't even have a suspect or a tree."

"What about the pizza delivery driver?"

"I visited Plaskett's apartment this afternoon; his reason for leaving town appears to be unconnected with Jenny's murder. He's definitely squirrelly but not a murderer."

The house was abnormally quiet; I heard no video game in progress or the pitter patter of my teenage sons' size twelve feet. "Where are the boys?"

"I sent them to the movies with Pete Raymond and gave them money to go to Baja Burritos for dinner. I didn't want them here if you were arrested."

Normally on Sunday afternoon, the house was redolent with the aromas of Sunday dinner cooking. Laura had been too upset to start preparing a dinner. "Why don't we go out tonight?"

"I don't feel like driving all out to Virginia Beach for dinner. We haven't been to the Bombay Curry House in years."

Our sons were not aficionados of Indian cuisine. When we were newly married and fresh out of graduate school, the Bombay Curry house provided a cheap night out. Located near campus, it provided a taste of home for CBU's large Indian student population. The restaurant was packed and the sari clad hostess told us it would be a minute for a table to be cleared when we arrived.

"My, it's just like old times," said Cynthia Wallach as she and her husband Stan came through the door.

As young faculty couples new to Norfolk, we had often shared dinners together at the Bombay Curry House and other inexpensive restaurants. Our friendship shifted as we became busy with children although we frequently crossed paths at PTA meetings, soccer games and Cub Scouts. "Shall we share a table," suggested Laura.

I noticed that for some reason Stan seemed less than enthused to join us but his wife won out.

"Have you made any progress in clearing your student?" asked Stan as we perused our menus.

"No, I've run into a brick wall now that Felton Snyder is dead."

"Who's Felton Snyder?" asked Stan.

Stan must've missed Shane's newscast on Saturday night. Snyder's murder received little coverage in Sunday's *Register* other than a small story about the body of a homeless man being found in a campus pond. It must've pleased Dick Torelli since it made no mention of any connection with Jenny's murder. "He's the homeless man who claimed that Brendan dumped Jenny's wallet in the alley behind Tait's Market. I think Jenny's murderer was paying Snyder off."

"No one besides Healy had a motive for murdering Jenny," said Stan after the turbaned waiter took our orders.

"Snyder was seen with a large amount of cash in the days before he was murdered," I replied.

"By whom?" he asked.

"One of my students plus a homeless man I encountered at the Ark Church."

"What were you doing at the Ark Church?" laughed Stan. "Have you joined the holy rollers?"

Cynthia gave her husband a withering look. "So what do the police think?"

"They chalked it up to one wino killing another wino."

"But, don't you think it's a stretch to link this bum's death to Jenny's murder? Those winos kill each other all the time over a bottle of Mad Dog 20/20. It just seems more logical," scoffed Stan as he ran his hands through his bleached blond hair.

"It's sad that Brendan killed Jenny; I mean she fell hard for him," said Cynthia. "My woman's intuition told me Brendan was dangerous. I saw that cheap tattoo of his over at the rec center and it made him look like an ex-con."

"Cynthia dear, he is an ex-con," corrected Stan in between bites of garlic naan bread.

Stan always seemed to treat Cynthia in a condescending manner. I wondered if Cynthia's recollection of Brendan's bicep reflected her opinion at the time she'd eyed it or had it been colored by Amanda Saltzman's distorted reporting of the murder.

"Laura, what's your opinion of Brendan?" asked Cynthia.

"I must admit I was taken aback when I saw them together last spring; he'd played fast and loose with the affections of a really darling student in the library science program last year. Kate caught him in bed with some sailor's wife and threw a book at Brendan's backside," recounted Laura.

"And did she hit him?" asked Cynthia.

"Dead center; the book left a nasty bruise from what I've heard."

I had to wonder where Laura heard about the bruise on Brendan's rear end.

Cynthia smiled smugly; obviously the young graduate student had avenged aggrieved women everywhere. Stan looked as if he'd just been hit by *The Decline and Fall of the Roman Empire* on his backside.

"Her membership in the American Library Association was revoked for improper handling of a book," I interrupted.

Stan and Cynthia laughed but it was my turn to get a withering look from Laura who didn't appreciate my jokes about librarians.

"Someone mentioned she seemed upset last winter after her breakup with that Polish student? Do you know anything about that relationship?" I asked Cynthia.

Stan squirmed uncomfortably in his chair and his face looked like he was suffering from indigestion, even though he hadn't had a forkful of lamb vindaloo yet.

"As I recall they started dating shortly after she arrived at the university; Tomasz was already in the doctoral program. You really need to talk to Barbara; she keeps track of the student romances in our department."

Stan's apparent indigestion seemed even worse or was it the topic of conversation? Rumors of Stan's extra-curricular activities had floated around campus for more years than I could remember. Rumors of a rift in the Wallach's marriage surfaced last year although he and Cynthia appeared to have patched things up, for now.

"Stan, were Tomasz and Jenny still together when she worked for you last summer?" asked Cynthia.

"Jenny worked for you?" I asked.

Stan took a sip of his beer. "I needed a research assistant last year to develop some economic models for an article I was writing. Cynthia recommended Jenny; she needed a job that summer since the econ department had no teaching assignments for her. Jenny was an immense help editing and proof reading the article; she was quite a polished writer. In fact, she's getting a co-author credit, posthumously, when the article comes out in January."

"Look who just came in," whispered Cynthia.

I discreetly looked toward the entrance and saw Art Campbell and his wife waiting for a table. Art pretended not to see us in the crowded restaurant. "It seems like old times; it wasn't all that long ago when we were all together on the third floor."

Cynthia sighed. "Unlike a wine, Art has failed to mellow with age; he's just become more acidic. I thought we were close to getting rid of him when Tollie threatened him with a post tenure review but then Art published that article this fall in some Marxist economic journal that no one ever reads, and of course, Art triumphantly threw it in Tollie's face."

"That rag is probably run off on a mimeograph machine in some commie's basement," scoffed Stan.

I laughed. "Is it even a peer reviewed journal?"

"The article was reviewed by an incestuous coterie of far left wing economists who are all pals of Art," Cynthia laughed.

"Was his article published in *The Journal of Marxist Economics*?" asked Laura.

Cynthia, her mouth full of chicken korma, nodded awkwardly.

"Well, due to the budget cuts the periodicals department wanted to drop that journal among others but Art and his band of true believers raised such an unholy stink that we relented."

"I'm sure he used the same irksome tirade about the stifling of academic freedom that he spouts off at every department meeting," said Cynthia.

"I was at the meeting with Dean Phelps; Art turned red in the face as he berated us for twenty minutes. Dean Phelps caved in and we're stuck with a journal no one reads. Only a handful of libraries in the country still subscribe to it."

"How did Art ever get hired?" I asked.

"Tom Hobart was the chair of the econ department at the time; Tom wanted to hire someone with a competing viewpoint to stir things up for the students. Believe me; he rued that decision until the day he died. Art wrote the obligatory book to get tenure that was really nothing more than a superficial reworking of his dissertation; he hasn't written a paragraph until this article."

"Didn't Art say he was writing a book on the exploitation of workers by multinational corporations?"

"Oh sure, he's talked about that book for at least a decade but I doubt he's written more than the introduction, if he's even gotten that far."

"Well, it looks like we're stuck with Comrade Art until they pry his copy of *Das Kapital* from his cold dead hands," I said.

Cynthia laughed. "At least he's gotten rid of that filthy shag rug. It drove me crazy every time I passed his office."

The smiling waiter came with our checks and we settled our bills. "We'll have to do this again sometime," said Cynthia as we walked to the parking lot next to the restaurant.

Stan paused and clicked a button on the key pad in his hand. The interior lights and headlights lit up a dark blue BMW 528i sedan at the end of the row of parked cars. Laura looked intently at the car and then looked in my direction. I nodded.

✿✿✿

We drove in silence until we were almost halfway home. "Do you think Stan was having an affair with Jenny?" asked Laura.

"It's possible; Stan drives a car similar to the one Melinda saw leaving the apartment but I was wrong about Reverend Franklin. Stan fits the bill in other ways."

"What does that mean?"

"Melinda said all of Jenny's boyfriends were cut out of the same bolt of cloth, Jenny liked them blond and blue eyed."

"But Jenny knew Stan was married. He's blond and blue eyed but for heaven's sakes, he's over fifty years old. What would she see in him?"

"Hey, I'm over fifty! I think women still find me attractive."

"Don't get any ideas about chasing after young grad students. You're not all that appealing," laughed Laura.

"Thanks! Who knows, Stan may've caught Jenny at a weak moment. Again this is second hand from Melinda. Jenny was upset after her relationship with Tomasz fizzled; she'd invested a lot in that guy. Also she felt her biological clock was running down."

"Excuse me, but Jenny was only 28."

"In waltzes Stan who's going through problems of his own and Jenny falls for him."

"I might as well tell you this but I don't want you sharing it with anyone. Last fall, I saw Cynthia at Nick's; she looked like she'd been crying. Stan had moved out and she needed someone's shoulder to cry on. Cynthia suspected Stan had been having an affair and confronted him."

"Did she know he was fooling around with Jenny?"

"I don't think so; she never mentioned her name to me. Cynthia thought Stan was boinking his Chinese research assistant, Lifen. Apparently she thought Stan looked like Brad Pitt."

I still couldn't figure out where Laura had picked up that word. "It would be rather brazen to have an affair with Jenny, a grad student from his wife's department."

"But like most men, Stan was thinking with his penis instead of his brain," Laura replied.

"Do you know when Stan and Cynthia got back together?"

"Cynthia told me Stan moved back home last spring."

"And that's just about the time Melinda caught Jenny with her mystery visitor. Father Novello mentioned that Jenny seemed distracted last spring, maybe she was having second thoughts about fooling around with a married man."

"Jenny hooked up with Brendan during the spring; maybe she gave Stan his walking papers and he had no choice but to go home with his tail between his legs. But do you really think Stan could've murdered Jenny?"

"It doesn't make any sense for Stan to have murdered Jenny six months after their affair had ended; if they even had an affair." I'd already been burned by drawing the wrong conclusion after seeing Reverend Franklin driving a BMW. I wasn't going to make the same mistake twice nor was I about to chase after every dark blue BMW in Norfolk.

"What if their affair hadn't ended? Don't you think Stan was acting a bit strangely most of the evening especially when Jenny was the topic of conversation?"

Stan's BMW fit with what Horace Meekins had told me this afternoon. Snyder was searching the parking lots at the university; he must've seen a car that night in the alley that stood out. Nothing else seemed to fit. Even if their affair had continued as Laura speculated, why would Stan have killed Jenny? Stan and Cynthia appeared to have reconciled, what would it matter if Jenny was screwing Brendan? And why would Stan have even been in Jordan Hall on Monday night? His office was in the College of Business on the other side of campus.

Wait! It was unbelievable but could Cynthia Wallach have found out about Stan's affair and killed Jenny in a jealous rage? Was that possible? Had I been looking in the wrong direction the whole time?

CHAPTER XXXII

At five a.m., *The Register* hit my front door with a loud thump and my eyes popped open. Unable to get back to sleep, I went down to my study. I took out a yellow legal pad and drew a triangle; I put Jenny at the top of the triangle and Stan and Cynthia at the other corners. It was hard to believe that either of them could be murderers; they'd been our friends for over twenty years.

Although guilty of adultery many times over, Stan seemingly had no motive for murdering Jenny. Their affair probably ended before Jenny embarked on her relationship with Brendan. Murdering Jenny in a jealous rage made sense only if he'd continued the affair after supposedly returning to Cynthia. Or had Jenny threatened to expose their affair to Cynthia and Stan murdered her to silence her? But was that really logical?

Cynthia, though aware of her husband's infidelities, appeared to have no knowledge of his affair with Jenny. She also seemed genuinely distressed when I first talked with her about Jenny's murder. I doubted she would've expressed that kind of grief if she'd known her husband was screwing Jenny.

But could Cynthia have gone over the edge when she discovered her husband had been cheating on her with one of her own students? Wouldn't it have made much more sense to kill Stan, not Jenny? Knowing Cynthia as well as I did, it seemed unlikely but on the other hand, rage coupled with a surge of adrenalin might've enabled her to overpower and strangle Jenny. But was that realistic? Jenny, though five feet, six, was a former collegiate athlete. Cynthia was maybe two inches taller but she was packing twenty years of professorial living on her frame. I'd give the edge to Jenny in a fight.

I went to the university's website and found Stan's webpage. All his classes were scheduled on Mondays, Wednesdays and Fridays. He held offices hours on Monday afternoon from two to five. Cynthia scheduled her classes and office hours on Tuesdays and Thursdays; no wonder Stan had time to fool around. I decided to pay Stan a visit on Monday afternoon; I hoped I wouldn't have to question Cynthia.

***

Tollie had scheduled a department chairs meeting for Monday afternoon beginning at two to discuss the impending budget cuts. Due to cutbacks in our state funding, eight of the eighteen faculty positions under recruitment in the College of Arts, Social Sciences and Humanities would have to be eliminated. The meeting dragged on for over two endless hours; each department chair claiming that his positions were essential, and by implication, another department should take the hit. Sitting at the head of the table like Zeus on high, Tollie watched bemused as we slashed each other to ribbons. Finally as the clock neared five o'clock, Tollie mercifully ended the meeting and said he would announce his decision from Mount Olympus by the end of the week.

I walked across campus to the College of Business and found Stan in his office answering emails. The recently constructed College of Business building was palatial compared to the aging Jordan Hall. It was easy to see which college was the fair haired child of the university's administration.

"So what brings you to the College of Business?" Stan asked cheerily, thinking I was merely paying a social call.

I closed the door to his office behind me; there was no sense beating around the bush. "Look Stan, I know you were having an affair with Jenny Biggio?"

Stan sat more erect in his chair. "That's none of your business!"

I decided to push him a little harder. "When Melinda Kroger came home early and caught you in Jenny's bed, I bet your heart must've skipped a beat or two. That was your BMW she spotted from the bathroom window, wasn't it?"

"What are you trying to insinuate?"

"I'm sure Harley Simpson will find it interesting that you were having an affair with Jenny."

"Why is that lesbo bitch stirring up trouble?"

"She only told me what she saw last March. As I said before, the police have been looking in the wrong direction."

"You're not going to pin Jenny's murder on me! Healy strangled Jenny!"

"Yesterday I talked with a homeless man, Horace Meekins, outside the Ark Church. Felton Snyder saw Jenny's killer toss her wallet in the alley behind Tait's Market the night of the murder. According to Meekins, Snyder walked around parking lots at the university looking for a car. Something stood out about the car Snyder saw that night. Don't you think a shiny BMW qualifies?"

"Jeez! You really are a piece of work! I never go anywhere near Tait's Market; no one in their right mind goes there unless they're looking for drugs or hookers. In fact, I was at Wal-Mart the night Jenny was murdered; Art Campbell saw me there."

"So when did your affair with Jenny end?"

"Cynthia and I were having our problems the summer Jenny worked for me. Shortly after he arrived in New York, Jenny's Polish boy friend dumped her for some art student from Pratt Institute he met at a gallery opening in Greenpoint. One thing led to another; you get the picture. It was great sex with Jenny while it lasted but it was over six months ago. Jenny made me feel like I was twenty-five again."

Or had Stan merely overdosed on Viagra? "The truth, Jenny dropped you when she started seeing Brendan, didn't she?"

"Our affair had simply run its course several weeks before that. Jenny was having second thoughts about being involved with a married man and I came to my senses and decided to try and patch things up with Cynthia."

But still, it seemed that Stan only came to his senses after Jenny dropped him. "Did Cynthia know you were involved with Jenny?"

"You're not going to tell her, are you? Give me a break!"

I had no intention of hurting Cynthia. "Your secret is safe with me."

"I've been walking on eggshells for the past two weeks fearing the cops might dig up my affair with Jenny and knock on my door one night."

For some warped reason, I found Stan's anxiety almost amusing. "Melinda mentioned your visit to me but she didn't think it was important when the police questioned her.

Stan breathed an audible sigh of relief.

"Did you break into Jenny's apartment? Making sure you'd left nothing for the police to connect you to Jenny?"

"No! I was always very discreet."

"I'm sure Cynthia is grateful for your discretion."

"No doubt you've scored with a few coeds in your time. It's an occupational hazard of being a college professor; they're just like sweet ripe fruit ready to pluck from the trees."

"Some of us know where to draw the line!"

Stan laughed. "Spare me the moral lecture."

I had one final question to ask. "Where was Cynthia on the night Jenny was murdered?"

"She went to Baltimore that weekend; her mother underwent arthroscopic knee surgery on Friday. I picked her up at the airport on Tuesday morning. Are you implying that Cynthia murdered Jenny?"

"Of course not!" I was relieved that Cynthia was not involved in Jenny's murder.

"All the evidence proves that Healy murdered Jenny. Talk to Barbara, the econ department secretary; she overheard him screaming at Jenny the morning she was killed. Healy showed his true colors; he's nothing but a scum bag."

I resisted the urge to laugh at Stan's observation. My efforts to clear Brendan had come to a dead end; I left Stan's office with the sense I'd failed again.

***

Walking across the parking lot after leaving Stan's office, I found myself in front of the library. It struck me that Jenny had been murdered only two weeks ago on Monday night. It was almost six, o'clock, the hour Jenny left the library.

Laura was covering for a sick librarian; so I went to the Reference Department in search of her. The tables and computer stations were sparsely inhabited. Only after the dining hall closed at six-thirty, would the students would start flooding into the library. Laura was seated at the reference desk, chatting with one of her colleagues. She motioned for me to go to her office so we could talk privately.

"How did things go with Stan?"

"He admitted to having an affair with Jenny but claims it ended six months before she was murdered."

"Did Jenny throw Stan under the bus in for Brendan?"

"Stan's version, take or leave it, the flames of passion had burned out before Jenny and Brendan got together."

"Oh sure, it would puncture Stan's enormous ego to admit that Jenny dumped him for a younger guy."

I'd noticed that every time Stan mentioned Brendan, there was always a bitter edge to his voice. "For Cynthia's sake, I hope he's sincere about saving their marriage."

"Hmm! Stan won't change; he's nothing but a low down dog sniffing around for a bitch in heat," laughed Laura.

"Is Henrietta working tonight?"

"She just went upstairs to help a student. Why?"

"I thought I'd try to retrace Jenny's steps the night she was murdered. None of the other leads I've followed have panned out."

"Face it, Sherlock Holmes you're not."

"And you're not exactly Doctor Watson."

Laura looked crestfallen. "No help at all, huh?"

"I wasn't talking about your detective skills. You're put together much better than Nigel Bruce."

"That's a quick recovery Sherlock, very clever."

"I keep going back to the moment that Jenny saw someone from the window of the periodicals room that night; she abruptly left and went to Jordan Hall. The police's theory is that she saw Brendan with Tiffany Finley, but that doesn't hold water. I just can't figure out who she saw."

"Sorry, I can't help you there but I'll call the boys and tell them you'll be home in twenty minutes to fix dinner."

I took the elevator to the second floor. Henrietta was helping a student find a journal in the stacks. A fluorescent light fixture in the ceiling hummed with an irritating buzz; the periodicals room had changed little during my twenty years at CBU. Only two of the tables were occupied; with many academic journals on line, the periodicals room was not as busy as in past years.

"Good evening Andrew," Henrietta greeted me when she finished with the student. "What brings you up here tonight?"

"Could you show me where Jenny Biggio was sitting the night she was murdered?"

"Are you still trying to help that hoodlum; Healy is as guilty as sin."

"Jenny Biggio's murderer attempted to kill me Friday night and he bumped off Felton Snyder. Don't you think that's proof that Jenny's murderer is still on the loose?"

"I saw the police fish that creepy old wino out of the pond on Saturday morning. No doubt some other wino killed him, no real loss there," scoffed Henrietta.

"And who tried to murder me? Washington Irving?"

"Humph! If you must know, she sat at that table by the window." I followed Henrietta to a battered wooden table with three chairs on each side at the end of the periodicals room near Jordan Hall. "She sat on the end." Henrietta pointed to a chair next to the window.

Something hit me as odd as I sat down in the chair and looked across to the second floor of Jordan Hall. Even if I tilted my head downward, I couldn't see the plaza below, not even a square foot of it. Despite Jenny being six inches shorter than me; she would've had the same problem. I looked to my left; a row of trees along the side of the library blocked my view of the parking lot. Jenny couldn't have seen anyone from that position. The only thing she could've seen was someone in the windows of the upper floors of Jordan Hall.

"Tell me again, what did Jenny say?"

Henrietta fiddled nervously with one of the pins that held her hair bun together. "As I told the police already Jenny stared out the window and said, 'That no good lying bastard; I can't believe he's cheating on me!' Then she slammed the journal down and I told her that's not the way to handle library property."

What I said to Brendan about the waitress at Nick's suddenly came back to me. "Eyewitnesses to history are often confused about what they'd seen." Brendan complained that the waitress would tell her grandchildren she served cherry pie and coffee to the infamous CBU strangler. Actually the waitress served Brendan only a cup of coffee while I had a slice of apple pie and coffee.

"Where were you standing during Jenny's outburst?"

Clearly miffed, Henrietta replied, "Over there by the compact shelving." She extended her arm and thrust out a long bony index finger.

If she'd been ten feet from Jenny, could Henrietta have mangled what she thought she's overheard? Or, was her memory colored by all the media coverage of the murder?

Frustrated, I was ready to head home and call it a day. I asked my final question to tidy up one last detail. "Do you remember what journal Jenny was reading?"

"She was reading *The Journal of Marxist Economics.*"

Where had I heard that journal mentioned before? Of course! It was the journal that Cynthia and Laura had discussed at dinner last night; it had recently published Art Campbell's article. "Do you recall what issue?"

"The fall issue; it's a quarterly publication. Dr. Campbell and his little band of sycophants are the only ones that read that rag. He's too cheap to subscribe to it."

"Do you know where can I find that issue?" Why was Jenny reading that particular journal? She wasn't one of Art's followers. From Henrietta's earlier account, it appeared that something she read in that issue upset her to the point that she slammed the journal down on the table. But what? Or was her anger caused by something unrelated to the journal.

"It's over there on the rack gathering dust, no one has touched it since that night," pointed Henrietta's bony finger again. She left me alone in the periodicals room.

I picked up the journal and went back to the table. Thumbing through it, there were three book reviews and four articles in the journal's one hundred pages. Art's article, the longest one in the issue, compared the decline in industrial wages from 1970 – 2000 with the rise in multinational corporations' profits. Scanning the article, I found it surprisingly lucid. The article was even supported by several graphs and statistical charts. It was amazingly readable and logical unlike Art's usual rants and raves.

Suddenly a thousand thoughts flooded my mind all at once. Cynthia had indicated that Art was under pressure from Tollie due to his lack of research productivity since achieving tenure. Failure to meet the goals set in the post tenure review process would mean termination. Publishing this article staved off a post tenure review for several years and now Art could coast into retirement.

But was it possible that Art hadn't written the article at all? Jake had said that Jenny was an extraordinary student; praising her statistical and mathematical modeling skills. When Jenny had assisted Stan with his article, earning a co-author credit, he'd praised her writing ability. Desperate, did Art claim credit for a paper Jenny wrote while under his tutelage before Jake took over supervising her master's thesis? But how could Art have hoped to get away with it?

Jake, normally dismissive of Art's point of view, probably gave the article no more than a cursory reading, if that much. Knowing that, Art probably believed that he was taking no risk plagiarizing Jenny's work. Since Jake had stolen Jenny from Art's orbit, he also assumed there was little chance that she'd come across her article in a little read Marxist economics journal.

Henrietta reported to the police that Jenny exclaimed, "That no good lying bastard; I can't believe he's cheating on me!" Enraged when she discovered that Art had expropriated her article, it was more likely Jenny blurted out, "That no good lying bastard; I can't believe he cheated me!" Henrietta only had to garble two words and thus send the police and me off on the wrong tangent. Jenny's murder had nothing to do with spurned lovers or illicit affairs; an even more basic human emotion was behind it all – greed. Something an economist like Art understood all too well.

I looked out the window at Jordan Hall; lights were on in only a few faculty offices. Naturally Jenny was furious when she discovered what Art had done. Throwing the journal down on the table and seeing that Art was in his office, she foolishly went over to Jordan Hall to confront him. Then what? Art panicked and strangled her?

But how could I prove Art murdered Jenny? Before going to Harley Simpson with another of my suspicions; I needed evidence. I put the journal back on the rack and used one of the computer terminals in the periodicals room to access the library's catalog. I looked up the citation for Art's only book.

Taking the elevator to the fourth floor, I found it in utter chaos. The worn out carpeting in the reading areas was supposed to have been replaced over the summer. Due to the late delivery of the carpet from the mill, the project was still not finished over two months into the semester. Chairs were stacked on tables and shoved around the walls. The old carpet was still being removed from the concrete floor. Huge rolls of new carpet were stacked at one end of the building along with plastic buckets of glue. Several lengths of heavy rope were strewn on the floor; left over from tying up the dry rotted carpet for disposal. With no seating available, the floor was eerily deserted. The rows of faculty carrels, enclosed metal cubicles serving as private space for faculty members using the library, stood deserted; no lights were on in any of them. A Marxist poster in Russian covered the glass window in the center of the door to Art's carrel; three doors down an aging poster of medieval London covered the window of Tollie Monroe's carrel.

I quickly located Art's book in the stacks and scanned the first chapter; the book was vintage Art. Having read thousands of student term papers over the years and reviewed articles for journals, I immediately noticed the difference in style and sentence structure between the book and the article. Art had an uncanny way of stringing phrase after phrase together, simply put, he overwrote.

An English professor like Tollie would be able to render an informed opinion that different individuals authored the article and book. After supervising Jenny's masters' thesis and reviewing her dissertation, Jake would be familiar with her writing style. Hopefully the two of them would back up my accusation that Art plagiarized Jenny's work. But what did that prove?

Standing there reading Art's book, other details started to come into focus. No doubt Art was behind the burglary at Jenny's apartment. He needed to obliterate all traces of Jenny's authorship by removing any extant copies and destroying any computer drives that may've contained the paper. It also explained why her laptop was still missing; Art no doubt destroyed it.

After murdering Jenny, Art cunningly implicated Brendan. Overhearing the fight between Brendan and Jenny that morning, he knew the police would find out about it from Barbara, the loquacious economics department secretary. To throw suspicion on Brendan, he moved Jenny's body to the restroom across the hall from the history graduate students' office and planted Brendan's Marine Corps ring in the office. Art probably strangled Jenny in his office necessitating the replacement of his beloved shag rug. Stan reported that Art had purchased the new rug at Wal-Mart on Monday night, no doubt after disposing of the incriminating rug in the Jordan Hall dumpster. The old rug must've contained DNA evidence linking him to Jenny's murder. Like a puzzle, all of the pieces were starting to fit together.

Hedging his bets, Art tossed Jenny's purse in the bushes in case the police didn't buy Brendan as a suspect; he also dropped her wallet in the alley behind Tait's Market figuring that one of the addicts or winos that frequented the alley couldn't resist the temptation to use her credit cards. But that proved his undoing. Felton Snyder saw Art's car that night and thought he could play the deal both ways. The police needed Snyder to corroborate the case against Brendan and he was more than willing to oblige to escape jail. From hanging around CBU, Snyder had probably seen Art's red Volvo decorated with a plethora of left wing bumper stickers and figured he could make a quick killing by blackmailing its owner. It was no accident that I bumped into Art at McDonald's on Friday after my confrontation with Snyder. Due to bad timing, I'd arrived a few minutes too early or I would've caught the two of them together. Snyder underestimated Art. He figured Art was just another fuzzy headed intellectual he could push around. That misjudgment cost him his life. I'd underestimated Art too; his cleverly improvised attempt to kill me with the pumpkin came within inches of succeeding.

Taking no chances, I looked out the window and saw the lights were off in Art's office; he'd gone home for the day. After dinner, I'd send an email to Tollie and Jake suggesting we meet first thing in the morning and I'd outline my suspicions about Art plagiarizing Jenny's paper. Then I'd call Harley.

Out of the corner of my eye, I sensed something, some movement behind me. Before I could turn around, my head exploded, a dizzying pain and then a black void enveloped my mind.

CHAPTER XXXIII

My cell phone vibrating in my coat pocket against my chest brought me out of my stupor; my head throbbed painfully. Opening my eyes, I found myself lying on a linoleum floor and unable to move. My ankles were trussed together and my arms were bound tightly behind my back. I tried to speak but my mouth was gagged with my tie, the gold tie Laura had given me for Father's Day. As my eyes adjusted to the light, I realized I was in the cramped confines of a faculty carrel. The yellowing English travel posters on the wall and the chipped plaster bust of Charles Dickens sitting on the desk were the signatures of Tollie's carrel. Art Campbell, wearing latex gloves, was sitting nonchalantly reading a book; a bottle of Russian vodka sat on the desk next to the book.

He seemed surprised that I'd regained consciousness. "Hitting someone on the head with a vodka bottle is an imprecise science; it only took one blow to kill Snyder. I'm sorry I had to tie you up but I couldn't take any chances if you came out of it."

I tried to say something through my gag but it did not quite sound like English.

"The lock to Tollie's carrel is keyed the same as mine. Your reprieve is only temporary," he replied after taking a swig of the vodka.

My bound state didn't give me a lot of options. Art noticed me looking at the carrel's door.

"The library closed thirty minutes ago; you've been out cold for hours. Security has already checked the floor and shut out the lights.

It's just you and me and Charlie." Art patted the top of the bust and laughed.

I kept still and tried to figure out my options. Art picked his book up off the desk and held it up. "I should be flattered that you chose my book as the last book you'll ever read."

Again my attempt to say something was thwarted by my once expensive tie.

"Don't take what I'm about to do to you personally. I always found your sophomoric jokes over the years mildly amusing. Since you have only a few minutes left until the cleaning crew finishes downstairs, would you like me to fill in the blanks for you?"

I nodded my head in an effort to buy time while I tried to figure out a way to get free. My arms were bound tightly behind my back and my chances of escaping like James Bond seemed slim to none.

"You didn't realize that I'd followed you after you left Jordan Hall this evening to see Stan Wallach. I'm guessing Stan had a dalliance with Miss Biggio?"

I nodded affirmatively.

"Poor Cynthia, Stan never could control his overactive libido," he sighed theatrically.

He bent down and removed my tie from my mouth. I gulped in air in an effort to clear the fog in my brain. Art helped me sit up; I leaned my back against the metal wall of the carrel and stretched out my legs. Yelling for help seemed pointless; who would hear me.

"Should I expect the headless horseman to be along in a minute?"

"When I saw you talking with Snyder on Friday in McDonald's, I knew you'd blundered onto my trail. The only weapon available was Tammie's pumpkin. I must've been inspired by Washington Irving; someday I'll have to visit Sleepy Hollow."

I felt my phone vibrate again; Laura was trying to find me!

"I knew you'd put two and two together when I tailed you to the library tonight and watched you reading *The Journal of Marxist Economics*. Why did Henrietta have to remember what journal Jenny was reading? When I checked the computer and found the citation for my book on the screen, I followed you up to the fourth floor. I couldn't believe my good fortune that no one was up here." Art flashed his teeth; it was not a pleasant smile beaming down on me.

"So Jenny did write that article?"

"As you've deduced in your clumsy fashion, she came to my office and accused me of stealing an independent study paper she wrote under my tutelage. I've not figured out how she found out about the article, probably the damned internet; modern technology can be a curse. One second she was screaming at me, threatening to tell Jake everything, thirty seconds later she was lying on my rug. Of course I couldn't very well leave her in my office for the police to find. I also had to replace my rug; my martial arts instructor never warned us if we strangled someone they'd piss all over themselves. What a mess!"

I shuddered at Art's callousness. "You strangled her for God's sake!"

"Was there any other option? If my plagiarism was discovered, Tollie would've gleefully fired me and no accredited college would've touched me with a ten foot pole. I've become too accustomed to academic life; where else can I espouse my Marxist beliefs? I can't do it at the barbershop."

"You're insane!"

"By your criterion, so is half the faculty."

"You're going to kill me and let Brendan go to prison for the rest of his life."

"Why not pin it on him? Brendan helped my cleanup efforts by having that disgusting little row with Jenny on Monday morning. I decided to dump Jenny's body on the sixth floor to draw attention to Mr. Healy; of course our feminist friends were using your conference room. So after throwing my rug in the dumpster, I went to Wal-Mart to kill time and bought a new rug as well as a box of these gloves figuring they'd come in handy."

Art chuckled at his pathetic puns.

"I bided my time until the sixth floor was deserted; I put Jenny in an old desk chair I found in the custodian's closet and rolled her down to the service elevator and placed her in the bathroom figuring that no one would find her until morning."

"Then you framed Brendan to take the rap."

"Being built by the contractor with the lowest bid, Jordan Hall has some interesting features. When we were down on the third floor, I discovered that each department's master key opens any door in the building. I used the key to drop the ring in Brendan's office and then stuffed Jenny's messenger bag in the ceiling."

"Everything was going fine until I had to go poking around and Snyder began blackmailing you."

"That derelict wanted $10,000 to keep his trap shut; I decided to silence him permanently instead. Murder is like a jar of olives, once you get the first one out of the jar, the rest tumble out quite easily. Like you, Snyder underestimated me."

I needed to keep Art babbling away till Laura found me, hopefully alive. "Don't you think the police will find three murders in two weeks more than just a coincidence?"

He took another swig of the vodka. "Our campus gumshoes haven't shown a capacity to think outside the box, excuse the cliché. Once Chief Simpson determined Healy murdered Jenny nothing was going to sway him from that conclusion. I did Norfolk a favor by eliminating one of the winos that infest the streets. Believe me, no one is going to waste any time investigating Snyder's murder."

Art killed Jenny in a moment of rage and had no qualms about killing a derelict like Snyder. Art was steeling himself with vodka to stomach killing me in cold blood after his attempt to kill me with the vodka bottle failed. "We've been colleagues for over twenty years; think about my family!"

"There's no faculty discount this time."

"For God's sake man, come to your senses!"

"I'm quite rational; if I was fired, I'd have to scrape together a living teaching econ courses at $2,000 a pop for some internet university that doesn't bother to check the references of it faculty."

"Don't you think my murder will be investigated? I'm not a wino like Snyder."

"Well, at first, people will find it odd that you committed suicide because you showed no outward signs of depression. Brendan confessed to you before he was arrested that he'd murdered Jenny; he'd found out that Stan was tapping her too and she was playing him for a sucker. In a moment of anger, he strangled her. Your suicide note details how you can't live without Brendan. People will be stunned to find out you were much more than his mentor."

I'm going to commit suicide? What in hell was Art talking about?

"It seems that Jenny had a hidden talent for photography; I found a number of nude pictures of Mr. Healy on her flash drive. While you were out cold, I went over to your office. You should have logged off your computer when you went to visit Stan."

Art jiggled my key ring.

"When the police find the pictures on your computer, coupled with the suicide note, I'm sure they'll draw the obvious conclusions."

"Don't you think a typed suicide note would immediately raise a red flag with the police?" Although that would do me little good after I was dead.

Art sneered menacingly at me and held up an envelope addressed to Laura. "Don't worry Andy; I've forged your signature on the note."

"Is forgery one of the crafts they taught you at the Young Pioneers camp?"

Art laughed. "When I was in high school, I was quite good at forging my teachers' signatures on hall passes."

My cell phone vibrated again in my coat pocket. Laura must be trying to find me. But would she find me in time? "The police have ample evidence of Brendan's womanizing but there's nothing to suggest he's gay and as for me, that's nuts!"

"Everyone will be shocked just like they were when Ian Henson dumped his wife and moved in with that adjunct theatre instructor. Harley Simpson will follow his standard operating procedures and after a cursory investigation close the book on this whole tawdry affair. Barry has served as a useful conduit to Amanda Saltzman and tomorrow morning she'll have all the sordid details of Stan screwing Jenny and Brendan's little love triangle."

I had to keep Art talking. "You're as mad as a hatter!"

"I'm disappointed that your last words were so trite. Your suicide note will wrap everything up into a nice neat bundle for the police. I'm going to enjoy watching Stan being eviscerated by Amanda; he'll no longer be Doug Clayton's fair haired boy."

"How are you going to make it look like a suicide?"

"A bullet through your skull; when I searched Snyder's pockets to retrieve my down payment on his blackmail demands I found this handgun." Art held up a battered black 9 mm pistol. "No one will suspect me; after all I'm the chairman of the campus chapter of *Professors Against Handguns*. Don't worry; I'll knock you out again before I blow your brains out. There won't be any pain; I'm not a cruel person."

Art was so engrossed in his drunken ramblings that he failed to hear the elevator open at the other end of the floor. Swinging my feet around, I pushed them through the glass panel of the door shattering it. The poster covering the window fluttered to the floor.

"What in the hell did you do that for?" Art stood up wielding the vodka bottle. "I'm going to crush your skull and be done with it!"

I thrust myself up and head butted Art in the crotch. The gun discharged and the bullet pierced the thin metal ceiling of the carrel.

"Aaggh!" The blow momentarily staggered Art. Then the darkened floor was flooded with light.

"Drop it Dr. Campbell!" Harley Simpson and Officer Benton came running toward the door, pistols in hand. Laura trailed behind them, afraid of what they were going to find.

"You can't treat me like this, I'm a tenured professor. This is a violation of academic freedom," Art protested as Officer Benton handcuffed his arms behind his back.

Harley took out a pocket knife and went to work on the rope around my wrists and ankles.

"Art hit me over the head with that vodka bottle and knocked me unconscious. He was going to shoot me and make it look like a suicide."

"Don't listen to him! He's a raving lunatic running around campus with his conspiracy theories!"

Harley rolled his eyes. "I'll call for an ambulance."

Laura hugged and kissed me. "How did you figure out where to find me?"

"The boys called when you didn't come home to fix dinner."

"Thank God for hungry teenagers."

"When you didn't answer your cell phone I began worrying and started retracing your steps in the library. No one at the circulation desk recalled you leaving. Henrietta reported your interest in Art's article in the *Journal of Marxist Economics*. She also noticed that you looked up the citation for Art's book. Her prying led us to the fourth floor."

"It's all wild speculation," snarled Art.

"I have enough tonight to hold you on assault and attempted murder charges," replied Harley. "In the morning you'll be arraigned for the murder of Felton Snyder. We found your fingerprint on a crisp fifty dollar bill concealed in a plastic bag in his backpack."

"It's not a crime to help a homeless person. Who doesn't believe in Christian charity?"

"I didn't know atheists practiced Christian charity," Laura answered.

"Snyder was blackmailing you. We arrested a prostitute, Venus Reid, last night; she told us about a red Volvo covered with bumper stickers in the alley behind Tait's Market the night Jenny was murdered. Snyder beat her to the wallet that you pitched out of your car. You were already a person of interest when Mrs. Stanard called," said Harley.

"A hooker is hardly a star witness. You have no evidence!"

"We have your fingerprint on the bill; it matches fingerprints that were taken in 1975 when you were arrested for cannabis possession in Boston. I believe you were a student at Emerson College at the time."

"That doesn't prove I murdered that wino!"

"The coroner removed skin scrapings from under Miss Biggio's fingernails. When the DNA results come back from the lab, we'll be able to confirm who strangled her."

"Amanda Saltzman proved that Healy murdered her!"

Officer Benton led Art away.

"When will Brendan be released?" I asked.

"Probably in the morning, I'll call Sergeant Milkowski tonight and get the probation violation charge dropped. You need to tell me how you figured out that Dr. Campbell murdered Jenny Biggio; I've only tied him to Snyder's murder so far."

"Capitalist lackeys! You're nothing but stooges for the globalization cabal," Art screamed as he was shoved in the elevator.

Laura gently rubbed my head and kissed me again; it didn't seem to hurt as much after her ministrations. In the distance, I could hear the sirens of the ambulance and police cars converging on the building.

EPILOG

SUFFERING FROM A CONCUSSION, I was kept in the hospital overnight for observation. I was released late the next morning about the same time Brendan was freed from jail.

On the way to the hospital, I called Shane Alvarez and gave him the details of Art's arrest; within weeks Shane was picked up by the CBS affiliate in Washington D.C. Barry Sanders using his key to Amanda Saltzman's apartment, found her bedded down with Dave Chen. Amanda had been looking for a scoop to put the final nail in Brendan's coffin. Dave, never able to resist the allure of a redhead, was more than happy to oblige her journalistic endeavors. Judge Warren sentenced Amanda to ten days in jail for contempt of court for illegally filming Brendan's arraignment and shortly afterwards her byline quietly disappeared from the *Register*. According to Mitch Blackwell, Amanda surfaced next as a reporter at a television station in Anchorage, Alaska.

Stan Wallach, relieved that he'd not been dragged into Jenny's murder investigation, became, for the time being at least, a model husband.

Jenny's parents were awarded her doctorate posthumously at the commencement in December to a standing ovation. As they had reconciled with Brendan, he was invited to accept it with them. Even Brad Biggio, once eager to punch out Brendan's lights, took Brendan out for a beer. Brendan celebrated his redemption with a ginger ale.

Brendan received his doctorate in May and found a position as an assistant professor at a university in North Carolina. President

Clayton, suffering from remorse for his treatment of Brendan, pulled a few academic strings to help Brendan secure the position.

Sergeant Milkowski took credit for solving a cold case when the DNA results came back on the bat used to kill Sean's rival; the DNA belonged to a drug dealer already serving time in Rahway. Milkowski's antipathy toward Brendan had been understandable as his daughter's husband had been killed by an IED in Afghanistan three months before Jenny's murder. Sally still carried a torch for Brendan and they were wed eighteen months after Jenny's death, Brendan becoming the father to her two young sons. Begrudgingly Sergeant Milkowski accepted Brendan as his son-in-law.

Tollie ecstatically signed the letter terminating Art for plagiarism after Jenny's parents found a copy of the paper among her effects. Making use of the stolen master key, Art had destroyed the official copy in the econ department office and thought he was home free after strangling Jenny.

Charged with two counts of murder and two counts of attempted murder, Art never went to trial. Depressed, facing the prospect of life in prison without parole, he fashioned a noose out of his bed sheet and hung himself from a steam pipe in his jail cell three weeks after his arrest. Harley told me that it had not been a quick death but I'll spare you the details. Art's suicide saved the university from a seamy, protracted trial; conspiracy theorists on campus saw Dick Torelli's hand in it but I never gave the rumors much credence.

FINIS

Made in the USA
Lexington, KY
17 June 2013